The Gypsy Queen

L. V. Gaudet

This book is a work of fiction. Names, characters, places, and events are products of the author's imagination or are used fictitiously. Any resemblance to actual events, locales, or persons, living or dead, is entirely coincidental.

ISBN 978-1-9992823-2-5
Library and Archives Canada
First edition published October 2019
Printed by IngramSpark

Cover art by Erskine Designs
https://www.facebook.com/pg/erskinedesigns/posts/
https://erskinedesigns.weebly.com/

Discover other titles by L.V. Gaudet:

Garden Grove
The Gypsy Queen
Old Mill Road

<u>The McAllister Series:</u>
Where the Bodies Are
The McAllister Farm
Hunting Michael Underwood
Killing David McAllister

Acknowledgements

Inspired by Sign of the Gypsy Queen by April Wine.

Heed the spirit that brought despair – April Wine,
Sign of the Gypsy Queen

Table of Contents

End of an Era

It is the end of an era, the era of the paddlewheel riverboat; flat-bottomed floating pleasure boats serving people seeking to escape their mundane lives for a few hours of indulgence. The showboats propelled lazily down the river by large rolling paddle wheels powered by steam-belching boilers have mostly vanished from the waterways.

The proliferation of the railways and invention of the automobile have taken over the transportation landscape. Most people travel across country by train now and, with the exception of the occasional aging paddlewheel, the riverboats that used to move people from one city to another up and down the rivers have nearly all been decommissioned over the years.

Only the ugly rust-stained barges used exclusively for transporting goods up and down the river fill the docks and waterways now.

It has been a bad few years for jobs, and many of the lower working class have found themselves out of work. Transient men willing to do anything for a meal, bed, and a few dollars in their pockets, mill around at the edges of the docks next to the barges in hopes of landing a job on the dock or one of the boats. Large sacks on their backs hold everything they own.

Dwarfed by the larger barges surrounding it and looking out of place, a lone paddlewheel boat is moored at the dock.

The Queen Rhiannon resembles a garishly decorated small cruise ship, its small size compared to the barges and the telltale paddle wheel on the back gives away its purpose. The crowds of well-dressed people arriving to embark on it are out of place amid the bustling dockworkers and boatmen.

1   All That Glitters

1952

Two men hunch inside their coats against the cold. They are huddled against the worn wooden wall of a building at the edge of the dockyard. Beneath their worn coats they wear the shirts and trousers of working class laborers.

The shrill cries of the ever present seagulls add to the cacophony of noise as they hover above, gliding in the air with the occasional flap of their wings.

Travis looks across the crowded docks, taking the sight in, his eyes eager despite his attempt to keep the excitement from showing in his expression.

"Are you ready?" He turns to his partner, looking for a response. He is fairly buzzing with the adrenaline coursing through him.

Darius shakes his head grimly. His eyes are nervous, not sharing in Travis's excitement. "I can't believe I let you talk me into this."

"It will be a piece of cake," Travis grins.

"We won't get past security." Darius frowns doubtfully.

"She is launching soon. We have to make our move now," Travis says.

Travis studies the dock once more, looking for some sign it is the right time. He gives his partner an encouraging nod and a "let's go" signal, and bolts through a gap in the crowd as it opens.

With a resigned sigh, Darius follows, the crowd closing again to swallow them both up.

The stink of the river hangs over the docks with a thick musty odour that clings heavily in the nostrils. People bustle about the crowded dockyard like bees buzzing around each other in a hive, their movements bumbling against one other in a jumble of bodies moving past each other, each with their own purpose.

Large barges lay waiting to be loaded with goods for transportation. Heavily laden trucks trundle through the crowded docks to have their cargo transferred to their decks by looming cranes; the crane's hooks dangling from above like giant anglers' rods waiting to hook one of the two-legged fish below. Longshoremen reach for the hovering cargo containers dangling from the cranes with their longshoreman's hooks, swinging them into place before the crane settles the heavy load on the boat deck.

More longshoremen work together to roll heavy trolleys piled high with smaller containers up the gangplanks to fill the boats' bellies. Other workers are arriving and making their way to their respective boats.

Adding to the confusion crowding the docks are the hopefuls. Men standing in groups in their work clothes, some holding their hats in their hands and wringing them anxiously, watching for anyone who might be in a position to offer them work. The depression has put a lot of men out of work. Desperation has led them to be willing to take any job, experienced or not, and to do anything to feed their families.

***

A man sits at a heavy mahogany desk inside a richly elegant over-decorated stateroom in the upper floor of the three-story paddlewheel riverboat, the Queen Rhiannon. His chair is turned backwards to the desk as he sits looking out the window. When they are on the river, the view allows him to watch the river retreat behind the boat, churning beneath the large blades of the paddle wheel on the stern.

Now moored at the dock, the view is the hull of a massive river barge looming next to the Queen Rhiannon, its metal hull sickening with rust and the growth of the river life that always clings to anything that spends too long soaking in its depths.

It is not a view he enjoys. It makes him anxious to be moving and to return the splendor of the river to his view.

A knock at the door interrupts him.

"Enter."

Malcolm Barlow turns his chair around as the door opens silently to face the intruder of his thoughts. He looks dapper in a well-tailored dress suit, his hair slicked back in the current in-style fashion only somewhat hiding the salt and pepper of his hair. His expression is cold and calculating. Malcolm is past his prime, now on the downward slope after reaching the mid-point of life.

Malcolm smiles at his visitor. The smile does not reach his eyes.

The man who enters with a deferential bow is dressed in the formal uniform of a boat captain, his hat held respectfully in his hands and the balding crown of his head laid bare.

"Mr. Barlow, sir, we are almost ready to cast off," the captain of the boat says, unable to hide the inevitable nervousness he always feels in his boss's presence.

"Right on time." Malcolm glances at the ornate clock on the wall. "I do like promptness. Keep the ship shipshape and all that, right?"

He smiles at his own poorly quoted cliché. The captain only nods agreement.

"All right then," Malcolm dismisses his own attempt at a joke, "let's get started loading the money."

The captain bows and backs out of the room. He waits for his boss to lead the way to the wheel room.

Malcolm gets up and walks past him.

***

Dodging through the crowd, Travis leads the way towards the boat slips where the barges are being loaded. Moving swiftly to avoid being run over by a large heavily loaded truck, he looks back for Darius and pauses.

Stepping back a few steps quickly, he urges Darius to hurry.

"You are a fool Travis," Darius says when he catches up.

Travis grins. "I will be a fool with money in a couple of hours. Come on."

He grabs Darius's arm, dragging him along and trying to speed up their pace.

Darius lets himself be pulled along, still regretting his choice to follow his friend.

Travis ducks into the line of wealthy people, dragging Darius with him and causing their neighbours to give them sour looks.

"There she is." He stares at the boat with awe. The Queen Rhiannon. She is larger than he imagined and ugly in her richly ornate decorations.

Darius shakes his head.

"You and your get rich quick schemes. The only thing they ever get you is in trouble. This won't be any different."

"Positive thoughts, my friend, positive thoughts." Travis grins at him.

***

From his place of honour in the wheel room, Malcolm looks down at the crowded dock, smiling.

"Look at all that money getting ready to board my boat."

The Queen Rhiannon is a floating casino owned by Malcolm Barlow.

Malcolm grins broadly.

"Where else would they go to lose their money? Oh yes, in my casinos on land. But this is all the rage now. They come because I am here. This is the only place they can see me in the flesh."

He looks at the boat captain.

"You know; I am a powerful man in more ways than wealth alone can explain. I own the waterways. I own the port officials, the Dock Workers Union, and the Dock Master. I own all the gambling houses around here and I keep the gaming officials close, in my pockets."

He pats his pocket for emphasis.

"Yes sir," the captain agrees blandly. He has heard the speech many times.

Malcolm returns to looking out the window at the docks.

The line of people waiting to board the Queen Rhiannon starts at the top of the gangplank, descends the length of the plank, and stretches in a snaky line through the endlessly moving crowds of workmen and trucks filling the docks.

A scrawny ill-kept young boy darts through the crowd below, looking for the chance to steal anything he might eat, his presence ignored by all.

The people lining up to board the Queen Rhiannon in their fancy dress clothes, showing off their wealth with the men finely dressed in well-tailored suits and hats and silver-tipped custom carved walking canes are conspicuously out of place in the midst of the rough looking dock workers. The women are older women, since it is unseemly for a young woman to be seen at a place of gambling or any other less than respectable public place. They wear fancy dresses and hats and glitter with gem-laden jewelry dripping from ears and draping from overstuffed necks.

Two young men waiting in the line are conspicuous both for their overly exuberant eagerness and their unrefined clothes.

Among the passengers dressed in their finest and standing there looking haughtily superior to the dockworkers surrounding them, these two men are more likely to be mistaken for dockworkers than passengers. If the poor quality of their clothes is not enough, their excitement is out of place in the crowd of bored wealthy gentry waiting in the queue to board.

Their excited antics, gesticulating, talking too loudly, and even drumming on the railing, draws attention to them.

People around them give the two young men annoyed glances, purposely not looking right at them and making it clear they do not belong among the upper class citizens. The two men seem oblivious to being out of place.

Malcolm frowns at the two unwelcome guests attempting to board his boat.

He turns his attention back to the line of wealthy people lining up to lose their money on his gaming tables.

"Look at them. They are not just the wealthy. They are the moneyed, influential people, corporate leaders, politicians, and those whose wealth is enough to be influential on its own. And they are here to mewl and ingratiate their selves to me."

***

Two beefy looking dark-suited men lean on the upper deck railing of the Queen Rhiannon, looking out over the docks. They study the guests waiting to board. One of them has a stout straight cane with a heavy ornate carved ram's head leaning against the railing next to him. He does not look like he needs the support to walk.

On the main deck below them, two men in lesser suits resembling a shipmate's uniform stand next to the closed gate at the head of the gangplank. They are watching the crowd of wealthy guests snaking down the plank and through the crowded dock while waiting for the signal to start letting the people lining the gangplank board.

They are not seamen. They have one job and one job only, security. The men above are the head of security for Malcolm Barlow. All of the security guards are dressed in business suits, except those few imitating the ship's crew for the amusement of the guests.

One of the men at the gate nudges the other, indicating the two overeager young men with a motion of his head and a smirk. The other man shares his smirk.

"We've got another pair. These working class guys just don't seem to get it. Every month we get a few trying to board. Hey, buddy, no one wants you here." He laughs.

"That's why part of our job is to keep them off."

One of the gate security men turns and looks up. He can just make out the hands of the two men watching from the deck above, their arms resting on the railing and their hands protruding before them. He has been glancing up every minute, watching for the signal to start the boarding.

One of the hands moves. It waves.

He turns to his partner and nudges him, "That's the signal."

He moves to take his position on one side of the gate, while his partner takes the other side. Placing his hand on the gate, he lifts the latch and swings the gate inward against the railing.

The first sign of life stirs through the bored crowd as their murmuring voices move down the line, announcing the opening of the gate.

***

Travis is staring at the Queen Rhiannon wistfully. Images play in his head of the anticipated grandeur of what he imagines the casino room on the boat will look like. The dealers calling out for bets, bells ringing, and the dull bop bop of the roulette ball bouncing around the wheel to the silky ticking of the wheel spinning. The soft sliding of cards being dealt and clink of chips changing hands.

"You can walk in with little and walk out rich," he murmurs hungrily.

The eagerness slithering down the line of the bored wealthy elite stirring them to life sends excitement washing through him when it reaches them.

"Here we go." Travis looks eagerly at Darius.

"It's not too late to turn back," Darius says. "They aren't going to let us on. Look at us." He looks Travis and himself up and down for emphasis. "Everyone knows they won't let anyone without a large bankroll on the Queen Rhiannon."

"You only live once, my friend. You only live once." Travis nudges Darius to move in anticipation of the slow forward motion of the line reaching them.

Gentlemen and ladies start the slow shuffle up the gangplank, boarding the boat with a regal air of entitlement.

The burly security guards stand to each side of the opened gate, silently watching the passengers board, nodding a greeting to the occasional guest. They miss nothing, ready to give silent signals to others waiting discretely on deck in case a passenger is to be quietly removed after boarding or taken to see Malcolm in his private office onboard.

Travis has eyes only for the goal ahead.

Darius keeps looking back anxiously, keeping an eye on their exit route.

When the line of boarders finally brings the unlikely pair of young men almost to the front of the line, one of the security guards raises a bushy eyebrow at their less than proper clothing.

Seeing the reaction and knowing it is meant for them to see, the nervous young men try to stay calm, not looking at the security men but not looking away either, as if they too are just another pair of bored wealthy passengers.

Just as the young men are about to move through the open gate, amazed that they are actually pulling it off, a heavy stick thumps down across the opening and blocks their path.

They look down at it. It is made of stout wood, rod straight from tip to tip, and crowned with a heavy deadly hook on one end. The other is attached to the meaty hand gripping it. The gaffer hook bears scars that they prefer not to find out how they got there. They follow the arm attached to that meaty hand up to the stern face of the burly man dressed as a seaman.

Behind them, they can hear snickers at their expense from those waiting to board.

They glance at the other man dressed in an identical faux seaman suit, and back to the one with the gaffer hook.

Without a word, the security guard shakes his head 'no' and points back the way they came, down the gangplank.

Travis opens his mouth to plead their case, but Darius gives him a warning jab from behind.

With a regretful shrug, they sheepishly turn around and squeeze their way down the gangplank past the glares of annoyed passengers who have to wedge themselves against the railing to let them pass. Looks of relieved disdain and a few nasty snickers follow them down.

When they finally reach the bottom and break free of the crowded gangplank they turn to look back with regret.

"Well, Travis, we tried," Darius says.

Travis shakes his head. "We will find another way. Darius, there is one thing you need to learn in life, and that is when there is a will, there will always be a way."

"They will never let us on board," Darius says. "The whole idea was crazy."

"We just have to not get caught," Travis says with a grin. "What are they going to do once they are under way? Toss us over the side?" He shakes his head. "We sneak on board and hide until they are on the river, then they are stuck with us until they dock."

"How do we get past the security?" Darius asks.

"I haven't figured that out yet," Travis admits. "I will find another way onboard," he vows, looking lustfully at the ornate paddlewheel boat.

They wander dejectedly around the dock, Travis unwilling to give up just yet on their hopeless cause.

Travis spots another gangplank running across from the dock to the rear deck and an open doorway into the bowels of the Queen Rhiannon. Longshoremen are struggling against gravity with the weight of heavy crates on wheeled trolleys being carefully drawn across the plank into the boat, gravity trying to pull the crates down with dangerous speed even as the men fight to control the slow steady pace of the rolling cargo.

Travis stops, the grin coming back to his face as his eyes twinkle with mischief.

"Oh no," Darius groans. "I know that look. You always get that look when you come up with some crazy idea."

"There, the cargo door." Travis thrusts his chin towards the gangplank.

Travis and Darius exchange a look.

Before Darius can try to talk him out of it, Travis quickly lowers his head and pulls his hat down low to cover his face. He rushes forward purposely, moving eagerly and having to force himself to slow down.

With an unhappy sigh, Darius follows suit, following him into the crowd. They lose themselves in the group of workers

Darius following Travis's lead, they each grab a corner of one of the heavy crates being rolled into the boat's belly on wheeled trolleys and lean into pushing it, putting their backs into it.

"Won't get far with hats like those," one of the longshoremen struggling with the cargo mutters. "Must be trying to press their way into getting hired instead of waiting for the Dock Master to pick them out of the group of hopefuls."

"They have to be inexperienced if they ain't even got no proper hats. Probably just laid off elsewhere and desperate for work." He shrugs. "It's not my problem to chase them off."

Once inside the boat, Travis and Darius take advantage of the hectic activity in the rush to load quickly, breaking away from the workers and slipping off down a narrow passage. They cross to another, looking back with relief to find they are not being followed.

"Okay, now what?" Darius asks. He feels a little dizzy and out of breath with the rush of sneaking onboard.

Travis looks up and down the passage. His heart is beating fast with excitement and his eyes are bright with his eagerness to make their way up to the deck.

"We will hide and wait until the boat is moving before sneaking up to the casino floor," Travis says.

They move down the passage checking doors. Most are locked.

They come to one marked "Utility" that opens and slip inside the very tiny closet. The two of them barely fit, Travis standing with one foot inside a large bucket that luckily is empty at the moment as Darius tries to squeeze in with him.

Travis looks down at the awkward spot his foot is wedged in

"Lady Luck is already shining on me."

The closet turns black as the door clicks shut.

"I hope this doesn't take long," Darius says, trying to shift so that whatever is digging painfully into his back will stop.

They wait, holding their breath every time they hear someone approaching and exhaling in relief each time the person continues on past.

"How long is this going to take?" Darius whispers after what feels like an hour wedged in there. "I'm getting a cramp."

"It shouldn't be much longer," Travis whispers back. He pushes down an urge to open the door and peek.

At last, they realize that they feel a rolling pulling that might be the motion of the boat moving down the river.

"I think the boat is moving," Travis whispers.

"I'm not sure. It might just be the waves against the dock," Darius whispers back.

"No, this feels different; I think it really is moving."

After an uncertain pause the decision is made. "We have to check it out," Travis says.

"Ok," Darius agrees reluctantly, but with anxious relief. "I don't think I can spend much longer wedged into this closet."

Darius slowly opens the door a crack, peeking out and expecting to have the door yanked from his hand at any moment by one of the two burly security men up top.

Stepping out of the closet, they pause in the passageway and listen, feeling the motion of the floor.

"It is definitely moving," Travis nods. "Let's go. They open the tables as soon as the boat leaves the dock."

He leads the way up the passage and down another until they find a sign marked "Stairs". They look up a narrow set of steep stairs.

"This place is big," Darius whispers, amazed at how big the boat seems below deck.

They duck through and go up the stairs.

The top of the stairs opens to the deck level of the boat.

Hiding in the stairway opening, they look around. On their right, a walkway runs between the railing and the wall, behind which they are sure the casino tables are housed. To their left, the open deck at the front of the boat sprawls. Lights that will be lit before dusk closes in are strung elegantly above the deck. White clothed tables with elaborate settings are strategically scattered at one end near a closed door that has to be the galley. Dinner will be served on this cruise. An open space that appears to be a dance floor is bordered on one side by chairs, presumably for musicians.

Travis nudges Darius, nodding towards the path between the railing and wall.

The ringing and clanging of machines, babble of bets being made, and calls of the card hustlers running the tables of the casino floor comes from doors left open to the railing and cooling river breeze.

The young men imagine they can feel the warmth of that room already embracing them with its warm lights and the heat of sweating bodies clamouring to win or lose their money.

With a grin at each other, they sidle up the passage and slip into the room, staying close to the wall as if that might prevent them from being seen before they are ready to start gambling.

They stare in slack-jawed awe around the casino room.

The walls are painted in off white with gaudy golden trimming everywhere. The thick trimming seems to roll in every direction. Carved trimming runs parallel to the floor around the entire room. It runs up and down the walls every six feet, bordering every doorway and window, and matches the heavy painted carved bases of all the wall lamps and trim circling the ceiling lights. Large glass chandeliers drip from the ceiling.

In contrast, the carpet is a dark patterned red and black mosaic. Richly red heavy curtains hang open and drawn back with golden tasselled tiebacks at the sides of the windows and the open doors leading to the deck. Staff doors are painted to blend in with the walls.

Slot machines lined up against one wall glitter in the lights, their bright colors and rolling wheels of pictures of cherries, grapes, and coins promising happiness and fun while they play happy music.

Dark stained wood tables with rich red felt table tops suggest wealth and prestige with the fine dark leather stools sitting stoically before them. Men in striped dress shirts and slacks call out the chances as men and women lay down their bets in the form of coloured discs.

Like a carnival game, the roulette table wheel spins, clicking and clacking around and around like a spinning wheel that ran out of wool, its dark wood and sleek frame giving the impression of something meant only for the wealthy.

Statues and plants are placed strategically, adding regal elegance to the room. The sleek design of the tables and machines give them a modern feel.

Even more awe inspiring are the people themselves. Wealthy men and women showing off their status with their rich clothing, gold watches, and gaudy jewellery dripping from the women, all flashing their money around.

The two security men dressed in business suits standing unobtrusively in a corner notice the two conspicuously under-dressed men the moment they slip into the room. The guard with the stout ram's head topped cane nudges his partner, nodding towards the two intruders. They move together, working their way discretely towards them. They are already moving in on them while Travis and Darius are still taking in the room's ornate gaudiness.

Travis and Darius are drawn forward by the excitement filling the room. They step away from the wall, moving through the crowded casino room and looking around like little farm boys who have never seen the wonders of a bustling city.

Their presence has not gone unnoticed, and curious looks are already being passed their way.

"It is not proper for deck hands to be seen on the casino floor," one woman whispers to her husband. They watch them along with a few of the other guests, feeling a little alarmed that something might be wrong.

On the floor, Travis and Darius are even more awed by the flagrant wealth being tossed around and lost on the gaming tables. Stacks of high value coloured discs pass back and forth between dealers and players as bets are called and closed, cards are played with deft precision, and dice are tossed.

Their eyes sparkle and their minds reel with the imagined possibilities, Travis's in particular.

Travis is dazzled by the sheer sickness of wealth surrounding them. Just making money betting on the tables is no longer enough. He burns with a new desire.

"This could be us. What if we could be running the show and raking in all this easy money?" he thinks, excitement coursing through him as he absorbs the elaborate furnishings and money everywhere.

"Let's try this table first," Travis nudges his partner.

Darius looks doubtfully at the wealthy people playing at the table.

"Maybe we should try the machines first," he suggests, nervous about going face to face with these people.

Grabbing his arm eagerly, Travis pulls Darius along to the blackjack table. The people there shift over nervously, giving them space but unwilling to abandon their game, uncertain about their presence.

Travis fishes some bills out of his pocket and plunks them down on the table.

The dealer looks at the crumpled handful of bills then at Travis, his mouth creasing into a snide grin. He makes no move to touch the offered money.

A heavy hand falls on Travis's shoulder followed by another on Darius's. They both turn to look at the burly suited man standing between and just behind them.

Darius gulps, his eyes immediately moving down, half expecting to see the man somehow holding some weapon in a third hand.

Travis smiles sheepishly at the security guard, Frank, although it is more like the sheep who just found itself surrounded by wolves. He is trying to look casual, like he belongs, and is failing.

"Gentlemen," Frank says with a smile more suiting a shark about to eat a baby seal, "how are we this evening?"

Darius reflexively glances at the open doorway and the sky beyond. The sky is still bright with the late afternoon sun, the deeper evening dusk still a couple of hours away.

Frank continues without pausing to let them answer.

"If you fine gentlemen wouldn't mind coming with me for a moment, my boss would like to meet you."

His hands resting heavily on their shoulders tighten into a vice-like grip as he directs them around and away from the game table, leaving the crumpled bills behind.

Travis glances back at his money, wanting to reach out and snatch it off the table, but he is drawn away too quickly and isn't given the chance.

"Damn," he thinks, "that was all the money I had."

As they turn and walk away, Frank's hand releases their shoulders and he casually grabs the heavy cane with the ram's head ornament he left leaning against a table behind them on the way past.

The other guard waits behind them. The moment they step away, he reaches out and casually pockets the crumpled bills. He nods to the dealer to continue with the betting and follows them.

The dealer immediately goes back to business, calling out the bets. The gamblers close their ranks on the hapless pair as if to prevent them from intruding on their table again.

"Mr. Barlow is waiting for you gentlemen in his office," Frank says as he leads them casually out of the casino room.

Instead of taking them to the deck as the two men expect, he directs them to one of the staff doors blending in with the walls. On the other side lies a narrow passageway with doors opening off it. They pass those doors, not given the opportunity to pause and see what might be inside any of them, and round a corner that brings them to a set of stairs leading up.

At the top of the stairs is an elaborate smoking room for special guests, and Mr. Barlow's office. The dark wood lustre of the smoking room beckons to them as they pass through it, pausing at the closed door to the office.

Frank knocks on the door and a voice beckons them to enter.

Opening the door, he directs the two men to enter ahead of him. The two security guards follow Travis and Darius in, closing the door behind them.

The office is as richly decorated as the rest of the boat with oiled wood panels and a large mahogany desk. It is more richly decorated and substantially less gaudy than the casino floor, flaunting wealth, not flamboyance.

Elegant pieces of art are displayed safely behind shallow glass cabinets.

The man sitting behind the desk is wearing an expensive suit. His carefully barbered hair has not a strand out of place and smile wrinkles crinkle at the corners of his eyes.

He is not smiling now.

Malcolm Barlow looks them up and down with a steady gaze, measuring them up. His disdain for the pair of loafs sneaking onto his boat is clear. His confident air also makes it clear he is accustomed to being obeyed.

"What makes you pair of nitwits think you can come on my boat?" he asks, his eyes deadly cold on them.

Darius looks at his shoes, trying hard not to fidget awkwardly.

Travis tries to meet his eyes, shifting nervously.

"Um, sir," Travis starts.

Malcolm holds up a hand, stopping him.

"Did you have a good time down there?" he asks.

Darius swallows the lump in his throat.

Travis nods, stiff with fear.

"How do you think it looks to my guests, people who can afford to be on my boat, when I let someone like you on board? It is not exactly good for my reputation, is it?"

"Um, no sir," Travis mumbles.

"People like those pompous asses below do not want to rub elbows with the likes of you, do they?"

"No sir," Travis manages. That the man they have been brought before is showing disdain for the wealthy guests with that last comment makes hope stir in his chest.

"Ok, maybe this won't be so bad after all. Maybe the guy is reasonable after all, a regular guy like us," he thinks.

Malcolm continues.

"The wealthy clientele who come to a boat like this," he spreads his arms to indicate the luxuriousness of the vessel, "do not want to taint their reputation by being seen appearing to cavort in an establishment with penniless oafs who do not know their station."

Travis's heart sinks. He only hopes they will get out of this with only minor injuries. He knows Malcolm Barlow's reputation. Unfortunately for Darius, he had kept that information to himself.

"I have to protect my reputation, and that of my establishment," Malcolm says. "You understand, don't you?"

He leans forward, raising an eyebrow in expectation of an answer.

Darius nods, swallowing the bile threatening to come up his throat.

"Yes, sir," Travis stammers. "We are sorry sir."

"You won't try something like this again, will you?" Malcolm says, more a statement than a question.

"No sir," Travis says.

Malcolm looks to Darius, waiting for a response.

"No sir," he mimics.

Malcolm nods.

"See, we are all reasonable gentlemen here," Malcolm says, smiling. He turns his smile on the two security guards, a signal he expects a response from them.

They both nod agreement, their expressions as bland as before.

"Yes, reasonable gentlemen," they say in unison.

Hope stirs again in Travis.

Darius feels it too, but pushes it down, afraid that any hope is futile.

"Now, please remove these gentlemen from my boat," Malcolm says, dismissing them..

"Thank you sir," Travis simpers nervously.

Darius nods. "Thank you," he manages.

The two security men step forward, one opening the door, and they indicate the two young men should come with them.

Travis and Darius go submissively, following the two larger men's leads, one security man ahead and one behind them.

After they turn down the second hallway and are still unharmed, Travis dares to breathe an internal sigh of relief.

"So, how are you putting us ashore? Are you docking? A dinghy?"

The security men remain silent as they lead the pair down a set of narrow stairs to the deck. They exit to the deck towards the front of the boat. A narrow passageway leads the way between the boathouse and the railing towards the front of the boat.

They are led along that narrow walk, the wind whipping at their clothes and rustling their hair. Here, mooring lines are carefully coiled and lifeboats are hung.

"So on a lifeboat then," Travis says, eying the boats doubtfully. None of them have been prepared to be set in the water.

The security men stop next to the rail where there is a space between two lifeboats, the two young men between them.

"It is time for your departure, gentlemen," Frank says. The emphasis he puts on the word 'departure' makes both their stomachs turn sour.

Darius leans over the rail, watching the fast moving current slipping by the boat. He pulls back. The current is strong and the waves seem higher than they should be.

"Is it from the wind whipping them up?" he wonders. "I thought the wind I felt was only from the forward motion of the boat." He cannot deny the stronger buffeting of a real wind that is blowing.

Darius starts turning towards the others.

Before either man can react, the two security men grab Darius. Using the railing as a focal point to spin him over the railing, they drop him over the side of the boat.

He vanishes with a shocked cry and a splash.

Travis stares at them in surprise, flapping his mouth a few times before he manages to find the words to express his shock.

"But, the current..."

The security men step forward.

"We will never be able to swim against it to shore!"

They grab him just as he moves to flee, on one each side of him.

Travis struggles. "We won't make it, we'll drown!"

Frank presses his face close. "You are not expected to," he says wryly.

They fling him overboard using the same motion, flipping Travis's weight over the railing like a teeter-totter someone forgot to fasten down.

His scream is swallowed by the splash below.

They turn away from the railing, satisfied with a job well done.

"How much did they have?" Frank asks.

The other man grins in amusement, jamming his hand in his pocket at the crinkled bills.

"Enough for a couple of drinks I think," he jokes.

2   The Plunge

The suddenness of the attack catches Darius off guard. The swift motion just as he is turning from the dizzying rush of water below to look at the others as the world suddenly spins upside down, the railing hard against his back.

Then he is weightless for a few surprised heartbeats before he feels himself falling with a sickening feeling.

The icy splash is instantly numbing. He hits the water head first, swallowed up and tossed end over end by the freezing current.

With no idea which way is up, Darius tries to hold his breath as he fights to stop rolling. The murky water is dark. One direction seems less dark, so he takes a chance, arms and legs pulling against the current still rolling him, fighting to swim towards what he hopes is the surface.

He breaches the surface, disoriented and in shock.

Darius struggles against the current, the icy chill of the river already making his arms and legs numb and his mind still reeling from the shock of hitting the cold water. He tries to call out but gets a mouthful of water instead. Up and down he goes on the water, slipping quickly past the boat as the strong current drags him bouncing against its side. The Queen Rhiannon is moving against the current, making it slip past him that much more quickly.

He scrabbles at the smooth surface slipping swiftly past him, but there is nothing to grab.

Choking on the water and being bounced and banged against the hull, Darius tries desperately to not be pulled beneath the boat.

Suddenly he is at the back of the boat, flailing, and manages to grab the side of the cage housing the lower part of the large paddle wheel propelling the boat.

The sucking of the large wheel churning the water is pulling him down, trying to drag him beneath the wheel.

Darius looks up for a moment, watching the wheel turning lazily, water cascading down after being scooped up, raining down on him.

He works his way along the cage to the back, clinging to it against the drag of the turning wheel and the current pulling him down.

Darius feels the suction pulling at him with each blade of the wheel. Luckily for him the boat's forward motion is drawing the water away from the boat. If it were going in reverse, he would be sucked beneath and into the turning blades the moment he lets go.

Trying to catch his breath and get his bearings, he watches the rolling wheel, trying to time this right.

"On five." He watches the wheel endlessly turning. "One, two…"

He lets go too soon, losing his precarious grip on the slippery surface.

Darius goes under, sucked beneath the surface before his flailing hands can grab the cage again.

***

Travis has the fortune to see it coming. It doesn't help.

Grasping for anything, the railing, the guards, he misses. Speed and momentum keep the railing just beyond his reaching fingertips.

Travis is screaming the moment he feels that sickening weightlessness a heartbeat before he plunges down.

His mouth is open and screaming when he hits the water headfirst, the blow stunning him as his head is swallowed beneath the thrashing waves. He is enveloped in an icy shock.

The current and the moving boat slipping by roll him in the water, leaving him disoriented.

His mind working dully, he swallows a mouthful of water, choking on it and fighting to keep his mouth closed against the reflexive need to open it and gasp for air.

Travis flounders under water, turning in circles and upside down, first going the wrong way before realizing he is swimming down and turning around in an attempt to fight his way to the surface before he can no longer fight the urge to open his mouth to cough out the choking water and gasp for air.

The paddle wheel turns endlessly, rolling through the water, the water lifting up to fall back to the river as the paddles go up and over.

His lungs are burning before he breaks the surface. His head bursts through and he is gasping and choking, trying to suck air in, and is immediately tossed by the waves and pulled back down by the strong undertow.

Travis hit the water further from the boat and does not bang against it as the current takes him swiftly past the boat.

The large turning paddle wheel sucks the water down and him with it, rolling him under the water again.

Unable to catch a breath before being sucked under, Travis fights against the pull of the undertow, desperate to reach the surface again. His lungs feel like they are going to explode with the need for air.

Travis can't stop it. His mouth opens reflexively, gasping for air and only choking on the mouthful of water he sucks in.

Finally, he breaks the surface of the water, staring up at the looming paddle wheel, water cascading down from it as if in another attempt to drown him.

His whole body is wracked with powerful heaving and gagging coughing in his body's attempt to vomit out the water in his lungs.

He came up right behind the boat, almost close enough to touch it if it were not moving away from him.

Travis spins momentarily in its wake, alternately watching the boat slip away up the river and staring at the river behind. Then, a few feet behind the Queen Rhiannon, the current of the wake combined with the undertow conspires to drag him beneath the waves again.

He thrashes desperately against the water, still struggling through the rough heaving coughs and gasping through his water-logged lungs for air, his head dipping beneath the water and coming back up a few times before he breaks free. He has no idea which way the nearest bank is.

With a silent prayer he digs in and begins to swim for his life. His legs kick woodenly and his arms flail, turning numb with cold and unable to get into the rhythm of swimming.

Travis pushes on in desperation, forcing his arms and legs to keep moving.

Exhausted beyond anything he has ever imagined possible, choking and gagging on swallowed water, Travis finally reaches the shore long after he has reached that point where he is certain there is no riverbank and the whole world has become one massive ocean of endless icy water.

Focused only on moving his arms and legs, Travis flails when his arms are suddenly getting caught up in soggy slimy stalks bent on tangling him up.

He barely manages to clumsily grab the thick grass and reeds growing on the bank, his hands slipping on the algae slime. Pulling his way through and scrabbling his way up the slippery bank, he slips back a few times into the dark water before finally making it.

He lays there, violent coughs pummelling him as his body tries to expel the inhaled water, too exhausted even to roll over.

Travis has no idea if Darius made it to shore or not. He is too dazed with exhaustion for the thought to enter his mind.

He closes his eyes, letting the blackness fill him.

3   Surviving the Swim

Darius groans, waking up feeling like he has just been put through a giant blender. Every muscle in his body hurts and his cheap bed doesn't help either.

He holds his head against the pounding that woke him up and groans again, sitting up. He had managed to get as far as stripping his wet clothes down to his underwear before collapsing into bed.

The pounding doesn't stop.

Darius looks up, groggily looking around the small room he rents, and finally realizes it is not just his head that is pounding.

Dragging himself stiffly to his feet, he staggers to the door, not caring that he is wearing nothing but river-crusted underwear.

He fumbles for the door, unlatching and opening it, cringing at the glare of the sun from outside.

Travis rushes inside past him, closing the door behind him.

He is vibrating with excitement.

Blinking, Darius opens his eyes a crack, staring at his friend.

He is a mess. Travis looks like he had been beaten by a gang of burly security men with stout canes instead of just thrown overboard.

"I see you made it to shore," Darius grimaces against his own pain as he turns and stumbles to the table against the wall, where he finds a cup and tin of coffee grounds.

Taking the cup to the bathroom, he fills it with hot tap water, stumbles back to the table, and spoons grounds into it.

"That's disgusting." Travis makes a face at the makeshift coffee.

His expression brightens again. He is painfully hyper, filled with excited energy. His eyes sparkle with it.

"Oh no," Darius groans knowingly.

"Did you see all the money?" Travis gushes. "The wealth? The riches those people showed off and the money they tossed around like nothing?"

Travis is pacing now with the nervous energy burning through him.

"The magnificence and beauty of that boat." He seems to be talking to himself now, Darius an unwilling theatergoer watching a one-man show. "The free flowing money going back and forth between dealers and men."

He rounds on Darius, staring hard at him with the excitement burning in him, the large smile on his face seeming like it will eat him up.

"We want that. We can have that. It would be so easy."

Darius shakes his head. "You are certifiably nuts," he mutters. "You must have banged your head too many times on the way down and are delirious with concussion."

Unfortunately, he knows Travis is entirely serious.

"We can do it!" Travis says eagerly, pounding the bottom of his fist into his open palm. "We just have to find a boat, get some gaming tables, and start gambling, and we are rich."

"Where are we going to find a boat?" Darius asks, wishing he has peace and quiet to sooth his aching head. He feels more dead than alive and half wishes he was so he would not hurt so much.

"We don't have any money," Darius adds.

"Don't worry my good friend," Travis says with a grin. "When there is the will there is always a way. We will find a boat."

"Whenever you say that, I know we are going to be in trouble."

Travis grins bigger. "Hey, you only live once. You only live once."

"Now I know we are going to get into trouble." Darius grimaces in pain. "We are doing nothing today but recovering from damned near drowning so we can go to work tomorrow."

"That's all right," Travis says, not losing any of the edge of his excitement. "I will let you rest. Don't you worry about it. I will find us a boat. You will see."

He lets himself out, almost dancing his way jogging down the steps.

"That's what I'm afraid of." Darius leans against the closed door. He can hear his friend whistling as he walks away and can picture his jaunty step as he practically bounces away from his door on a cloud of dreams that lack any sense, common or otherwise.

He steps away from the door and grimaces with pain as he lowers himself into a chair. He bares his teeth in a disgusted scowl as he takes another sip of the revolting water and coffee grounds mixture and puts the cup down.

Moving to the bed, he lets himself fall onto it, snoring moments later.

4 One Man's Heap of Crap is Another Man's Riverboat

Travis looks around the dockyard, absorbing the busyness of the crowds of people and trucks. Like the last time they were here, it is noisy and crowded. Everyone seems to have something to do or somewhere to go.

In the midst of the commotion, groups of men mill around watching the activity with a mix of hopeful and dour expressions.

The Dock Master and his clerk come out of his office, walking through the crowd with a sense of importance. They stop before one of these groups of men. Seeing this, the others press their way through the crowded docks to join them, competing for a position in front.

The Dock Master nods to his clerk and raises his chin, directing his attention over the heads of the gathered men.

"Can any man here work a crane? Does any one of you know how to operate a crane?"

Two hands are raised and he points at one, indicating towards his clerk. The other man gives the chosen one a sour look as he pushes through the crowd to the clerk, who starts taking down his information.

"Can any man here drive a truck?" The Dock Master, Basil Jacobson, eyes the scattering of hands that go up. He chooses one, sending him to see his clerk.

"I need five dock hands," Basil says.

The crowd almost pushes forward, each trying to get his attention.

Basil points to five at random, overlooking those who look old or weaker.

The remaining shift unhappily while they push their way through to the clerk to have their names taken down.

"I have two more positions to fill."

The crowd is hopeful again.

"These are positions on the Keelyhelm."

Unhappy looks and mutters spread through the crowd. Basil continues.

"It is true. The Keelyhelm experienced an outbreak of Tuberculosis among the crew. That is why the positions are open. Two more have been taken off the crew list. Make of that what you will. It is your choice. Raise your hand if you are willing."

Murmuring spreads through the crowd. They look at each other, wondering who among them are desperate enough. One hand goes up unwillingly, and then another.

The second is a boy no more than sixteen.

Another man grabs his hand and pulls it down, giving him a reproachful look.

"If you die of the Tuberculosis who will earn the money to feed your mother and your sisters?" he hisses at the boy.

The boy looks down sheepishly, a hot flush of shame staining his cheeks.

Another man looks around. He is skinny, his bones poking out where there should be meat to cover them. His eyes are slightly yellow stained with sickness and he looks ill kept.

He hesitates and then raises his hand.

Basil looks at him. "Are you strong enough to work?"

"Yes sir," he nods. His eyes shift away quickly. He is lying.

Basil motions the two men to see his clerk.

"That is all the positions I have today," he announces and turns away from the crowd, making his way back to his office.

"I've been here every day for bloody weeks and never got picked a single day," one man grumbles.

An older man looks at him. His eyes are as grey as his hair.

"Months," he says expressionlessly.

The crowd starts to disperse, milling around in hopes there is another calling later.

Watching, Travis focuses on the older man. He pushes through the crowd to him.

"You have been here months looking for work?"

The old man turns to him.

"Yes."

"They don't take you. Why? Is it because you have no experience?"

The old man's eyes have a hint of pain.

"Forty years working on the docks."

Travis notices now his ropy muscles and the hard edge to the man despite the thinness of malnutrition.

"So why don't they hire you?"

"I'm too old."

"Forty years. That is a long time. You must know a lot about the boat business."

"I know my fair share."

"How would I go about getting a boat? I mean, where can I buy one?"

The old man weighs him.

"You are in the wrong place for a little fishing boat. These here are river barges. And by the looks of you, you can't even afford a small fishing boat."

"I'm not looking for a fishing boat. I'm looking for a pleasure boat; a paddlewheel."

"You don't look like you can afford something like that. Who are you enquiring for?"

"I'm looking for myself. I'm buying it, along with my partner. The boat will pay for itself in no time."

"So, you want a showboat steamer. What kind? Theatre? Dinner and dancing? There's no money in showboats any more. That's why there aren't any around anymore."

"There is one."

Travis's eyes move to settle on the Queen Rhiannon, sitting quietly in her boat slip.

The old man's eyes follow.

"If it's a casino boat you are after. That one is not for sale."

" No, and I could not afford that one. I'm looking for a fixer upper. Something we can fix up and make into a casino boat."

The old man shakes his head.

"I will give you the best piece of sound advice anyone will give you. Stay out of the boat business. And, stay the hell away from casino anything."

The old man turns and walks away, chuckling under his breath about casinos and foolish young men.

Undaunted, Travis stares at the Queen Rhiannon wistfully and then continues asking around about where he can get a boat.

***

Darius is on his way home from work, walking the distance since he has no car, dirty and tired from a hard day's labour.

He stops in the road and pulls his boot off, shaking a stone out and examining the bottom.

"Damn, a hole in the bottom. I've worn the boot sole through and have to get it fixed."

Brushing the dirt off the bottom of his socked foot, he puts the boot back on and continues the long walk home.

He is wearily reaching the end of his trek on the last leg of the journey as he turns up the street where the house he rents an upstairs room at the back sits halfway up the block.

Travis comes jogging up from behind, catching up.

He is dirty too, but not from working.

Darius stops and looks him up and down.

His trousers are wet and muddy from the knees down. His boots are similarly soaked and muddy. One arm matches from the elbow down, as if he had fallen and braced himself with that arm. Mud splatters have dried on his face and in his hair.

"Where have you been? You haven't been to work in two days. The boss is ready to fire you."

It has been a full month since their little adventure onboard the Queen Rhiannon.

"I found it!" Travis says with a big grin, matching Darius's stride easily as they walk on together.

"Found what?" Darius asks.

"Her," Travis says excitedly.

Darius stops and turns to him.

"Her? Who?" He pictures his friend swooning over some woman, something that always ends badly, usually at the hands of the uninterested woman's husband or boyfriend.

Travis's grin spreads ear to ear and he nods dumbly.

"The boat." He practically yells it in his excitement. "I found the boat. Oh, she is so sweet. I don't know her name, but she is beautiful."

"The boat?" It takes Darius a moment for it to sink in. He had forgotten all about the ridiculous idea and thought Travis had too. He shakes his head doubtfully.

"Where do you expect to get the money for a boat? You probably don't even have enough for next month's rent."

"She won't cost that much," Travis says.

Darius eyes him warily. "What kind of condition is it in?"

"She is a little rough."

"How rough? Where did you find it?"

Travis looks down to evade his look. "She is abandoned up a dried up tributary."

"Abandoned. You want to buy an abandoned boat."

Darius wrinkles his nose, finally catching a good whiff of Travis.

"Where have you been?" He waves a hand in front of his face to ward off the unpleasant smell.

"Digging around off river," Travis says, still grinning. "That's where I found her. She needs a bit of work. That is why we will be able to buy her."

Darius shakes his head regretfully; sorry Travis had ever convinced him to try to get on that casino boat in the first place.

"You are on your own." Darius walks on.

Travis hesitates only a moment and speeds up to keep pace.

"I need you. I can't do this alone."

Darius looks him in the eye sternly.

"No. Absolutely not." He does not slow down.

Travis just grins, walking alongside him.

***

Two weeks later, after nonstop pleading and daily harassment, Travis finally convinces Darius to go take a look at the boat he found.

"I can't believe I let you talk me into this. Darius grumbles. "How much farther is it?"

"Not much further, it's just ahead," Travis says.

They have already been walking along the riverbank for a couple hours, after hitching a ride down the road some ways.

Not much farther turns out to be another two hours walk along the riverbank and then turning up a small nearly dried up tributary for another forty minutes.

The grass is long and full of brambles and prickly weeds that cling to their clothes and leave scratchy burrs sticking to their socks.

As they move up the tributary, the ground becomes increasingly impassable except for the low ground of the dried streambed. What remains of the stream trickles down the center of its dying path. Here, the cattails and thick water grasses are slimy with the foul smelling rot of dead vegetation that had been underwater decomposing for years and is now released to dry out in the air.

Getting the rot on their shoes and clothes as they go is unavoidable.

"No wonder you smelled so bad," Darius grumbles. "Does this boat even exist? Or are you taking me on a wild goose chase?"

"She is there, you will see," Travis says eagerly.

And then suddenly there she is.

The boat looms on the edge of the mostly dried up tributary, half buried in the trees and bushes overcrowding the edge of the drying streambed.

She had been grand in her day, but today grey rotting boards are being sun bleached, the bare wood vulnerable and exposed to the elements. Most of the paint had long ago cracked and flaked away, scoured by the winds and the rain.

There is not a single window that is not broken. Many are altogether missing, and some nothing more than shards of sharp glass in the edges of the frames like beasts baring their broken ragged teeth to the world. Rotting fabric curtains hang limply in the odd window frame. The boat is leaning heavily to one side because of the shape of her hull on the ground.

The wood itself is infested with a cocktail of dry rot, wet rot, and insects eating their way through it as they nest in the soft rotten lumber.

The large elegant paddle wheel on the back sags in the middle, some of the blades missing.

Some unseen animal scurries in the darkness within the large hole in the hull that looks like it may have been broken open on a large rock.

There are no rocks in the vicinity large enough to match the damage.

Darius stops in his tracks, staring at the monstrosity.

"I can't believe I let you drag me all the way out here for this piece of offal." He shakes his head regretfully. "This is going to be a very long walk home."

Travis's eyes sparkle with excitement as he stares at the boat, picturing what he imagines she must have looked like in the prime of her life.

"She is a beauty, isn't she?" he says breathlessly.

"It's firewood," Darius says, turning to start walking back the way they came. He is too tired from the trip there to bother getting angry.

Travis stops him.

"Come on; just take a look at her. See the possibilities!"

Darius doesn't need to.

"It has a big hole in the bottom, the wood looks all rotten. The thing probably has to be completely rebuilt from the frame out. You might as well just build your own boat." He regrets the words even as he is saying them.

"Damn," he thinks, "don't give him ideas. He will probably try to do just that."

"No, no, she is not that bad," Travis insists, pulling him along by the arm to take a closer look at the rotting vessel.

While Darius watches skeptically, Travis tries climbing a ladder to the top. With a dull crack, the ladder tears free and they both tumble to the ground.

"Ok, so she needs a little work," Travis grins as he gets up, pulling the ladder off himself.

Darius shakes his head.

"I don't know what I should feel right now. Shock and surprise would be suitable, but quite frankly I don't feel either. This is par for the course with you Travis."

Travis is climbing one of the trees the boat is resting against, probably where the current dragged the floundering beast before leaving her trapped there to die.

When he reaches the top of the tilted boat, he half steps-half jumps across onto the boat. He makes it to the deck, holding the railing to keep from sliding off the tilted surface.

"Come on up, take a look," he calls down.

Darius knows better, but he still has that boyhood curiosity about old and abandoned things that is an integral part of any boy. That little boy inside who just has to poke at that dead animal to see what it is like, crawl through rotting falling down sheds, and on top of dangerously dilapidated old boats.

Unwilling to admit he actually wants to; Darius grudgingly climbs the tree to the deck.

"See? She's not so bad," Travis says, bouncing on the wooden deck to prove his point.

With a dry dull crack followed by a thud and winded grunt, he vanishes beneath the wood floor.

Darius cautiously makes his way closer to the new hole that just opened up in the deck, peering over the edge.

"Ok, so she needs a lot of work," Travis calls up from the darkness below. "But she will be beautiful, you will see."

"This is not convincing me. I am going home," Darius calls down. He makes his way back to the tree and climbs down, leaping down the last few feet to the ground, and starts walking back up the tributary towards the river.

He makes a point of not looking back to see if Travis is following, though he listens to make sure he is, just in case he was actually injured inside that boat.

Travis catches up, a slight limp to his walk, and they start the long trek home. After a while, Darius has to tune his friend out. Travis chatters endlessly about his plans for the two of them to fix up the boat.

Darius stops at one point, turns to Travis, and asks, "Does anybody own that hunk of junk? Do you even know who you would have to buy it from?"

Travis shakes his head with a grin. "No, but I will find out."

***

"I can't believe you talked me into this," Darius grumbles, walking into the bank with Travis.

"You won't regret it, you will see," Travis says enthusiastically.

"Funny, I think I heard that before."

Darius is stone faced, thinking about the huge mistake he is about to make with a sinking in the pit of his stomach.

"Neither one of us has a hope in hell of getting a loan," he says. "Not alone or together. We both own nothing to put up as collateral, renting little rooms in other people's houses to live in, work for low wages, and have no money to put in a bank account. We have no equity and no prospects.

The only reason I agreed to this is to make you see reality and give it up. The man at the bank is going to laugh us out the door."

After a brief wait, a carefully coiffed headed woman ushers them into the loan manager's office where the man behind the desk directs them to sit in two uncomfortable wooden chairs before his desk.

The man behind the desk is balding with glasses frames that are too dark and thick for his face. His striped suit shirt only makes him seem more stiff and awkward.

A nameplate on his desk haughtily displays his name. Mr. Shannon Whitaker.

He looks down his glasses and long nose at the two young men who came to sit across from him like the principal might look across his desk at a pair of misfit boys caught toilet papering the school mascot.

"So, Misters Wright and Marek, you want to take out a loan for this, um," he pauses as if having trouble with the word, "investment idea of yours."

Travis nods eagerly. "Yes sir. She is a beauty of a boat. Just a little work and we will have her on the water earning money in no time."

The loan officer's lips tighten and his eyes narrow, a vein in his forehead throbs with an anger tick.

"I took a look at this investment of yours." He clears his throat. "Ruined a pair of shoes too."

Darius knows at that moment the only reason the loan officer even agreed to meet them is to make a point of letting them know that.

"Gentlemen," Shannon says evenly, "the only service you can do for the world with that boat would be to light a fire to it."

"What about the loan?" Travis asks, being unbelievably obtuse about the man's intentions.

Shannon smiles a cruel little smirk, stands up, and reaches into his pocket.

He tosses something on the desk top.

"Here is your loan."

It is a single matchstick.

He stares down at them, indicating the open door to his office with a motion of his head.

Travis feels the heat of anger rising in him. He looks at the loan officer's name plate. Mr. Shannon Whitaker.

Darius jabs Travis in the rib with an elbow, nodding at him to get up, feeling his own flush of shame under Shannon's contemptuous glare.

They rise, feeling his stare on their backs as he walks them out. They feel the shame of every set of eyes on them as they walk through the bank, Shannon following with a spiteful sneer.

Shannon opens the door for them, laughing them out of the bank just as Darius imagined, following them outside with a barrage of cruel jokes and insults.

Looking back insolently as Darius tries to get them walking on, Travis gives the loan officer the best parting shot he has.

"You have a girl's name."

Shannon's lips tighten into an angry line and his eyes narrow. He is not laughing any more as he closes the door on them, returning to his bank and putting a forced smile on his face as he turns to his audience inside.

Travis and Darius stand outside the bank looking back at the loan manager, who is sharing the joke of the ruined boat and a matchstick with everyone else inside, laughing openly at them.

Travis kicks dejectedly at a rock on the ground.

"Well, I guess that's it then," Darius says with relief.

Travis looks like a little boy who had just had his best slingshot taken away. You can see his mind working.

He spins on Darius, the dejection replaced by determination.

"We won't give up, not just yet!" he says.

Darius shakes his head. "What harebrained idea do you have now?"

"We start with buying the boat," Travis says eagerly. "I already know where we can keep her while we fix her up. I found who owns her and the guy is willing to let us have her for a really good price, almost giving her away. He is just happy to see her finally getting fixed up, so he is willing to do us a favour on the price."

Darius is sceptical. "This sounds more like the guy is doing himself a favour. What do you even know about the value of boats? I don't know anything."

"A couple of weeks, some extra jobs, and we will have the down payment for her." Travis is pacing now in his excitement. "He said we can pay some of the money up front and we can start working on moving her and pay the rest later."

"You are beyond reasoning with," Darius complains.

Travis spins again on Darius.

"We can still do this. We just have to keep working and do extra jobs for the money to fix her up."

Darius groans. "What have I gotten myself into?" He is not seeing any way he could have avoided it.

5   Life Changing Transaction

The Dock Master leaves his office, walking across the dockyard to the docks. Without pause, Basil starts up the gangplank to the Queen Rhiannon. The single man watching the gate is roused out of his half slumber by the sound of footsteps on the wooden plank. He quickly opens the gate before Basil reaches it, nodding deferentially.

"I am here to see Mr. Barlow."

"Yes sir." The security man in a faux sailor suit whistles a piercing whistle to get the attention of a man some distance away. He signals to him and the man jogs off to announce the Dock Master's visit.

Basil walks on and is met by Frank, Malcolm Barlow's head of security, before he reaches the door to the casino room.

Frank half bows.

"This way, Mr. Jacobson."

He leads the way through the casino room, through a door, and up the stairs to Malcolm's office. He knocks on the door and waits for Malcolm to invite them in.

"Enter."

Frank opens the door and nods Basil to go on in, following him in and standing by the door.

"Mr. Barlow." Basil half bows to Malcolm from the doorway.

"To what do I owe the pleasure of this visit?" Malcolm says, not bothering to get up from his desk.

Basil approaches the desk, his anxiety showing.

"Mr. Barlow, sir, I have heard reports of a gentleman inquiring around the dockyard about buying a showboat paddlewheel steamboat for a pleasure business."

Malcolm's eyes harden almost imperceptibly.

"What kind of pleasure business?"

"A casino operation, sir."

Malcolm's mouth tightens.

"I run the only casino business in town."

"Yes sir."

"And they are asking here?"

"Yes sir. They must be new to the area if they don't know where to buy a boat."

"Not at the docks," Malcolm snickers humorlessly. "Thank you Basil. Keep me apprised."

"Yes sir." The Dock Master turns and leaves, walking quickly in his anxiety at meeting Mr. Barlow face to face.

Malcolm's face hardens.

"Frank."

"Yes sir."

"I run the only casinos in town and it is going to stay that way. Find out who this is."

"Yes sir." Frank bows and leaves.

***

A truck pulls over on the side of the road at the entrance to a dirt road, letting Travis and Darius jump out of the truck box. Travis waves a thank you as the truck drives away.

Having hitchhiked most of the way, they walk up the dirt road and finally arrive at a house. They stop in the road, looking at the property.

The house is more a rundown shack than a house, barren wood stained dull grey with little remnants of the paint that had once coated it. Stained curtains hang limply inside the streaked dingy glass of windows that must do little to allow the light in.

The yard is unkempt and littered with the skeletal remains of old cars and tractors. A dog sits panting inside one windowless truck, watching them from the driver's seat. Nestled against the trees and bushes invading the edge of the property, derelict sheds and a barn lean dangerously.

A crow flies from the hole in the barn roof, cawing loudly.

A truck parked in front of the house doesn't look much better than the remains of its deceased brethren littering the yard.

"Are you sure this is it?" Darius asks doubtfully.

"This is it," Travis says.

"That figures," Darius says.

"Come on." Travis waves him on to follow him and starts walking up the driveway.

Darius hesitates, wondering if anyone really lives here. Against his own instincts to turn and leave, he follows Travis into the yard. It looks just as bad closer up as it does from the road.

A trio of scruffy looking aggressive dogs appear from the debris cluttering the yard, barking loudly. Their stomachs heave with the barks, their legs and tails stiff.

The door of the house opens on hinges that cry loudly for oiling and a man steps out from the relative darkness inside onto the porch.

Darius envisions the man falling through the rotting wood, wondering how it can hold up the weight of a man.

The man is large, his round belly hanging like a mushroom over the belt of his pants, and looks as dirty as his torn shirt. His long hair is dirty and probably hasn't seen a comb in at least as long as it has been since his stained teeth have seen a toothbrush.

Looking around, Darius more than half expects to see a puppy mill next to an illegal moonshine still next to the backyard home taxidermy shack. He sees no evidence of any of these, although he does see a scrawny sickly looking rooster trying to mount a half bald chicken walking along pecking away at the ground, seemingly oblivious to her suitor's presence.

"Welcome, welcome, gentlemen," Norman says loudly, waving them over as he sits heavily in a chair on the porch.

Eying the aggressive dogs nervously, Travis and Darius step forward, moving one cautious step at a time. The dogs hover just outside of stone-throwing distance, their hackles raised and legs stiff as they glare distrustfully at everyone including their owner.

Travis and Darius mount the steps, the soft wood bending and creaking beneath their weight.

Darius looks at the sagging porch uncertainly before risking his life crossing it.

"Who is your friend?" Norman asks, pulling out a pocket knife from his trousers pocket, pulling the small blade out, and indicating Darius before he starts cleaning under his fingernails with it.

Travis hesitates briefly in his excitement.

"This is my partner, Darius. We are buying and rebuilding her together. Darius, this is Norman, the boat's owner."

The fat man continues with his unlikely nail cleaning as if their arrival is interrupting the very important task.

"Have you got my money?" Norman asks.

Another man, just as dirty and unkempt, skinny and long-haired, comes out of the shack to stand leaning against one of the posts holding up the roof.

Darius wants to beg him not to, picturing the man's weight knocking the support beam down and the whole porch roof collapsing on top of them.

"I have it right here," Travis says, stepping forward too eagerly to hand over their hard earned cash.

Norman takes the wad of bills, counting it slowly.

"How are we supposed to move that thing?" Darius asks.

"That's your problem, not mine," Norman says, followed by a loud belch.

"What is her name?" Travis asks eagerly as if buying the man's prized hunting dog.

Norman looks up from counting the money with a confused look.

"Who?"

"The boat."

"Hell if I know," Norman mutters. "Picked 'er up with a bunch of other junk." He blinks, a sly smile creeping across his face. "She was the pick of the litter though. Yeah, you'll be happy with her, I think."

"Do you have a bill of sale?" Darius asks, having a bad feeling they are being taken for the pair of fools they are.

Norman's look turns stern as he pulls out and signs a stained and crumpled piece of paper and hands it over to Travis.

"When are you giving me the rest of my money?" he asks. "I'm doing you a pretty big favor, you know, letting you have her so cheap."

Travis nods dumbly, agreeing.

"Every week. I will bring you a payment until she is all paid up."

"Don't make me come looking for it," Norman warns, his tone threatening. "You fall behind on the payments and I take her back just like a bank, just like we agreed."

"No sir, I mean yes sir," Travis says. "Don't worry; you will get your payments."

"Cash," Norman reminds him.

"Cash," Travis nods.

Norman nods, satisfied.

"Now get your damned boat off my property," he says, dismissing them with a smirk.

Travis practically dances down the porch steps in his excitement, causing the nervous dogs to dart around barking at him.

Darius follows at a more tempered pace.

"What have I gotten myself into?"

The moment they are out of earshot the skinny man stands up.

"That piece of shit isn't even salvageable, you know," he says to the fat man.

Norman coughs out a chuckle.

"Hey, the authorities told me to haul it out of there, so it's getting done. At least I don't have to pay to get it hauled out."

"How much are you skinning 'em for?" Floyd asks.

Norman almost chokes on his laugh. His eyes light with the shadow of the greed that had gleamed in them days before at the thought of these two rubes taking the boat off his hands when he first offered to sell it to the eager and very naive young man for a great deal more than a boat half as decrepit would be worth.

"Ten times what it cost me when I picked it up. Hell, I am getting rid of it before the authorities fine me and even if they stiff me for the rest I've already made a profit off the old bucket."

"Salvage value on a boat that can be stripped for parts and materials isn't much more than you paid for it," Floyd chortles.

He looks at his partner slyly.

"Are you going to let it go if they can't pay? I mean, look at them. There is no way those two rubes can come up with that kind of money."

Norman chuckles.

"Exactly. Look at them. Hell no, I'm not going to let them slide. I'm going to keep an eye on them. We are going to squeeze them for every penny of what they owe, plus interest. Those idiots are a prime set up for failure. They'll never get that boat out of there. It's sunken in the mud and going nowhere. The only way it's being moved is to rip it apart or burn it."

"And if they do manage to move it?"

"They won't."

"If they do?"

"If they manage to move it, I might just have to hire them." Norman laughs again, this time at the absurdity of the possibility.

"Even if they move it, they will never get that boat back in the water. They will have the Shipbuilders' Union and the Dock Master to deal with. And then there is the question of the original owner of that boat."

Floyd raises an eyebrow and Norman gives him a devilish grin.

"Let's just say that I will be there to kindly offer to take their problems off their hands for a very low price. Either they will pay for my help or, if by some miracle they actually get far enough rebuilding that hunk of firewood to make it worth anything, I will make a nice profit off selling it again."

***

"I still can't believe our luck," Travis enthuses as the pair make their way home, walking along the road and hoping for a vehicle or wagon to come along and possibly hitch a ride.

He is puffed up with pride.

"We got her for such a cheap price, at less than salvage value."

"How do you know?" Darius asks skeptically and feeling a little ripped off.

"The fat guy that sold her to us said so," Travis says, talking like the man is something of a saint, a reputable salesman.

"I don't know," Darius says, "it seems like an awful lot of money for a boat that won't even float. How do you expect to even move that thing?"

"I don't know," Travis says dreamily, "We will figure it out."

"How much more do we owe the fat man for that thing?"

"You leave that to me," Travis beams.

***

A few days later, Travis and Darius are standing in the mostly dried up tributary staring up at the boat.

"Is it just me, or does the boat look a little sunken?" Darius says skeptically.

They walk around the ruined boat, trying to work out how to move it.

"This is going to take a lot of work. I don't think it's even moveable."

Travis looks at him. "We will find a way."

"Yeah yeah," Darius mutters, "where there is the will there will always be a way."

"You got it," Travis grins.

"I don't have the will. I think we should just forget the whole thing."

"We will lose our deposit." Travis looks almost pouty.

He straightens himself.

"We will figure this out. Some ropes and pulleys..."

He walks around the boat, prodding at the rotting hull to test the wood's softness.

Darius does the same. "The wood is too soft with rot. This thing will just fall apart the moment we try to move it."

"She will hold up."

"How are we going to move it? Drag it out of here? With what?"

"We get some poles under her and roll her out." Travis's eyes are gleaming with ideas.

"With what? There is no way we are getting trucks in here."

"Mules," Travis says distractedly, his attention on studying the condition of his new prize. "We rent mules to pull her out."

"This is going to take a lot of hard work to move this boat," Darius says, shaking his head doubtfully. "A lot of hard work and a lot of man hours that will have to be spent in between working our jobs."

"And the extra jobs," Travis says.

Darius looks at him and he looks back.

"You know," Travis continues, "the extra jobs to make the payments on her and to buy tools and materials to rebuild her."

Darius groans.

"Who is going to rent us mules?"

"Leave that to me."

Darius does not like the twinkle in Travis's eyes.

42

6   Beginning the Move

Travis and Darius are again standing in the mostly dried up tributary staring up at the boat. A thin stream of water trickles down the middle of it, muddying the center strip.

"This thing is definitely sunken," Darius says, studying it critically.

The rotting boat sits exactly as it did before, looming on the edge of the mostly dried up tributary, half buried in the trees and bushes overcrowding the edge of the drying streambed, and leaning heavily to one side because of the shape of her hull on the ground.

The broken ladder lays on the ground where it fell on their last visit.

The one difference is that now a series of ropes and pulleys are draped around the hull of the boat. Ropes are tied off to any part of the boat that looks sturdy enough to take the strain.

"It's still firewood," Darius says, feeling like this whole thing is a big waste of their time and money. It feels like a bad dream and he wants to wake up.

Travis does not hear him, absorbed in the task of preparing his prize to be moved. He moves around the boat, checking knots and adjusting pulleys.

"I think we are ready to line up the logs," Travis says. He waves to Darius. "Come on."

The two men are a sharp contrast in their movements, Travis with a happy skip to his step, and Darius the unwilling participant.

The logs were left where they dragged them, ahead of the boat in the mud and laid haphazardly across the bow of the boat, the trickle of water running past them a tease of what the boat once was. The logs are long, full trees stripped bare of their branches.

Darius doesn't know where Travis got the logs. They look like they should be floating down a river somewhere to a sawmill after the tree cutters chopped them down and stripped the branches off.

He doesn't want to know. He doesn't ask where they came from.

Two teams of four mules each stand patiently grazing not far off, still rigged in their harnesses and tack.

"Grab the other end of this one," Travis instructs, grabbing the other end of a log.

Darius complies and together they drag the log and lay it out across the bow of the boat.

They continue this, creating an untied line of long logs laid out side by side against each other before the bow of the boat.

They stop, sweating from the heavy work, inspecting their handiwork.

Travis wipes a gloved hand across his forehead to wipe away sweat threatening to drip down his face.

"Her bow is sunken lower than the logs in the mud. I think we are going to have to dig it out and get these logs under her."

Darius frowns at the boat.

"That's going to be a lot of work."

"Then we had better get started digging."

They grab shovels and get to work, digging and slowly working on getting the logs jammed under the bow as far as they dare go.

Hours later, sweating, mud-spattered, and exhausted, they look at each other over a log that is giving them a particular difficulty.

"Let's take a break," Darius huffs.

Travis nods, letting the log go.

Darius shoves the blade of his shovel into the ground, leaving it standing up.

Travis does the same and makes his way over the logs across the front of the bow.

He is just passing the bow when his shovel falls to the ground. He pauses, turning back to look at it. With a shrug, he keeps going to the tall grass on the other side where they left a wagon with their tools and equipment, the mules still grazing nearby.

Darius glances back at the sound too and keeps going, grabbing his lunch from the wagon bed and plopping down in the grass.

"I guess she doesn't want us to take a break," Travis jokes, grabbing his lunch from the wagon bed and dropping down next to him.

Darius just looks at him then puts his attention on hungrily devouring his lunch.

They sit silently eating, each contemplating the boat with his own thoughts.

***

Their break over; they return to straining over the boat. After another hour spent positioning logs Travis stops and looks across the bow to Darius.

"I think she is as good as she is going to get."

Darius shakes his head doubtfully. "Are you sure?"

"We have to give it a try sooner or later. What can it hurt?"

Leaving their shovels, they retrieve the mules and get them into position, hooking up the ropes to their harnesses. The ropes lay on the ground behind them, strung to the old boat.

Each standing at the head of a team, they nod across to each other. Taking the lead animals' bridles, they walk the teams forward, taking up the slack on the ropes until the slack is gone.

Looking across to Travis, Darius calls out.

"Ready?"

"Ready!" Travis calls back.

"Heeyuh!"

They both shout to the animals, urging them forward.

The mules step forward and the ropes go taught. The mules stop, unsure what to do at the hands of their inexperienced drivers.

Travis and Darius pull on the bridles, urging the mules on. They pull and stop, stamping their hooves and stepping uncertainly.

They go behind the animals, taking up the long reigns left lying on the ground. Slapping the reins on their rumps and urging them on again, the mules make another effort to pull, this time leaning their weight against their harnesses.

The rotting wood of the boat creaks and groans, the thick ropes groaning against the hull. The mules whinny unhappily, the sound ending in a donkey-like bray, and they stomp their hooves. Their load not budging, they start backing up, leaving the men to scramble to stop them before they tangle up the ropes and harnesses.

"It's stuck too deeply into the mud. We are not going to break this thing out with just two teams of mules," Darius says, going back to inspect the boat.

Travis joins him. They walk around the boat, shoving on it and testing for any signs of loosening.

"She is in there pretty solid, all right," Travis says.

He grabs one end of a log and starts dragging it.

"Help me with this."

"What are we doing with it?" Darius grabs the other end.

Travis swings his end against the hull of the boat.

"We are making a lever to see if we can break her loose. Lift your end while I try to jam it in underneath."

With Darius holding his end up, Travis digs and claws at the mud with the shovel, and they work the log under the boat until it becomes impossible to get it any deeper without digging under the boat.

Travis looks at their handiwork.

"We can't go any further without making a tunnel to get it in there," Darius says.

"A tunnel might be better," Travis jokes.

Darius slaps him in the arm with his work gloves and Travis just grins at him.

"Okay, let's see if we can budge this thing." Travis points to the end of the log hanging in the air.

They lean on it, putting all their weight into trying to push and pull it down. The log bends a little with their efforts and they stop, pushing up instead of down.

"Let's try it again. Down and up. If it works and we get a rocking motion, it should rock the boat loose from the mud," Travis says.

They return to trying to push and pull it down, alternating up and down, trying to get a rocking motion going.

"It's too big. It will never work." Darius stops, standing back and studying the boat.

"We need more levers," Travis says.

"All right," Darius sighs unhappily. "How are we going to push them down all at once?"

"I have no idea. Maybe one at a time will work?"

Digging more logs in as levers at different points along the hull, they alternately try to push and pull each one into rocking the boat loose.

They continue the same process for the next couple hours until the lengthening evening shadows have stained the ground with the shadow of what looks to be some strange contraption with sticks sticking out on both sides.

Still, the boat has not budged.

"It's getting late and we haven't budged this thing at all," Darius complains. "It's going to be too dark to work soon."

Travis looks at the darkening sky.

"We will quit soon." He grabs a shovel and starts digging away at the ground beneath the edges of the boat as if he might dig the whole thing out.

With a regretful shake of his head, Darius grabs the other shovel and starts digging.

Darkness falls and they are still digging, tripping over the rough ground with the occasional curse.

Darius stops, tossing his shovel on the ground.

"That's it. I am calling it. It's time to stop for the night."

"All right," Travis says, his voice strained with exhaustion and a hint of desperation.

They wrap their exhausted bodies in blankets and lay on the ground staring off into the darkness. The soft sounds of the mules nearby are the only thing making them aware they are still hobbled nearby.

"What do you think her name might be?" Travis asks wistfully.

"I have no idea. It doesn't matter. It's your boat. You can name it whatever you like."

"Yeah, I guess."

Darius's snoring is the only response.

Travis lays there sleeplessly staring into the dark. He is too eager to get this boat home to sleep and has to push down the urge to get up and get back to work on freeing her from her muddy prison.

A sharp yip-yip-yipping cry in the night makes his head snap up. He looks around nervously.

"It's just a coyote," Darius mumbles, not opening his eyes.

Another cry answers the first.

"They won't bother us," Darius says.

"How do you know?" Travis's voice shows his anxiety.

"The mules are calm. They are too far away to bother us. Now go to sleep."

Travis lies down and closes his eyes, trying to make himself sleep. Eventually his exhaustion wins and he falls asleep.

***

In the morning, the sound of grunting wakes Darius. He blinks sleepily, sitting up and stretching out his stiff muscles, looking around.

It is not just grunting he hears. He can hear the low sounds of a voice whispering. The voice is coaxing and urgent at once. It sends a chill down his back, although he does not know why.

A low fire crackles inside an imperfect ring of rocks not far away and a tin coffee pot sits balanced precariously on a couple rocks at the edge.

His eyes roving the area, Darius spots the mules across the field, having roamed some distance off in search of water and forage despite their hobbles.

Further searching soon finds Travis toiling away at digging the boat out of the mud. He is saying something, but Darius cannot make out what.

"Who are you talking to?" Darius asks, still groggy with exhaustion.

Realizing Darius is awake, Travis points to the fire.

"Coffee."

"I'm just talking to myself," he grunts, straining against one of the poles.

"I thought I heard you say something about doing something to someone," Darius says.

"No, I didn't say anything like that."

"I'm going to get you something. Something like that."

Travis shakes his head. "I was just muttering to myself about getting the boat free." He keeps working, grunting with the strain against the pole as he heaves against it again.

Darius shifts with a groan, finding a tin cup near the fire and pouring himself a coffee. He rubs one hand through his messy hair and dried flakes of mud fall from it.

He digs in his bucket for something to eat, chewing the drying out food and swallowing bite after bite, washing it down with the black coffee and a grimace.

When he's done, he gets up stiffly, tries to stretch his cramped muscles out, and joins Travis.

Together they spend the morning struggling to push, pull, dig, and rock the boat out of the mud it had slowly settled into over the years.

With the sun beating unseasonably hot above, the insects chirring, and exhaustion taking its toll, frustration mounts. They spend the morning repeating yesterday's efforts of digging out what they can, jamming logs under the boat to act as levers and heaving on them, and even hitching up the mules to those levers.

That last only succeeds in pulling the levers out from under the boat.

They try pulling the boat in different directions, left, right, forwards, and even backwards.

Their efforts are met with the mud's resistance and a series of mishaps from mislaid shovels to snapped ropes, slipping and falling in the slimy ooze that is left beneath the small trickle of water that is all that is left in the tributary and a kick in the shin from one of the mules that leaves Darius limping.

She stubbornly refuses to budge.

Now they are each standing at the head of a four-mule team harnessed to the front of the boat.

"Okay, let's try it again," Travis says. "Maybe we can get enough momentum going. We will run the mules hard to the right until they are lunging at the ends of the ropes, then fast hard to the left and the same."

Darius nods and they cry out, urging the mules on, running alongside them.

They reach the end, the mules are brought up short, the ropes strain and groan, and the beasts start fussing at their inability to go forward with the men continuing to urge them on.

"Now!" Travis cries. "The other way!"

It takes too long to get the confused animals turned and galloping the other way. They reach the end and the ropes go taut, the mules whinny-braying and stomping their hooves in complaint.

"Again!" Travis cries.

They repeat the process again and again, the mules learning from repetition what is expected of them and starting to rear up and stomp their hooves and balk in exhaustion and frustration before the ropes grow tight. They noisily complain and finally refuse to cooperate altogether.

"Come on, you damned mules," Travis yells, pulling and pushing on the lead animal for his team.

The mule just looks at him with annoyance and gives him a loud long donkey-like bray in the face.

Finally, with a growl of frustration, Travis whips his work gloves off and throws them down on the ground with as much force as he can, stomping off to pace angrily.

The mules chuff and bob their heads as if laughing at him, the lead mule obligingly stepping on his gloves and pressing them into the mud.

Travis drops down and sits in the grass on the edge of the tributary, dropping his head into his hands dejectedly.

Darius stands for a long moment just watching him.

"This might be a good time to suggest we give up," he thinks.

But the abject look of rejection on his friend's face and the slouch of his unhappy shoulders stops him.

Darius walks over to stand over him, looking down at Travis for another long moment.

Travis ignores him, sulking in his own miserable thoughts of dejection and failure.

Darius looks at the boat, studying their predicament and thinking. He wants more than anything to give up and abandon the boat to remain in its grave in that dried up tributary.

"Some water would help. Soften up the mud and maybe partially float it out of here," Darius suggests.

"We don't have water," Travis says sulkily. "Not that much water."

Darius looks at the trickle of water steadily flowing past them, turns and stares up the tributary then down the other way. He looks down at Travis again, a pang of guilt tugs at him for wanting to quit something his friend so desperately wants.

"We will keep at it," Darius finally says.

Travis looks up at him and Darius sees that he is fighting back tears.

"I have an idea," Darius says. "It will take time. Days, maybe even weeks; if it works at all. But I have another idea too, and between them we might just be able to break this bitch free."

A gleam of hope lights Travis's face.

"What is your idea?"

***

Frank knocks and enters Malcolm's office.

Malcolm looks up.

"Mr. Barlow, sir," Frank says, bowing deferentially. "There is no information on the two men looking for a showboat."

"What do you have?"

Frank shakes his head.

"Nothing. Really. There are no investors. No families with money looking to get into the business. No leads at all."

"You are telling me they don't exist? That the Dock Master told me a story about two men looking for a boat and they aren't real?"

Malcolm arches an eyebrow, questioning, disbelieving.

"They exist. There was a man asking around about boats. But he is a nobody. No money, no backers, no family; just some poor sod with big dreams and nothing to back them up."

Lost interest, Malcolm waves him off.

"So it is a non issue then."

7   Moving the Boat

Travis and Darius are leading a couple of the mules along the grassy embankment above the mostly dried up tributary towards the mouth where the water once flowed into the river. The mules have minimal harnesses and ropes and the men are carrying shovels and axes slung over their shoulders.

The shallow water running down the tributary is little more than a ribbon of wet mud here.

"Do you really think this plan of yours will work?" Travis asks hopefully.

"No, but it's our best bet; and I know what a betting man you are." Darius grins at Travis.

The new project is a welcome change from fighting with the boat trapped in the mud and has Darius in a better mood.

They reach the mouth of the tributary and stop, looking down at the river. There is a drop from the tributary mouth to the river where the water has worn down the riverbank.

"All right, let's get to work," Travis says.

The next hours are spent chopping and dragging bush and small trees and packing them with mud, creating a manmade beaver-like dam.

Sweaty and tired when they finally finish, they stop to examine their handiwork.

Travis frowns doubtfully.

"You really think this tributary is going to fill up?"

"That depends on what is on the other end."

"So we could have wasted time damming up this end for nothing." Travis frowns deeper.

"It is possible. There is only a trickle of water running down the tributary. It won't be enough if there is no water at the other end. With luck we will find some kind of blockage preventing the water from flowing this way. If it's just a re-routed stream, we can hopefully block off the dried stream and re-route the water this way. We let it build up, then release the water to wash the boat out."

"Okay, let's go check out the other end."

They head back the way they came, bringing the mules and tools with them. It is a long walk and their sweat is attracting biting flies, adding to their discomfort. Insects buzz and chirr in the grass around them as they walk past the boat in search of whatever lies upstream of the small ribbon of water trickling past them.

As they go, the ribbon of water changes little.

After a few hours of walking, Travis and Darius reach the cause of the lack of water flow, a gnarled mound of sticks, branches, and mud.

"It looks like someone beat us to it," Travis says.

They stop and stare, then approach and climb up to get a better look.

The construction is more solid and expertly built than their own attempt to dam up the other end. A small trickle of water makes its way around the damn on both sides, flowing down from the top into the tributary to join together in the middle, becoming the thin ribbon of water flowing slowly past the boat.

On the other side, the water level sits high, creating a murky pond that sprawls out to flood the land around, turning it into a marshy habitat.

Travis cautiously steps out onto the dam, testing it with his weight. He gives a careful bounce. It is solid.

An irritated slap of a tail on water and swift motion gives away the owner of the dam.

Travis grins. "Thank you beavers."

"This is going to save us a lot of time waiting for the water to build up," Darius says. "Now we have to get ready to release the water. But, we have to somehow get it to release at the right time while we are at the boat ready to break it free and get a rush of water. We have to figure out how we are going to make the boat float. The boat hull is just going to fill up with water with that big hole in it."

Travis studies the dam thoughtfully.

"We could try patching the hole, but that will take longer."

"Without doing it properly, I doubt it will hold. Who knows how many more leaks are in that thing."

"We build a raft," Travis says.

Darius looks at him skeptically."

"Even if we can build a raft, how would we get that thing on it? And the water would have to get deep enough to float it. I don't think that would work to get it from where it sits to the river. I don't think the tributary will fill with enough water. At best I expect the water might break it free."

Travis shrugs.

"We break her lose and roll her out on logs. When we reach the drop at the river, we shove the raft under her. Then we just sail her home."

Darius considers this.

"Maybe. It might just work. Either way, we still need to put at least a temporary patch on the hole in the hull, and figure out how we are going to take out the beaver dam at just the right moment and break the boat loose from the mud."

"How do we blow this thing?" Travis asks, studying the beaver dam.

"Dynamite and a long fuse," Darius jokes.

Travis gets a reckless gleam in his eyes and smiles at him.

Darius groans.

"We need more logs, another couple teams of mules," Travis starts making a list of what they are going to need.

***

It takes Travis and Darius a few weeks to get more logs, build the raft, and patch and prepare the boat to try to break it free. Their time off in the evenings is spent on this project after spending the days working at their jobs. They lash logs together, building the raft in pieces to be put together on location so it is moveable.

At last they are ready.

With the logs loaded onto two wagons, a four mule team pulling and another tagging behind each wagon, they make their slow way to the boat.

The wagons bounce and rock over the uneven ground when they leave the road to travel overland to the tributary where the boat waits to be freed from her muddy prison.

Driving the wagons first to the mouth where the tributary will once again flow into the river, they get to work. Unloading the raft sections, they lash them together and tie the raft off to sturdy trees and ease it into the river. Dragging and positioning the raft just right, they tie off more ropes to hold it there, knotted so they can quickly release the ropes when the time is right.

Leaving the empty wagon, they return to the boat with the other wagon and mule teams.

They start rigging the boat and adjusting the logs laid out before it. The logs they had previously dug in under the bow are still there, if looking a little sunken into the mud.

Darius studies the logs already dug under to bow.

"Travis, do those logs look a little off to you?"

Travis comes to take a look. He goes to one side of the boat, grabs a log, and starts moving it side to side.

"What the hell?"

He moves on to the next and does the same, repeating again on the next. He looks at Darius, his expression serious. He looks like someone who just discovered his home vandalized in a demoralizing way.

"These are all snapped. What could have done that? Do you think someone is messing around with us?"

Darius frowns at the broken logs.

"Are you asking if I think someone sabotaged us?" He shakes his head. "Not likely. What would they gain from it? It's not likely anyone even knows this boat is here, except the fat man you bought it from."

"So what do you think happened?"

"My best guess…" Darius pauses, thinking. "The weight of the boat must have snapped them. They were probably bending under the weight and eventually snapped from the stress."

"Maybe," Travis says doubtfully. "This will leave us short on logs."

"We will make due. Let's get set up."

The next hours are spent replacing the ruined logs beneath the bow of the boat and tightening the line of loosely rolling logs before the bow.

Next, they build framework to support the warped used lumber they managed to salvage and attempt to seal the large hole in the hull as best they can.

Finished, they study their handiwork.

"It's not going to hold." Darius stares at it skeptically.

"It will hold," Travis says. "It has to."

They move on to securing more ropes to the boat and preparing the logs dug in under the hull, roping them off with a series of ropes and pulleys so when the mules pull the boat forward, they will also be pulling the logs.

They are checking the ropes previously tied to the boat while tying off more ropes.

"I'll go up top," Travis says. "You throw the ropes up to me and I will secure them."

"Make sure you double check the ropes already up there," Darius says.

Using a makeshift ladder, Travis climbs up to the boat deck. He walks awkwardly, trying to balance on the tilted surface, while Darius gets the ropes on the ground ready to throw up to him.

"What the hell?" Travis yells from above.

Darius stops and looks up. "What is it?"

Travis's face appears over the edge of the deck, looking pinched. He holds a rope over the edge, waggling it for Darius to see.

"It's a rope," Darius calls up.

"But look at it," Travis calls down.

"I just see a rope."

Travis tosses it down for his inspection and Darius has to dodge it.

Darius picks it up, inspecting it.

"It's broken." He looks up at Travis. "So, tie off another to replace it."

"There are a bunch of them broken like that," Travis calls down. They look like they were snapped."

Darius scratches his head, thinking. "What could have snapped them? They are thick strong ropes. I thought we left them with one end tied off to the boat and coiled and ready to throw down."

"We did. But they are tossed all over and are snapped like something pulled on them hard until the ropes gave."

"That's impossible. It would have taken a lot of force to snap them. Something very strong. Are you sure they weren't cut or sawed?"

"Yeah, a bear played tug of war with our ropes." Travis's voice has an edge of sarcasm.

Travis looks around. He returns to look over the side again, pacing the edge and studying the hull. He returns to look down at Darius.

"There are no signs of claw marks. How could a bear have got up here and done this?"

Darius inspects the rope again, frowning at it.

"Or maybe it was cut and then frayed, made to look like it just snapped," he says quietly.

Darius is regretting their decision once again, hoping for something that will convince his friend to abandon the boat so they can just go home.

Travis shrugs unhappily and continues lashing the ropes to the boat and throwing the other ends down for Darius to harness to the mule teams.

Finished, Travis climbs off the boat to join Darius.

"That just leaves the dam." Darius looks at him. "You said you had that figured out. What is it?"

Travis almost does a little happy jig and goes quickly to the wagon. Reaching into the back, he pulls out a bundle wrapped in old cloth.

He turns to Darius with a huge smile, holding up the bundle for him to see, and Darius has a sinking feeling in his stomach.

"No," Darius says.

Travis nods eagerly.

"You didn't," Darius says.

Travis doesn't wait. He turns and starts the trek upstream, a giddy bounce in his step.

Darius groans and shakes his head. He follows.

"He did it," Darius groans. "He got dynamite with a long fuse."

When they arrive at the beaver dam, they start inspecting it.

"Do you even have any idea how to set that stuff?" Darius asks. "Do you know where to put it so it works?"

"The guy I got it from gave me a few pointers." Travis is leaning over the dry side of the dam, testing for loose branches.

"I have a feeling all we are going to do is kill a couple beavers blowing the roof off this thing," Darius says doubtfully.

"It will work, trust me."

"How are you going to get that thing to blow in the right direction? We need it to blow out from the other side. It would be under water."

"Out and down," Travis says.

"Huh?"

"Out and down. If the charge is set right, it will blow down through the dam, blowing it out this side. The blast will weaken the dam and the weight of the water will do the rest. The water flowing through will erode the mud and the dam will crumble, the weight of the water will push it out, and it will tear apart."

Darius looks beyond the dam with misgivings.

"We don't even know how long this thing has been here. We could be doing some serious damage to the area. Maybe draining water someone relies on or flooding someone out downstream."

"It's all good. There is nothing upstream except land that is already flooded, and the river downstream. This thing was meant to flow to the river. The beavers dammed it up."

Darius comes closer, inspecting the dam.

"So, where do we put it?"

Travis finds what he thinks is the spot. He carefully shoves the dynamite in, pulling on branches to crack the spot open more to make it fit.

"That's a big coil of fuse you have there," Darius says, eying the long fuse rolled up.

"You said we need a long fuse," Travis winks.

Travis tests the placement of the dynamite.

A beaver eyes them coldly as it drifts by in the water on the other side of the dam, not impressed with their meddling with its dam.

"Let's go," Travis says, uncoiling the fuse as he goes and heading back downstream towards the boat.

Darius follows uneasily, adjusting the fuse so it lies along the least grassy path of the mostly dry streambed.

"Hopefully we don't start a grass fire," he mutters.

Behind them, a curious beaver clambers up the dam, inspecting the new addition left behind by the interlopers. It sniffs it, not liking the human scent. It paws at the dynamite, tries biting at it, and starts digging out the mud around it.

They move along, laying out the very long fuse until they reach its end.

"That's it," Travis shrugs.

"Now what?"

"Now we run."

Travis smirks, kneels down, and lights the fuse.

"Oh Hell!" Darius exclaims. He turns and starts running.

Travis bolts after him with a joyous whoop, adrenaline pumping through his veins.

The crackling and fizzling of the flame consuming the long wick retreats the other way, towards the dam and the waiting dynamite.

Arms and legs pumping, their ragged gasping breath scorching their throats, they run as if for their lives.

They hear the distant muffled boom and the ground barely shakes, and then nothing.

They stop and look at each other.

"It didn't work," Travis says. His voice and expression show his disappointment.

"Plan two I guess." Darius shrugs; almost relieved.

"What is plan two?"

"We carry on and try without the water?"

"You sound unsure."

"Or we start trying to break it loose with the ropes and pulleys and mules, and one of us goes back to try to break the dam apart by hand."

"That might work."

They start walking again

Travis points when they arrive at the boat.

"You take that side and I'll take this one. Just as we planned it, work the mule teams forward and right and left."

"What's that?" Darius looks back upstream.

"I don't see anything," Travis says, looking upstream too.

"Listen."

They both listen.

"I don't hear anything."

Then it comes, a light trickling sound.

They look down in unison to see the small ribbon of lazily moving water moving faster, grown in intensity.

They look at each other.

The trickling intensifies and so does the water's movement.

"Is that?"

"Rumbling?"

"Move!"

With a look of shocked panic, they bolt for the mules, startling the animals.

The mules are not cooperative in their agitated state and it is a fight to get them to move the way the inexperienced men want them to. One of them tries to bite Travis when he reaches for its bridle. He pulls his hand back quickly, moving behind it at a cautious distance to grab the long reigns.

He snaps the reigns, yelling to urge them on.

The mules dance and jerk forward, taking up the slack in the ropes.

The growing distant rumbling adds to the animals' nervousness. They chuff and stamp their hooves, moving in agitated motions as the men urge them on.

Travis and Darius keep urging them on, calling to the mules and each other.

The first wave of water arrives with a louder trickling as it washes over the ground an inch deep, gurgling and dancing over the uneven ground, slowly spreading across the dry streambed.

"Is that it?" Travis complains.

"I don't think so." Darius looks back uneasily. "I have a bad feeling it worked."

"Let's get to it then!" Travis shouts excitedly.

They push the mules, driving them forward, left, and right, working frantically to try to break the boat free from the mud imprisoning it as the water soaks into the mud and softens it.

The water reaches the bow and trickles around the poles laid out ahead of the boat. As the water slowly rises it starts trickling over the poles, not yet deep enough to make them float.

One pole almost floats, shifting but still held in place for now.

The mud the boat sits on now under water, the running water washing over it is weakening its grip.

Further ahead short pieces of wood wedged into the ground hold the poles in place until a great enough force comes along to move them forward. They are anticipating that this will be the forward momentum of the boat rolling over them.

"Come on, we have to get this thing moving before the water washes away the poles!" Travis shouts.

With a series of ropes and pulleys and the rented mules, they struggle to roll the boat onto the unattached free rolling logs.

They pull and heave on long ropes attached to the boat, leading the mules first on one side and then another, jerking the bow in opposing directions as they try to break the hull free of the mud, grass and bushes trying to grow through it, the boat-eating vegetation not willing to give up its prize easily.

Upstream, water is gushing over the ruined beaver dam into the tributary. The force and speed of the water with the weight of the water the dam is holding back pressing against the weakening structure is slowly tearing the dam apart. A large section is leaning out increasingly, threatening to break off altogether and release a new torrent of water.

The water flowing steadily grows, widening its path as they work. The flow comes faster, the water slowly inching deeper. The dancing trickle starts to overtake the rest of the logs. Logs move and bump together, still held in place for now.

They renew their efforts, attacking it and working furiously to break the boat free.

The wood of the boat groans and cracks, sounding like it will break apart, but finally it budges a fraction.

Travis whoops with joy, pumping his arms in the air at this minor victory.

They keep at it, exhausted and afraid to rest.

The boat creaks and groans, the logs threatening to break free, and it finally budges again.

Travis whoops in excitement.

"It's working!" His grin is huge.

Upstream, a piece of the crumbling dam breaks off, flowing downstream on a fresh cresting wave of water released after years of captivity behind the dam. The water rushes down the easiest path right down the middle of the once flowing streambed.

The debris breaks apart as the water floats it downstream.

The distant roar of the water grows louder with the approach of this new crest.

"Go, go, go," Travis cries. "We have to get this before the water washes away the logs."

Frantically, they attack the poles jammed under the hull, putting all their weight on them. They urge the mules in every direction, left then right and left again.

Darius slips in the growing wet, almost falling beneath the hooves of the straining mules.

He turns and looks upstream. Watching the coming tide, Darius wraps the reins around his hand, gripping them tightly.

Another surge of water hits them, almost washing Darius off his feet. He saves himself only by gripping one of the mule's tack and holding on until he can get his feet under him again, the mules digging in their hooves and leaning against the current.

The next surge is the biggest yet. The water hits the boat, the wood groaning with the soft splintering sound of wood on the verge of snapping.

The team of mules lose their footing as the water surges around them and would be swept downstream if not for the ropes tethering them to the boat. The mules slip and fall, thrashing in the water. They are dragged with the rushing surge until the ropes stop them.

Darius is washed with them, grasping for anything he can grab and trying to not be crushed under the falling animals. The reins wrapped around his hand is the only thing that stops him from being washed away, stopping him short with shoulder-wrenching force when he reaches their end. The mules bray in a sound the men have not heard them make and flounder until they get their footing again.

Darius struggles against the current, pulling himself along the reins and fighting to get his feet under him. He manages to get back to the mules, using them to pull himself to his feet.

The stream continues rising, spreading to fill the banks faster than it rises.

The unhappy animals are stumbling and getting stuck in the increasingly slick mud beneath the rushing water.

"Get them out of there," Travis cries, jumping over low hanging ropes and racing for the teams on the other side.

"I'm trying," Darius yells back, struggling to lead the mules to the grassy ground outside the stream's banks.

Finding their front hooves finally on solid ground, the lead mules surge forward, pulling those behind along as they slip and nearly fall in the slick mud beneath the grass of the bank.

With the mules on dry ground, Travis runs back and wades into the water, trying to get on the boat.

"Stay off it," Darius yells the warning too late, still struggling to get his mules established on the bank.

The boat slips forward, butting against the logs, and Travis slips down and into the moving water.

The sucking motion of the boat with the rushing water pulls at him, trying to pull him down under the slipping boat. Travis kicks one foot out, savagely kicking at the hull and pushing himself off, narrowly avoiding ending up partially under it.

Debris is flowing past, snagging on the poles and hitting the boat, threatening to puncture holes in the rotting wood.

With the grinding creaking of wood on wood, the front curve of the hull drags up onto the logs and the boat stops dead in its tracks.

Darius is looking for Travis anxiously. He can't see him past the boat.

"Are you all right?" he shouts.

"I'm good," Travis shouts back. "We have to keep it going."

Travis wades out of the water and scrambles back, charging to the head of the two mule teams on that side and finally back into Darius's view.

Relief washes over Darius's face.

Another surge of water comes, washing downstream from another break in the deteriorating dam, bringing with it a new wave of debris from the ruined dam.

The fresh swell of water hits the boat, pushing it forwards another inch.

"Now!" Travis screams the moment the water hits the boat.

They both urge the mules on hard. The mules surge forward, their harnesses creaking, the ropes groaning, and the ropes and pulleys straining.

Incredibly, the front of the boat pulls up onto the logs, the logs cracking and splintering beneath its weight, bending and pressing into the ground. A couple logs snap completely, but they finally manage to drag the boat partially onto the logs.

"Keep the momentum going," Darius screams over the sound of the water and grinding wood.

They keep the mules moving steadily, the boat moving slowly over the logs. The logs start to roll slowly with the boat.

A final swell of water washing downstream threatens to undo all they did, but miraculously the logs keep close enough together and the boat keeps a slow forward progress. It washes past in a wave leaving a weakened flow in its wake, the water level dropping quickly.

With the boat finally on top of the rolling logs, the wooden hull crackling and bending as the unhappy mules drag it, their job has only begun.

The posts holding the logs in place bend forward with the pressure of the rolling logs and boat. The water levels are levelling out quickly to mere inches, still spreading to fill the bottom of the stream bed.

The flowing stream has stopped growing in surges, instead rising more slowly. The still flowing water adds its strength to their effort, trying to wash the boat downstream, but does not get deep enough to float the boat.

Travis and Darius scramble to release the ropes and pulleys that pulled them forward but would now hold them back; leaving them to the sturdy trees they are tied to.

Urging the reluctant mules forward, the boat rolls very slowly along the top of the logs, the logs bobbing and cracking as they roll on the uneven ground beneath the weight, holding the boat above the sucking mud of the ground.

Just like in the old riverboat days before steam engines powered them, when barges were pulled along the river by animals, they have two four-mule teams tethered on each side of the boat. A long thick rope runs between the animals and the boat, dragging it forward as evenly as they can from both sides.

They pull the boat forward very slowly, stopping to race back to drag the trees left behind to the front of the boat, struggling to pull them across the tributary to roll the boat over them again. Every time they stop it is a struggle to start the forward motion again, the mules slipping as they strain to pull.

The rise of the water has slowed to be almost imperceptible as the marshy area's water slowly drains off, redirected back now to its natural flow while the new channel cut by the damned up stream still takes its flow in another direction.

It takes days just to roll the boat to where the tributary flows into the river; that trickle now the steady flow of a creek gradually deepening by the day.

Every now and then the curious fat man who sold them the boat and his skinny friend make the trip out to watch their progress, walking away with their shoulders shaking in laughter.

Aware of their interest, Darius watches them go, feeling the brunt of some private joke.

Travis never even notices; he is so focused on getting his baby home.

At last, they reach the river.

The two men and the rented mules are sweating from the hard labour. They stop to survey the river and try to figure out the next step.

"It looks like the dam didn't hold," Travis says.

Their loose damn of sticks and mud washed away easily with the increased flow of water.

"That explains why the water leveled off and never rose any more," Darius says.

"We still have to get her into the river to float her down river."

"How?" Darius studies the drop from the tributary to the river. The water is cascading down in a steady mini-waterfall to the river below. "This thing is not going to float. And when it hits that raft, it is going to just split it apart. The drop is too much."

Travis studies the river, turns, and studies the boat. You can almost see the light bulb turn on in his mind.

"We lash the logs together into a ramp and then slide her down to the raft. Then we can float her down the river with the mules, just like we dragged her down the tributary."

Darius looks doubtful.

"We won't be able to put an animal on each bank. It will just keep getting pulled to shore and getting hung up."

Travis sits down. He has to think this out. There has to be a way.

"How do boats get steered down the river?"

It comes to him.

"One of us will have to ride the raft. We can make a thing on the back to steer it, and use a long pole to push off the bank when we have to."

"A rudder," Darius says.

"Huh?"

"A rudder," he repeats.

"Yeah, a rudder."

"It's getting late," Darius says, looking up at the sky. "We need to quit for today. "

"We need something to lash these logs together anyway," Travis agrees.

He looks at the waiting mules.

"One good thing about the money we are spending on renting the mules is that we can ride them back."

They secure the boat to sturdy trees, unhitch the mules, and each climbs on the back of one, leading the others behind. The animals plod along slowly, heads falling to snatch vegetation in their teeth as they go, tired from the hard day of pulling the old boat.

8   Ramp Building

Days later, after working long hours at their jobs and doing extra jobs for cash, Travis and Darius are up early Saturday morning and on their way with the teams of rented mules to start lashing the logs together to build a ramp to slide the boat down to the raft.

The difficult task is made harder by the fact that neither man actually knows how to build a ramp.

They work diligently, binding logs together, tightening them up, and binding them again.

At last, they proudly inspect their job. Once again, they set up ropes and pulleys to drag the boat forward. They lower the ramp into place, hook up the mules, and start dragging the boat forward onto the ramp.

Things are going well until the boat actually starts dragging onto the ramp.

Darius clicks at the mules, urging them forward. The animals pull until they feel the resistance of their load and then stop.

He urges them forward again, and this time the animals dig their hooves in, put their weight against the harnesses, and pull.

"Keep them going, that's it," Travis calls.

Darius keeps urging the mules on, slow and steady, looking back to make sure they are not pulling the boat sideways off the ramp.

The wet mud makes the footing difficult for the mules and they struggle to keep their footing in the slippery muck.

The bow drags across the sloppy wet ground, the mud making it easier to slide, and the rounded edge inches forward a little at a time, finally connecting with the edge of the log raft.

"That's it!" Travis cries excitedly the moment the boat touches the raft.

It looks like it will glide onto the raft easily.

The boat presses against the edge of the ramp, pauses, and then slips forward an inch, pushing the ramp ahead of it. The far side of the ramp digs into the mud, stopping its movement. The ramp groans and buckles as Darius urges the mules forward. The lashings are strained to their limit and begin snapping with a dull sound, the logs clattering against each other as they fall loose.

"Stop! Stop!" Travis cries.

Darius looks back, sees the damage, and pulls on the reigns to stop the mules. The animals look back at him with bored looks that suggest they are merely suffering his foolishness.

He races back to survey the extent of the damage.

Travis is already crawling over the ruined ramp. Nothing seems broken except the lashings.

"We are going to have to rebuild it," Travis says. "We don't have enough rope to do the whole thing over."

"Maybe we don't have to," Darius says, studying the ramp lashings. "They only came apart at one end. We just need to re-tie this end. The other should hold up, I think."

Travis nods. "Let's give it a try."

They work quickly with what they have left of the rope. With the ramp repaired and the day waning, they try again to get the boat on the ramp.

Darius urges the mules on. They dig their hooves in; put their weight against the harnesses, and pull.

The boat hesitates and then slips forward against the edge of the ramp. It stops again as the mules pause to pull again, and then slips forward, pushing the ramp ahead of it again. The far edge of the ramp digs into the mud again, bringing them to sudden stop. The logs groan and the lashings snap, the logs clattering loosely against each other.

"Stop!" Travis calls.

Darius pulls the mules to a stop, looking back and shaking his head. He comes back to inspect the ramp.

"We have to get the ramp to stop digging in," Travis says.

"I don't think that's it," Darius says. "If the boat just pushes it, we will end up with a ramp in the water and no boat on it to slide down to the raft. We have to get the boat to stop pushing the ramp."

"But if it doesn't push the ramp to the water, we will just be stuck on dry land with the boat on the ramp. We need it to slide onto the ramp and slide down it to the water."

Darius thinks about this.

"It's too late to do anything more today." He looks up at the sky. Dusk has settled on the land and the sun is hanging lower on the horizon.

"We will try to figure it out tonight and come back tomorrow."

"Do you have any money to buy more rope?" Travis asks.

Darius narrows his eyes at him. "What happened to the money you had left?"

Travis looks sheepish. "I thought we would be celebrating. I bought a bottle."

Darius gives him a look. "It's a little soon for that, isn't it?"

9 A Woman's Advice

The next morning, they arrive at the hardware store. Darius and Travis automatically nod a polite greeting to the old man sitting on the bench in front of the store, wondering at his seeming to be oblivious to the gesture. The old man just sits, watching as though he is waiting for someone.

They enter the store and turn their attention to inspecting the various ropes and arguing over how to get the boat on the ramp, and thus onto the raft.

A young woman approaches them.

"Excuse me," she says. "I could not help but overhear. You are trying to get a boat in the river? Why don't you just drag the boat to the river and float it without the raft?"

Darius points at Travis with a teasing smirk.

"This guy bought a boat with a big hole in the bottom," he says.

The young woman nods, her look becoming thoughtful.

"Where is the boat?" she asks.

"By the edge of the river," Travis says.

"On a dried up tributary," Darius adds.

"If you wait for the rains, you could get the boat on the raft, tie it up, and then when the rain comes and the water level goes up it will float itself to the river," she says.

Darius looks at her, impressed. "It's too much of a drop and we can't lift the boat onto a raft."

"We tried floating it. The water never gets high enough for that," Travis says. "We have to move it now."

"Hmm," she taps her lower lip. Her eyes flash brightly with an idea.

"Why don't you make the raft into a ramp?"

"A ramp?" Travis scoffs. "We tried that. It didn't work." He chuckles at the absurdity of an idea coming from a woman.

He looks at Darius in amusement, his look asking what would a woman know about these things.

The young woman nods, flashing a quick look of annoyance at Travis.

"Build the raft and drag it to the very edge of the water. Dig the end nearest to the boat into the mud at the edge of the river and tether it off so the boat does not just push it. The other side will be raised a little like this," she holds her hand up to demonstrate, angled up just a little.

"Instead of catching on the edge and pushing the ramp, the boat will slide right on it and push the other side down. By the time the buried side pops out of the mud, the boat is already past the edge and sliding onto the raft." She slides her other hand up the first one smoothly in demonstration. "If you tie the bow to the rear of the raft, the ropes will make sure the raft goes with the boat. Then you just have to drag it onto the water. It might even pull itself into the water by the time you get the boat all the way onto the raft."

Travis sneers and starts to chortle at the idea but Darius stops him with a warning elbow to the ribs.

Darius bows his head towards the woman with a smile.

"Thank you Miss," he says. "We will consider your wise counsel."

She flushes and turns away, pretending to be inspecting a pile of farming tools a little distance away.

They bring the rope to the counter to pay for it. Darius keeps looking back at the young woman. They are arguing the merits of the young woman's suggestion all the way out the door.

"It is absolute nonsense," Travis complains. "It won't work."

"It's a better idea than any we've come up with so far," Darius counters.

"A woman cannot possibly come up with a solution to a problem like ours," Travis insists.

Darius just keeps going back to the image of the young woman deep in thought and tapping her finger on her bottom lip. They are nice lips in his opinion.

"Forget where the idea came from," Darius says. "Just think about the idea itself. I think it will work."

A small smile lights the young woman's face as she surreptitiously watches the young men leaving, listening to their arguments.

***

Travis and Darius argue about how to get the boat on the raft all the way to the boat.

"Some of it might work," Travis grudgingly admits, "but we will have to change stuff to make the plan work."

"You are just stubbornly refusing to let a woman outsmart you," Darius teases.

"I have no doubts of any woman's ability to outsmart me in many other ways, but not when it comes to something like this. Hard labour and issues of engineering are the domain of the man and the man's mind."

Darius shakes his head at him.

They repair the ramp, drag it to the edge of the river, and moor it to a strong tree. They dig the end towards the boat into the mud, raising the other end so that it hangs in the air just above the water, supporting it with branches that will give and break before the strong wooden logs will beneath the weight of the boat.

They tie off ropes and pulleys on trees growing on the edge of the riverbank, tethering them to the mules and the boat.

Wait." Darius clambers down the bank. He pulls the raft there in and starts digging at the mud.

"What are you doing?"

"Digging the raft in too. I have a feeling we will need both. It won't do us any good if it hits the raft in the water and just pushes that away too."

Travis clambers down too and together they dig and pull the raft in, burying one end in the mud beneath the overhanging edge of the ramp.

Finished, they study it. The ramp should come down to cover that end of the raft. With luck, the boat will simply slide down the bank onto the raft, bringing the ramp with it to float on them both.

When they are finally ready, they look at each other.

"Okay, here goes," Travis says.

Darius nods, matching his serious expression.

Darius urges the mules on. The animals dig their hooves into the sloppy mud of the riverbank; put their weight against the harnesses, and pull.

The boat pauses and then slips forward half an inch.

"Keep going," Travis shouts, keeping a hand on the boat as if he can somehow direct it where he wants instead of just being dragged beneath its weight or pushed aside like a small child.

Darius urges the mules again. They heave against their harnesses and the boat slips forward another inch.

They keep at it, moving the boat forward inch by inch. The edge of the boat comes to the buried edge of the ramp.

"This is it," Travis cries. "It's at the ramp."

Darius looks back, says a silent prayer, and urges the mules forward.

Travis holds his breath and almost closes his eyes.

The boat inches forward and glides across the slippery mud over the buried edge of the ramp without a hitch. The wet mud lubricating the bottom of the boat keeps it sliding as it is pulled onto the ramp.

The mules continue to strain, Darius urging them on, as Travis watches the boat with an expression of fear and delight as it continues its slow forward progress.

The boat reaches the mid-point. The weight of the boat tips the ramp flat, bringing down the edge hovering over the water and dragging the buried end out of the mud. The boat balances precariously at the edge of the drop, its bow hanging weightlessly for a heartbeat, and then it tilts forward, teeters, and tips.

Its weight thrusts it forward, dragging the ramp with it, wood on wood grinding together with the weight.

Instead of the ramp tipping and the large boat gliding down it, everything drops with a suddenness that leaves Travis feeling his stomach drop with it.

"HOLD," Travis yells. His face is a mask of panic.

The momentum speeds and the boat ungracefully skids down the bank, tearing branches and bushes out with it, the ramp dragged ruthlessly beneath it.

It comes down with a gut-wrenching splash against the water, landing mostly on the raft with a dull crack that echoes off the sky, bowing down and pushing the raft beneath the water. The water washes over the raft, ramp, and boat from the weight of the boat coming down hard on its surface, the water immediately beginning to dissolve and wash away the lubricating mud. The mud-less boat bottom against the rough logs acts like a brake, stopping the boat's forward motion before it slides right off the other end of the raft.

The weight and forward momentum has boat, ramp, and raft shooting forward together, brought to a sudden groaning stop when it hits the end of the ropes tethering them to sturdy trees, protecting the mules from being yanked forward and dragged with it. The force yanks the trees hard with a shuddering jolt that makes them crack and creak. The trunk of one tree cracks; tearing a jagged raw wound up its length. Another tree is pulled partially loose from the ground, leaning as if bowing to the mastery of the decrepit vessel. Two ropes groan and snap under the weight, the ends snapping back viciously to drop impotently on the ground.

Darius ducks instinctively at the snapping ropes, keeping his focus on the mules.

Brought up short, the boat rocks in its own waves; waves licking at the bank.

"Stop! Stop!" Travis is yelling.

Darius is pulling the mules to a stop, afraid to look back. He is expecting a repeat of the previous day's failure, only this time with devastating results. He turns and gapes in surprise.

"It worked. We followed that woman's suggestion and it worked perfectly," he says.

Travis is jumping, whooping, and gesturing in excitement.

Darius walks back to inspect their progress.

"It is still too soon to celebrate. I am still not sure if the raft can hold the weight of the boat without falling apart," he says.

He walks around it, inspecting their lashings. Some of the lashings are weakened, and some have snapped, pulling the lashings loose in places. There are gaps in the raft now, and some of the trees are broken and crushed, but so far it looks like it is mostly holding up. The other edge of the raft is tipped precariously into the water with one edge still on the riverbank.

"Ok, let's see if we can get it the rest of the way into the water," Darius says. "The mules will pull it along the shore since we have nothing to pull it out further into the river. You will have to use the pole to try to push it out into the river while the mules drag it so it doesn't get stuck on shore."

"How are we going to keep them from just pulling the boat off the raft?" Travis asks, looking the boat over.

"Good point," Darius says. "The best thing would be if we can tether the mules to the raft instead of to the boat.

Travis walks around the raft studying it, trying to figure out how they might do that. The weight of the boat has the raft pressed down into the slick mud beneath the surface of the water.

"There is nothing to attach to," he says finally. "What if we just loop it through the bindings?"

Darius looks it over. "That might just pull the raft apart, or it might work. We will wrap the extra rope around and re-lash below where we tether the mules to it. Lashing the ramp to the raft so it does not pull out might help with its buoyancy too. Maybe that will make it strong enough."

They make the adjustments and get into position. Standing on the bank, Travis wedges a pole under the raft towards the front on the side nearest him, ready to throw all his weight into using it as a lever and pushing the raft off the shore.

Darius has the mules ready and looks back for the signal Travis is ready.

Travis waves and Darius urges the teams of mules forward.

The raft and boat shudder for a moment, hesitating, and then it slips forward just a fraction on the wet sloppy mud.

"Good. It's working," Travis calls. "Keep them going."

Darius urges the mules forward. They strain, trying to pull the flat raft is harder than the curved boat hull against the ground.

He urges the other teams on, straining against the weight of the boat.

The water flowing down the once empty tributary helps, the water washing past the boat and beneath it where it can, adding its push to the effort.

The boat shivers again and the raft slips forward again. Darius keeps urging the mules and they pull steadily. The boat and raft move again. This time they both keep moving very slowly forward as the mules strain to pull.

Travis stands ready to release the ropes lashed to the boat while Darius is ready to release the raft.

Travis throws his weight against the pole, pushing up on it as the raft slides forward. The boat and raft edge further into the river. Pulling out the pole, he jams it under the raft towards the front again, pushing his weight against it again, slowly edging the boat laden raft towards the middle of the river again.

"It's working!" he yells to Darius. "Keep going!"

The raft is groaning with the strain, the trees rubbing against each other and the lashings straining on the edge of their breaking point. A few ropes snap, but the raft so far holds together as it is dragged forward along the riverbank and pushed over further into the river.

The edge dips down, the boat and raft rocking precariously as the shore side is pushed up by underwater roots as it scrapes over them. The wood of the raft groans and the ropes moan with the strain.

The weight of the boat pushes the raft down below the surface of the water.

Travis feels the jerking motion of the raft slipping beneath the boat and realizes suddenly that the boat could be pulled right off the raft in the water.

They pass over the roots of trees beneath the water and the boat and raft settle, leveling out and sinking further under the weight. Instead of floating, it is being dragged on the bottom.

His mind reels and he starts to panic.

It is harder for the mules to pull now and they are starting to balk at the added strain of pulling the raft miring in the river bottom.

"Stop," Travis yells. "It's sinking!"

Darius does not hear above his own shouts as he keeps urging the mules forward.

The animals strain and the raft keeps going. It is approaching the edge of the tributary's mouth and the bank looms up like a miniature cliff before the sliding raft. The boat and raft start turning slowly on a crash course with the riverbank.

Travis runs ahead frantically, digging the pole into the mud and driving it against the raft, trying to keep it from being pulled up the bank and tipping the boat off.

"Stop," he screams. "It's going to go over!"

Darius keeps urging the mules on, hearing only his own voice yelling at the mules.

The raft slides forward, Travis heaving and screaming, and the edge of the raft comes up against the side of the riverbank. It is pulled up and the boat teeters precariously.

Then with a sudden motion, it goes.

The raft slides sideways into the river, Travis falling with it, and the mules suddenly lurch forward when the weight of their load suddenly changes. The raft is yanked forward, the front rising and splashing down, almost catching Travis beneath the edge.

"Stop! Stop!" Travis is screaming.

Darius pauses when the mules suddenly lurch forward, looking behind him, and pulling the reigns back to stop the animals.

One of the mules turns to look at him and makes a rude noise at him.

He races back to the raft and Travis floundering in the water at the river's edge.

"Why didn't you stop?" Travis demands. "I was yelling at you to stop."

Neither man notices the raft is floating beneath the surface with the weight of the boat pushing it down. The current takes it and it swings out from the edge, being drawn downstream.

Darius turns to watch it in blank surprise.

The raft is yanked to a sudden stop when it reaches the end of its mooring rope. The tree it is tied to lurches and bends from the sudden tug, but it holds.

Darius helps Travis out of the water with a huge grin.

Travis's face is a mask of fury.

"I was yelling at you to stop," he spits. "We lost the boat off the raft."

Darius's grin makes him angrier. "What are you smiling at?"

Darius points to the raft and Travis turns to look. His expression changes to confusion then wonder.

The raft is submerged beneath the water from the weight of the boat, but it is floating.

Travis leaps into the air, whooping with joy.

He runs out into the water, remembers, and comes back for his pole.

He stops and turns to look at Darius. "Well? What are you waiting for?"

Going back out into the water, it takes a few tries before Travis finds a spot to stand so he can use the pole to push the raft away from the shore as it is dragged upriver. His feet are submerged beneath the water with the raft.

Darius goes back to the mules, re-rigs them, and brings them around to pull the boat up the river. He signals to Travis that he is ready. Travis signals back and Darius races back to cut the mooring line.

The mules shift uncertainly and then start backing up with the boat pulling them backwards on the drag of the river current until Darius races back to them and starts urging them forward. The animals start pulling and the boat and raft begins its slow trek up the river to what will be its new home while it is being rebuilt.

Crews on passing cargo barges whoop and point; laughing at the men pulling the half sunken rotting steam boat up the river.

Travis keeps pushing against the riverbank with his pole, preventing the raft from being dragged to shore as the mules slowly bring it home.

The drag of the water slows their progress, and at times they run into obstacles of trees and bush. The way proves difficult, with the mules pushing their way through the growth along the riverbank and tangling up the ropes in it. Each time they have to stop while Darius cuts them loose.

They continue for hours, slowly dragging their precious cargo upstream.

10   It all Falls Apart

They are nearing the end of their trip upriver when the lashings begin to give.

Travis is poling the boat when he feels the raft shudder beneath his feet. A log slips a little, the ropes groaning and the wood grinding. A lash snaps.

The log slips more, dragging another with it.

Travis looks around urgently for the source and another lashing snaps.

He looks around him as he feels the logs beneath his feet sag apart. He cannot see them. His feet are underwater on the raft, but he knows what he felt. His eyes widen and he starts yelling to Darius.

"Faster! Go faster! We are not going to make it!"

Darius looks back to see what he is yelling about and sees Travis gesturing frantically.

At that moment a log floats loose, drifting backwards away from them on the current, and Darius knows what the problem is. He turns back to the mules, urging them faster. The raft lurches and Travis almost falls off.

Darius urges the mules faster again and they grudgingly pick up their pace, pulling the raft faster. All his attention is focused now on the mules.

Another rope snaps and then another. Logs spread further apart and the boat sinks deeper. It is a race to the finish, man and beast against the deteriorating raft and the cool unforgiving waters of the river.

People passing on cargo barges and on the shore watch the frantic men, laughing. Some cheer the men, others cheer for their predicament. Logs are starting to float to the surface and the boat sinks deeper as its hull tries to slip between the raft logs, putting more strain on the ropes.

The logs groan and creak, the boat shifts sideways, and more ropes snap as they close in on their destination.

They are just nearing the spot they were to stop when part of the raft gives and pops to the surface in a jumble of logs lashed together in threes and fours haphazardly.

One moment Travis is standing on the deteriorating raft, his feet beneath the surface of the water, and the next he is gone; dropped through the separating logs.

One log popping up to the surface connects with his head and back with the force of a strong mule kick, sending a flash of pain through him and almost knocking him unconscious.

The boat sinks lower, water flowing in through the holes in the hull dragging it down, and it hits the river bottom, the weight of it making it slide against the bottom until it comes to a stop. The current grabs it, trying to pull it back the way they had come.

Travis flails groggily under the water, fighting the blackness closing in. His arms and legs move instinctively but without direction or purpose.

He sucks in a breath of water, choking and gagging on it instantly, causing him to vomit it up and suck in another, threatening to fill his lungs with water.

Travis manages to break the surface, choking and gagging, and swims weakly for shore, floundering in the water. When he realizes he can touch bottom he comes up waterlogged and running.

"Bring them away from the shore!" he yells through choking gasps of air as he runs at Darius and the mules.

Darius looks behind him, sees the ravaged raft, and angles the mules away from the water to drag the drowned boat to shore.

"The raft," Darius yells, pointing. "We need the logs to move the boat!"

Realizing, Travis turns and runs back to the river, wading back in and fighting the current, trying to salvage as many raft logs as he can. Many have already been carried off downriver, some are held against the boat's hull by the current.

The boat is resting now against the edge of the riverbank, its weight holding it in place while the exhausted mules rest.

The spectators on the shore seem almost disappointed the show is over, and even more so that the men actually succeeded in bringing their prize in. With nothing more to see, the spectators start to mostly disperse to return to going about their business.

Gasping and panting, Travis falls to the ground next to the river.

The mules stopped and eating grass, Darius walks back to join him, standing over him.

"We almost lost you there again, didn't we?"

Travis looks up at him, shielding his eyes from the sun.

"Nah, it would take more than that."

Darius eyes the boat then looks back down at him.

"Do you get the feeling this thing doesn't want you to rebuild it? How many times has this boat almost killed you now?"

Travis thinks, tilting his head to consider. He grins up at Darius.

"Six?"

Darius shakes his head, wondering if his friend will ever learn.

"We need to rest the mules," he says.

"And you," he adds after a pause.

Travis pats the ground beside him and Darius joins him on the ground.

"You know, we could just leave it there," Darius suggests.

"The river would eventually pull it all apart and drag it downstream."

"That might not be such a bad thing."

Travis gives him a mock horrified look, then grins, not taking him seriously.

Darius looks at the boat longingly, considering the idea of just letting the river take it. Even after all they have been through to get it this far, it still feels like a good idea to him.

They sit staring out at the river contemplating it and their next moves.

"How are we going to get her up on shore?" Travis asks finally. "It's going to be a lot harder to drag her up than to drop her in."

Darius thinks.

"The same way we get a heavy mine cart up when it jumps the tracks?"

Travis nods thoughtfully. "It might just work."

Getting up wearily, pulled down by exhaustion, they get back to work.

Using what remains of their logs as a makeshift rail ramp, logs laid out beside each other to run the hull up their length. Travis and Darius stretch ropes between them to hold them from pulling further apart and start pulling wet slimy mud from the river bottom and coating the logs heavily with it to grease them.

With their makeshift rail line ramp ready, they bring the mules around. Taking the end of one rope and looping it around his waist and tying it off, the other end tied to the ends of the other ropes fastened to the mule teams, Travis jumps into the river. The current pulls his feet from under him, leaving him swimming to the beleaguered boat. The current swiftly pulls him downstream and he misses the target. Fighting the current back to shore, he jogs upstream before trying again.

Working with the current this time, he reaches his goal, banging into the boat and scrabbling for something to grab, and finally catching one of the ropes still tied to it and dangling down into the water.

Using the rope to climb up, he makes it to the boat deck and reels the rope tied around his waist in until he has the ends of the other ropes. He ties them off at a few points on the boat and jumps back into the river, swimming back to shore.

"Okay, let's do this."

With Travis watching the boat and willing it to work, Darius urges the mule teams on. They take up the slack, pause, and lean into their harnesses. Hooves digging in, the mules strain to pull. The ropes are taught and groaning and the boat does not move.

"Come on, baby, you can do this," Travis urges, clenching his teeth and fists as he wills harder for it to work.

Darius urges the mules to pull harder and they strain harder against their harnesses, putting effort into it this time.

The boat shifts, sliding on the muddy river bottom, hull grinding against the rocks and submerged dead trees and branches.

Travis whoops eagerly, looking back at Darius and waving.

"It's working! She's moving!"

Darius urges the mules on and the boat is slowly pulled to the shore.

Just as it is about to hit the riverbank, Travis screams.

"Now! Harder!"

Darius lashes at the mules, snapping at their rumps with the end of the long reins and yelling hoarsely at them. The sting makes them jump and surge forward to escape the biting.

The boat slips forward faster, the weight and momentum sending the curved bow skidding up the slope. It hits the makeshift rail ramp, slipping up the groaning poles. They bend and bow out, but the weight of the boat is partially lifted from the ground as it slides up the mud-slickened poles, allowing it to glide more smoothly.

"Keep going!" Travis yells. "Don't stop!"

The boat keeps moving, the mules and its momentum pulling it awkwardly up the logs. The bow passes the top of the riverbank and Travis watches with baited breath, scared it will fall back into the water.

It slips up and over, reaching the halfway point, tilting precariously to one side, and skids along the mud-slick poles, grinding them down.

The ropes snap and logs are forced further apart, the weight of the boat dragging it to a stop and leaving a groove of ruined ground behind it.

The boat comes to a stop and the straining mules pull futilely.

"Stop! We're good!" Travis shouts.

Darius looks back and reins the mules in. He walks back to join Travis staring up at the boat in shock.

"We did it," Travis says, incredulous. "We actually did it."

"Yes we did," Darius says, already regretting it.

A cold chill runs down Darius's spine.

"I don't know how, but we did it," he thinks. "This should not have been possible for just two guys like us alone."

The next days are spent struggling through the day at their jobs while they recover from the strain of moving the boat, their muscles screaming with the pain and stiffness and the extreme abuse served upon them.

11   Reconstruction Begins

Basil leaves the Dock Master's office, hurrying through the crowded dockyard. He gets in his car, cranking the engine over with an impatient grimace. He honks his horn at a couple men who do not move out of his way fast enough, narrowly missing running them down.

Gripping the wheel hard, he urges the car to move faster as he leaves the dockyard behind.

When he reaches the entrance of a large home, he pulls to a stop in front, shutting off the engine and getting out.

Basil moves with the same urgent pace as he mounts the stairs and knocks on the door.

The door opens to a butler bowing humbly.

"How may I help you, sir?"

"I am here to see Mr. Barlow."

"This way," the butler nods, leading him inside.

He deposits him in the parlour.

"I will see if Mr. Barlow is available to greet guests.

Basil nods, waiting impatiently. He is pacing by the time the door opens again. He looks up at the opened door, almost startled.

"Mr. Barlow will see you," the butler says. "This way."

He leads him to Malcolm's home office, bowing before entering the open door.

"Mr. Jacobson," he announces, motioning the Dock Master to enter.

Basil enters hesitantly, turning to see the butler closing the door.

Suddenly he feels trapped and regrets rushing over here.

"What if it is nothing? What if I am wasting his time?" he thinks.

Malcolm's expression is bland, giving no insight into his thoughts. He looks at the Dock Master from behind his large desk.

"I presume from your anxious expression that you have something to tell me." He does not offer the Dock Master a seat.

Standing awkwardly, Basil nods.

"Yes sir. It might be nothing, but…"

"If it is nothing then you are wasting my time."

Basil looks frightened now.

"There have been reports, sir, of a boat being ferried down the river."

"There are a lot of boats on the river. Why should I care about this particular one?"

"She's a showboat, sir. A paddlewheel."

Malcolm looks less bored now. He nods at him to continue.

"This paddlewheel, what business does she run?"

"None sir. It appears someone has brought the boat in from somewhere."

"Do you have any suspicions where from?"

"It has to be a salvage purchase. The boat is decrepit. The reports are that she is sinking, sir."

Malcolm laughs at this.

"Why would I care about a boat sinking in the river?"

"I believe it is the two young men who were looking for a boat."

Malcolm arches an eyebrow at him.

"And you believe they bought a salvage; an old decrepit sinking salvage. There have been no sales or auctions of salvage lots. They must have got this boat from somewhere else."

"Yes sir."

"They are brazen; I have to give them that. I am not concerned about some sinking salvage. You are wasting my time."

Basil turns, startled to realise someone is standing behind him. The office door is open and the butler waiting patiently outside. Malcolm's security man, Frank, is standing too close for comfort behind him.

"Out." Malcolm waves him out, dismissing him.

"Yes sir. Sorry sir." Basil bows and hurries out, letting the butler lead him back out the front door.

"A sinking boat," Frank laughs.

"Check it out anyway," Malcolm says.

***

Travis is back in the lumber store buying materials to start rebuilding the boat. Standing before the wall with his back to the store, he is busily digging through a barrel of nails, scooping them into a bucket.

Taking his bucket, he moves on to inspecting saws standing up in another barrel and hanging on the wall. Putting down his bucket of nails, he takes down a long two-man saw with jagged teeth and handles on each end to reach the smaller saw behind it.

The young woman from before walks into the store; pausing briefly and to look around. She smiles with surprised pleasure.

Changing direction, she approaches Travis.

"How is the boat moving business?" she asks.

Travis jumps, startled by the intrusion, and turns to face her. A flush burns across his face the moment he meets her gaze.

"Um, good," he manages, finding it hard to look her in the eyes. He swallows the dry knot in his throat along with his pride and confesses.

"We tried your suggestion."

"And?"

"It worked." He is flustered and feels the urge to kick himself for it.

She looks around. "I don't see your friend with you today."

"He's busy," Travis says.

After an awkward moment, she looks at what he is holding.

"You are not going to use that are you?" she asks.

Travis looks down at the saw in his hand and back up at her.

"Yes."

"What on earth are you going to use that for?" she asks.

"We are rebuilding the boat." He feels foolish under her scrutiny.

She chuckles, reaches forward, and takes the long two-man saw from him.

"And just how big is the tree you and your friend are cutting down?"

With a smirk, she selects a different saw and hands it to him.

"This will work much better." She winks and turns, leaving.

"Wait!" he calls after her, "What is your name?"

"Amelia," she says just before the door closes behind her.

***

Travis and Darius are studying the boat to determine how damaged it is. She rests on the grass leaning to one side, still in a puddle of the remaining water that had been filling the hull as they dragged the boat up the river.

Darius shakes his head regretfully.

"I can't believe I let you talk me into this," he groans. "I don't think we can even sell this thing for salvage. The smartest thing we can do is cut our losses now and just burn it."

Travis stares at the boat as if it is the most fabulous thing in the world. He is enamoured.

"She's not so bad," he says. "She just needs a bit of work."

"A bit?" Darius coughs up a cynical laugh. "I'm amazed it survived the move without falling apart with all the rot."

He looks at Travis and sees the eagerness. Travis is vibrating with it.

"All right," Darius sighs, knowing he is going to regret this even more in the days to come. "Let's get to work."

Travis scoops up tools eagerly and practically dances to the boat.

"Where do we start?"

"You haven't figured that out?"

"I thought we would sort that out together." Travis's wide grin is annoyingly giddy.

Darius frowns, studying the rotting vessel. "Well, I imagine the first thing we need to do is to prop it up so it stands upright with some sort of base to hold it steady."

"Then we can figure out which boards are too rotted and have to be replaced," Travis says.

"That would be all of them," Darius says cynically.

"How are we going to prop it up?"

It takes another two days, more lumber and nails, and renting the mule teams again to pull and brace the boat upright.

Finished, Darius frowns up at it.

"I sure as hell hope this holds."

After returning the mules, they go to work on the boat, starting with scraping off the scraps of old paint and testing boards for their sponginess. Over the next days, boards are pried off; the pile of insect and dry rot ravaged boards growing as the boat gradually becomes more and more a skeleton of her former dilapidated self.

The weight of the boat slowly pushes the boards propping it up into the ground, leaning more each day.

She leans sadly to one side, as if too tired to do anything but melt back into the ground and let it consume her rotting hull.

Travis and Darius work diligently day after day, getting up early to spend long hours laboring at their jobs, and then picking up any odd jobs in the evenings they can find for the extra money they need for tools and lumber and supplies. When they cannot find any extra jobs, they work on scraping down the boat and prying off rotting boards.

It is a long slow process that has taken weeks so far. The boat is beginning to look more like a whale carcass than a boat, its flesh picked clean to reveal the bones of its ribcage and spine.

Each Friday night they put their money together, carefully counting it.

Today is Friday, the sky outside is growing dark, and the money is laid out on the small table in Darius's rented room.

They both look down at the meager offering with frowns. Exhaustion has worn both their faces into haggardness.

"It's not enough," Darius says as Travis counts their money again. "Re-counting it is not going to change that. We don't have enough for this week's payment to Norman."

Travis looks at him in alarm.

"Norman is not happy. Last week he threatened to repossess the boat. He wants what we are short plus this week's payment in full."

"This is all we have," Darius shrugs. "Let him take the boat. We will be done with this madness."

"We have to work more jobs. We have to find the money." Travis looks up at him urgently. His eyes are full of worry that Norman will take the boat back.

"We are spending too much on buying tools and lumber," Darius says. "We have been short every week on the payments to Norman. We have to cut back on buying stuff for the boat and work on paying off the debt."

A wild look of panic crosses Travis's eyes. "I'm not ready to give up on her yet." The words are on the tip of his tongue, but he clamps his mouth shut. Darius is right, and it does not have to mean giving up on her; just slowing things down a little.

Travis paces the floor anxiously.

"You are right," he says. "We have shorted our payments to Norman too much already and need to catch up. But the faster we get her fixed up, the sooner we can start making money with her."

"Norman's threats have grown more severe each week we are short on the payments," Darius says. "You have to stop buying stuff for the boat for a while."

"But we need the stuff to fix her up," Travis complains.

Darius gives him a stern look.

"You can't fix a boat you don't have. We would lose the boat, tools, our jobs, everything. For what? Your impatience, your dreams, and your newest wild get rich quick scheme.

I have a bad feeling about this guy. I don't think he will stop at just threats. If we don't pay, I have a feeling he will follow through on those threats.

For now, on all the money that does not go to our rent and food goes on the payments until they are caught up. After that, we put it to the payments first and buy tools and materials only if there is anything left."

He pauses.

"Or we just let Norman have the boat back."

"We have to find more jobs," Travis says miserably.

"We can't do more jobs than we already are," Darius says wearily.

He is already exhausted beyond words. Every waking moment is spent working; laboring hard either to earn money for the boat or on rebuilding the boat. They work late into the night and are up early, getting half the sleep they should be getting. He is burning out with exhaustion.

"Besides, odd jobs are getting harder to find each day. There are too many people out of work. Some men have even taken to brawling over jobs."

"Maybe we can borrow from somewhere?" Travis suggests.

"Borrow against what? A boat that is unusable? That heap of junk is worthless." Darius shakes his head.

Travis's mind is working, but it is going in a direction he knows better than to share with his partner. He feels desperate.

"I can't give up on fixing her," he complains. He can feel the draw of the boat even now, the urgency to get her on the water, the lights and glitter, money flashing as it changes hands, and them living in the lap of wealth and luxury for once instead of in poverty.

Mostly, he can feel the physical tug of the boat pulling him, the low persistent need to be with her.

"You just have to be patient," Darius insists.

He goes to the door and opens it.

"I need to get some sleep."

Travis nods. Leaving their pooled money on the table, he pauses in the doorway and turns back.

"See you tomorrow."

"Tomorrow."

Travis leaves and Darius closes the door behind him.

With a weary sigh, Darius cleans up the money, stuffing it into an old coffee can and putting it on a shelf.

Too exhausted to bother changing, he lies down on his bed and in minutes is snoring.

12   Night Activity

Travis moves stealthily in the darkness, sidling up alongside the building. It looks more like a big barn than a warehouse and is about as secure. There is a line of small windows down the side of the building. They are too high to reach easily, and just big enough to fit a man.

He looks at the building guiltily.

"That old planer I have been using to scrape the paint and smooth the warped wood is broken and not repairable. We need other tools and materials too, but with not enough money to make the payments on the boat; our work has ground to a halt with no ability to buy what we need. I have to solve that problem."

Surveying the warehouse for the best way in and out, he drags over an old rain barrel, turning it upside down and placing it beneath a window. Climbing on it, he stands and tries the window.

It is locked.

Jumping down, he drags the rain barrel to the next window, climbing up and trying it. When he finds it locked, he continues down the line of windows.

The sixth window he tries is not locked.

"Good. I don't want to damage anything getting in. I don't want them to know anyone was ever here."

Sliding the window up, he grunts as he tries to maneuver himself around and slides through the window feet first.

Once he is in, Travis looks around, rubbing his hands like a little boy set loose in a toy store.

He starts gathering things and piling them up on the front counter, starting with a new planer. Up and down the aisles he goes, collecting tools and materials; rope and nails. He picks up a new hammer, pauses to look at it and thinks it over again, and grabs a few more.

"I can sell the extras."

By the time he is done Travis has made a large pile. He looks at it in surprise, not realizing just how much he had gathered.

"How am I going to get all this out of here?"

Shrugging, he goes to the back of the shop. Picking up a large heavy bag of feed from a stack by the rear barn door, he brings it to the window and drops it on the floor with a thud. He returns for another and a third, piling them below the window to reach better.

Satisfied, Travis starts passing his loot through the open window, dropping it on the ground below. He cringes when some of it clatters loudly.

Travis pokes his head out the window, looking around to make sure no one is coming to investigate the noise.

He starts climbing out and stops, glancing back inside.

As a last thought, he slips back in and runs to the back of the store. Grabbing some burlap sacks and twine, he jogs back to the open window and drops it out the window.

Finished, Travis climbs out the window and closes it behind him. He bundles the stolen goods the best he can, filling the sacks and tying bundles of larger items together.

He looks down at the pile.

"This is going to take a few trips. I need to move it away from the warehouse to someplace less visible. Then I can try to get it home."

He looks around for a likely spot then remembers.

"I know where to hide it. There is a place in a field just behind the warehouse where the bushes and trees grow thickly enough to hide it."

It takes him three trips to bring his stolen treasures there; shoving the bundles under the bushes until no more will fit without being visible. Then he finds another spot a little further along and fills it too.

Travis is wired with anxiety and just wants to get far away from there.

"I'll come back for it later to bring it to the boat. But first…" He searches the sacks until he finds it.

"The new planer." He takes that and a sanding block, re-ties the sack and shoves it back out of sight under the bush and heads for home.

"I will sleep for the last few hours before I have to go to work."

13   Burglarized

Mr. Roman Bukowski whistles as he walks to the lumber store to open it for the day. He is the second generation to run the store and was counting on his own son to take it over from him; if his wife would only provide him with one.

He crosses the street, arriving at the store. He pauses to nod greeting to the old man on the bench.

"Morning," he says

The old man does not respond.

It takes him a moment to fish for the key and unlock the door.

Stepping through the doorway, he closes and locks the door behind him. He has an hour of preparation work to do before opening the store.

Roman walks through the store, stopping to straighten the items on a shelf. He is meticulous in his care and running of the store.

Going to the front counter, he hangs up his coat and hat on a coat rack and then pulls out the ledger from beneath it, flipping to yesterday's entries. This is the ledger where he tracks items he needs to order to replace stock. There are two deliveries expected today.

He nods approval and closes the ledger, sliding it back on its shelf below the counter.

Roman hums to himself as he pulls out the slate board and chalks. He notes today's sale on the slate and slides it into its holder on the wall; baling twine, five cents off per roll.

He turns and starts walking to the twine samples to rearrange it in a more attractive display.

Roman stops before he reaches it, staring in confusion at a couple of feedbags lying on the floor by the window.

"Those do not belong there."

He grunts as he picks up one of the heavy bags, carrying it awkwardly to the back of the store, where he deposits it on the stack of feed back by the back barn doors.

Returning for another, he stops when he notices a hammer out of place on a shelf of garden sheers.

"How did you get there?"

He picks up the hammer, looks at it in his hand, and walks to the tools section.

Putting the hammer back where it belongs, he stops to straighten a chisel that is misaligned, turns, and stops.

Taking a step closer, he keeps staring at the wall where saws hang. A couple of hooks are conspicuously empty.

A red flush creeps up his neck and his face hardens.

Roman returns to the remaining feedbags piled out of place beneath the window. He looks at the bags and then at the window and purses his lips.

Stepping on the bags, he inspects the window. He tests it, sliding it up, and poking his head out, looking down.

On the ground beneath the window are a couple of nails laying on the grass.

He pulls his head back in, straightening up and stepping off the feedbags.

"I have been robbed." The revelation is a shock; a violation.

Roman scurries to the front counter, grabbing his coat and hat in a hurry. He puts them on as he rushes to the front door, unlocking it and stepping outside. Closing and locking it behind him, he walks quickly back the way he came.

When he arrives at home, he rushes into the house, closing the door quickly behind him.

He hangs his hat and coat on the coat rack inside the door.

"Why aren't you at the store?" his wife, Lena, asks, coming from the kitchen.

He looks at her, his expression bland with shock.

"I have been robbed."

"What do you mean you have been robbed?"

Her expression turns from confusion to alarm.

"Were you mugged? Are you all right?"

She rushes forward, fussing over him and looking for injuries.

"Not me, the store. The store was robbed." His shock is starting to turn to anger.

Amelia stops in the hallway just before stepping into view, listening in horrified shock.

"How? Who?" she thinks.

Roman brushes Lena's hands off.

"Stop fussing over me woman."

"Who could have robbed the store?" Lena asks, looking at him intently with the same shocked expression.

Roman's face is growing redder with anger. He scowls, thinking.

"There have been a couple of young men in the store recently, claiming to be rebuilding an old boat. It sounds unlikely. I would bet it was them. By their clothes, they haven't two red cents to rub together."

Amelia puts her hand to her mouth in shock to stifle a gasp. She leans against the wall as if her legs might not hold her, blinking back shocked tears.

Roman pounds his fist into his hand angrily, looking at his wife.

"I will see those hooligans put in jail for this." He grabs his coat and shrugs into it, putting his hat on his head.

"Where are you going?" Lena asks.

"To see the constable."

14   Visit from the Constable

Darius arrives at the boat Saturday morning to find Travis already there hard at work.

"You started early." His eyes move to the planer, noting its newness.

"I was eager to get started today, I guess." Travis nods towards the toolbox of worn tools with a grin. "Did you come to jaw at me or to help?"

Travis looks down at the new planer he is holding, noticing Darius eying it. He holds it up.

"I borrowed this from a guy. Pretty good, huh?"

Darius is doubtful but decides to let it go. He picks up a pry bar and moves around the boat, testing boards. Finding a rotten one, he digs the pry bar in and starts working it off. The wood crumbles before the nails give and he has to try prying it off in another spot.

"Every board we pry off reveals more rotting lumber," he complains.

They continue working at the boat, Travis lost in his work and Darius wondering where he got the money for the new planer.

It is in the afternoon when Travis looks up from his work to see two men approaching from a parked vehicle. He quickly hides the planer and sanding block. He picks up a hammer and chisel and starts working the wood with it.

Spotting Darius first, the approaching men make for him.

Darius is busy in his chore and does not notice the men approaching until they speak to him.

"Sir, can we have a word?" the constable says.

Darius looks up in surprise to see the local police constable and the man from the lumber store where they have been purchasing most of their tools and supplies.

The shopkeeper, Mr. Roman Bukowski, looks angry enough to reach out and grab him, throttling and shaking him like a dog does a rabbit. Darius pictures the man's calloused hands reaching for him as if reading his mind.

He puts down his tools stiffly, sensing trouble, and nods acknowledgement to the two men.

"Afternoon," he says in greeting, nodding to them each in turn. "Constable Graham, Mr. Bukowski."

The constable looks around at their handiwork and the mess it is leaving behind as if interested in their project before speaking.

"Good afternoon Mr. Marek," the constable says. "This is quite a project you have going here."

Darius nods. "It sure is."

"It must be costing you a fair bit of money for all the materials and tools."

"It is. We have both been working extra jobs."

Mr. Bukowski is fidgeting angrily; impatient the constable is not just getting to the point. He opens his mouth to let loose a tirade, but the constable motions him to back off.

Constable Graham wanders over to where Travis is working and glancing at them out of the corner of his eye, pretending to not have noticed them. Darius and Mr. Bukowski follow the constable.

Graham watches Travis work for a few moments, noticing the poor state of his tools.

It takes a conscious effort for Travis to not look up.

"Doesn't look like you have much for tools there," the constable says.

"We are making do," Travis says, pausing in his work to look at the constable.

"What are you using for a planer?" the constable asks, looking down at the broken tool lying on the ground next to Travis.

Travis points down at the broken tool. "It's not ideal, but I manage, until I can buy a new one anyway."

Darius looks down at the broken tool. He purses his lips, trying not to show his anger.

"I don't suppose you gentlemen have seen anything unusual lately, have you?" the Constable asks.

"No sir, nothing that comes to mind. Why?"

"It seems there have been some thefts in the area."

Travis and Darius both look properly shocked. Darius is already suspicious this visit has to do with his partner's 'borrowed' tools.

"What has been stolen?" Travis asks, feigning innocence.

The constable looks around their worksite casually.

"Mr. Roman Bukowski's store was burgled. Building supplies, tools, some other stuff," the constable says. "The kind of stuff you might use to build or renovate a house, or maybe fix up a boat." He levels his gaze at the two men meaningfully.

Darius almost sputters in his nervousness.

"You haven't noticed anything on your worksite go missing?" The real question veiled behind the constable's words is clear. He continues.

"You should keep an eye on those tools of yours with these thefts going on." The hint is clear in the constable's words and look that he suspects them. There is no reasonable way these two could afford the project they have undertaken.

"We haven't noticed anything go missing yet, sir," Travis says. He can feel the hot flush creeping up his neck. "Thank you for warning us. We will certainly be on the lookout for anything missing or anything unusual happening."

Roman is fairly humming with anger. He cannot hold it in any longer.

"Aren't you going to do anything?" he demands of the constable. "You know they broke into my store and stole from me."

"I have no proof they did anything. Look around at their tools," the constable says.

The constable nods towards the tool in Travis's hand and the broken planer on the ground.

"All I see here are broken and old tools and no new supplies."

He studies the boat.

"It looks to me like they are still tearing this thing apart. It doesn't look like they will be ready for new lumber and tools for some time."

The constable turns to Roman.

"Does any of this look like it was stolen from your shop?"

Roman's jaw clenches and his eyes burn with anger. He shakes his head; an admission the constable is correct.

He turns to Travis because he is the last of the two to speak.

"I want my property returned," Roman demands, glaring at him angrily. "Every last nail and board. Every tool. I know it was you two."

He leans in close. His voice is a low growl. "I will have my ounce of your hides."

Travis instinctively stands on the balls of his feet, making himself look larger, and leans towards to the shopkeeper.

"Best you keep your suspicions and threats to yourself mister, and leave this to the constable. I do not take to anyone accusing me of something I did not do."

The constable puts himself between the two men, pushing them apart and making them both back up a few paces.

"That is enough of that you two," he says, giving them each a stern look. He gives Travis and Darius a warning look. "I will be back to check on you two. I will be watching."

"Let's go," Constable Graham says, turning to the angry shopkeeper.

Roman gives them a final angry glare before grudgingly turning to follow the constable. They can hear him grumbling about thieves and the constable not doing anything about it as they walk away, his complaints finally cut off when they get into the constable's car and close the doors.

They watch Roman still gesticulating in the car as the constable drives away.

Darius turns on Travis angrily. "You stole the stuff, didn't you?"

Travis tries to deflect, but it is pointless.

"That old shopkeeper is just accusing us because he knows we don't have a lot of money. We stopped buying stuff at his store, so now he is angry."

Darius shakes his head.

"No more," he says angrily, turning away. "Maybe I should not trust you with the money for the boat payment. If you steal from the only store we can get supplies at…" He does not finish, leaving the rest of it hanging unsaid in the air between them like a foul smell.

Travis tries to look innocent and remorseful. It is not a very successful attempt.

"Don't be like that," he says. "You know I would not steal from you. It's just that we ran out of money and we can't just give up fixing her up after everything we have been through to get her this far."

Darius walks away without looking back, returning to the work that had been interrupted, angrily tearing off rotting boards.

Travis goes back to scraping the hull of the boat. Pulling his new scraper out, he climbs up to sit on a platform hanging from ropes near the top rail, and works with renewed energy, burning off the stress of the moment and the fear of being caught.

He is scraping away, moving up the hull a little and scraping more when he stops and stares at the rotting wood.

He studies it, running his fingers delicately over the wood as if caressing a lover. His mouth works as he concentrates on making out the faint lettering that is there, its paint barely legible where it had once been stencilled in vivid letters on the hull.

His face works itself into an expression of incredulity then joy.

"There you are," he breathes. "There you are." He caresses the wood.

Looking for Darius, he shouts down to him.

"Darius, come see this. I found it. I found her." He waves Darius to come up.

"What?" Darius calls, jogging over at the urgency in his voice. He looks up at him. "What is it? What did you find?"

Travis is staring at the boat hull, running his fingers lovingly over the rough rotting wood.

"I found her," Travis says in deference. "I found her name."

Darius steps closer, sees nothing, and climbs up to sit next to Travis on the platform. He studies the mostly bare wood until he too can make out the faint traces of the lettering that had once stood out proudly in bold stencils.

Gypsy Queen.

"Well, I guess now we know what to call it," Darius says. "We will have to check the registry now that we have a name, just to make sure someone else does not have a claim on the boat."

Secretly, he is hopeful someone does and that they take their claim and the burden of fixing this thing up from them.

***

A sleek car stops along the road, the people inside looking at the decrepit boat some distance away.

"So that is it?" Malcolm says, a lopsided grin lifting one corner of his mouth.

"Yes," the man sitting next to him in the back seat says. "These are the men who were looking to buy a paddlewheel.

Malcolm starts a low chuckle that breaks into a full-hearted laugh.

"I don't think I have anything to worry about. Drive on."

He motions his driver on and the car starts moving again.

In the front passenger seat, Frank looks out the window at the boat with two men sitting side by side on a platform near the boat's rear deck.

***

Travis is elated over finding the lettering on the boat. He holds on to that excitement for the rest of the day and by the time they decide to stop working, he has an uncontrollable need to share the news.

"This is killing me. I have to tell someone," Travis says. He looks at Darius eagerly.

"Who are you going to tell?" Darius asks, packing tools away.

"I don't know. Maybe the woman we met in the store? She seemed interested."

Darius flashes a look at him, quickly looking down to hide it.

"She probably isn't that interested," he mutters.

"She is the only person I can think of." Travis cannot stop grinning.

"I'll see you later," he says.

"You are going straight to see Norman to make the payment, right?" Darius says.

"Straight away," Travis says, patting the money in his pocket.

Darius watches him go with an unhappy look and returns to cleaning up the tools.

Travis goes to the store where they bought their supplies and tools, the only place he has seen her. He nods to the old man on the bench and stops in the road, looking in the windows. He does not dare go in after the confrontation with the owner at the boat.

"She isn't there," Travis mutters.

He starts down the road.

"Where else would a young woman go? One who was found in the most unlikely store for a young woman?"

Travis turns a corner and spots her walking ahead.

With a big grin, he jogs after her, a little out of breath when he catches up.

"Hi there Amelia," he greets her excitedly. "I found it. I found her name. The Gyp-." He is cut off by her angry look when she stops walking and turns to face him.

He takes a step back, looking at her in confusion and wondering why she is so angry.

"How dare you?" she demands, her eyes bright with fury and her lips puckered in a tight frown.

"W-what?" he stammers. "Why are you angry?"

She advances on him, making him take two more steps back, brandishing an accusing finger at him like a dangerous weapon.

"You stole from my father." The words come out stilted with anger, each one a stab to his guilty heart, their meaning sinking in a little deeper with each successive word.

"That is why she was in the store," he thinks with a sinking feeling.

He waves his hands in front of him in supplication and denial, as if he might ward off her anger.

"No, no, I didn't," he says as if denying it will help.

Her angry look is cold and ruthless.

"Someone broke into my father's store and stole tools and supplies." Her eyes meet his, studying his reaction and apparently seeing the guilt she expects to see. Her eyes narrow and she nods to herself, such a slight nod that he almost thinks he imagined it.

He cannot fight the raw flush that creeps up his neck.

Her suspicion is confirmed. The guilt in his eyes gives him away.

"Just the kind of tools and supplies you might need if you were rebuilding a boat," she finishes.

She turns and walks angrily away from him down the street, walking at a brisk pace.

Flustered, Travis blubbers at himself for a second before realizing she is no longer in front of him and breaks from his state of frozen fear, following her. He has to jog to catch her.

"No, no, you have it wrong," he pleads, following along after her. "Please just stop and listen to me. I wouldn't, I couldn't-," he breaks off.

She stops and turns to him.

"You are a terrible liar. You could. You did. Do not ever talk to me again." She turns and walks away angrily; tossing her head as if to toss away any thought of him with it.

Travis helplessly watches her go.

"I didn't know," he says to her retreating figure, too quietly for her to hear.

He looks dejected. Then the thought occurs to him.

He shoves his hand in his pocket, feeling the money wadded there; the money for the boat payment.

"I am supposed to go see Norman tonight to give him the payment."

Travis turns and races down the road, reaching the store just as Roman is locking the door from inside. Roman turns, walking away to vanish into the store's interior, not seeing Travis.

Travis stops out front, banging on the door to catch the shopkeeper's attention.

Roman stops and turns around, his expression turning to fury the moment he sees who is on the other side of the door.

Returning to the door and opening it, he glares at Travis.

"Come to rob me again?" he demands.

Travis tries to give him his best compassionate look.

"No sir," he says quickly. "I just feel so badly that a hardworking man like yourself has suffered such a loss at the hands of some," he almost chokes on the word, "degenerate. Please, I only want to help."

He shoves his hand out, offering what he holds in his fist.

"Take it, please. A gift. To help with your loss."

Roman looks down at Travis's hand doubtfully, still suspect, and extends his hand, palm up. Travis drops what he holds in it.

Roman looks down at the wad of bills in his hand. He looks at Travis in surprise and suspicion.

Travis nods. Not waiting to find out if he will thank him or punch him, he turns and leaves quickly. He wants to put as much distance between him and this man as he can.

"Darius is going to be furious when he finds out I didn't make the boat payment."

15   Registering the Gypsy Queen

The following morning Darius goes to the Dock Master's office at the docks. The dock is as busy as it was the day they tried to sneak onto the Queen Rhiannon.

He arrives at the docks and stops to take in the hustle and bustle with a feeling of dread. Darius looks at the boats currently docked. The gaudy casino paddlewheel boat and its wealthy patrons are not present today.

A small relief washes through him at not seeing that boat at the docks.

"After being thrown overboard to drown, I would rather avoid the owner of that boat and his men."

He makes his way through the crowds and stops uncertainly outside the Dock Master's office, looking up at the building's façade. Like the rest of the buildings fronting the docks, it is well worn and in need of repainting.

Darius enters, pushing the door open. The bell over the door jangles to announce his arrival. He looks around, not sure what to do.

The clerk sitting at a desk on the other side of the counter looks up. He is past middle aged, a bit plump in the belly, with thinning hair and trousers and a striped dress shirt that have seen better days. He adjusts his thin round wire-framed glasses.

Seeing Darius and his worn clothes, he assumes he is another unemployed hopeful looking for work.

Getting up, he grabs up a clipboard and pen from the desktop lining his side of the counter and plops it down on the counter while looking for something else behind the counter.

"Fill this out," he says without looking up at Darius.

"What?" Darius looks at him in mild confusion.

"Fill this out." The clerk looks up at him. "You can write, can't you?" He steps closer, taking the pen and spinning the clipboard around, ready to write. "Never mind. Name?" He looks at Darius expectantly.

"Darius," he says hesitantly.

The clerk starts scratching at the paper on the clipboard with the pen. "Surname. Do you have any skills?"

"Marek, uh, I'm not here for a job, sir."

The clerk stops scratching at the paper and looks up. "All the jobs on the dock go through the Dock Master. If you aren't here for a job, I doubt there is much I can do to help you."

"I'm building a boat."

"You need to see the Ship Builders union. Their office is at the shipyard."

"What I mean is I, we, bought a boat."

The clerk looks him up and down skeptically.

"Are you building one or did you buy one? Those are two very different things. Either way you don't look like you have the money. Is this some sort of a joke? You can see I am not laughing."

"We didn't pay much," Darius says apologetically, although for them it is a lot. "It was a salvage. You are the Dock Master, right? I want to look up the boat's name; just to be sure no one has a claim to it."

The clerk nods.

"Right then, and no, I am not the Dock Master. I am his clerk. He is out right now. But that is smart thinking. We have seen a few, you know, boats sold as salvage without the rightful owner's knowledge. The downturn in the economy, lack of jobs and all, has people doing desperate things. Usually they are abandoned, but that does not mean the rightful owner won't try to get their pound of flesh out of you for stealing their boat just to turn a little extra profit."

He puts the clipboard away and turns to a side table where a large leather-bound ledger lays. He turns to look at Darius.

"What's her name?"

"Who?" Darius looks confused.

"The boat. What is the boat's name?"

"Gypsy Queen I think. The paint is mostly gone, but that was lettered on the side of it."

"Any idea when she was built or decommissioned?"

"No, we have no details on it."

The clerk starts leafing through pages, looking for the boat name.

Darius's thoughts turn to the abandoned state the boat was in. It appeared to have been abandoned, and may very well have been. The man who sold them the boat seemed shady at best.

"If you are going to own a boat, you should know to call her a she, not it," the clerk says as he studies the pages.

"Why is that?"

The clerk looks up. "You know, I'm not entirely sure. Nobody has ever asked me that. It is just the way it is. A boat is always a she. Some romantic notion, I suppose; the boat being the mistress of the sailor, in light of spending his life at sea. Women on board were always frowned on in the old days. Thought of as bad luck, you know." He chuckles. "I guess it would make the mistress mad."

He returns to studying the ledger.

"Ah, here she is." His attention on the ledger becomes more intent as he reads the entry scrawled within the ledger.

"The Gypsy Queen is listed as having been decommissioned and sold for salvage. That was years ago. She should have been destroyed for scrap a long time ago. You have a bill of sale; I trust? No matter if you do not. If she has not been scrapped yet, she is considered abandoned by now, without an owner. Open salvage she would be. Any man would be in his rights to claim her if she were found on no man's property."

Darius digs the document from his pocket and hands it over.

"The bill of sale."

The clerk looks at the offered rumpled paper being held out to him and shrugs, taking it. He turns to the current page of the ledger and starts carefully printing in the information, adding it to the history of the Gypsy Queen. He takes Travis and Darius's names and fills them in under registered owners.

Before signing the ledger, he turns to Darius. "You do have money? There is the registration fee to be paid."

"Yes, right here." Darius digs out the money and hands it over.

The clerk takes it and counts it, nodding. He returns to the ledger, signing it and making it official. He pauses, looking up at Darius.

"I am assuming she is not seaworthy? She will not float?"

"No sir. We need to rebuild it. Her, I mean."

The clerk nods again, making a note in the ledger. He takes a form and fills it in, signing it and bringing it to the counter.

"Sign here."

Darius signs it and the clerk sets it down.

"It is official. There is no question of the Gypsy Queen's ownership. You and your partner have her by rights."

Darius's biggest fear, that once they got this boat fixed up and worth some money, the previous owner would show up demanding the return of his vessel, is eased at last. He almost lets out a sigh of relief.

The clerk continues.

"I have noted for the record that the boat is in dry dock indefinitely for repairs and is not seaworthy. Before you can set her in water, you must come back here to the Dock Master's office to have her officially registered as seaworthy. There will be dock fees, and if you dock here," he gives him a meaningful look, "and this is the only dock around, all dock workers are hired through the Dock Master. This is not optional."

The clerk looks for his stamp, giving the form the official Dock Master stamp, and holds it out to Darius along with his bill of sale.

"I recommend you visit the shipyard and see the Union Master. Just to avoid any trouble rebuilding her. The Shipbuilders' Union will also have to approve her to be seaworthy. And do keep these in a safe place."

Darius takes the papers, carefully folds them, and puts them in his pocket.

"Thank you sir," he nods.

Darius leaves the Dock Master's office with that weight lifted off his shoulders only to have a new one take its place.

He is walking alone through town, whistling with his spirits raised, when he suddenly finds himself face to face with the fat man who sold them the boat.

He stops in his tracks, staring at the man blocking his path, feeling instantly defensive.

Norman's posture is aggressive.

16   Bad Deeds Bring Bad Deeds

Amelia pauses at the bench outside the lumber store. She sets down a plate wrapped in cheesecloth next to the old man sitting there and continues on to enter the lumber store. He seems oblivious to her presence. She comes every day to help her father for a few hours. She looks around and finally finds him at the back of the store filling out a list.

"Are you still working on taking stock?" she asks. "You have to be the only shopkeeper there is who actually counts each nail." She says it light-heartedly. It is something she teases him about regularly.

Roman turns around to look at her and returns to counting. His look is serious. He is in no joking mood today.

"I have to take a complete stock of the store so I know what was stolen."

Amelia frowns.

She takes one of the pages of his list and moves to a nearby shelf where she starts counting items on the shelf and marking the number of each on the list.

They work in silence for a while. The heavy weight of her father's mood has turned hers sour too.

"That young man you talked to in the store," Roman starts, breaking the silence.

Amelia stops counting and looks at him, her expression curious but her eyes guarded.

"Which young man? There are a few who come in here."

"Don't play coy. I saw how you looked at him."

Amelia watches to see if there is any smile in her father's eyes. There is none. His expression is cold.

She flushes, thinking about the two young men who came into the store. One had angered her, talking down her idea of how they might move their boat as idle nonsense. She had told herself at that moment that she disliked him. The other listened to her, taking her idea seriously.

Although she despised him, she could not help the flush she felt when he came back again, even as she wished it had been his friend who came back instead, the nice one.

Her father notices the heat rising in her cheeks.

"There were two of them the first time. You talked to them. Then one came back. What do you know about the young man who came back? He is not a regular."

"Are you talking about the man you accused of robbing us? I don't know anything about him."

Amelia keeps her voice casual, as though the matter is unimportant to her. She feels a mix of angry indignation at the thought of the young man, but also a flush of attraction.

"You talked to him twice. You must know something."

"I helped him like I do any other customer." She looks at her father. "Do you still think he is the one who robbed the store?"

He looks at her levelly.

"He came by and gave me money. That, my dear Amelia, is the act of a guilty man."

She looks away quickly, not wanting him to see the pain in her eyes.

He watches her for a moment and then resumes taking inventory.

***

Darius stands there staring at Norman.

"You haven't been to see me," Norman says, the threatening tone underlying his voice putting Darius further on edge.

"Travis was just out at your place last night," Darius says. "We didn't think it was necessary for both of us to come."

He is thinking fast. He has not talked to Travis since they parted ways at the boat yesterday. Travis was supposed to go straight to see Norman to pay him his money.

Norman chuckles a low mirthless laugh.

"It isn't necessary for you both to come, but it would be nice if just one of you did; especially when you owe me money. It makes me think you are avoiding me."

"But, Travis-," Darius starts.

"Did not show up," Norman finishes for him. "You are already overdue for your last payment. That is not good. That does not make me happy, and it does not make my friend happy either."

Darius stiffens at the word 'friend'. He is about to look around for a second man when his head explodes with the brilliance of stars and light ringing through it and he drops limply to the ground.

Norman's friend had stepped out from where he was hiding right behind Darius as they talked, swinging a board like a batter going for the home run. The wood thunked dully against the back of Darius's head an instant after the word "friend" and Darius dropped like a sack of potatoes.

Floyd smiles at his fat friend.

Barely clinging to consciousness, Darius tries to keep his eyes open. The world is a spinning blur fading between black and grey. His head screams with the ringing in his ears that tells him he is probably still alive. The sharp pain filling his head sends waves of nausea through him as he fumbles weakly on the ground, trying to crawl to his feet.

Norman and Floyd watch him fumble and mewl like a dying kitten with wicked sneers on their faces.

Darius manages to get to his hands and knees, the motion causing him to vomit on the ground. He fumbles around, fumbling in his own hot vomit, trying to get up.

"This will help you remember not to miss any more payments," Norman says. "I want double. That's interest only. Plus, the two payments you are late on. You have two days." He spits on the downed man and the two of them go to work on him, kicking him brutally, Floyd beating him with the board.

It is all Darius can do to curl up into a foetal ball and try to protect his head.

***

The Dock Master's car pulls up in front of a restaurant and parks. Basil gets out, walking into the restaurant. He looks around, spots who he is looking for, and is already moving towards the table before the maître d' can reach him to try to seat him.

Two men are sitting at the table; one of them elderly. Both are well dressed in expensive suits. They look up when he stops at their table.

"Basil," the younger man says, nodding a greeting.

"Mr. Moloney," Basil nods to him. "Mr. Randall," he addresses the elderly man.

Basil continues, addressing them both.

"I believe you will be interested to know that a young gentleman has been in my office registering a boat."

"I am not aware of any boats ready to be registered," Desmond Moloney says. "It must be a purchase being shipped in."

"No sir. Apparently, the two young gentlemen have purchased an old salvage. My clerk said the young man who came in seemed to be very inexperienced. They are planning to fix up the salvage, rebuild it."

"What kind of boat is it?" Desmond asks.

"A steam boat. A sternwheeler. She used to be a showboat."

"They must be a couple of wealthy lads playing with their family money," Eugene Randall says, his voice papery and cracking with age. "It is always good when they get themselves into a constructive hobby."

"I don't believe so, sir," Basil says. "My clerk said this young man seemed, well, poor."

"Poor? And they bought a boat?" Desmond is incredulous.

"A salvage, sir. Likely abandoned and left to rot. They probably bought her for a fairly low price."

"And she was a showboat? I don't remember when we had a showboat around here last, except for the Queen Rhiannon."

"What is the name of the boat?" Eugene looks at him with more interest.

"The Gypsy Queen, sir."

Eugene's eyes lose focus for a brief heartbeat and he reaches for his wine glass with a hand that has a tremor to it. He takes a sip, changing his focus to his wine glass.

When he does not respond, the others turn their attention back on each other.

"Poor or not, these boys will need to see us for the proper permits and help to rebuild this boat of theirs," Desmond says. "Do you think they will reach out to us?"

"I don't know sir," Basil shakes his head. "As I said, my clerk believed them to be inexperienced. He did advise them they should visit you at the Shipbuilders' Union office."

"Thank you. I believe we will need to pay those young men a visit. We need to make certain they know they cannot rebuild a boat without union labour."

Basil nods and takes his dismissal, turning and leaving the restaurant.

"What was that?" Desmond asks, turning to Eugene, hearing him muttering under his breath.

"Nothing. It is nothing," Eugene says, still looking down at his wine glass.

Feeling that something is bothering him, Desmond cannot help but keep looking at his boss, the CEO of the Shipbuilders' Union, Eugene

Randall, who was once a formidable man before age turned him into a shell of his former self.

"Is something about that boat bothering you?" he asks.

"She is just a boat," Eugene says.

"Yes sir. The name does have a familiar feel, like I should know it."

Eugene looks at him.

"There was a steam boat running in the area with that name. A long time ago."

"So, you remember her." Desmond is pleased that his memory rings true. "What was she about?"

"She was a casino boat."

"Like the Queen Rhiannon. I did not think the Barlow family would allow another casino to operate in the area. They have operated the casinos in this area for a few generations now."

"Yes. Mr. Barlow built an empire out of his father's small casino. He would not allow any competition. Now his son Malcolm Barlow runs the Barlow empire."

"So, the Gypsy Queen…"

"Was Thaddeus Barlow's boat."

"Should we let Mr. Barlow know?"

"I do not see the point, unless they plan to make her a casino boat again."

Desmond nods, processing the ramifications of the situation.

***

Amelia is sitting in the parlor sewing when the front door bangs open, startling her. She looks up in surprise, craning to see who came in.

Roman walks heavily with anger, closing the door too hard behind him. He fumbles with his coat, angrily jabbing it onto the coat hook in a motion Amelia half expects to tear the fabric.

She puts her sewing down, half getting out of her chair in alarm, and pauses to watch him in shock.

Roman mutters angrily as he turns and struggles more than a man should with his shoes.

"Something very serious is wrong," Amelia thinks, standing and taking a few tentative steps forward.

Her father's rage holds her back. She has never seen him this angry and it frightens her.

Relief floods her at the sound of her mother's footsteps coming from the kitchen.

Her mother stops in the entrance, looking at Roman with dismay; alarmed by the fury etched in his face and movements.

"Roman, what is wrong?" Lena's voice reveals the alarm on her face that Amelia can't see from her vantage point. "Has something happened?"

Kicking his shoe away, Roman stomps past her to the parlour where Amelia is anxiously watching and drops heavily into his chair.

Lena follows him in, looking at him with concern.

Roman rubs a hand over his hair and then his face, and finally looks at the two women.

Seeing their worry, he tries to control the anger in his voice. He stares straight ahead, not looking at either of them.

"The store was robbed," he says flatly, unable to avoid the tremor of anger that still resonates in his words.

"We know the store was robbed," Lena says. She blanches. "Was it robbed again?"

They both look at him in shocked disbelief.

Amelia blinks back tears, shocked and upset someone could do this to her father.

"But-but how? Who? You work so hard, who would do this to you?"

Roman waves them off.

"No, it is still the same robbery. The constable is not going to arrest them. He says there is no proof of who did it."

"But you know who did it," Lena complains.

"Does the constable think it was him?" Amelia asks, afraid the answer will be yes. "Was it him?"

Roman looks at her, his eyes cold with anger.

"Can't say that I know, but I have already talked to the authorities and now I must take other action to get recompense. It will be dealt with."

There is something in his look that Amelia does not like. Some unspoken message meant for her, but meant to be kept to himself.

She takes two quick steps towards to him.

"What do you mean?" she pleads.

"That hooligan, the both of them, will not get away with robbing me."

Amelia looks at him with panic. She is filled with disbelief. Despite her better judgement, she voices it.

"It cannot be him, or them." She looks at him imploringly. "They are good and kind and decent. They are not the sort to rob stores."

"They are criminals." He glares at her. "Are you taking their side over mine?"

"No Father, I just do not believe they could have done this. I do not believe they would ever do such a thing."

Roman looks at her with a new realization.

"She is smitten with the bugger," he thinks. It sends a new dark anger down to the pit of his stomach, raw and fresh.

"Face the fact woman," he says, forcing himself to begrudgingly acknowledge that she is no longer a child. That she is indeed a woman, and a headstrong one at that.

Amelia is the daughter he raised her to be. Strong willed and fair minded, and one who thinks for herself. Her obvious interest in the young man only makes him dislike the thief even more.

He continues.

"Those two are poor. Without means. Somehow, they managed to get their hands on some worthless heap of scrap and, by some strange nature of their quirks, have determined they will rebuild it. That takes a lot of time and money. Mostly a lot of money. They need tools, and when tools break, they need more tools. And as they progress, they will need even more tools. They need a great deal of supplies. Where are they going to get all that money for all those supplies?"

He stares at her, giving her a chance for it to sink in.

Amelia frowns, looking away.

Faced with the evidence of Travis's guilt, all circumstantial, she grudgingly has to admit that it is likely, although she admits it only to herself. She is furious with Travis.

With a heavy sigh as if he regrets turning her against the young man, while secretly relishing it, Roman continues.

"When he was confronted with the theft, he came back and tried to pay me off. Compensation, even if a poor compensation. You do not pay a man compensation for a crime for which you are not guilty."

He looks at her, studying her for a reaction.

"That man tried to make a gesture of making things right."

Amelia looks back at him, meeting his look and seeing that Travis's effort only angered her father more, sealing both his guilt and his fate in her father's mind.

"He is right," she thinks. "Why would Travis try to make things right if he is not guilty?"

The thought is a knife to her chest. The pain of his betrayal is a sob welling up that she pushes down.

"He is guilty. He robbed my father's store," she thinks.

A flicker of hope burns deep inside her.

"I have also seen the remorse when he learned it was my father he stole from."

That piques her interest.

17 My Gypsy Queen

Travis is working on the boat alone. He looks up again, looking for Darius, and still sees no sign of him.

"Where is Darius?" He shrugs it off. "He must have picked up a job." He goes back to work.

He is sitting on the plank platform hanging just below the deck level, carefully tracing out the name on the hull with black paint, the brush leaving ragged lines across the uneven rotting wood. Dipping the brush in the paint, he carefully traces over it again and again, strengthening the line as the paint fills into the cracks in the wood. It is a start. The name is now visible for the world to see.

He pauses to examine his handiwork, feeling pride surge inside knowing that anyone passing by will see the name and know the Gypsy Queen belongs to him.

"I know it's pointless to repaint your name now. These boards are rotting and will have to be replaced. But you have a name and you should wear it proudly."

Leaving the paint to dry, he climbs down and starts working on tearing apart a section of rotting hull.

As he works, Travis keeps sounding out her name in his head.

Gypsy Queen.

"My Gypsy Queen," he whispers, working with care, gently prying off boards.

That is when the first strange thing happens.

Travis pauses at the faint sound of a noise behind him. He turns around, looking for the source of the sound, but sees nothing. Thinking nothing of it, he goes back to work.

A few minutes later, he pauses again. Travis sets the pry bar down, turning to look behind him. He looks around suspiciously, unable to shake the feeling that someone is sneaking up on him.

"I could swear I heard something behind me," he mutters.

He shrugs, picks up the pry bar, and goes back to work pulling off boards.

Travis feels the hairs on the back of his neck stand up at the light touch of coolness on the skin of his neck. Like someone just breathed a cold breath on his neck while standing behind him very closely and looking over his shoulder.

He freezes, expecting a blow to the back of his head from an attacker, and spins around, wielding the bar as a weapon to defend himself.

There is no one there.

He looks around, listening, but there is no sign of anyone. His nerves are jangling, the sensation of being watched stronger.

"I'm going loopy," Travis mutters to himself, trying to shrug off the unpleasant feeling.

He puts down the bar and picks up another board, leaning it in place against the cross beams it will be nailed to.

"This won't hurt, I promise. But we have to support these beams so they don't collapse."

Travis kneels down, grabs some nails, and reaches for the hammer.

His fingers brush only the ground. He looks down.

"I could have swore I put the hammer right there," he mumbles. He looks around him for the hammer.

Travis scratches his head in confusion. The hammer is nowhere to be found.

"Well, bugger." He gets up, searching all over for the hammer. Finally, he gives up and looks around, scratching his head in confusion.

"I guess I need another hammer. I just can't figure where it went to."

***

Amelia slips into the house quietly, looking around furtively and hoping neither of her parents noticed her gone.

"I am a grown woman," she thinks in annoyance. "I should not have to sneak about to leave the house."

Her mother is supposed to be out for another hour and she is unsure if her father has returned yet.

Taking off her shoes and hanging up her coat, Amelia straightens herself and looks at herself in the mirror hanging on the wall by the front door. Her cheeks are still flushed. She rubs them to rub the rosiness away, and it only makes them rosier.

She freezes at the sound of voices in the other room. They are men's voices coming from the kitchen.

"Don't worry, Mr. Bukowski," a man's voice she does not recognize says. "When we are done teaching this Travis fellow a lesson, he won't be bothering nobody again."

"He won't be robbing no more stores or talking to the young ladies after we are finished with him," another strange voice says.

Amelia moves just as she hears the rustling of movement and the scrape of a chair, ducking into the parlour just as they come from the kitchen. She slips behind the parlour door, hiding out of sight and listening to their approaching footsteps.

They pause in the front entrance.

"I want that son of a bitch to pay for robbing me," Roman says angrily. "The police won't make him pay, so I guess it is up to me."

"Your payment will speed us along nicely," a third man grins. "When we find him, the beating we will give him will be something he won't ever forget. He won't come near your store ever again."

"Or your daughter," one of the other men sneers.

Roman gives him a disproving look. He does not like this unpleasant man even mentioning his daughter.

"Make sure that he thinks twice before he ever thinks on robbing anyone again," Roman says. "And I don't want this to come back to me. I am paying you good money for this to keep my hands clean."

Amelia's heart flutters fearfully at the thought of those rough men cornering Travis in the dark. She pictures Travis laying broken and bleeding on the ground in the darkness. She imagines garbage fluttering by as he reaches weakly toward the sound for help that is not there. Would he live? Will they leave him dead or horribly disfigured?

She has the urge to burst into the midst of them and order her father and his thugs to leave Travis alone. She wants to beg her father not to hurt him.

Amelia starts to move and stops.

"It would do no good," she thinks. "I can't let them know I am here, that I overheard. I should not have been here listening to begin with and any attempt to plead for Travis will only make Father more determined to teach Travis to leave what is his alone."

Amelia moves quietly, slipping off to her bedroom and softly closing the door.

Throwing herself down on the bed and burying her face in the pillow to muffle the sound, she sobs herself to sleep that night, sick with worry.

***

It is dark. Travis waited for the cover of night to move some more of his hidden stolen goods to the boat when no one will be around to see. He only makes one trip, not wanting to risk bringing too much at once.

Finding his stash, he carefully selects tools and nails, stuffing them into a sack. He pulls out some boards of wood, all that he can carry. Making sure the stash is still well hidden; he shoulders the wood and picks up the bag. Travis moves off through the night, depositing it at the boat.

It is not very late when he finishes. There are still people on the streets; although in the darkness of the unlit route he is taking it is very unlikely anyone has noticed his movements. Or, if they had, they most likely are not interested enough to take a closer look at who is moving what in the darkness.

"This went rather well. I think this calls for a stop in at the pub for a few drinks."

He almost makes it to the pub when he is confronted in the street.

Travis eyes the group of men loitering ahead of him, trying to decide if they are just casual loafers or up to no good. He steels himself for a possible confrontation as he approaches the group, looking past them to his goal, the worn door of the pub.

He can hear the music coming from inside and the voices talking too loudly and laughing too heartily. He imagines he can smell the smoke-filled room and the funk of stale liquor soaked into the floor.

Travis nods to the men as he reaches them, intending on moving past quickly, and purposely not looking them in the eye. If they are looking for trouble, then looking them in the eye would be like trying to stare down a nasty dog. He would see either fear or challenge reflected there. Either way, it would be sure to attack.

"Hey, are you the guy with the boat?" one of them calls out as he is passing them.

"Damn," Travis thinks, "if I don't acknowledge, it will be obvious I'm avoiding them."

"Yeah, I'm the guy with the boat." It is not the first time Travis has been asked that question since they brought the Gypsy Queen to fix up. Some people are genuinely curious about their attempt to rebuild her, but most just want to laugh or tell them they are fools.

This time the question feels threatening.

"That's quite a piece of work you have there," the man says. "It's nothing but a big heap of firewood, if you ask me."

Travis pauses, prickling at the insult to the Gypsy Queen. He feels the urge to turn around and confront the man, but a part of him does not want to. That part wants to keep going, do not look back, and do not say another word. Just walk on.

"That is your opinion I guess," Travis says as he is walking past them.

"Might be we decide to have a bonfire tonight," the man says. "Nice night for one."

Travis stops and turns around, studying the group of men, staring down the speaker.

"Good thing we know where to find a big heap of fire wood," the man says.

Travis clenches his fists, stiffening, and is about to take a step forward. A gut feeling stops him.

"Do I know you?" Travis asks, trying to place the man's face. He is familiar, but Travis is not sure from where.

"You've got some fine fresh firewood too." The man leans forward aggressively. "Wood you didn't pay for."

It clicks. He had seen the man working at the lumberyard. The men's intentions are now as clear as his insinuation. The man whose store he stole the materials from sent them to teach him a lesson, Amelia's father.

Travis's face stiffens and his whole body tenses.

"Don't show fear, don't show fear," he repeats to himself while he takes a quick head count. "Five-to-one. I'm screwed."

He turns and runs.

With a whoop like coyotes chasing prey, they sprint after him.

Travis is running for his life, feet pounding and heart pounding faster. He concentrates on just running, hearing his pursuers behind him.

He dodges up another street and down an alley, watching for any likely hiding spot, anything that might help him lose them.

He is getting frantic.

Travis is gasping for air, his tortured lungs sending a sharp pain slicing through his side, and his legs feel like he cannot possibly take another step.

"Damn those guys have endurance," he thinks, too breathless to utter the words.

The pounding feet following are like the pounding of drums in his ears.

Then he sees nothing but darkness ahead and the looming shapes of trees. With nowhere else to go, Travis says a silent prayer and forces his legs to continue pumping, dodging trees as the darkness engulfs him.

The men follow him into the trees, cursing the darkness.

He hears one of them run into a tree with a thud, a yelp, and swearing.

Travis trips into a gully, suddenly finding himself falling forward. His stomach twists with the endless feeling of foreboding that comes with falling and not seeing what, if anything, lies below.

He flounders, grasping at air, wondering how far the fall will be. He would have yelped if he had the breath. Instead, he falls with a soft airless wheeze.

It turns out to be a short fall. Travis thuds to the ground. What little wind he has left is knocked out of his lungs, possibly saving his life.

Travis rolls reflexively when he hits. It is an ungainly awkward move, expecting a swinging weapon to be coming down on him, his pursuers close behind. He moves blindly and finds himself up against the craggy mud side of the ditch, the wall going straight up and over in a bit of a lip above overhanging the side where water regularly rushing through after storms had cut away the earth.

He tries to gasp for air, instead feeling the frightening refusal of his body to cooperate. He manages only to choke out a breathless cough, quickly covering his mouth to deaden the sound, trying to catch his breath.

Panic buzzes through Travis.

"I can't breathe!" he thinks wildly.

He claws at his throat, trying to suck in air, to gasp and pant. His whole body suddenly feels like it is shrinking in on itself with the need for air that will not come.

"Stop," a hoarse whisper above commands. "Listen for him."

Above, the men stop, listening for any sound that will give away the man they lost.

Realizing they are right there above him, Travis manages to force himself to stop and lie still, pressed against the cold bank.

"I don't hear anything," the voice above whispers. "We lost him. Let's go. Search the woods."

Travis hears their footsteps move away, moving more cautiously through the trees in their search for him.

The pain in Travis's lungs is unbearable by the time his shocked body finally composes itself enough to let him suck in that first faint breath of air. Frantically he gasps and pants until he realizes it is doing no good.

Forcing himself to concentrate on slow small breaths, he begins to take the first shallow breaths. His breaths get bigger as the seconds tick by. His heart rate slows as his breaths deepen and he keeps focused on taking that next slow breath of air.

He lays there for a while just breathing until the dizziness goes away.

He does not feel like going to the pub now and slinks his way home.

18   After the Dark

Amelia is walking to her father's store purposely, staring ahead and her expression stony. She does not realize how quickly she is walking, her mind lost in conflicting feelings and dark thoughts.

"I feel like I did not sleep at all last night worrying over what those men will do to Travis and Darius if they find them."

"When they find them," she corrects herself.

Amelia hesitates on the corner, looking off in a direction she is not intending to go. She yearns to go that way. That way leads to the boat they are rebuilding.

"It won't take so long; just a quick detour to see if they are there to make sure they are both all right."

Her cheeks redden with a flush, thinking about the two men.

"I don't know who I want to see more. Darius is kind, attentive when he talks to you, and does not dismiss my thoughts as silly just because I am a woman. Travis is distracted and has too much ego, but has shown interest in me."

She looks back the other way towards her father's store.

"No, I have to get to the store to help Father. I will have to find out later if they are okay."

She looks back once more to the path leading to the old boat and hurries on her way to the store. Worry for the two men sits as a tight heavy knot in her stomach.

"I am sorry I'm late," Amelia says as she bustles into the store, the bell over the door jangling her arrival. She looks around quickly for her father and spots him sitting on a stool and crouched over a low shelf doing inventory.

"You are just in time," he says, not pausing from his task. "We need to finish inventorying the store. The other clipboard is on the counter."

Amelia fetches it and gets to work counting.

The bell over the door jangles again to announce someone's arrival and she looks up to see two men entering the store.

They are two of the men who chased Travis the night before.

Roman looks up to see who came in.

"I will look after them," he says, putting his pencil and clipboard down and getting up quickly to intercept them.

It is not lost on Amelia that he is moving more quickly than normal.

"He does not want me to talk to them," she thinks.

"This way, gentlemen, it's on this shelf," Roman says, pretending he is bringing them to show them something."

He ushers the men to the far side of the store and behind a shelf.

They look at him in confusion and follow him.

He waves them to stop when they are out of Amelia's sight and drops his voice to a whisper, looking at them with a mix of anxiety and irritation.

"Why are you here?"

One of the men looks down sheepishly.

"We didn't get him," the other says, trying to sound apologetic.

"What do you mean you did not get him?" Roman whispers hoarsely.

Hearing the whispered voices, Amelia is suspicious. She pretends to continue taking stock, while straining to listen. She shifts closer to them, moving halfway up the next aisle.

"We had Travis but he got away."

"He got away? How many of you were there? You could not catch one man?"

The man shrugs. "He was fast. We had him and he escaped. He outran us and hid. We couldn't find him."

Roman's face twists into an angry scowl.

"Do you want us to try again?"

"No," Roman spits out. "Once looks like a mugging and can be argued as such; a criminal robbing a criminal of his stolen goods. No harm, no foul. If you try again it will be too obvious to the police if he goes to them."

He turns away angrily.

"Just get out of my store. We are done."

"We scared him pretty good, I'm sure," the apologetic man says. "I think he learned his lesson even if we did not get to beat him."

Roman just gruffs at them, waving them on to leave.

"We didn't have what they want," he says for his daughter to hear as he leaves the aisle, watching them leave the store.

Amelia moves quickly away, nervously glancing in his direction to make sure he does not know she was eavesdropping.

"Travis escaped his attackers," she thinks, the opposing feelings rushing through her dizzying. Amelia is filled with curiosity. She feels instantly elated that he might be okay. She also still feels the burn of anger at him for his betrayal in robbing her father's store.

"I need to see him," she thinks, "to see for myself that he is okay."

She can think of no excuse to take her anywhere she might see Travis even at a distance.

"How is that inventory coming?" Roman asks, coming around the corner into her aisle.

Amelia looks up, trying to control her reaction and feeling startled.

"Good," she says, almost choking on the word. "I think we should be done by tomorrow."

***

Travis arrives at work and looks around for Darius. There is no sign of him among the men arriving for work.

"Hey, have you seen Darius? Has anyone seen Darius?" He asks worker after worker only to get head shakes and answers of "No".

The foreman seeks out Travis halfway through the day.

"Where is that buddy of yours?" he demands angrily. "He missed his shift today. You tell him he had better have a good excuse or he's fired."

He stalks off angrily, leaving Travis to watch him go.

"This is not like Darius. He never just does not show up."

When the shift ends, Travis hurries out to go looking for Darius. He goes to the house where he rents a room upstairs off the back of the house and knocks on Darius's door. When there is no answer, he tries the door. It is locked.

He tries peeking in the window, shifting and craning for a view. He catches a partial view of what he is sure is a body laying on the bed.

"Darius, Darius!"

He bangs on the window.

"I know you are in there. I can see you."

He bangs and rattles the door.

"Darius, I see you. Open the door."

The sound of banging and his name being called rouses Darius. He opens his eyes as much as his swollen lids let him, groggy, the room spinning. All he can see is a slit of fuzzy light and dim shadowy shapes.

Managing to get into a sitting position, waves of nausea rush through Darius. He pushes himself up off the bed where he had lain for a full two nights and days, unable to get up.

Darius groans, wishing the noise pounding into his head would go away.

Travis continues persistently banging on the door and calling him.

"Quit all that racket and banging." Darius's landlady yells at Travis, appearing from the front of the house. She is a small frumpy woman, overweight and perpetually tired looking. She comes around the side of the house, squinting up at him angrily.

"If he is not answering then he isn't there."

"Ma'am," Travis nods to her and she goes away. He waits, intent on the locked door, and bangs and calls again after she is gone.

"Darius, come on. I know you are there. Open the door. Darius."

Hearing him, she waves her hand in the air in irritation, muttering to herself as she walks away.

Darius trembles with the effort and manages to get to his feet, stumbling forward. He finds the door only by the sound of banging and the voice on the other side.

Fumbling blindly against the door until he finds the latch, he manages to unlock it. A brief moment of searching and his groping hand finds the doorknob. He stumbles back, almost falling as he opens the door, using it as an unreliable support.

Travis exclaims as he rushes forward, grabbing Darius before he falls, steadying him. Darius leans limply against him.

He is in shock at the sight of his friend. Darius's face is almost unrecognizable, a monstrosity of swelling mottled with bruises. He is covered with crusted blood, his eyes swollen shut, and his lips swollen to impossible size, his upper lip split open.

"What happened to you?" Travis demands in alarm as he half carries half drags him across the room to the bed.

His first utterance, "Norman", is unintelligible.

"What?"

"The fat man," Darius manages, saying it slowly, his words sounding like he is talking through a mouth stuffed full of cotton.

More frightening than his appearance is the garbled words that slur out of his mouth and his obvious disorientation and grogginess.

Travis looks around the room in shock as if he might find the answer there before him.

Darius falls heavily to the bed as Travis lets him down.

"When? How long have you been like this?" Travis's voice quavers.

"Don't know." Darius spent most of the last two days drifting in and out of consciousness.

"You need a doctor."

Travis kneels next to the prone man.

"Do you have any money?" he asks, searching his own pockets. He has some, but not enough to pay the doctor.

He looks at Darius. His eyes have closed again and he is not moving. Travis gently shakes Darius, trying to get him to wake up to listen.

"Do you have any money?" he asks again. "You need a doctor."

Darius moans an unintelligible sound.

Travis gets up and searches the room. He finds a few bills in a coffee can, but not even close to enough for the doctor.

"I'll be back," he says. "I'm going to get the doctor."

Travis rushes out and races down the street to the doctor's house. He stops there, panting and knocking urgently at his door. The doctor opens the door.

"What do you want?"

"I need you to come. My friend, Darius, is hurt bad."

The doctor shakes his head. "I can't help you. I know you two well enough to know that neither of you has any money to pay me."

"Please," he looks at the doctor imploringly, "he is in a really bad place. He is all beaten up bad. He needs a doctor."

"I don't work for free," the doctor mutters, shaking his head again as he closes the door on Travis.

Travis stares at the closed door and purses his lips. He cannot force the man to come. He returns to Darius's room, letting himself in.

He leans against the wall in despair.

"The doctor won't come. I tried, but he won't come."

Travis looks around, lost and uncertain. He stands and searches for a washcloth. Wetting it, he starts gently cleaning up Darius.

While he is cleaning him, Darius waves weakly at him, waving him off. He starts trying to roll onto his side, but cannot.

Travis gently helps him roll and, at that moment, Darius's body is hit with a gagging convulsion pushing the first hot wave of vomit splattering to the floor with stomach bile. Little comes out of his empty stomach. There is already drying vomit there. He groans with the pain the motion is inflicting on his damaged body.

Instinctively jumping back, Travis looks around in a hurry, grabs the trash can, and shoves it under Darius's mouth as his body continues to be wracked with waves of nausea. Bile splatters into the wastebasket again and again until there is no more to come, leaving him dry heaving.

Darius's whole body convulses with the effort of vomiting, his empty stomach sending up nothing more than stomach bile that drips from his mouth in strings of mucous. He tries to grit his teeth against crying out from the pain of his ribs rubbing together with the coughs and surges of dry vomiting. He is trembling and pale, having eaten little or nothing in days and unable to keep down even water.

Travis gets up wearily from his chair to clean up the mess, starting with wiping down his friend's mouth.

Finished, he sits in the chair, leaning forward and hanging his head.

"What do I do?" he moans. "I don't know what to do."

He looks at Darius, worried.

"Don't die on me buddy, don't die."

He sits back, his head back, and holds the sides of his head in despair. His eyes are red and his face haggard and drawn. He blinks back the tears.

"We aren't family, but you are all the family I have."

Travis sits up.

"Amelia. Maybe she will know what to do. I'll be back."

He rushes out the door.

***

Travis goes to Amelia's house. He stands in the street looking at the house uncertainly.

"There is no way they will let me see her. I can't go to the door. What do I do?"

He tries to see in the windows without approaching the house. Walking around to the side, he tries the side windows.

As Travis is reaching the back of the house, the back door opens. He ducks out of sight, watching the door.

Amelia comes out with a basket full of laundry. She goes to the clothesline and starts hanging the laundry.

Travis watches her surreptitiously, glancing at the house.

When she is almost finished, using the hanging clothes as cover, he jogs into the yard, staying low.

"Amelia," he hisses, keeping his voice quiet.

She jumps, startled, brandishing a pair of trousers before her like a weapon.

"Who is there?"

"It's me, Travis," he whispers. He ducks his head around a dress and back into hiding.

Amelia steps forward, looking around the dress.

"Why are you hiding in my laundry?"

"I had to see you."

A thrill races through her, at the same time trepidation fills her. She glances at the house. Further conflicting her emotions is relief to see that he really is okay and the burn of anger and betrayal.

"My father would be furious if he knew you are here. You should go." She hisses.

"And I am still angry with you," she adds.

"I need your help."

"I do not want to see you or talk to you. You broke into my father's store. I cannot forgive you for that. You are a louse. A horrible person. You are a thief and a criminal."

"Please Amelia," he begs. "I don't know what to do."

"You can start by not breaking into other people's property and stealing from them."

"It's not about that." He waves to her. "Come closer. Please."

Her heart beating faster and her breath catching in her throat, Amelia hesitantly takes a few steps towards him. She looks around the clothes he is hiding behind and looks into his eyes.

What she sees startles her more.

He is haggard and drawn, his face pinched with pain and fear.

"Please Amelia, I need your help. It's Darius."

"What about Darius?" Fear courses through her, leaving a tight knot in her stomach.

"He is hurt. The doctor won't come. I don't know what to do. Please come with me and see him."

Amelia glances at the house anxiously, looks into his pained eyes again, and cannot say no. She suspects it's a trick to get her to talk to him, but the fear and pain in his eyes looks real.

She nods wordlessly.

Travis backs away and she follows him.

Once they are out of sight of the house, they walk quickly towards Darius's rented room. Amelia's feet move quicker to keep up with his longer legs. Fear for what she will find keeps her silent until they reach Darius's door.

Amelia stops outside the closed door, stopping Travis before he can open it. She looks at him. He looks at her, his eyes anxious.

"Did you bring me just because I'm a woman?"

He hesitates. "What?"

"Do you assume I am going to know how to care for him just because I'm a woman?"

He nods.

"You know how to look after kids and stuff. I thought you would know what to do."

She purses her lips at him, her eyes flashing anger.

Making a hasty retreat, Travis opens the door and ushers her inside before she can change her mind.

Amelia hesitates before going in.

Inside, she looks around at the small room and quickly spots Darius lying on the bed. She stares at him. He really is there. It is not some ruse.

It takes a moment to register.

She rushes over, seeing the full brutality of his injuries. Her mouth opens in a shocked O.

"What happened to him?" Amelia manages. Her mind is working, thoughts whirling.

"Father's men said they had Travis," she thinks. "They said he got away. They didn't say anything about Darius."

"Some guys beat him bad," Travis says, his voice hoarse with emotion.

Amelia looks at him in alarm.

"Who?"

Travis's face reddens. He looks ashamed.

Amelia's lips tighten into an angry line. Her eyes go hard. She glares at him.

"Was this because of my father's store?"

Travis shakes his head woodenly. The denial is not entirely true. He swallows.

Her accusing look makes his shame worse.

"I gave your father money I was supposed to pay someone else."

Amelia gives him a cold look of fury. She turns her attention on Darius, dropping down to sit on the edge of the bed, examining his injuries.

"Can he stand? Walk? Can he see? Is he vomiting?"

Travis stares at her in shocked numbness.

Amelia turns to him, her eyes cold with fury.

"Answer me."

Travis swallows.

"He is vomiting. He cannot walk or stand. I-I don't know how much he can see. He is mostly unconscious, sometimes drifting on the edge of consciousness, but mostly out of it."

Amelia turns her back on Travis, pointedly ignoring his presence, and returns to examining Darius.

She gets up, finds a cloth and wets it, putting the cool compress on his head.

"He probably has a bad concussion," she says to herself.

"When is the last time you ate?" she asks the unconscious man. "You need to eat. Clear liquids only. You need warmed broth."

"Find him some broth," Amelia says without looking at Travis, her voice cold and angry.

Travis nods, feeling awkward, and leaves in search of broth.

Darius is laid up for days suffering the effects of a severe concussion as his other injuries heal. He has bruises and swelling everywhere, but by a great strike of fortune no broken bones except for cracked ribs.

Amelia and Travis spend much of the following days looking after him, Amelia slipping away whenever she can to come sit by his side. She lets herself in when she gets there, bringing warmed broth she tells her parents is for the sick mother of a friend.

Darius spends those days vomiting and delirious, Travis and Amelia unsure if he is aware of their presence as they nurse him. They do their best to get soup broth into him, but manage little of that.

Alone with Darius, Travis is attempting again to feed him, the now cold broth seeming to somehow come up in greater volumes than it went down.

Fevered and with chills, Darius is trembling and the motion of rolling and vomiting causes the cool damp cloth on his forehead to slip to the floor.

Travis pulls the wastebasket closer, allowing the vomit to splash into it. When Darius is finished, he wets the cool washcloth again, replacing it on his forehead and grabs the other washcloth to clean him up again.

He is in the middle of cleaning Darius's face when angry knocking starts at the door.

Travis looks up, startled at the angry pounding. He looks around quickly for anything he might use as a weapon to defend himself, settling on the broom. Putting down the cloth, he gets up to answer the door, grabbing the broom next to it.

He opens the door to reveal the angry face of Darius's landlady, Mrs. Solomon. She purses her lips at Travis, obviously displeased to see him.

"I don't know what you two are up to in here," she scolds, "but somebody needs to pay me rent."

She looks Travis up and down the way one might a giant cockroach if it were entirely normal for one to answer the door.

"And if you are both living here now, the rent is going to be double." She crosses her arms angrily over her chest, waiting for a response.

Travis is taken aback. Not so much by the woman's unpleasant disposition, he is used to that, but by the fact that neither of them has any money to give her. A hot flush burns his cheeks and his stomach clenches into a knot.

"You look lovely today Mrs. Solomon," he says, trying to sound like he genuinely means it. A little flattery often works on his own landlady when he is late with the rent.

Mrs. Solomon harrumphs at him and purses her angry lips tighter.

"Mr. Wright, don't think your mediocre charms will work on me like they do Mrs. Moreau. Mr. Marek is late on his rent and if I don't get some money he is going to be out of here."

She cranes her neck, trying to look around Travis, who is blocking the doorway, suspicious.

"Where is Darius? Why isn't he answering the door?"

She glares up at him suspiciously. "Just what are you up to in there?"

She sniffs the air, getting a whiff of the unpleasant stench of vomit.

"What are you two doing in there?" she demands. She tries to look past him again.

Travis tries to shift to keep her from seeing anything, but she spots the prone form of the other man on the bed.

"What is the lack about doing in bed?" she demands. "Mr. Marek, come to the door and talk to me yourself."

She looks up at Travis.

"What's wrong with him?" Her voice is accusatory.

"He is sick Ma'am," Travis says, "very ill."

"Sick with what?" Mrs. Solomon demands accusingly. She pushes past Travis, moving the larger man aside as if he were nothing more than a child, forcing her way in.

She looks down at Darius and gasps, taking in the swollen face, split lip, and bruises.

"Now what trouble have you two gotten into?" She whirls on Travis with a look a stern schoolteacher might give a boy who stuck a tack on her chair.

Travis immediately feels like that boy. His face reddens, his heart quickens, and his bowels suddenly feel loose and watery with fear. He clears his throat that suddenly seems to catch with a knot trapped inside it.

"He was jumped by a couple of guys," he says. Telling the truth would only anger her further, so he decides to elaborate with a small lie. "I think they were robbing him."

She purses her lips even more, though it does not seem possible, and looks the injured man over.

"He needs a doctor," she snaps.

Travis shakes his head, lowering it apologetically. "The doctor would not come. I don't have enough money to pay him."

"He has a concussion," she mutters, examining the injuries and prying his lids open, looking into Travis's unfocussed eyes. He should be in a hospital."

She stands up, turns to Travis, and gets right in his face.

"I don't run a charity here either," she hisses. "I want my rent. Double if that Mrs. Moreau finally came to her senses and kicked you out and you are staying here."

She glances quickly at Darius.

Travis is not sure, but he thinks he might have seen the slightest softening of her expression. She turns her attention back to Travis.

"One week," she says harshly. "I'm giving you one week to pay the rent or he's out."

With that, she walks out, leaving behind the unpleasant lingering energy of her disagreeable personality.

Darius looks around groggily.

"Was that Mrs. Solomon?" he moans weakly.

"Yes, but don't worry about it. She is just looking for rent money. I will take care of it."

Darius tries to push himself up and swoons dizzily.

"H-how long? H-how long have I been laying here?"

"Not long," Travis lies. "Don't worry, everything is fine."

Darius tries to shake his head to relieve the grogginess, but even that slow motion makes the world dip and spin. He feels like he is falling even though he is still lying in bed. He tries to put his arms out to brace himself against the landing that will not come, but his arms are uncooperative.

"No." It comes out a hoarse whisper. "How long? Really?"

Travis sighs.

"A couple days," he admits, although not saying how many.

Darius blinks, trying to think, his bruised brain having trouble with the most basic cognitive functions.

"My job," he says. "I lost my job, haven't I?"

"I'm afraid so," Travis says. He does not add that he lost his too because he had stayed by his friend's side instead of going to work.

Darius closes his eyes wearily, drifting off to sleep. It is all he has done for the past days, sleep and vomit.

Travis suddenly needs fresh air in a bad way. He slips outside and sits on the stairs, his face lined with worry.

"I don't know where I am going to come up with the money. My own rent is overdue already and now I have to come up with money for Darius's rent too. And we are even more behind on the payments to Norman now."

Travis scowls. "That fat bastard did this to him, probably as a warning because we were already late paying him."

His anger is not directed at Norman. He is angry at himself.

"I should have paid Norman like I was supposed to. I should not have given it to Amelia's father. How stupid can I be? Giving away the money for the boat payment just to impress a girl; the shopkeeper's daughter who is angry with me and believes I robbed her father's store. She is right, of course, but I didn't know when I robbed the place that she is the daughter of the owner."

Travis feels more desperate now than ever. They both have not worked all week, he has two rents and Norman to pay; and the Gypsy Queen is sitting idle and alone. He has not eaten that day. He is out of money and food.

His stomach feels the tightness of hunger, but it is a different hunger that fills him. He feels the draw of the Gypsy Queen, the urgency of what she could be, the pull of the glamour and lights and money that will fill her.

"I have to do something," Travis mutters. "I have to do something now."

Getting up, he leaves, walking down the street knocking on doors. He begs for work, for any odd job no matter how small or unpleasant, even if the payment is only a simple meal. When they don't offer him a job, he begs for money, for food, for rubbish they have that they want carted away, anything he might fix up and sell, promising to give them a portion of the sale price.

At house after house, he is turned away, some apologetically, some angrily. Some outright threaten him with violence. One house sets three large brutish looking dogs on him. Travis runs for his life, finally climbing on top of a shed to escape the snarling animals, only slightly mauled.

He waits there, shivering, until the dogs finally give up and trot off home.

Climbing down, dispirited and desperate, Travis continues up the street. The next house he comes to proves to be empty. He looks around cautiously, walks around to the back, and begins looking for a way in.

Finding an unlocked window, he gently lifts it, stopping and looking around when the swollen wood lets out a squeal. He continues pushing the window up in its track. Hoisting himself up on the windowsill, Travis slides through headfirst, coming down on his hands on the floor inside a bedroom. He lets the rest of him follow.

Travis gets up and listens. The only sound is the dull thocking of a clock in the living room. He moves off through the house to the kitchen and starts searching the cupboards.

He finds an empty potato sack and starts filling it. First with food, then with anything small he might be able to sell. He checks the other bedroom, the typical room of a small child, the living room, and finally returns to the bedroom he entered through.

The family has little of value, living simply but comfortably in their tidy sparsely furnished home.

A quick search of the room gives him only a small jewelry box. He opens it, shrugs, and scoops up the few pieces, dropping them in his bag.

"I don't know if they are worth anything, but it's worth a try."

Travis returns to the window, putting one leg out to crawl out, and pauses. He looks back at the house he just robbed with guilt. The guilty flush burning his ears, he climbs out and carefully lowers the window back down.

He stops knocking on doors after that. It was getting him nowhere. He spends the rest of the night searching for houses that are dark and silent, breaking in to steal food and salable items. He returns to Darius's room when his sack becomes too heavy to carry, like a trick-or-treater unloading his Halloween goodies so he can go out to fill up again on more loot. Only his task is more solemn and surreptitious, sneaking through the night filled with sickening shame over his mission and fear of being caught.

19   Making Ends Meet

More days have passed as Darius slowly recovers from the vicious beating Norman and Floyd gave him.

Darius is sitting on his bed when there is a knock at the door. He gets up gingerly, always conscious that moving too fast will send shock waves of dizziness ringing through his head. Moving in a shuffling limp, he opens the door, grimacing at the brighter light. He has been sensitive to bright light since the beating.

It takes him a moment to place the face at the door, the features swimming from a haze into clarity.

He steps back, letting Travis enter, and returns to sitting on his bed with relief. Most of the swelling has gone from his face now and he is recognizable again. The bruising has deepened into brown, yellow, and purple deep tissue bruising as it spread and is slowly healing.

Travis comes in, putting a full sack down on the table.

"How are you feeling today?" Travis eyes him suspiciously. "From your expression, I would say not so good."

Travis's expression turns to concern.

"Are you still having the spells?" He clucks over Darius like a mother hen, looking into his eyes and holding up his hand with a few fingers splayed.

"How many fingers?"

Darius swats his hand away, his aim off, and grimaces at the motion.

"I'm fine. Yes, I am still having dizzy spells. But only if I move too fast."

"And the headaches?"

Darius's bloodshot eyes and perpetual look of pain tell the story. His head ranges from ringing with pain that seems to bounce from ear to ear, to dull throbs, to feeling like it is expanding and will explode with the pain.

Travis nods, turning to the table.

"I have something in here that should help with that." He unloads the bag, pulling out food and finally a packet of powder. He holds up the packet.

"For your head."

Darius nods gratefully.

"Thank you for this." He looks down awkwardly, not used to taking help. "For looking after the rent, bringing me food; everything. I will be up and looking for work as soon as I can."

Travis turns away to hide the guilt he is sure is sitting plain on his face. He feels the heat of it rise up his neck and burning his ears.

"It's my fault you were beaten." The confession is on his tongue like a foul taste. He swallows it, trying to compose himself, and fails. He cannot let him know. Keeping his back to his friend, he starts putting the food away in the only cupboard.

"You look like hell," Darius says, watching him. He can tell by Travis's tense posture that there is something he is not telling him.

Travis shrugs. "I've been working extra jobs. Until you get back on your feet, I have to pay both our rents and Norman."

"You smell like shit. Literally."

Travis turns with a scowl, it cracks, and they grin at each other. The seams of his boots and clothes are caked with the manure he shovels all day. A smudge under his cheek undoubtedly is dung as well.

"I have to go," Travis makes a move for the door. "I have to get cleaned up for work. I also have a second job working from the dinner hour rush to late into the night in the hotel kitchen, washing an endless stack of dishes. I can't go to work like this."

"Do they know you shovel shit before you handle their clean dishes?"

They both let out a dry chuckle.

"I'll see you tomorrow," Travis says and leaves.

He pauses outside.

"I have a few hours before I have to be at work. Let's see if I can make some money." He heads home to wash, change his clothes, and grab a bag of items to sell.

In addition to the backbreaking labour of shovelling manure and the endless hours in a steamy kitchen rinsing swill from plates and washing them until his hands are raw, Travis is picking up any odd job he can and selling the stolen property from his nighttime raids.

Travis is leaving his room when he is stopped by his landlady, Mrs. Moreau. He instinctively hides the bag of goods, a guilty flush burning his neck.

"We haven't been seeing much of you these days Mr. Wright," she says a little too loudly.

Travis cringes inwardly at her voice, picturing a harpy swooping down to devour his soul. The harpy wears the too large bosom and the face of the unpleasant woman.

He gives her a grin. "I've been busy of late."

"You look like something even the cat wouldn't drag in," she says. "Not up to any mischief, I hope. You will be on time with the rent next month?"

"I have been working hard Mrs. Moreau, so I can make the rent on time."

Travis flourishes a bow to her and heads on his way, grateful to leave her behind. He heads for the center of town.

With his bag of stolen property, Travis finds a spot on a busy street and looks around at the crowd hopefully.

Travis spies a possible mark. He watches the man approach through the crowd. When he reaches the optimal point, he pounces.

"Sir," Travis jogs after him, the ruse adding a level of urgency to the transaction. He easily catches up to him, panting breathlessly as though he had just had a great run.

"Sir, if I may, you look like a man of some means."

The man waves him off irritably, not looking at him, and keeps walking.

Travis follows. "A man of means also means a man with a wife with some needs, and perhaps one who is best kept happy?" His voice is carefully cheerful, lilting up in a question.

The man pauses and turns to him. "What rubbish are you peddling?" He scowls. His wife, indeed, has been miserable, and has been making his life miserable. Ever since they had been robbed, she has lamented the loss of her jewelry. He would rather replace the pieces without spending a small fortune on them.

Travis's eyes light up. "The fish is nibbling," he thinks.

"I have some fine combs and pieces of jewelry to make any woman's eyes sparkle."

The man comes closer and he opens the bag, pulling out a necklace for him to examine.

The man studies the necklace with a frown, considering it. "What else do you have?"

Travis pulls out an ornate comb and the man studies it. He shows him a few more pieces, thrilling with the attention. The man would not still be looking if he is not interested in buying. This is almost a sure sale.

Travis pulls out a broach, placing it in the palm of the man's hand.

The man frowns, looking down at it. He turns it, studying it. His eyes narrow and his lips harden into a thin line. A crimson flush of anger starts seeping up his neck to stain his cheeks.

He levels his eyes to meet Travis's.

Travis's smile falters.

"You stole this," the man says coldly.

"What? No," Travis tries to deflect.

"You stole this," the man repeats more loudly, "and now you are trying to sell me my own wife's broach!" He looks around indignantly at people who pause to watch the scene unfolding.

Travis takes a step back, mentally searching for an escape route.

"Sir, I assure you, this is not stolen. Perhaps your wife has a broach that is similar."

The man advances on him angrily. His face flushed with red.

"That is my wife's broach." He jabs a finger angrily into Travis's chest. "You sleazy little bag of dung. You robbed my house and now you are out here peddling stolen goods. You are trying to sell me my own property."

Travis waves his hands pleadingly in front of him. "No sir. I purchased these items from a respectable dealer in another town. Look, I feel for your loss. Why don't you keep the broach? A gift."

He is backing away, the man following.

"Police! Police!" The man yells, looking around.

Travis dodges and makes a run for it, the man's hand snapping out to catch him and catching the bag of stolen property.

Travis drops the bag, letting it dangle in the man's fingers, loot spilling out as the bag droops.

Necklaces slither out with a scattering of other jewelry and falls to the ground, bouncing and rolling to litter the ground around the man as Travis races away through the crowd.

He hears the slapping of running feet and does not look back, not sure if it is the police chasing him down. He dodges around a corner, puts his head down, and keeps on running.

Dodging around another corner, Travis finally stops, bending doubled over and gasping to catch his breath. He leans against a building for support, still doubled over and gasping.

His breath is just coming back and he is able to stand when a woman's voice makes him almost jump.

"Mr. Wright, you look a fright."

He turns and straightens to see Amelia standing there looking at him with an amused half smirk.

A blush threatens to creep up his neck and Travis clears his throat, trying to compose himself.

"You are entirely out of breath," she comments.

"Not entirely." Travis can't avoid panting despite his effort not to."

"Were you running?"

He nods. "I'm late for work. Sorry, but I have to go." He gives her a little bow and retreats, turning and jogging off. He breaks into a run and makes his getaway. Travis cannot stop the grin.

Amelia watches him go with a small smile for a moment and turns to resume her business.

20   Undressing the Queen

Darius moves through his routine, dressing carefully, eating stale bread and cold soup, and leaving his room.

His landlady catches him as he is leaving.

"Darius, you are up and about now, I see. It has been weeks. How are you recovering from your injuries?"

He blinks at her in the early sunlight, the light making him wince and sending pain shooting behind his eyes.

"Good morning Mrs. Solomon. I am afraid I am making a slow recovery. I have managed to find another job."

She looks at him, seeing what he is not saying in the pain and exhaustion reflected in his eyes. He is struggling with his job and still suffers from dizzy spells and severe migraines.

"You look like hell. Take it easy. I do not want you overdoing it."

"I will. Good day Mrs. Solomon."

He makes the walk to work, arriving on time and getting straight to work. When his day finally finishes, he takes his salary and stops, counting it. His shoulders sag with a deep sigh. He shakes his head.

"It is not enough. We continue to struggle with our payments to both our landladies and to Norman. Those weeks I could not work, when Travis sat by my side and neither of us worked, has put us so far behind."

He starts walking to his next job. In addition to the two jobs, he does what odd jobs he is able to manage, the long hours leaving him completely exhausted, pale, and weak.

Feeling guilty for the long hours Travis worked to pay his rent and food while he was incapacitated, Darius pushes himself every day to keep up. He feels he owes it to his friend.

***

The time away from the Gypsy Queen has only made Travis hunger for her more.

Now that Darius has passed his delirium and is up and about, Travis has become obsessed with spending as much time as he can spend working on her.

They work together on rebuilding the Gypsy Queen whenever they can. Travis spends every moment he is not working or sleeping there, and their efforts on the Gypsy Queen are finally starting to show despite being dragged down by their lack of shipbuilding skills and money.

Amelia comes by now and then, bringing sandwiches for them and quickly leaving. She avoids Travis, leaving the sandwiches without a word and refusing to look at him if he is there.

She has still not forgiven him for robbing her father's store.

The Gypsy Queen, once a rotting pile of worm-eaten dry rot wood, is now a partially skeletal frame like the bleached ribs of a great whale beached on the shore. They are working on shoring up and reinforcing that rotting frame, finding the soft wood to have a tendency to crumble and break away with decay.

When Darius is too ill to work, he goes to the local shipyard to hang out and watch the men build boats and ships. When he can, he brings a bottle of cheap liquor and sits with the men on their breaks, sharing his liquor and asking questions.

Today is one of their rare days off and they are both working on rebuilding the Gypsy Queen.

The sound of hammers reverberates inside the wood hull, stopping at the sound of a voice calling from outside.

"Hello," the voice calls. "Hello."

Travis pops his head out from a hole in the hull.

A man in a uniform that appears to be a cross between a peace officer and a ship's officer is standing outside the boat looking very official. It is the Dock Master.

"Hello there," Travis says, climbing out of the boat. Darius follows behind.

The uniformed man is looking the boat up and down.

"I did not think this heap could be repaired," he says, looking at the boat skeptically, "but it looks like you really are making a go of it. How much shipbuilding experience do you two have?"

"None," Travis says proudly.

"I have been learning from the men at the shipyard," Darius cuts in quickly, giving Travis a quick warning look. He has a feeling it is a bad idea to let on they don't really know what they are doing. The boat would have to be inspected before it can be put into the water again.

The Dock Master turns his attention to them, sizing them up.

"I am Mr. Basil Jacobson, the Dock Master," he says.

"She is registered, if that is what you are here about," Darius says.

"I know she is registered," Basil says. "I go over the registry myself to keep up on what boats are being decommissioned, which are in dry dock for repairs, or which are being added to my docks. I was quite surprised to see the name of this one in my books. She was decommissioned for salvage a very long time ago. I thought she had been torn apart for scrap, but from the look of her I would say she has been left to rot all these years."

"You are right on that," Darius says. "She was left rotting up an old dried up tributary."

Basil nods as if answering his own question.

"It looks like she still has a lot of work to go," he says. He wanders along the Gypsy's barren ribs, testing the rot. I am not so sure anyone can revive her."

"We have been working hard on her, sir," Travis says. "Do you want to come inside and see?"

Basil's look is guarded, but Darius thinks he saw a flash of fear. Basil shakes his head quickly.

"No need," he says. "I haven't the time for tours today."

Darius has a sense the man does not want to go inside the boat for some reason.

"I came to see how she is coming along," Basil says. "I see you are making surprising progress. How many men do you have working for you?"

"Just the two of us," Travis says.

Basil gives them a calculated surprised look.

"It looks like she is due for an inspection before you go much further. You can replace all of the rib cage, but before you do anything else she must be inspected."

Basil looks at Travis steadily.

"You don't know much about the business, do you?" The question is more of a statement.

Both men shake their heads. They are jumping into unfamiliar waters with both feet.

"That is what I thought," Basil says. He leans in conspiratorially. "Just a little suggestion, gentlemen, but green greases the wheels in this business."

Both men get his meaning immediately.

"I would say it is time to start thinking about making some payments to secure your slip at the dock," he says casually. "It can take months to get a slip, even years. It is better to reserve one early."

Travis and Darius exchange looks.

"How much money do we need to, uh, reserve a place at the dock?" Darius asks cautiously.

Travis's alarmed look moves from Basil to Darius, who shoots him a warning look back.

They both feel the stress in the pits of their stomachs. They are barely managing now. This is an expense they have not foreseen.

Basil ignores their exchanged look. He is expecting it. He has already sized them up and placed them as being men of no means, just as his clerk said. He will not get much out of them.

"A slip has come open, for the time being. I will go easy on you since you are new to this and give you a deal," he smiles. It is a predatory look despite his effort to look conciliatory. "One hundred will do."

"A hundred dollars?" Travis almost chokes.

"Space is money. I do not know how long it will be before another slip comes open. This really is a bargain." Basil's grin widens and it makes him look more predatory.

Darius steps forwards. "Sir, I understand and I appreciate you giving us this break. But, we really do not have any money. A hundred dollars is more than we can pay. We don't make much and we have rent and other expenses."

Basil frowns. "That is hardly my problem. I cannot just keep a slip empty and not earning." He turns as if to leave. "If you cannot pay, I will just have to let it to someone else."

He pauses, looking at them meaningfully. His voice holds a subtle warning tone.

"I would hate for you to go to all this work and not be able to put her in the water because you did not secure a slip at the dock."

Darius tries to think. "How much money can we come up with?"

Agitated, Travis shifts on his feet and starts speaking, to promise to find the money.

"We will-."

Darius cuts him off just as he starts.

"We can pay forty." He looks at Basil earnestly. "But, we do not have the money right now. Please, we are barely getting on now."

Basil sighs, shaking his head.

"Sixty and you pay me tomorrow."

"Done." Travis steps forward eagerly to shake his hand on the deal, relieved.

Darius flashes him a look. He was hoping to work out more time at least. Maybe bring the price down.

"Make sure you do drop by the docks with your payment tomorrow, or you will lose any chance you had of securing space at my dock."

"Yes sir, we will be there with the money." Travis is nodding too eagerly.

Basil turns and starts to leave, then pauses to look back at them.

"You know; a boat this size is not usually built without hiring labour. Have you been to see the Shipbuilders' Union yet?"

"We are all the labour we need," Travis says.

"That was not an observation," Basil says. "It is a suggestion. Boats of this size are generally built using a work crew." He pauses meaningfully so his next words will sink in. "A shipbuilding crew."

Travis looks at him blankly, not getting the meaning.

Darius nods. He knows. He has been spending time at the shipyard learning what he can about building a boat.

"A Shipbuilders' Union crew," Darius adds.

Basil tips his head to him, giving him a salute and a wink, his fingers almost touching the tip of his hat.

"This has nothing to do with me, but nobody builds without the Shipbuilders' Union." His words hang heavily in the air between them. "If you don't, you can expect trouble that will take a lot of greasing to fix. Trust me when I say, you do not want them to have to come to you."

He turns and leaves, leaving the two men to digest and fully realize his meaning.

He stops at his car, calling back to them. "By the way, this is just a down payment. This is space you are renting, not buying." He nods to the two shocked men, gets in his car, and leaves.

Travis turns to Darius.

"We don't have the money to hire any crew. There is no way we can pay a union crew."

Darius looks thoughtful.

"We are going to have to come up with a lot more money," he says. "That union plays dirty. If we are lucky we can get away with just paying the union off to leave us alone."

"If we are not lucky?" Travis asks.

"We have to hire one of their crews and pay them off to leave us alone." Darius's look is very serious. "We are in serious trouble if the union decides to give us any trouble."

Travis shakes his head in consternation.

"First we have to pay dock fees already, and we are months away, at least, from her being ready for the water. Now we have to buy off the Shipbuilders' Union."

"You really are innocent aren't you?" Darius says.

Travis gives him a confused look.

"That money for the Dock Master has nothing to do with dock fees. It is a bribe and it is going straight into his own pocket. But it is still a necessary fee if we hope to get a dock slip when the time comes."

"He said it's a down payment. He expects more."

"I don't know how much more or how we are going to get the money. Hell, I don't know how we are going to get the money for tomorrow."

Travis shoves his hands in his pockets, rummaging for money. He pulls it out and counts it. "Nineteen dollars and thirty-six cents."

He looks at Darius. "How much do you have?"

"Twenty fifty."

"So we are short. Twenty…" Travis starts trying to do the math.

"Twenty dollars and fourteen cents," Darius finishes for him.

Travis whistles. "Where are we going to get that by tomorrow?"

"I don't know."

"Maybe if we bring him what we have, he will let us pay the rest later."

"I don't think that's how it works."

A heavy tension hangs between them.

"Give me some time to think," Travis says. "Let's get back to work on the boat."

Darius goes back inside. Travis stands there staring after the Dock Master's now gone vehicle.

"What did you do with the pail of nails?" Darius calls from inside the boat.

"I left it right there," Travis calls back. He enters the hull, his footsteps creaking across the wood bottom as he walks to where he left the nail bucket.

"It's not here," he says. "Did you move it?" Travis looks around for the missing nail bucket.

"No, I did not move it," Darius says, annoyed, coming to where Travis is looking around for the pail of nails. "You had it before the Dock Master came. Where did you put it?"

"I am telling you I left the bucket right here. I swear, I left them right here."

"Well, they are not here now."

150

21   The Union Knows All

Eugene Randall, CEO of the Shipbuilders' Union, is sitting in his office at the shipyard, frowning as he reads a report on his desk. He is well past retirement age and probably should have retired and left the business to younger men. But Eugene is also a man who enjoys the power of his position and is not about to give it up readily.

He rings his receptionist.

"Send Desmond into my office."

"Yes sir," her voice comes back to him.

He sits back to wait. Desmond could be anywhere in the shipyard and it could take time to track him down. Desmond is second in charge beneath only Eugene, and more than twenty years his junior.

Desmond knocks and opens the door.

"Sir, you wanted to see me?"

Eugene does not bother getting up from his fine leather chair behind his desk when Desmond enters his office. Not a man to mince words or waste time, he gets right to the point.

"I noticed a guy who is not on our crew hanging around watching and talking to the guys. What do you know about him?" Eugene asks. "What union is he from?"

Desmond had spotted the man the first day he came and immediately started checking around with his sources to find out who he is working for.

"Nobody seems to know who he is or who he works for," Desmond says. "I checked my sources and he is an unknown."

"He could be from a competing union from another yard trying to steal away skilled workers. This recession has left a glut of unskilled workers looking for work. It makes it harder to find the skilled ones to hire. It makes them more valuable too."

"Maybe," Desmond agrees with a doubtful look, "but I don't think so. The guy does not seem to know anything about the business of shipbuilding. I think it is more likely he is just a guy looking for work. He probably thinks if he hangs around enough he will get on."

"You could be right. It does not make much sense though. He has to know he will not get hired without experience."

"We are in desperate times. A man will do anything for work these days. Let's go see what the men know."

Eugene gets up and moves out from behind his desk. Desmond follows him out to the yard where they wave over some men who are milling about the area.

"Have any of you seen a guy hanging around the yard who does not belong?"

They all nod and make sounds of agreement. They have all seen him.

"Have any of you talked to him? Who is he? What does he want?"

"He just watches," one man says.

"He asks questions about shipbuilding," says another, who has shared a drink with the man on a few occasions. "Goes by the name of Darius."

"What kind of questions?"

"How to build a boat. He does not know anything about building boats. Seems pretty keen to learn, though."

The strange man's apparent lack of knowledge leaves the union boss scratching his head.

"Why is this guy asking all these questions?" Desmond asks. "Has he said anything about trying to get a job here? Or about maybe someplace else that a shipbuilder might want to work?"

"They're rebuilding a boat," one of the men pipes up. "A paddlewheel steamer."

Eugene turns to the man who spoke.

"A boat?" Eugene mulls this over. "A paddlewheel."

He looks at Desmond.

"There is only one boat that can be. What crew is working for them? One of ours?"

"I forgot about them," Desmond says. He turns to the men. "Have they approached anyone about hiring a crew?"

The men look at each other in confusion. None of them has heard a thing.

"No, I don't think so," one of them says.

Eugene turns to Desmond.

Eugene looks a little pale and waxy. He has been in the business much longer than his underling. While anyone who has been in the business for any amount of time has heard the old stories and rumours about the Gypsy Queen, he was there. He knows the stories that have not been told in years, the ones that are not rumours. He witnessed some of them first hand.

"They have no idea what they have gotten themselves into," he says.

"The Gypsy Queen was owned by Thaddeus Barlow," Desmond says thoughtfully. "I wonder how these guys got their hands on her."

"Old Thaddeus Barlow had her decommissioned and sold her for salvage decades ago," Eugene says. "She was to be destroyed. I remember he was insistent that she never be allowed in the hands of any man and she was never to be put back in the water."

"Obviously the salvager didn't destroy her," Desmond says. "But how did these guys get her? I heard some of the rumours of the Gypsy Queen. I never heard the boat's fate until now.

I always assumed by the stories that old Thaddeus Barlow never would have allowed the boat out of his family. I heard she was his pride, his treasure."

"She was that," Eugene says. "He valued that boat more than he did his wife or his business. She was the first floating casino; a paddlewheel boat commissioned to be built by Thaddeus Barlow, a powerful man in his day who ran multiple casinos. This was while the rest of them were being decommissioned and destroyed because they were aging and no longer in popular use. His son Malcolm now runs his gambling empire and owns the only floating casino boat presently on the water in the area, the Queen Rhiannon."

"I had the Dock Master do some digging. After she was decommissioned and sent to be destroyed, the salvage yard sold her in a salvage lot. They bought her from Norman, a slimy fellow who buys and sells just about anything."

"The Fat Man," Desmond nods. "I heard of him."

Eugene continues.

"The salvager was selling scrap in lots of combined items and Norman happened to buy the lot that included the Gypsy Queen. The salvager failed to tear her apart first.

I do not know why, but instead of re-selling her or tearing her down for materials, Norman just left her moored up a tributary that eventually dried up. He just left her to rot."

He shakes his head sadly as though it were someone he had feelings for who had been left to die.

"Maybe he thought old man Thaddeus or his son would decide they wanted her back and pay a nice price to get her," Desmond suggests. "I don't get why he would have just let her rot like that. I heard she was still in excellent shape when Thaddeus sold her for salvage."

"If he thought Thaddeus would want that boat back, then he could not have known why he wanted her destroyed in the first place," Eugene says.

Desmond nods his agreement, unaware that his understanding of the situation is lacking some of the information Eugene is reflecting on.

"She was a grand boat in her day," Eugene thinks, "and Thaddeus tried to have her destroyed for very personal reasons. Only some of which were guessed at in the rumours and speculation that followed her sudden departure from the waterways."

"Basil said these guys are completely naive and innocent," Desmond says. He feels a little bad for the two over-eager young men. They are about to receive a lesson they will never forget.

Eugene meets his look. His own is cold and hard.

"They won't be so innocent and naive after a visit from their friendly local union representative," he says. He pauses, then adds, "That will be nothing compared to what will happen when the Barlow family learns they are planning to put that boat on the water."

"Is Thaddeus even still alive?" Desmond asks.

"For their sakes, they had better hope not," Eugene says.

He turns to Desmond.

"Take the boys and go pay these two gentlemen boat builders a visit. I have a few calls to make."

Desmond nods and calls a couple of men out from the crowd that has been growing around them as they spoke to accompany him.

They are large burly men. They nod and step forward.

"We are going for a ride."

The men get into a vehicle and drive out of the shipyard.

Eugene returns to his office.

22   Union Business

The car with Desmond and his union thugs pulls up by the Gypsy Queen, rocking over the rough ground as it drives over the grass to stop closer.

Desmond looks at the boat through the car windows with a grim expression.

"They are rebuilding her in the grass next to the river?" Desmond shakes his head. "That is irregular. How are they working with the boat just leaning on the ground like that? All their angles are going to be off and the floors and walls won't be straight."

They hear the sound of hammers through the closed car windows and doors. The two men they have come to see are here.

Getting out of the car, Desmond takes the lead and approaches the boat. He studies the progress that he can see, grinning at the absurdity of two lone men without boat building experience trying to rebuild a boat like the Gypsy Queen.

He walks around the boat, finding one of the two men pounding in nails to secure a board.

Travis finishes hammering the board in place and moves on to the next board; pausing and lowering his hammer to look around when he has the feeling he is being watched. He has been having that feeling off and on all day and it is unnerving him.

Every time he looks, there is no one there.

This time there is and the surprise on his face when he sees the men standing behind him is almost comical.

"Hello there," Desmond says, approaching with one hand extended for a friendly handshake. "Would you be Mr. Darius Marek?

"No sir, that is my partner," Travis says stepping forward and clasping his hand.

"I am Mr. Desmond Moloney. And you are?" Desmond asks, looking around. The sound of a second hammer can still be heard knocking on the boards inside the boat. They release hands, each stepping back a pace.

"Travis."

"That must be your partner I hear? Might I have a word with the two of you?" Desmond asks, keeping his tone friendly.

"Darius!" Travis calls, "We have visitors!" He looks the man in the business suit up and down, wondering what business he has with them. The rough looking men standing behind him, their postures tense like they are ready for a fight, sets off warning bells in his head.

Darius comes out of the boat, squinting in the sunlight.

"Hello Mr. Marek," Desmond says, extending his hand again. "I am Mr. Desmond Moloney with the Shipbuilders' Union. I just stopped by to see how things are going with your endeavor here."

Darius walks forward, grasping the man's hand in a firm handshake and releasing it; both again taking a step back.

He avoids looking at the rough looking men standing behind Desmond. He recognizes them from the shipyard and has an immediate suspicion what the purpose of the visit is.

Desmond looks around, surveying the area.

"What exactly is your purpose here Mr. Moloney?" Darius asks, already suspecting the answer.

"I am here as a representative of the local Shipbuilders' Union," Desmond says. "I came to offer you what help I can. I heard about a couple of young gentlemen rebuilding a boat on their own and thought that could not possibly be true. But here you are and it is. You, gentlemen, could use some experienced shipbuilding workers. You wouldn't want to spoil a boat like this by not having skilled labour."

"We are doing just fine on our own Mr. Moloney," Darius says.

"Gentlemen," Desmond says, "we are all friends here. You cannot just build a boat like this without experienced shipbuilders." There is an undercurrent of threat in his tone, a mild warning to be read between the lines.

Darius feels the tinge of fear but he is not about to show it. As hard as it is, Darius keeps his expression calm. His effort to hide his fear gives a tone of defiance to his words.

"I will be straight with you Mr. Moloney," he says. "We are just a couple of average guys who are probably in over our heads as it is with the materials for this boat. We don't have the money to pay laborers."

Desmond smiles a bland condescending smile.

"What do you do for a living Mr. Marek?"

"I build wood crates."

"You own a crate building business?"

"No, I build crates at one."

"So you have no money then?"

"Just my pay every week and what I can pick up doing odd jobs, mostly as a handyman."

Desmond turns to Travis.

"And you Mr. Wright, what do you do for a living?"

"I'm working at the slaughterhouse," Travis says, "shovelling shit. Whatever odd jobs I can pick up on the side too."

Desmond looks from one to the other, unable to keep the smirk from invading his face. He can feel the laugh bubbling up.

"Well, you gentlemen certainly are in pretty deep over your heads, aren't you?"

"Yes sir, we are," Darius says. "So if you don't mind, I will have to thank you for your offer of help, but we just cannot pay the wages to hire anyone. We will just have to go at it alone."

Desmond shakes his head regretfully.

"That really is too bad," he says. "You see, the union has rules and those rules are that a boat this size cannot be built, or rebuilt, without union labor. So, that puts us in a bit of a jam here, doesn't it?"

The men standing behind Desmond step in closer, sending the threat level up a notch.

"I will let you gentlemen have a little time to think on that." Desmond turns to leave. "I expect I will be hearing from you soon. Let's go boys."

Without another look back Desmond walks away, gets into the car with his men, and drives away.

The moment he is gone Darius lets his guard down, turning pale and shaky with the fear he suppressed during the confrontation.

Travis stares after the car until it is out of sight and then turns to him.

"We are screwed," he says.

"Yes we are," Darius says reflexively.

"What are we going to do?"

"I don't know. We can refuse to hire his union laborers and risk the consequences. He will send men after us and they will put the boots to us; maybe burn the boat down. If we are lucky they will let us live."

Travis looks at him, alarmed.

"Do you really think they would go that far?"

Darius's return look says it should not be a surprise.

"You have heard of the Shipbuilders' Union, haven't you? As a laborer?"

"Everyone has."

"So then you know as any other laborer does how ruthless the Shipbuilders' Union is. You know the unspoken truth about their political ties. Who runs it."

Travis turns pale and looks a little green around the gills. This is not something he had thought of when he came up with this whole plan to fix up an old boat and start his own casino boat.

"The men running the union are not just teamsters, they are mobsters. This man's boss answers to another much more powerful boss," he says sickly.

"Right."

"Our only choice is to hire them. We will have more than the union on us when we can't pay them." Travis looks like he is going to vomit.

"We have to pay the union too, on top of the men's wages," Darius says.

They both think about this, their hopes sinking in to the pits of their stomachs.

"Neither option is doable. We have no money to pay for labor or the union. And not hiring them will leave us in just as much trouble," Darius says.

"Once we start dealing with the union they will own us." Travis says. "You know that, don't you?"

"Yes I do," Darius says gravely. "And if we don't..." It is not necessary to finish the sentence.

"What if we just pay the union guy to not make us hire his crew?" Travis suggests.

Darius looks at him doubtfully.

"It is really just about money, isn't it? We hire his crew and pay their wages. The crew kicks back some of the money to the union. We pay the union. It's just about them, the union, getting their money. They get it from their workers, and from anyone who hires them. Maybe we can bribe this Mr. Moloney to leave us alone. He gets his money and we are not stuck paying wages we do not have the money for."

Darius mulls it over.

"It does make sense," he says. "We don't have the money to pay bribes either, but it will be a lot more manageable than trying to pay wages and union fees. Hell, those guys make more than we do."

He looks at Travis for a moment, his look guarded.

"You know; we could also walk away. Abandon the boat, hitch a ride to another town, and get new jobs there. We could do the smart thing and end this now."

Travis's eyes widen and his face tenses. He looks at the Gypsy Queen as if he is being asked to abandon his beloved to the depravity of a living grave.

The look of panic on Travis's face is all Darius needs to know.

"Even if I walk away, Travis won't," Darius thinks. "Travis does not stand a chance on his own. He would be dead within the month, if not sooner."

Darius lowers his head regretfully.

"We will pool together as much money as we can and go see Mr. Moloney tomorrow," he sighs. "Hopefully he will take the bribe and leave us alone."

He knows, though, that once that first dollar changes hands, the union man will indeed own them. They will be paying a lot more bribe money before they are done.

***

Eugene is sitting in his office delving into past memories.

He pictures the grandeur of the Gypsy Queen when she was new and fresh; the excitement and the wealth filling her decks. Old Mr. Thaddeus Barlow as a younger man, powerful and domineering. They are all old now, but Thaddeus Barlow somehow never seemed to be young.

The Gypsy Queen was a princess, enigmatic like a foreign beauty. Something about her was refined and delicate despite the darkness that hung over her.

The darkness hiding within her belly.

Desmond knocks on his open door before entering, bringing him back to the present.

Eugene looks up. "So, what kind of shape is she in?"

"They have made surprising progress stripping rotting boards off the hull."

Eugene nods thoughtfully. "Pour us a couple of brandies." He indicates an elegant bar table on the other side of his office.

Darius moves to do as he is bid.

Eugene almost smiles, thinking about the grandeur of the Queen who once reigned over the rivers.

"I remember both the Gypsy Queen and her master. She was an elegant creature, rich and beautiful.

The Gypsy's master, Thaddeus Barlow was a smart and powerful man. He was a businessman in more ways than one. He ran the casinos in the area with an iron will that no one dared question; wealthy beyond most men's imagination, and powerful. The unions did not run him; he ran the unions. He owned the politicians, the police, and the judges.

Nothing happened without Thaddeus's permission and no one denied him anything he wanted. He was a man accustomed to having his way and getting what he wanted. He did not bother wasting time asking, he just took what he wanted. No one ever questioned his right to do so.

He had the Gypsy Queen built, watching over every little detail, making sure every inch of that boat was perfect; and ran her more like a lover than a business. She was his pride and joy, his love."

Desmond hands him a tumbler with a few fingers of brandy and he brings it to his nose, smelling it appreciatively before taking a sip. Desmond rolls the liquid around his tongue before swallowing.

Eugene waves Desmond to a richly leathered seat before his desk and continues his story.

"That was the first time I dealt directly with Thaddeus Barlow. I was not the head of the Shipbuilders' Union then. I was a lower level union boss, lower than you. I was sent to talk to him about hiring union workers when he was commissioning the boat to be built.

Fortunately for the union, and for me, Thaddeus had no interest in getting into the shipbuilding business and our business dealings remained as brief interactions over the years once she was completed.

His son, Malcolm, runs his empire now. Malcolm is a shadow of his father; and a mediocre one at that, more bully than powerful. Just as his father commissioned us and oversaw the building of the Queen, Malcolm built Queen Rhiannon, his own private treasure. And just like her master, Queen Rhiannon is a shadow of her predecessor's glory, a lot of flash and show, more gaudy than beautiful."

He turns his attention directly on Desmond now.

"What are those fellows planning to do with that boat if they do ever get her fixed up?"

"I don't know sir. I will find out."

Desmond nods acceptance and slips back into his memories of the past.

"The Gypsy Queen. She was the princess of the waterways in her day, until Thaddeus suddenly had her put in dry dock, decommissioned her, and then sold her for salvage.

He became reclusive after that, vanishing from the watchful eyes of the public to run his empire from the shadows.

He put his son in place as his puppet as soon as he determined the young man was old enough to be taken seriously, pulling his strings and controlling the empire through him.

The Gypsy Queen herself had her own secrets, stories that will remain forever in the memory of her once polished wood."

"Thaddeus never intended her to ride the waterways again," he says softly.

His thoughts turn back to the business at hand.

"How did they take your offer?"

"They tried to say no," Desmond says. "They are just a couple of nobody hacks with no money and no benefactor rebuilding the Queen."

"I can't let a couple of small time guys get away with rebuilding a boat that size without union labour," Eugene says. "It would not look good. If they got away with it, others might get the idea they should too."

But at the same time, Eugene is reluctant to send any of his men to that particular boat.

23   Prankster

"I will be back later," Travis says. "I have some errands to run."

Darius waves him off, continuing to work on the Gypsy Queen.
He shakes his head wryly.
"More likely Travis is really just trying to see Amelia."
A surge of jealously fills him and he pushes it down.
"It's not my business," Darius mutters. "She will like who she likes. He is no good for her. Travis is no good for any woman, but they always want him anyway. He will hurt her like he always does, leaving me to pick up the pieces."
He looks around at the rotting wood inside the hull.
"He will leave this piece of junk too, eventually. In worse shape than he found it, just like every woman he has chased after. But I'm not sticking around to pick up the pieces this time. When Travis finally gives up on this boat and moves on, they can burn whatever is left of it."
Darius is feeling edgy. He has been having that unsettling feeling that makes the hairs on the back of your neck stand up with an indefinable chill down your spine; the feeling that he is being watched by someone unseen.
Darius is also getting frustrated. The unnerving sensation is affecting more than just his nerves. He keeps misplacing things.
He puts down the measuring tape on a nearby plank of wood. Holding his finger to the spot he needs to mark, he reaches for the pencil. Scratching a small line in the wood with the pencil, Darius puts it down and reaches for the measuring tape. His questing fingers find only the flat surface of the board.
He looks down, looking for the measuring tape.
"Where did it go? Damn, I'm getting punchy. I am sure I put it right there."
 He spends fifteen minutes searching for it only to find it on the ground under the board.
Darius scratches his head. "I looked there. I know I did."
He goes back to work, measuring and marking along the length of that section of hull.

Finished marking, Darius fetches some boards and sets them down near where he was marking. He goes back and grabs the hammer and bucket of nails.

He sets the bucket down, turns, and takes a board and sets it in place. He carefully lines it up with the pencil marks. Holding the board in place with his hammer wielding hand, he stoops down to scoop a couple of nails from the bucket only to reach for empty air.

Darius looks down with a confused look. The bucket is not there.

Angry frustration burns through him.

"I put it down right there." He plays out the last minutes in his mind. "I walked up. I put the bucket down right there on my left."

He holds up the hammer that he still holds in his right hand, looking at it.

"I had the hammer in my right." He looks down at his empty left hand. "The nail bucket in my left. I put the bucket down to set the wood board in place."

He looks down to his left. "And the bucket is not there."

Darius shakes his head.

"I need to get more sleep," he mutters, walking around the area in search of the bucket he had just a moment ago. "I swear I put it down right there on my left." He checks outside the hull where he got the bucket and hammer from, finding no bucket of nails.

Shaking his head and muttering, Darius returns to where he was working inside the hull and stops. He stands there staring in confusion.

The bucket is right there where he was working. Only, it is where it would be if he had held it in his right hand when he put it down. He looks down at the hammer, still held in his right hand.

"I must have switched the hammer to my other hand."

Darius returns to work, moving the bucket so he can use his left hand to retrieve nails while hammering with his right. He sets the board in place again, carefully lining it up with the markings, and hesitates before reaching down to scoop a few nails from the bucket.

He looks down and the bucket is still there on his left. Scooping up a few nails, he hammers the board in. Darius hammers the rest of the boards in without incident.

"I need more boards."

Darius puts the hammer down, making a conscious mental note of its location, and goes out to bring some more boards in to where he is working.

Leaning the boards in a row where he needs them, Darius turns to pick up the hammer and it is gone.

He looks around, frowning.

"I know I put it there," he mutters. He looks under the bench and all around it.

He roams the inside of the boat, searching for the hammer. It is nowhere to be found.

Giving up the search for the mislaid hammer, Darius goes outside to the toolbox to get the other one, muttering under his breath.

There, leaning against the open toolbox in the grass and not even close to anywhere he has gone since using it, is the missing hammer.

The other hammer is in view in the open toolbox.

Darius picks up the mislaid hammer, looking at it and hefting it to feel its weight. He looks around suspiciously, expecting to hear someone snickering at him.

"Someone is playing tricks on me."

Wielding the hammer like a weapon, he begins searching for the prankster. He searches the area surrounding the boat; sure the person has to be hiding nearby. Finding no one, he stalks off angrily searching the boat inside and out.

He can't find anyone and goes back outside to stand there looking around.

"When I get my hands on you," he mutters angrily, "I will show you about playing games on someone."

Tense and angry, Darius goes back inside the boat, scoops out a small handful of nails, and sets the first board in place, carefully lining it up perfectly with the one already nailed down beside it.

He raises the hammer, holding a nail in place, and stops, stiffening.

He turns quickly, lowering the hammer, sure he heard a noise, but sees nothing.

Turning back to his work, he raises the hammer again and hears the noise again.

It is the soft scrape of a shoe.

Darius imagines someone sneaking up on him and whirls around, seeing no one. Only his eyes shift as he stays perfectly motionless; listening.

He hears the sound again. Putting the nails down soundlessly, he raises his hammer and moves forward stealthily to catch the intruder.

Darius jumps at the sudden hollow clattering sound behind him. The sound echoes inside the boat.

He spins quickly. One of the boards leaning loosely in a row is lying on the ground. He stares at the board then looks around to see what or who might have knocked it down.

Another board falls on its own, clattering with the hollow sound of wood bouncing against wood.

Darius stares; dumbfounded.

"How?"

Another board falls and then another, each falling before the one before it clatters to the floor, coming faster with each successive board as if someone were running behind them with a hand out knocking them down until they reach the end of the loosely leaning boards.

With a creak of the wood, a brief squeal of metal against wood, and a popping sound, the first nailed down board follows its loose brethren. It pops free of the wood behind it, hovers there for just a heartbeat, balancing, and then falls and clatters to the floor. The next one follows and then the next and the next, popping loose with increasing speed and falling, all down the line until the hollow clattering of the last board is the only sound still ringing in the ship's hull.

Darius stands there, gaping in open-mouthed shock. He swallows the knot in his throat and slowly backs away, tripping over the hammer he didn't know he dropped and spilling the bucket of nails when his foot hits it as he falls.

Scrabbling to his feet and looking behind him, leaving the felled boards, tipped bucket of nails, and the abandoned hammer, and watching to make sure nothing else strange happens and nobody is following him, he rushes outside.

Darius is breathing heavily when he bursts out of the boat; his heart pounding in his chest despite the tightness that makes it feel like each breath is a struggle.

He takes one last look around before turning to run, and realizes he is still holding the hammer. He looks down at it in shock.

"But, I saw-." He pictures the hammer he remembers seeing on the floor where he must have dropped it. The hammer he tripped over. "I know I saw it."

Darius sidles over towards the toolbox, looking cautiously into it. The other hammer that was there earlier is gone.

"I am going nuts," he whispers, half afraid there is someone there after all and they might hear him.

He backs away until he feels he is far enough away and turns and runs, feeing idiotic.

24   No Missed Opportunity

Travis is loitering up the street from the lumberyard, hoping to catch a glimpse of Amelia. He knows she stops by there daily, but it was late afternoon when he got here.

"I hope I haven't missed her."

He ducks out of sight when the door opens; peering around the corner of the building he is hiding behind.

Roman leaves the store, locking it up and walking away.

"I missed her." Travis weighs his options, thinking of what places a young woman might go to.

"She might be at home of course, but that is probably where her father is going. Even if her father has somewhere else to be, I doubt I would be allowed to see her if I show up on her doorstep."

With no other hope, Travis wanders off, wandering around town.

He tries the grocer and the general store, dawdles outside the dressmaker's shop while trying to look inconspicuous glancing in the windows, and then strolls up past the bakery.

Travis tries the park, finding a few young ladies tossing pieces of bread to the ducks at the pond, but none are Amelia. He walks back up towards the bakery and checks the restaurant.

Travis is about to give up and go home to his lonely single room when he sees her coming out of the bakery just as the baker is locking up.

She is smiling as she chats with the large man. The baker's whole stomach shakes as he laughs too loud at something one of them said and Travis cannot help the sudden flush that rushes through him.

"Jealous of a fat old man," he mutters to himself, feeling completely foolish. "Obviously Amelia would have no interest in the baker."

He waits until she leaves the bakery, the baker going in the opposite direction, and starts walking up the street towards Amelia. She is coming towards him.

When Amelia turns away from the baker, heading for home, she sees Travis up ahead walking towards her. Her breath catches and her heart lurches in her chest.

Travis has an urge to duck out of sight to watch her.

He stops and stands there for just a few heartbeats, and then steps to the side out of her sight, moving to hide. He considers abandoning his quest without talking to her.

"That would be dumb after spending the last three hours trying to run into her." He steps back, half giving in, to stand where she won't see him until she is almost on top of him.

"Should I go? Should I stay? Go, just go. You are making a fool out of yourself. No, stay. Take a chance. Talk to her."

"He is waiting for me," Amelia thinks, trying to ignore the sudden elation she feels. She straightens her back and stiffens her walk. "Look straight ahead. Don't look at him. Pretend he isn't there."

The distance is closing while Travis argues with himself, taking the decision out of his hands. Now he can't do either without her seeing him.

He sucks in a nervous breath of air, reminds himself not to spit it all out the moment he opens his mouth to talk, and steps out when she gets close. Travis makes a show of it, looking away as if oblivious to her presence, and then looking up to look directly at her, managing to look more startled than the pleasant surprise he is going for.

"Amelia," he smiles, "what a happy coincidence that makes us run into each other."

The look she gives him is one of a woman suffering an absolute bore that she would much rather not have run into and be forced to exchange idle pleasantries with.

"Hello Mr. Wright," she says icily, not slowing down.

He falls into step beside her, following her.

Her heart flutters at his closeness as he walks beside her, desperately trying to get her attention while she purposely puts an invisible barrier between them.

"He stole from my father," she thinks, fanning her anger.

She continues; flip flopping to make excuses to forgive him.

"But I am sure it was out of desperation," she thinks. "It has to be. He regretted his actions. So, he is good after all. Of course, I am still angry with him for stealing from my father."

"Would you like me to carry that for you?" Travis asks, eying her lightweight parcel from the bakery.

"I can manage," Amelia says, purposely not looking at him.

"How is your father? I hope my little gift helped. It probably was not enough to cover his losses, but it must have helped a little. I felt bad when I heard about the theft. A hard working man like him should not have to suffer such a loss in times like these when money is tight all around. I wanted to help him out after he was robbed."

Amelia purses her lips.

Despite her cold rudeness towards Travis, Amelia is marginally more inclined to talking to him this time. She has been thinking about the young man a lot lately. When she first met him, she had found his bumbling incompetence amusing. She had felt an attraction to the man. His dismissal of her ideas just because of her gender irritated her. Now she has every reason to be furious with him.

"Do you think your father still blames me for his store being robbed?" Travis asks.

Amelia stops walking and turns on him, her eyes flashing anger.

"Do you really think your little handful of money could make up for breaking in and stealing from my father?" she demands. "Do you really think I, I mean he, will forgive you? That did not even come close to paying for what you stole and now there can be no trust. My father will never trust you."

He stares at her angry lips, wanting to kiss them.

On an impulse, he reaches out suddenly, grabbing her and pulling her to him, kissing her.

She drops her parcel from the bakery in shock and immediately begins pummelling him with her purse and her fists, getting in a few solid blows to his head.

Travis releases her and backs away, cringing and trying to cover himself with his arms, her words lashing out just as hard as her blows. She follows him with her continued attack.

"Who do you think you are to take such liberties with me?"

Flushed and worn out, Amelia finally stops beating him, straightens her clothes, and picks up her parcel. She turns and strides away without another word, her head held high.

"Now I will have to explain to Mother and Father how the cake was ruined," she thinks angrily, her heart pounding in her chest with excitement and her cheeks glowing with a rosy flush.

Travis grins and watches her go, smarting from her attack. "She is stronger than I imagined."

25   Paying Dues

The shipbuilding yard sits large in the distance, slowly growing with each step that takes them closer to it. Without a vehicle, Travis and Darius are making the long walk there.

"I still don't like this," Darius complains. "I don't know where we are going to get the extra money to keep paying off the Shipbuilders' Union. I think we are better off cutting our losses and abandoning that boat."

A chill runs through him at the thought of the boat. Try as he does, Darius cannot come up with any rational explanation for what happened the last time he was at the boat.

"We can't give up on her now. We have come so far." Travis's voice is high with tension. The threat of losing the Gypsy Queen is a physical pain. It runs though him, leaving him feeling empty with a loss he has not yet experienced.

Darius glances at him. He does not want to go back to that boat.

"He has become too obsessed with that damned boat," Darius thinks, worrying over his friend. "It never ends well when he gets too obsessed with something."

"I should tell him what happened the other day," he thinks. "No, it sounds ridiculous. Your imagination was playing tricks. There was too much strain on the wood, too much bend. That must be what made the boards pull off."

"I just hope bribing them to leave us alone works," Darius says. He frowns. "I have a bad feeling it will not be enough. If they force us to hire union labour, we are sunk."

"We are here," Travis says hopefully. "Try to look confident."

Travis and Darius enter the shipyard. No one pays them any attention as they walk across to the squat building that holds offices for the union and the shipyard management.

They enter the building nervously and the secretary looks at them over the rims of her cat's eye glasses, which make her look even more severe than she does naturally. The building looks as old and tired on the inside as it does on the outside.

"How can I help you?" she asks, sounding as if helping them is more of an annoyance than her job should entail.

"Yes, hello Ma'am," Darius says nervously. "We are here to see Mr. Desmond Moloney."

She looks them up and down, pegging them as labourers probably looking for a job, and purses her lips at them.

"Do you have an appointment?"

"Yes Ma'am."

She does not bother looking in her appointment calendar.

"I do not have you listed in my appointment book," she says.

"How does she know?" Travis wonders. "We haven't even given her our names."

"We do not have a set time," Darius says. "Mr. Moloney is expecting us though."

She looks down her nose at him despite her shorter height with an expression that says, "You had better not be playing me," and reluctantly gets up from her desk and goes down the hall. They hear her knock on a door and some murmured words.

She returns, giving them a distasteful look.

"Mr. Moloney will see you," she says, returning to her desk. "Second door down the hall."

"Thank you Ma'am," Darius says politely. They head down the hallway, afraid of what lies ahead.

"She really does not like you," Travis whispers with a chuckle to Darius as they enter the hallway.

Behind them, the secretary purses her lips even tighter. She heard that.

They slow as they approach the second door. The door is open.

"Come in gentlemen," Desmond's voice rings out from inside.

Travis pokes his head around the doorway before placing his whole body in front of it. He nods greeting. Darius follows close behind and the two step inside to stand shifting nervously like a couple of little boys called into the principal's office for punishment.

The furniture in the office looks like it belongs in a much newer and richer looking building.

"Come in, sit down," Desmond says, waving them towards a couple of chairs strategically situated before his desk.

Both men look at Desmond then at the chairs, having an instant flashback to being hauled into Malcolm Barlow's office after sneaking on board his casino boat, the Queen Rhiannon. That meeting did not go well.

It gives them a feeling of foreboding about this meeting.

"I presume by your presence here that you have thought over my proposal," Desmond says as they nervously take their seats.

"Yes sir we have," Travis says. "As we said before, we just do not have the money to pay any man's wages. Frankly, your union men earn more than either of us does."

Desmond shifts in his chair, leaning forward, his expression stiffening.

"Can I be frank here sir?" Travis asks.

Desmond nods, waiting to see what the man will say.

"We understand that as a union you have to make sure your union interests are looked after. You cannot have anyone thinking that a couple guys like us can get away with building a boat without the union. So we thought that maybe we could just pay you the union fees without hiring the union crew."

Desmond slowly inhales and exhales a deep breath and looks at them levelly.

"How do you think that would look?" he asks them heavily.

They both look like they are about to say something and he waves them to silence.

"Don't think that I do not understand where you are coming from, I do. But you have to understand where I am coming from. This is the union. If I let you build your little boat without using union labour, people are going to notice. Tongues are going to wag. People might think I was taking a bribe. That would be risky for both you and me." He pauses, giving them a chance to say their piece.

Darius digs in his pocket, pulling out a wad of cash.

"Please, sir, just understand. We can't pay union dues and union wages. We don't make enough, either of us. We will join the union if that is what we have to do to make it look good on your books. We will become members, pay our dues. Here, take this for now, to show our good intentions." He puts the money on the desk, pushing it forward towards Desmond.

Desmond ignores the money, looking them over.

"You are not even skilled shipbuilders," he says. "I cannot admit you as a union member unless you apprentice. Believe me gentlemen," he looks down at the wad of money with a sour look, "if this is the best you can come up with, then you cannot afford it."

They both feel their stomachs sinking.

"If you had a lot more money, then you might be in a position to bargain. However, it would be cheaper just to take my offer of help and hire the union labour. You will pay the men's salaries including their union dues. There is also the matter of the dues you will have to pay as a union employer."

Travis and Darius are both feeling ill now and look pale and waxy.

"The union does, on occasion, come to a special business arrangement with some of our larger sponsors. You, however, certainly could not even be considered one of our smallest. You could not possibly hope to pay the necessary fee for such an arrangement.

I will do you a favour, however; in good faith. I will send only a token crew of a few men to help you out, rather than a full crew."

Desmond smiles at them as he gets up and comes around his desk, waving them up from their chairs and towards the door, scooping up the cash and pocketing it on the way.

"Now if you will excuse me gentlemen, I have other business to attend to."

They look at him, numb with shock and still clinging to the hope they will get their money back. They are disappointed he obviously intends to keep it despite refusing to consider their desperate request.

Desmond laughs good-naturedly as he ushers them out of his office.

"You two gentlemen have a good day," he chuckles. "I believe you have some business of your own to attend to. After all, boat building is a big money business."

Travis and Darius walk out of his office woodenly, feeling the world closing in on them. They head down the hall back to the entrance.

"The men will show up Monday for work, bright and early," Desmond calls out to them from his office doorway, still laughing. "You really should have come to us first, not making us come to you. We maybe could have worked something out then."

Desmond is turning to go back into his office when an office door further up the hallway opens and Eugene steps out into the hallway. His timing is as perfect as if he had been privy to the exchanges of the entire meeting.

Eugene stares after the two men. He calls out after them. Travis and Darius pause and turn back at the sound of Eugene's voice.

"Whatever you do, do not tell the workers the name of the boat. Scrape the name off the hull. Tell them anything you like, but do not tell them she is the Gypsy Queen." He stares at them for a moment after calling out that parting warning.

Desmond turns to Eugene in surprise. He isn't surprised the older man has such impeccable timing, but that he would even bother getting involved in dealings with two nobodies.

Eugene steps back into his office and closes the door.

Desmond looks completely confused as he steps back into his own office.

Travis and Darius exchange a look and head for the exit, walking quickly past the disapproving look of the cat's eye glasses secretary. They don't feel safe yet as they cross the yard, heading out of the shipyard.

"What was that about?" Travis asks.

"I don't know," Darius says, just as confused. An eerie sense of foreboding creeps up his back like an icy finger.

***

Travis's mind feels like it is stuck moving in fast forward. His visions of glamour and excitement and piles of money flowing into his hands seem impossibly unattainable now. The brilliant colors of the Gypsy Queen in his mind are muted and dulled, the clinking of game chips sound muffled, and the lights have an eerie cast to them. The music from the band sounds tinny and unreal. His whole world is suddenly a little unfocused.

He runs through the possibilities, each one ending in dismal failure.

"We have only days before the union workers will show up and we have no way to pay them or buy materials. They will be sitting around doing nothing," he says.

"Don't forget the fat man," Darius adds. "We have to keep up the payments to Norman. And the bribe payments to the Dock Master to ensure we will have a slip for the Gypsy Queen when it is ready to start taking passengers."

Travis feels ill.

"Norman, the Dock Master, and now we have to pay bribe money to the union, the union labourers' wages, as well as the increased cost of materials once the construction of the boat speeds up with the added hands.

We are going to need a lot more money."

"We will have to start with the bank," Darius says as if reading his thoughts.

The truth is that Darius's thoughts are somewhat mirroring his partner's, only he does not fantasize about the glamour and riches of the boat, but instead worries about keeping his friend from getting himself killed in his new scheme.

"You know," Darius says thoughtfully as they walk, "for one of your get rich quick schemes, this one is proving to be neither quick nor likely to leave us with anything but in a very deep hole of debt."

"Do you think the bank will give us any money this time?" Travis asks, his cheeks burning at the memory of the loan manager laughing and mocking them all the way out of the bank.

"Probably not, but we have to try. At least now the boat isn't just a pile of rotting lumber abandoned up some dried up stream. We have done a lot of work on it, enough to show that we are serious about this. And with the union involved, maybe the guy at the bank will take us a little more seriously. If not, maybe we can play the union card a bit. You know; drop a hint that we have union backing; that the union wants this project to happen. It might just make him think twice before laughing us out the door again."

"You might be right. Even the guy at the bank has to know the Shipbuilders' Union is probably run by the mob. He might be too scared to turn us down for a loan if he thinks they have a stake in this boat getting built."

When they enter the bank they are greeted by a friendly woman who seats them off to one side to wait for the loan officer after they tell her why they are there.

When the loan officer comes out to greet his new customers, they recognize each other immediately.

Darius's hopes sink. Shannon Whitaker. He was hoping the loan officer would be a different man this time.

Travis meets Shannon's smug look with a guarded one.

"Hello sir," Darius starts, extending his hand in greeting.

Shannon ignores the offered hand, instead waving them off.

"Don't even waste your breath buddy," he says, cutting him off before Darius can begin to tell him why they are there.

"I know exactly why you are here. Do you need another match? You are still playing about with that pile of driftwood and think I am going to be foolish enough to give you a loan you will never be able to repay."

He shakes his head, his shoulders already moving up and down with suppressed laughter.

"There is no way in this world I would give you two a loan. I would not loan you the money for a cup of coffee, let alone enough to build a boat. Get out of my bank you bums and don't come back." He directs them towards the door.

Just like their first visit, the loan officer cattily laughs and mocks them all the way out of the bank, calling insults out to them as they walk red-faced down the street away from the bank and laughing so hard he is wheezing.

They spend the rest of the week and the weekend trying to figure out how they are going to come up with the money.

Travis and Darius go from job to job trying to scavenge better paying jobs, second and third jobs, and any kind of casual labour they might be able to do in between.

They go up and down the streets from sun up to sun down, knocking on the doors of any house that looks like they might be able to pay, offering their services. No job is too big, too small, or too low.

They are desperate.

Even if all their efforts succeed, it will not be enough.

Monday morning rolls around and Travis and Darius both get up earlier to stop at the Gypsy Queen before going to their jobs building crates and shovelling shit.

The union men are arriving on the job already.

Stopping at a distance from the boat, they turn and skulk off with heavy hearts and a sick sinking feeling in the pit of their stomachs.

"It isn't just one or two token guys," Darius mutters. "It is a whole bloody crew."

"We are screwed," Travis agrees.

They walk together in silence until they come to the point they must go their separate ways. They part without a word, each lost in his own sullen thoughts.

***

Darius leaves work at the end of the day with a heavy heart. The decision he made weighs heavily on him.

He goes to the shipping yard. Alternating jogging and walking and managing to hitchhike part of the distance, he arrives there just in time to see Desmond getting into his vehicle in front of the office building.

"Wait, Mr. Moloney," he calls, chasing the car as it pulls away.

Hearing the sound of someone calling his name, Desmond looks in his rear view mirror and spots Darius chasing his car. He watches him as he turns around in a wide circle towards the exit.

Desmond entertains the thought of ignoring him and just driving by him, but decides to stop instead. He rolls down the window just as Darius reaches the car out of breath.

"How can I help you Mr. Marek?"

"You say you were going to send only a token crew, just a few guys. A whole crew showed up."

Desmond shrugs as if the matter is out of his hands. "That is how unions work sometimes."

"We can't pay just a few guys. How are we going to pay a whole crew?" Darius pleads.

The desperation in Darius's eyes almost touches a soft spot in the union boss. He nods understanding.

"I will see what I can do about reducing the size of the crew. It will cost you, however. There will be a penalty charge."

Darius blanches, feeling sick. This was no mistake.

He shakes his head.

"Look, we can't do it. We just can't do this. We can't pay your dues or these guys' wages."

"That is unfortunate. You do not want to fail to pay." Desmond's tone carries a clear warning.

"Can't you just give us a small break? At least take the crew back and let us just pay the union dues?"

"That is out of my hands, I am afraid. Union rules. I cannot allow you to build, or even rebuild, a boat without union men on the roll."

Darius sighs heavily.

"I only hope I can get Travis on board," he thinks. He is exhausted with this whole thing. "I have a feeling Travis is not going to give up the boat no matter what."

"You win," Darius says. "We will sell the boat, or abandon it or burn it, whatever we have to do. Whatever you want us to do with it. We will do it. We give up. We just can't do this. We are not boat builders and we have no money. We are done."

Desmond shakes his head regretfully.

"I am afraid it is too late for that. You are signed on to the end. There is no quitting."

Darius looks at him, alarmed and trying to muster up defiance.

"We will burn it down and just walk away. If we have no boat, there is no boat for the workers to build."

Desmond levels a steady look at him.

"You do not want to do that. The consequences will be," he pauses, "decidedly unpleasant. For both you, and your partner. I hope neither of you has any family."

He lets that last comment hang in the air.

Darius feels like the world is tilting. He has to swallow to stop himself from vomiting.

"I will tell you what," Desmond says. "I like you. You have a lot of gumption. I will see if there is anything I can do to make things easier for you."

"Thank you sir," Darius nods his head to show appreciation.

Have a good day," Desmond says, rolling up his window and driving away, leaving Darius to try to find his legs and walk home.

Darius staggers the first few steps, feeling unsteady, and stumbles off home.

***

Travis goes to the Gypsy Queen after work. He walks around her, inspecting her. There is nothing left of the materials. Not even scraps, except a partial bucket of nails.

"The union crew must have worked until they ran out of materials. Who knows what they did after that. Sat around."

He walks along beside the boat, sliding his hand along her hull as he goes, caressing the wood.

"They are all against us. They are trying to stop us from bringing you back to life; from making you grand and elegant again, from making money with you."

He leans in close, whispering. "I won't let them. I will do whatever it takes. I will never abandon you."

Travis looks the Gypsy Queen over reluctantly. "We have no materials and no money. I can't even work on rebuilding you now, not until we can get more materials.

I don't want those strange men all over you, rebuilding you. I want to do it myself. Make you grand again. I will find a way. I will find a way."

Travis turns to leave. He takes two steps and stops. He feels the draw of the Gypsy Queen; the lure of her promise pulling him back. He looks back at her.

"I will be back."

***

Arriving at his small rented room, Darius packs up his meagre belongings, locks the room, and knocks on his landlady's door.

She answers the door and looks him up and down.

"From the packed bag, I take it you are leaving us," she sniffs.

"Yes Mrs. Solomon. I am afraid I have to move on."

She puts her nose up. "Well, there will be no refund for the rest of the month. It will take me time to find another renter, you know."

Darius nods. "Yes, Mrs. Solomon. I understand. You have a good evening."

She closes the door on him without saying goodbye.

"She is going to miss me," he says ruefully, unhappy with the situation he finds himself in.

He walks away, carrying his worldly belongings in a sack on his back.

"It looks like I will be sleeping in the boat now that I am homeless. The rent money will have to go towards paying the work crew. It won't be enough."

***

Travis waits for it to be dark to slip into his small rented room and collect his belongings. He feels guilty and, although he has every right to be there, he feels like a criminal; like he has no business being there.

Giving the small room one last regretful look after packing his things, he slips downstairs and around to the front door. He leaves a note on his landlady's door promising to pay what he owes. He is already behind in his rent, as usual. He slips off into the night.

Travis arrives at the Gypsy Queen to see a dim light glowing inside.

Approaching cautiously, he puts down his rolled blankets and the large duffel bag he carries slung over his back. Picking up a hammer from the toolbox, he approaches a large hole in the side of the hull silently, watching for any intruder.

Travis raises the hammer, ready to use it as a weapon, and steps inside.

Inside, Darius is sitting on a makeshift bed of blankets and a pillow spread on the curved floor of the hull, reading by lantern light.

Darius looks up when Travis enters the hull, putting his book down. His expression is a mix of surprise and guilt.

"I see we both have the same idea," he says as he takes in his partner's skulking posture and raised weapon.

"I guess we do," Travis says, lowering the hammer. He slips out to get his things, bringing them in and making his own makeshift bed on the floor.

"They did a lot of work in just one day," Darius says. "They have gone through more lumber in one day than we do in a week."

Travis lights another lantern and starts walking through the boat, inspecting the work the union men have done.

Darius gets up and follows, adding the light of his lantern. He is still amazed at how much progress the crew made in only one day. The rib bones of the boat are more exposed to the open air. Gaping sections where the rotten wood has been removed are more plentiful than the hull now. They go outside, taking stock of the dwindled supplies.

"We are out of materials."

"What are we going to do tomorrow?" Travis asks.

"Nothing," Darius says. "There is nothing we can do. We have to see if we can find materials somewhere. I doubt we will find anyone who will let us take it now and pay later."

26   Dark Morning

Morning comes early after a night of fitful sleep and the union men are already arriving before Travis and Darius leave.

The foreman looks around with a dry chuckle at the lack of building materials as his men settle in for a long day sitting around doing nothing. He is a large brute of a man with meaty hammers for fists and a hard face.

Travis and Darius come out of the boat at the sound of voices outside. The foreman looks up to meet their eyes.

The foreman holds out one large paw. The tension coming off Travis and Darius is strong.

Darius takes an awkward step forward, letting him wrap his larger hand around his, the foreman's grip too strong. He tries not to wince at the pain.

"I'm Herman." The large man nods and releases Darius's hand. "I'm the Foreman running this crew."

It takes Darius a conscious effort to not rub his hand and check for broken bones, although he knows there is none.

"Darius, Travis," he indicates himself and his partner.

"Just because there is no work to do, it doesn't mean we don't get paid," Herman says. His tone is a clear warning. "The union said we come, so here we are. We aren't leaving and we expect to be paid Friday as usual. Providing tools and materials is your problem."

Darius nods understanding and the two of them duck out to head for work, certain the laughter that follows is entirely at their expense.

Travis walks next to him, his shoulders slumped despondently.

"Desmond kept his word," Darius mutters, somehow not feeling relieved. "There are only four men today."

This is their second day with a union crew and it hangs over them with a dark pall.

That night Travis and Darius spend their evening scavenging separately for materials.

Darius manages to convince the owner of the lumber store to sell him a small amount of lumber and nails. Roman Bukowski postures and threatens him before relenting. Darius has to show him the money first, of course.

Travis raids his stash of stolen tools and supplies, and uses whatever means he can to find scraps of lumber.

By the end of the evening they have managed to get enough material to keep the workers busy tearing rotting boards off for a day or two, they hope. As long as the crew does not grow to more than three men and a foreman.

But they still have to come up with the men's wages and have only two more days to do it.

Friday rolls around, and Travis and Darius meet up after work before going back to the Gypsy Queen.

"How much money have you come up with?" Darius asks.

"Not enough," Travis says unhappily.

They both pull out their money and pile it together in a mound of crumpled bills and coins, counting it carefully. Between their full time jobs, second jobs, and the odd jobs, it still is not enough to pay the men's wages.

Darius pulls another wad of money from his boot. He nods at Travis.

"That's the money we put aside from our extra jobs over the last weeks," he plunks it down on the pile. "The money that was supposed to pay for the boiler, furnishings for the boat when we come to that, and the money for the dock master's bribe."

"It's still not enough," Travis groans. He pulls out his own wad of bills, tossing it on top. "The payment for Norman."

"How are we going to pay Norman?"

"I haven't figured that out yet." Travis shakes his head, feeling lost.

"That's everything," Darius says. They count it.

"Just enough," Travis mutters unhappily. He looks up at his partner fearfully. "We are completely cleaned out. What are we going to do next week?"

"I don't know." Darius shakes his head. He feels hollow inside with desperation.

"I found us work for the weekend. It will be a start for next week, but two men working eighteen hour days seven days a week still will not be enough to pay even a small crew of men earning more than them."

Silence hangs heavily between them for a moment.

"They are also going to be out of materials again by now," he adds. "We are going to need more by Monday or we will be paying them to sit around."

"I knew we wouldn't have enough to get past today," Travis says. "I made arrangements for materials. We just have to go pick it up."

Darius looks at him doubtfully.

"How did you get the money?"

"It's on credit," Travis says. "I arranged for a wagon. It will be a bit of a drive. The store is in another town. It's going to take all night. One of us will have to drive there while the other sleeps. We will switch off for the trip back."

"You sure wouldn't get credit in this town," Darius says wryly.

Travis nods. He is grateful Darius did not bring up the store owner's accusations against him.

"Going further into debt is something we don't need," Travis says. "But on the other hand, we are stuck paying the crew until the job is finished, whether we have the materials for them to work or not. An idle crew will cost a lot more in the long run."

"Ok, let's go," Darius says reluctantly. "We will go pay the men and then head out."

He looks at Travis. "We still have to come up with money to pay Norman."

Travis nods and looks down guiltily. When he gave away the payment to Amelia's father, the fat man beat Darius nearly to death.

"My stupidity almost got him killed," he thinks. He looks back at Darius. "We will figure something out."

"Let's go, we have to be back by morning."

***

After stopping at the Gypsy Queen to pay the waiting men, they walk the distance to the livery stable.

Darius looks around.

"It doesn't look like anyone is here."

"I got it," Travis says. "My guy said to just hook them up and go. The wagon should be around back."

Darius looks at him doubtfully.

Even with the horses well accustomed to the routine, it still takes the two inexperienced men some time to manage to corner one of the horses in the pen and get a lead on it.

Tying it to the fence, they make out only slightly better cornering a second horse. Leading them out and around to the back of the large barn, they find a couple of wagons parked there.

It takes them a while to maneuver the horses into place before one of the wagons, the animals balking because of their inexperience despite knowing what to do better than their handlers do. It takes longer to figure out how to hitch the horses up and they are finally on their way. Travis drives the wagon and Darius sits on the bench seat beside him, the wagon bouncing and jostling on the rough road.

When darkness starts closing in, Darius crawls into the back and settles himself in the flat wagon bed with a pillow and blankets. The constant rocking motion of the wagon and gentle creaking of the harness and wheels eventually lulls him to sleep.

The wagon moves off through the night.

Some hours later, the wagon comes to a stop and Travis rouses Darius.

"Rise and shine sleepyhead. Time to get up."

Darius opens his eyes, looking around groggily. Above him, the sky is speckled with stars and the moon hangs over its apex, beginning its slow descent back behind the earth.

"We are here," Travis says. "We better get loading fast. It will be slower going on the way back with the heavy load and tired horses. We have to be unloaded before dawn. I promised to have the wagon back before the livery opens."

Darius gets to his feet and jumps down from the end of the wagon, stretching stiffly and surveying the area. There are piles of building supplies everywhere. This lumberyard is bigger than the one in their town.

"Over here," Travis calls, indicating a nearby pile of lumber, "this is the pile."

"Are you sure about this?" Darius asks doubtfully. He has a bad feeling about this. "It seems odd we are loading in the middle of the night."

"Yes, I arranged it around us being able to work," Travis says as he starts grabbing as many boards as he can carry and loading them into the back of the wagon.

Darius shrugs and joins in, giving him an uncertain look, the two of them transferring the stack of lumber to the trailer bed. They work hard and fast, Travis casting nervous glances around every time one of them puts the lumber down too hard, making it clatter noisily in the night.

"Keep loading. I have some other things to grab," Travis says.

With Darius loading the last of the lumber, Travis starts adding other supplies to the load.

Darius is busy loading another armload and doesn't see Travis slip around the corner of the building and pry open the back door. He enters and comes out minutes later carrying buckets of nails and sacks of tools.

Darius eyes the sacks Travis is putting in the wagon.

"What is in the sacks?" he asks.

"Tools for the crew," Travis says, avoiding looking at him. "My guy left them sitting in back for us to grab." He feels bad lying, but he knows Darius would refuse to take this stuff if he knew the truth.

Darius can't shake the dark feeling hanging over him. The feeling that Travis is lying to him and what they are doing has nothing to do with any arrangements.

"The longer the union workers sit idle, the more debt we will rack up with the union and Norman," Darius thinks, "and that might just put us both six feet under."

He pushes his doubts down and continues working unhappily.

Loaded full, they use some long lengths of rope Travis produces "from his guy" to tie the load down. Darius climbs into the driver seat and Travis into the back on top of the lumber.

"Remember, we have to make good time," Travis says as he settles himself in. He does his best to make himself comfortable on top of the piled lumber in the back, cushioning his bed with a blanket and pillow as Darius drives the wagon out of the yard. "Just follow this road out, take the road left at the corner, then follow the right fork. That road will take us home. I have to have the wagon back before dawn."

Darius starts the horses moving.

"We have to take a count of everything we loaded so we know what to pay the store later," he says.

"It's already covered," Travis mumbles from his perch.

Travis's expression hardens.

"I still want a count."

***

The orange light of dawn is beginning to spread across the horizon to announce the coming of the rising sun when they arrive at the Gypsy Queen.

Darius wakes Travis up and they quickly unload, Travis glancing nervously at the sky often. The last of it is barely off the wagon when

Travis leaps to the driver's seat and urges the horses on, rushing down the road to town to return the horses and wagon before the livery opens.

Arriving at the livery, he hastily unhitches the horses, gives the animals a speedy wipe down to remove the obvious sweat and foam from their long night of exhaustive labour, and puts the animals back in their pen.

The livery owner will be at a loss to explain why the animals seem so tired and unable to work, thinking they must have come down with some illness overnight.

***

After Travis leaves to return the wagon, Darius looks over their newly acquired supplies.

"I have no idea how we are going to pay for it, but I hope it is enough to get the work crew through the week. In the meantime, we have to figure out how we are going to come up with the union crew's wages by next Friday, as well as the payment for Norman that is overdue now."

He goes inside, finds paper and a pencil, and returns outside to start taking stock of every board, tool, and nail.

27   Borrowing Against the Odds

"Who are we going to see?" Darius asks, walking next to Travis in the dark night. "And why do we have to meet him so late?"

"We need money we don't have and we can't get a loan from the bank," Travis says.

"That does not answer my question."

"We are seeing a guy about a loan."

"A guy. An unconventional loan, you mean." Darius eyes their surroundings with misgivings.

They have entered the roughest part of town. Here the houses are little more than shanties. Children who should be in bed sleeping are hanging around outside. A group of them stops whatever they are doing to watch them hungrily as they walk past.

"Why do I have the feeling those kids are as likely to eat us as rob us?" Darius asks. He watches the kids warily, half expecting them to attack.

There are men and women too, all watching them suspiciously while they go about their business. Some doing little more than sitting on their front steps. The same as they do during the daylight hours with no jobs to go to.

"This part of town never sleeps," Travis says. "Is it me, or has this area grown?"

"It's the depression," Darius says. "Everyone is out of work. Jobs are getting harder to get every day and more people are losing their jobs as more businesses shut down. When they can't pay their bills and lose their homes they either leave town or end up here."

"I have noticed a lot more houses shuttered around town."

"Two were shuttered on Mayberry just this week."

"We are almost there," Travis says. "This way."

He leads Darius down a dark narrow road where a building that looks like it was abandoned and possibly condemned some time ago sits some distance from the nearest home. Dim light spills out the grimy windows to light the road in front of it. They can hear the muffled sound of many voices and the strains of a poorly played out of tune guitar coming from inside.

"What is this place?" Darius asks. "I don't think we should go in there."

"It's the pub." Travis pushes the door open and the raucous noise inside escapes to greet them.

The air inside is smoky and stale with the stink of unwashed bodies, stale tobacco, and alcohol.

He leads the way in, Darius following a little too closely and eying the inhabitants nervously.

Travis moves through the room with a cocky arrogance. Those who notice them watch them with the distrust reserved for someone who does not belong there.

He stops at a table in the back. A rough looking man sits there. His clothes are well worn, beard scraggly, his hair uncombed, and he looks like he has not had a bath in some time.

The man looks up and nods to the seat across from him.

Travis slides in, urging Darius to follow.

Darius slides in next to him reluctantly.

"This is Walter," Travis says. "My partner, Darius."

Walter looks Darius up and down and turns his attention to them both.

"You two don't look like you could afford to fix up a fishing dingy," Walter grimaces. "And now you got trouble with the Shipbuilders' Union."

Seeing hope, Darius leans forward. "They are forcing us to pay them off. They are forcing us to hire their crew to rebuild the boat, and pay union dues to them for the crew and as employers."

Walter chuckles.

"I guess you shouldn't have picked a boat. Of all the kinds of businesses you could have tried to get into. You could have tried to have a go at anything else and it would have cost you less. Why a boat?"

"We did get her pretty cheap," Travis says.

"And you thought you could make some easy money," Walter says. "Yeah, I've seen it more times than I can count. Some young penniless dandy picks up something cheap, a wagon maybe, thinking oh hell, it ain't costing me much at all. I can make some easy money off this.

But then it ain't so easy. You can't run a wagon without something to pull it. And now you got to find animals, feed them and care for them. And the work turns out to be more work than they bargained. And they didn't think on having to pay the cost of feed and the livery when they need it. And the wagon throws a wheel because it's old and all rotted out and that's why it was so cheap. Now he's got to buy a wheel.

And now, this sod is stuck with a wagon with a broken wheel, animals he can't feed, and he's sleeping under the wagon because he ain't got a home no more because he couldn't pay the bills and he lost that too."

"Yes, so you understand," Darius says hopefully.

"I understand you fools got yourselves into a tight spot you can't get out of. You don't get out from the Shipbuilders' Union until they are done with you."

"How do you get them to decide they are done with you?"

Walter looks at him evenly. There is no pity or forgiveness in the look. Only cold knowledge.

"You build the boat or you die trying."

"And if we just walk away?" Darius swallows the lump in his throat.

Travis glances at him quickly, a look of fear that he might mean it in his eyes.

Walter shakes his head slowly and chuckles a low humorless sound.

"You don't. You don't walk away, you run. And it won't matter. They are mob run. The only organization you need to fear more than the Shipbuilders' Union is the Gaming Commission and going up against old man Barlow, who's got the Gaming Commission in his little pocket. Running won't matter. They will find you. And if you have family, whether they are here or someplace else, they will find them too."

Silence falls on the table. Darius blinks at him. It all feels unreal.

Walter grins.

"Now, let's get to business. That's why you came to me, right?"

"Yes," Travis looks at him earnestly. "We are working day and night and we can't keep up. We need to borrow against our future earnings. Enough to pay off the Dock Master, the Shipbuilders' Union, the union crew's wages, and for the materials to rebuild the boat."

He looks at Darius and remembers.

"Yeah, and the rest of what we owe on the boat."

Walter's smile spreads wider and he laughs a full-bodied laugh, throwing his head back in the throws of unbridled humor. He sits up, staring them both down with a wolfish grin.

"It is going to be a pleasure doing business with you."

They start working out the terms of their commitment to the loan shark, Travis and Darius both feeling more ill as the negotiations proceed.

***

Travis and Darius manage to muddle through the next weeks working exhaustive hours, begging, borrowing and stealing to maintain the unforgivable grip the Gypsy Queen has over their lives.

While the boat de-evolves to a barren skeleton; the ribs, framework of the boat, removed and re-built, and the hull an empty husk being reborn fresh and new in sections around them, they sleep in the boat for the few hours at night when they are not working.

Images of what she will become haunt their dreams when their exhausted slumber allows them to dream, with the gleam of lights and colors and the clink of gambling chips; the endless muted drone of the players' voices sounding more like a hive of manic bees and music that seems strangely distant and menacing despite the cheerful melody playing in the background.

For Travis the dreams are a promise of the lifestyle she offers.

For Darius they are a foreboding promise.

Travis has become a man possessed, driven with the need to make the Gypsy Queen come alive. His eyes fill with a strange look whenever he is near her. He goes over every nail hammered in by the union crew, obsessing that each detail must be perfect. He talks endlessly of what she will become, the riches and the glamour that will shine like her very soul.

Darius sleeps only fitfully every night, worrying over the depth of the impossible hole they have found themselves trapped in with no way out. He worries over Travis's failing sanity. He wants only to walk away from it all, to abandon the boat to whatever her fate may be. But he knows that if he does he would also be leaving Travis to his fate, one that seems tied to the boat he refuses to abandon.

Days meld into weeks and weeks into months, a blur of endless hours labouring to earn money, begging, borrowing, and Travis resorting to stealing for it without Darius acknowledging knowledge of it, all for their greedy mistress the Gypsy Queen.

Around them, the Gypsy Queen is taking shape and her raw fresh wood is starting to show the vitality and glamour she is intended to have. Their dreams are beginning to be realized for the first time, coming alive as the Gypsy Queen begins to look alive.

***

"It is a new day," Travis says. He is standing with his back to Darius examining a potential flaw in the perfection of the boat's hull frame. "I'm only working at the slaughterhouse today. Today when I return, we will have time to work together on bringing us closer to our dream."

"I don't think so," Darius says, not turning to look at him. He is busy folding his blankets to put them away before the crew arrives. "I don't have the evening off and you have to see Walter to borrow more money and then you have to see Norman to make the payment on the boat. We both won't be back until late."

"What?" Travis asks, turning to look at Darius. "Did you say something?"

Darius turns and looks at him. Travis is standing facing the inner wall of the boat hull. He is standing close as if talking to someone on the other side of the wood barrier, one hand resting gently on the wall.

"You weren't talking to me," Darius mutters under his breath. "You were talking to the damned boat again."

"Nothing," Darius says. He changes his mind. "Don't forget to go see Walter and Norman today."

"Right after work," Travis smiles, turning to look at him now. "We have to get going. We will both be late for work."

They leave the boat to find the first of the union crew showing up.

Always the first to arrive, the foreman is standing leaning on his truck. The crew will not start work until the designated time. He gives Darius and Travis an unsmiling nod and they head off walking down the road.

Behind them, they hear the foreman, Herman, calling the men to get ready to start working.

They pass some of the crew on the road. Some are riding in a union truck, others are walking.

Darius groans, feeling dispirited and suddenly more exhausted when they pass yet more men.

"The crew is larger today," he says. "It's almost like they know we somehow found a source to borrow money and are intent on drying up the supply."

"It just means they will finish sooner and we will be rid of the Shipbuilders' Union." Travis tries to give him an encouraging smile.

Darius only looks sick.

"It means we need even more money. We have to go even further into debt to that snake, Walter."

"I saw Amelia again yesterday," Travis says, trying to change the subject.

"She still isn't talking to you?"

Travis can't help the grin that spreads across his face.

"The moment she saw me she looked mad enough to drive off a swarm of angry bees; gave me the most inspiring withering glare and stomped off."

His smile slips.

"No. She still won't talk to me."

"You did burglarize her father's store," Darius casts a quick glance at him.

Travis does not respond to either deny or confess to the crime.

"Give her enough time. She will come around," Darius says. "They always do for you."

"It's time we part ways," Travis says. They have reached the corner where they go separate ways to work.

They give each other a parting nod and go their own way.

Darius's thoughts turn to Amelia, her eyes, her hair, her hands. The light trill of her laugh, the sound of her voice. Her scent. She has not been coming by the boat anymore.

"No, I can't go there. I can't even consider it. Not when Travis is enamoured with her. I couldn't. It could end our friendship. And if he does get past this, makes her fall for him, and they always do…"

He burns with the knowledge that just like every woman he has chased, Travis will invariably break her heart and move on to the next conquest. Women and his get rich quick schemes all end the same way. Badly.

"Amelia deserves better than that."

Darius has the urge to go see her. To talk to her, warn her, and stop Travis from making a fool of her. To just see her.

The image of her looking up at him, a small smile on her lips, swims before him.

"I can't. Not after she has been with him. I just wish he was half as enamoured with her as he is with that damned boat."

***

Malcolm Barlow looks up from the papers on his desk at the knock at the door.

"Come in," he calls.

His office door opens and his head of security, Frank, enters.

"Sir, I have an update on the Gypsy Queen," Frank says.

Malcolm smirks. "They haven't given up on that thing? It's so rotted out it isn't worth the effort or money to fix up."

"They have not, sir. Quite the opposite."

Malcolm raises a questioning eyebrow.

"The Shipbuilders' Union got wind of their endeavor," Frank says.

Malcom's grin widens cruelly.

"I think I know where this is going."

Frank nods.

"Yes sir. The Union has them under their thumbs and they are putting the squeeze on them. They put a crew on rebuilding the boat and are forcing them to pay. They made surprising progress. The Gypsy Queen might actually come together."

The corners of Malcolm's mouth turn up into a big smile.

"This is delightful. So, you are telling me that my father's boat might become valuable again, and someone else is paying for it."

He laughs delightedly.

"We can't allow her to hit the water under anyone else's ownership. My father swore that boat would never touch the water again. We will let them make more progress, let her begin to realize her value, and then after the Union has broken these two idiots I will take their problems off their hands and buy the Gypsy Queen at a price substantially lower than her partially built value."

The gleam in his eyes is vicious with greed.

"She will be mine. My father's most prized possession, coveted by all in her days of glory, will be mine."

"What are you going to do with her sir?"

"That depends on how far these two get rebuilding her. I might have her stripped and burned. No man will own her but me."

"One of them will probably be glad to get rid of the boat," Frank says, "but from asking around it sounds like the other will never agree to sell."

"Oh, they will, long before the Union is done with them. They will fall to my feet and kiss them with relief that I am taking the boat and the Union off them.

I want to see this boat. Frank, we are going to take a drive out there."

Frank nods understanding.

28   Talk Sweetly to the Queen

Three men are working inside the hull of the Gypsy Queen while the others work outside the boat. Boards are spread across a pair of sawhorses, two men working together. One man holds the board still on the sawhorse while the other measures, marks it with a pencil, and cuts it to length.

The third man carries the cut board across the work area to the other side and sets the cut board in place, pounding the nails home with two powerful strikes each with the hammer, securing the boards. They will go over them again after to add more nails and secure them properly.

"Where do you think these guys are getting the money for this boat?" the man marking the board with a pencil asks.

"Must be family money," the man holding the board says. He laughs a harsh guttural sound.

"Did you see the look of fear when they passed us? The union has them good."

"I don't care," the man hammering mutters, "as long as I get a pay check."

"What do you think this old bitch used to be?" Pencil muses. "I heard the boat was found abandoned around here."

"They should have left it rotting where they found it," the board holder says.

Cutting the wood, Pencil mutters an oath and holds his hand up. A crimson drop falls to the floor as he inspects his finger.

"Damn, cut myself."

The red bead of blood soaks into the wood floor.

"What are you doing after work?" Holder asks.

"Visiting the ladies," Pencil leers, making a crude gesture.

"You got a lady right here," Hammer says.

"What do you mean?"

Hammer waves his hammer at the boat around them.

"She's more like the ladies you don't want to touch down in the camps," Holder grins. "She's rotting from the innards out."

"That's never stopped you," Pencil laughs.

"But this lady is a queen," Hammer says. He grins, pounding a nail home hard. "We should treat her like one."

He hammers another home, harder.

"You might need a bigger hammer," Holder sneers. "Look at the size of the holes in this hull."

"You guys should come with me," Pencil says.

"I got a wife for that," Hammer says.

"Your wife hates you."

"That don't matter. She does what I tell her or else."

He brings the hammer down in another forceful blow. The hammer glances off the nail head, bending the nail and cracking the plank.

"You broke her like your wife."

Hammer shrugs.

"She's my property to do with as I please. That's what they're there for."

They all laugh.

Hammer gets another board, lines it up, and sets the nail with a quick tap. He raises the hammer to strike.

He pauses, holding his hammer in mid swing and wondering at the sudden chill in the air. His breath comes out as a cloud of vapor as if it were winter.

He yelps. It is a guttural sound of surprise that has not yet registered a need to feel fear.

Pencil looks up curiously, his eyes focusing on something, and pales, his eyes widening in shock. The initial paralysis of fear grips his tongue, silencing it, holding him captive in its tight embrace.

Holder looks up to see why Pencil stopped working.

It is at that very moment the first thud of a nail embedding itself into the wall sounds.

Pencil's face pales. He is frozen in place with shock.

Hammer looks behind him in surprise, not seeing it at first.

Another nail thuds into the wall after a long pause of ragged heartbeats. Another comes after a shorter pause, and another and another, each nail coming closer on the dull thud of the last hitting the wall than the one before; a trail of nails leading across and up, moving towards the sawhorse.

With increasing speed, the nails lift one at a time from the bucket on the floor and fly across the room with the velocity of a bullet until they are flying like the spray of rounds from an automatic machine gun, straight and true, pointed end piercing the wall with a dull thud.

Hammer screams a warning too late, watching in horror as the nails fire soundlessly from an invisible gun and impact the wall with a dull thud in a line moving closer to the other men until they begin sinking into them instead of the wall. He starts to move one way then the other, unable to think with the shock and fear seizing his mind.

The two men at the sawhorse cry out and dodge, not moving fast enough, blood spattering as the nails strike flesh when the line of missiles reaches them. Scattered crimson drops spray across the floor and the wall behind them as they turn with the surprise of the impacts.

The two men in the line of fire run from the approaching spray, not running fast enough to outrun it, struck repeatedly with the pursuing line of nails. On hindsight, it may have been wiser to run into the oncoming path where the nails had already gone.

Hammer is waving his hands frantically at the other men.

"Run! Get out of there!"

He stops suddenly at the hollow sound of lumber being struck by a blunt force. He turns just as the pile of boards stacked neatly near one wall tumble over as if struck from the other side. The boards clatter and bounce in a cascade of falling wood and he leaps back out of the way, striking his head on something hard. The pain flashes through his head with an explosion of nauseating red light.

Hammer turns, stunned, feeling the room spinning. His world is a blur. He barely registers the sound of the other men screaming and running from some unseen attacker.

His shirt feels wet.

He reaches up with one hand, feeling where his head has struck something, and his hand comes away dripping with blood. He looks to see what struck him, but there is nothing there for his unfocused eyes to find.

Two men working just outside hear their screams and come running to investigate. They pause in the opening in the hull, staring at the scene before them in stunned disbelief. Two bloodied men are shrieking and dodging maniacally while the third stares blankly at nothing with blood oozing from a head wound.

Breaking the paralysis of shock, one of them jumps forward and wraps his arms around the nearest man, grabbing him in a bear hug and trying to pull him out to safety.

Hammer struggles and tries to swat away his attacker, seeing only the haze of pain and shock. Someone is grabbing him, arms wrapping around his chest from behind and dragging him backwards.

He struggles; swinging his fists, and realizes he still holds the hammer in his hand. He stares down at it in wonder at the crimson drops dripping from it which have no reason to be there.

The other worker pulls him towards the opening again.

"Stop fighting me," he yells at Hammer. "I'm trying to get you out of here!"

It is like trying to save a drowning man. In his haze of fear, Hammer fights again, lashing out blindly. A voice is yelling at him but he can't understand what it is saying. The room swoons and tilts and he feels himself being dragged across the floor.

The other worker who came to investigate the screams breaks from his own shock. He runs past the rest and grabs at Pencil, the furthest from safety, who looks like he had been shot multiple times, half carrying and half dragging him towards the opening in the hull. He grabs at the other man with his other hand as they pass him, trying to drag him along.

"Come on," he urges.

Pencil and Holder stagger with him, letting him help them to safety, while the other rescuer wrestles Hammer through the opening in the hull.

They all make it out of the boat, staggering away through the hole in the hull.

All that is left inside are scattered tools and lumber, and drips and splatters of blood everywhere, as the hull suddenly falls as still as death and as suddenly as it came the chill sucks into itself and out of existence.

***

Darius has two sides of the wooden crate he is building between his legs, using his legs to hold them together. Using one hand to clamp the corner together, nail held between his fingers, he deftly swings the hammer with the other. The hammer rings off the nail, sending it biting into the wood. Two more strikes and the nail is embedded, it's head flush with the wood.

He turns the crate and repeats the process, grabbing another square side to add to it. When he has all the corners of the sides tacked together, leaving one side open, he runs along the edges hammering in more nails to make the crate sturdy.

Finished, he inspects it, tosses it in the pile of finished crates, and grabs two more boards to start another. He lays them out, grabbing more boards, building each side before putting them together.

He pushes himself to work hard and fast. Paid by the finished crate, the more crates Darius can build, the more he gets paid.

With one side left to add to the crate, the hammer slips, glancing down the side of the board with the full power of the hammer strike, damaging it.

"Damn." He tosses the partially built crate aside, shaking his head in frustration. "That will come out of my pay."

Darius grabs more boards, expertly nailing them together to start a new crate. The ringing hammer glances off the nail and chatters down the board. He stops to inspect it. No visible damage.

Exhaustion pulls at his face, his eyes are bloodshot with it, and he is weakened from not eating.

"Hey, we need that stack of crates on the truck," the crate factory foreman calls.

"I'm on it."

Darius puts down the partially built crate and stacks as many creates as he can manage, picking them up and carefully making his way to the truck.

Exhaustion has drained him of some of his faculties. He is moving in a zombie-like state.

He does not see the other truck.

"Darius!"

He hears his name shouted, but it takes too long to register.

Someone runs at him, lunging to grab him.

The driver brakes too late, his eyes widening in response heartbeats before he can react to reach for the brake. He spins the wheel, swerving.

Instead of hitting Darius straight on, knocking him down and driving over him, the swerving truck hits him a glancing blow. Darius and the crates are hit by the side of the truck, sending both him and the crates falling back.

"Are you okay?" The foreman and other workers surround him, feeling him over for broken bones. The driver throws the truck into park, leaping out and racing back.

"Hey, are you all right?" He looks around in shock. "I didn't mean it. I didn't mean to. I mean, I didn't see him until it was too late."

"The crates... are they okay?" Darius asks, looking around in a foggy-headed daze. "Are they damaged?"

His foreman laughs a dry chuckle.

"He gets hit by a truck and all he cares about is the quality of his work. That's Darius for you."

Darius looks up at him.

"You aren't going to dock me for those crates, are you?"

"We'll see if they are damaged first."

The foreman looks around for help.

"Get him up. Get him out of here. We have crates to move."

A couple of men help Darius to his feet, half carrying him off.

"Look at him, he can't even walk," the foreman complains. "Darius, you are done for today. Go home."

Darius only manages a wave back in acknowledgement.

The men half carry him to the exit.

"Are you okay to walk?" one of them asks.

"I don't have much choice," Darius says.

He gets his balance, tests his weight on his legs, and starts the walk home.

***

The sky hangs heavily with black clouds threatening to spill a deluge on the world below. Trees in the distance are beginning to whip with the winds as the tip of the advancing storm approaches.

Darius's dragging feet kick up dust in the road as he limps along towards the Gypsy Queen. His body is wrapped in the numbness of a heavy exhaustion, closing out the world to some distant realm.

He reaches the boat before he realizes the air is silent of the sounds of saws and hammers.

Darius looks around curiously as he crosses the grass to the boat, too exhausted to think much of it, but wondering where the workers are. There are no trucks and no workers to be seen.

Most of the holes in the hull from the weeks before are closed and smoothly sanded, waiting for the coating that will keep them from soaking in the water from the river. The cargo doors in the side sit just above the water line of the floating vessel. They are closed, their seams nearly indistinguishable.

In a few more days the only way in will be to climb a ladder up to the deck above. Presently it is the only way to access the deck above.

Darius looks around.

"It is too early for the crew to quit."

"Hello," he calls. There is no answer.

He climbs the ladder with difficulty, his injury making the feat nearly impossible. When he finally reaches the deck, he walks to the open doorways on deck, calling out and finding it vacant.

"Hello. Hello? Anybody here?"

"Where is everybody?" he wonders.

Darius wants nothing more than to collapse on a soft surface and sleep, but he has the disconcerting feeling that something is wrong.

"I'm going to have to go talk to Mr. Moloney at the shipyard," he mutters. "They better not expect us to pay wages for men who aren't here."

With a dispirited groan, he climbs back down the ladder to the ground.

Darius starts limping for the road and the long walk to the shipyard, stopping when he sees a car approaching.

Grateful to have a reason to not make the trip, he waits, watching the approaching car grow larger, wondering who it is.

The car stops and the driver door opens. He recognizes the old man who gets out of the car, surprised to see that he came alone.

It is the same man who stepped out of his office to call out to them at the union office in the shipyard, warning them not to let the workers know the real name of the boat they are rebuilding.

"Good afternoon Mr. Marek," the elderly man says, tipping his hat in a gesture of greeting. "I am Mr. Eugene Randall, CEO of the Shipbuilders' Union."

"Mr. Randall," Darius nods greeting. "I recognize you from the office."

He approaches the old man, closing the distance with his limping steps as the other man advances. They shake hands politely.

"I was just coming to your office to see Mr. Moloney," Darius says.

"Then it looks like I saved you a trip," Eugene says, looking down at his bandaged leg. "It is probably a good thing too from the look of that leg."

He looks around. "I don't see a car. I presume you were going to walk on that leg?"

"Yes sir, I was." Darius looks at the old man, taking in his serious expression.

"Whatever he came for, it can't be good," he thinks.

"The union men were already gone when I got here," Darius says lamely, knowing the other man undoubtedly already knows that.

"Yes," Eugene nods. "That is what I came here to talk to you about."

He looks around as if studying the worksite, but with little to see outside the boat Darius suspects it is more of a delay.

Finally, Eugene takes another step closer and looks him in the eye, his stare steady and grave.

"You gentlemen are in way over your heads," Eugene says. "You know that, don't you?"

"Yes sir, we know," Darius says. He does not like the way this conversation is going already.

"If you have any sense you will quit now, while you still can," Eugene says. "Just walk away now and the union will leave you alone."

Darius studies him, sizing him up and trying to guess at the union boss's motive.

"I wish we could," he says at last, his voice weary with pain and exhaustion, "but I'm afraid it's too late. I do not see that as an option. We tried that at the start, but your Mr. Moloney would not allow it. He made that pretty clear. Now we are in this too deep. We owe too many people too much money. I don't think we could walk away now, even if we tried."

Eugene nods. He had expected as much.

"Claim bankruptcy," he says. "It will follow you forever, but it is better than this."

Darius shakes his head.

"You don't claim bankruptcy with the sort of people your union put us in a position to have to borrow from."

Eugene lowers his head, acknowledging guilt and possibly regret, but Darius doubts the man feels that.

"Why were the men pulled from the job?" Darius asks. "I hope we are not going to still have to pay them while they aren't here. We still have materials, so they could still be working."

Eugene's expression becomes graver.

"There has been an accident. The foreman shut down the site and left."

Darius pales.

"An accident? What kind? How bad?" He imagines what it might be, what kind of accidents might happen on a project like this. An accident with a saw or a crushed hand. He looks around anxiously.

"Maybe we should go inside and take a look Mr. Marek," Eugene says heavily.

Darius feels a fluttering in his stomach, his heart sinking to meet it. It has to be bad.

He nods and leads the way. He stops next to the boat, near the ladder.

Eugene stops at the base of the ladder, looking up at the boat looming above him. A chill fills him as if he were standing in the boat's deep shadow; a shadow, which does not exist on this cloudy day.

He motions towards the dark maw of the hole still in the hull.

Darius nods and turns, leading the way. They stop outside the hole.

"After you," Eugene says, waving towards the opening.

Darius steps over the lip into the dark interior of the boat's hull. He looks down. In the light coming in, he sees a trail of blood drops.

Eugene follows him in.

"It happened in here?" Darius asks.

"Below deck somewhere," Eugene says. He is not sure himself where it happened, taking what little he knows of the accident from the excited ravings of the men who came back to the shipyard.

They follow the drops. The trepidation builds in Darius as they move through the hull of the boat looking for the scene of the accident.

That the man who came to inform him about it doesn't seem to know where it happened is even more unnerving than the fact it happened.

"Could the accident have been that bad?" Darius wonders.

They turn a corner and poke their heads into a room that has yet to reveal its purposes. The room is spacious for a paddle wheel powered river barge and possibly has yet to have the walls built dividing it into smaller rooms.

The moment they look through the doorway; it becomes clear the accident is more serious than Darius imaged.

Dull light splashes in from a still un-rebuilt hole in the hull on the other side of the boat.

It is exactly what Eugene suspected but tried to convince himself was an over dramatization of the reality.

They both pale and look shaken as they absorb the scene before them.

Darius steps through the doorway first, not even realizing he stepped forward, numb with shock.

A line of nails runs up one wall at an incline as if sprayed from an automatic machine gun, the wall behind and floor spattered with blood, appearing as though some of the nails may have been shot directly through the victims to become embedded in the wall. They stick out of the wall to different degrees, from half sunken to completely embedded so that all that is visible is the hole left by the nail.

The surface of a pool of blood on the floor is already congealing and crusted over.

The room is in disarray. Tools and materials are spilled across the floor as if the men had frantically scrambled in panicked escape, knocking them over. Drips of blood trail from one end of the room to another and back, zigzagging towards the opening in the hull, chronicling the desperate dodging of someone injured fleeing from something that apparently chased them. Bloodied handprints, footprints, and smears add to the tale.

"What? How?" Darius is at a loss for words, his mind unable to grasp what he is seeing. "There is nothing save for a machine gun capable of doing something like this. I-I cannot see how one could even shoot nails instead of bullets. And who would do something like this?"

He stammers, trying to speak without knowing what else to say.

"The blood, the scattered tools, none of it makes any sense."

Eugene gapes; trying to match the scene to the men's frantic babbling.

He shakes off the sudden chill he feels tingling down his spine, trying to put the disturbing visions out of his mind. He looks at Darius with an almost apologetic look.

"It would appear she has taken her ounce of blood," Eugene says.

He looks at Darius seriously. The look sends a new surge of fear through Darius.

"Two of the three men involved did not survive," Eugene says.

He turns away and starts making his way out the way they came in, loath to step through the scene and get blood on his shoes.

Darius follows, feeling numb, stunned.

Eugene speeds up, hurrying. He feels the ill-fated past of the Gypsy Queen like an illness trying to find its way in to pollute him.

"The crew refuses to come back here," Eugene says when they step safely outside the boat. "The crew are pretty rattled by whatever happened here. I will have to talk to them and get their statements. Union rules. A boat this size has to have union labour. I do not know when they will be willing to come back, if at all."

Darius's head is ringing with numb shock over the blood-splattered hull. He follows Eugene away from the boat.

Eugene has to pause to catch his breath. Darius wonders if it is from the stress of what they witnessed in the hull.

"So what happens now?" Darius asks.

Eugene turns to him, his expression grim and his rheumy eyes holding a fear he cannot hide. He shrugs. It is more of a defeated gesture. He moves away, wanting to put more space between him and the boat.

"I guess until we find some men willing to work here you can do whatever you like with the boat. Under the circumstances…" He lets the sentence drop. It isn't necessary to say any more.

He studies Darius for a moment, sizing him up, gauging his reaction to the grisly scene inside the boat.

"My recommendation is to burn it to the ground, and I say this in the strongest terms," Eugene says at last, the words heavy with regret. "The men will be put on other jobs. Take a few days, or even weeks, to think about it. As long as you keep paying the union dues, the union won't be concerned. On the books it will show the work on her has been temporarily halted. You will not have their wages to worry about."

Darius weighs this over. Despite the gravity of the situation this is good news in that it gives them a reprieve to work at coming up with more money. He dares not voice this thought, even in his own head.

He gives the old man a solemn look and a small appreciative nod.

Eugene gives Darius a parting nod, an agreement to an unspoken understanding.

Darius limps after him as he walks back to his car. He watches the old man climb in and drive away, the chilling feeling of being watched from behind sending a shiver down his spine.

Alone at last and overcome with exhaustion, Darius finds his rolled up blankets and pillows and goes in search of a quiet corner to sleep in. He avoids the end of the boat where the accident happened, finding a spot as far away from it as he can on the opposite end of the boat.

***

It is late when Travis returns to the Gypsy Queen. The boat is in darkness and he has to fumble around to find a lantern.

He looks up at the boat looming above him.

"Let's see what work they have done on you today."

The cloudy night allows no moon or stars to light the way.

Travis finds a lantern and lights it. He steps inside the hull, entering through the same hole Darius and Eugene did earlier.

He spots Darius sleeping and decides not to wake him.

Travis turns the lantern light low and moves off through the hull to inspect the work done by the union crew.

With the low lantern light giving a soft glow that fills only a few feet of space, he goes around a barrier wall to the other end of the hull.

He crosses to the wall, holding the lantern up to it to inspect the work done. Travis runs a hand over it. The wood beneath his fingers is rough.

"Yes, I know. They are a bit rough. Here, I will fix it. I will smooth it out."

He finds a sanding block and goes to work gently sanding the wood.

Travis is engrossed in his work to the exclusion of all else. He is working the lower wall, sitting on the floor and sanding the wall down where it meets the floor, pausing now and then to caress his hand over the wood to test its smoothness.

There is a thud immediately behind him.

Travis turns, leaning back as he does so, and quickly leans forward the moment he feels something dig into his back.

He stands and turns to see a saw lying immediately behind him. It rests at an odd angle, propped against a heavy bucket full of nails he is sure had not been there before.

"Neither of those were there."

If the saw were lying at a different angle, it would have been the sharp teeth that would have dug into his back instead of the handle.

He scratches his head, confused.

"I better not tell Darius about it."

"You are back."

Travis turns at the sudden voice behind him.

Darius is standing there at the edge of the wall barrier, looking more like he is leaning than standing up. His face is more haggard than Travis remembers seeing it.

"You were sleeping. I didn't want to wake you."

Darius runs a hand roughly over his head and down his face.

"I must have been tired. I don't know how I can sleep."

Travis senses something is wrong.

"Did something happen?"

"Come. I have to show you." Darius bends down and picks up a lantern he had set down just on the other side of the wall. He turns up the flame and the light fills the open area with its warm yellow glow, revealing the trail of blood drops he and Eugene followed earlier.

His senses jangling a warning, Travis picks up his lantern and follows.

Darius stops in the doorway of the other section of the hull and looks at Travis, his expression grave and his face pale.

He holds the lantern up to light the area. He nods towards Travis's lantern.

Stepping beside him, Travis raises his lantern and turns the flame higher, adding more light.

Travis gapes. His jaw moves and he stammers, trying to speak.

"Wh-what happened?" he finally manages.

"I don't know," Darius says. "It looks like someone tried to kill them."

He shakes his head, his eyes hollow.

"I don't know. I just don't get it. I mean, one of the union bosses came. The old man. He didn't say anything about anyone trying to kill their men." He pauses. "He said it was an accident."

"An accident?" Travis stumbles forward, taking in the blood splatters and the trail of nails and holes running up the wall.

"Was this…"

Darius shakes his head. "It's nails. Nothing I know of could have done this."

"I heard of a guy working on something, Pynoos…" Travis trails off.

Darius shakes his head.

"Could they have faked it?" Travis looks at him, incredulous, trying to make sense of the senseless.

Darius shakes his head slowly. He meets his eyes. Darius's eyes are haunted.

"You didn't see the old man. You didn't hear his voice, see his eyes. He was, is, terrified of this boat."

"Who would do this? An enemy of the union?"

"I don't see how. I think he would have said something if someone attacked them and then hammered the nails in to make it look like this."

Travis stumbles forward, studying the scene. He reaches out, not quite touching some of the nails partially sticking out of the wall.

"It looks like these nails were shot right through them."

He turns to look at Darius.

Darius meets his look. "Yes, it does."

Darius looks away and back again.

"All I'm saying is maybe it was an accident. Or maybe it was some attack, some warning for the union crew. Or meant for us. But there is nothing I know of that can shoot a nail through a man, let alone a lot of them like they were fired from some kind of automated fast firing gun."

They stare at each other in the heavy silence.

Finally, Travis really looks at Darius and realizes it is more than exhaustion weighing him down.

A look of panic flashes in his eyes and is gone.

"You are hurt. Was it the Gypsy Queen?"

"Accident at work. I was hit by a truck."

Darius lowers his head wearily. "I'm tired. I'm getting some sleep. We will clean up the blood in the morning. I just wanted to show you. Tomorrow we will have to decide what we are going to do."

He sets the lantern down, turns, and walks off into the darkness.

Travis stares after him although he can't see him. He turns to take in the horror of the blood and nails again. The scattered lumber. The kicked over bucket of nails.

He walks slowly to the wall, delicately running his fingers over the nails embedded in the wall, mindless of the now dried blood dripping down it.

"What did they do to you?" he whispers, his voice a sweet caress. "What did they do to make you so angry my Gypsy Queen?"

Without another word, Travis takes the lantern and searches for a bucket and rags. Filling the bucket at the river, he returns and starts gently washing the blood away in the yellow light of the lantern.

29   Bad Debts

The day hangs heavy and dreary with dark clouds threatening the sky. Darius is alone after waking to find Travis gone.

His empty stomach feeling hollow and sick, he stumbles outside and vomits dryly. There is nothing in his stomach to vomit out.

With the gloomy light of the threatened storm that is still hovering in the distance, he goes to the blood splattered area.

The blood is smeared across the walls in a faded caricature of the gruesome aftermath of the accident.

"Travis stayed up trying to clean it."

Darius finds the blood splattered bucket and rags and takes them to the river to rinse and fill the bucket. Swishing and wringing the rags out, the river water turns red with blood, the stream quickly washing it away.

He returns to the boat to finish the job of cleaning up the mess.

Hours later, Darius steps wearily from the boat, sickened by the smell and sight of the blood.

He breathes in the fresh air in deep sucking breaths in an attempt to scour the smell from his nostrils and lungs.

A car approaches up the road, the dust from its wheels creating a cloud that blows away behind it in the wind that is picking up speed.

Darius turns, seeing the car. He watches its approach with dread sitting heavy in his stomach.

"Every time a car comes to the boat it's something bad."

A few minutes later the car pulls up, rocking over the rough grass to park twelve feet away from the boat.

The front doors open and two large men get out. One of them moves to open the rear door and another man exits from that door.

The back seat passenger stands there in his expensive suit and slicked back hair looking at the Gypsy Queen while the others come around the car to join him.

The sick feeling of dread in Darius's stomach falls with a greasy weightless sensation.

He immediately recognizes the two security men who threw them overboard the Queen Rhiannon and the man who ordered it.

"So, this is it," Malcolm says. "This is the infamous Gypsy Queen. Not much to look at, is she?"

He smiles at his entourage.

Malcolm looks around and spots Darius. He nods to his security men.

Frank steps forward, walking ahead of him to approach Darius.

Darius's eyes go immediately to Frank's stout straight cane with a heavy ornate carved ram's head gripped in one meaty fist. A cane the man does not need to walk.

The other security man steps forward, almost as large, pacing Frank.

His two security men creating a two-man wall between Darius and Malcolm, Malcolm waits until they have closed half the distance before he steps forward and follows.

There is no recognition in Malcolm's eyes. He smiles broadly at Darius.

"Do I know you from somewhere?" Malcolm shakes his head, dismissing the idea. "Is this your boat?"

"Yes, sir."

He looks pointedly around at the Gypsy Queen.

"This is quite the undertaking you and your partner have taken on here. Kind of a large project for two men without the means to complete it."

"We are managing," Darius says, gritting his teeth against the sick feeling of fear that threatens to make them chatter.

The two large men stop before Darius, watching him with the wary confidence of two such men who know he is too terrified to so much as flinch.

Malcolm stops a few paces behind them.

Malcolm looks directly at Darius, sizing him up. His weakened and injured exhausted state makes Darius look weaker against the strong confidence of the other three. He smiles at him.

"Let me give you a small piece of advice. Abandon this pile of rot. You cannot hope to finish her. Just pack your things, if you have any, turn your backs on her, and walk away."

Darius looks down at the ground, his feet shifting. His stomach roils sickly and he feels faint.

He looks up, meeting Malcolm's stare and trying to keep his eyes and his stance steady.

"With all due respect sir, I don't think so."

Malcolm laughs, looking at his security men as if they might point out the joke to him.

"Are you serious?"

He looks at Darius again.

"Really, it is not that difficult. Just…" He wags his hands in a shooing away gesture. "Walk away."

"We are well past walking away," Darius says, working to keep his voice and eyes steady.

Malcolm's eyes turn cold.

"If it will help, I could buy the Gypsy from you for a reasonable price. Reasonable for me."

"You mean a low price."

Malcolm's lips spread in a predatory grin.

"I did say reasonable for me."

Darius thinks for a moment.

"All I have to do is say yes," he thinks, "and we are out. We walk away."

His thoughts go to Travis. Travis talking to the boat in that way that sickens him, as if the boat is a person, sentient.

"Travis will not walk away," he thinks. "He will never walk away. Not at any price."

"The boat is not for sale," Darius says. "Not for any price."

Malcolm's smile drops. His mouth hardens.

"Perhaps I did not make my position clear. You don't really know me, do you Mr. Marek?"

"You are Malcolm Barlow. I know who you are."

Malcolm's mouth curves into a cold smile-less grin.

"Do you? I am not so sure. You know my name. You do not know who I am."

"Who are you then?"

"I am a man people do not say no to."

"Well, sir, I am respectfully saying no." Darius feels like his legs are going to give out in a puddle of fear sweat.

Malcolm's eyes and mouth harden.

"You will walk away. If I am feeling in a generous mood when you do, I might consider giving you a small reward for finding my father's lost boat. If you don't…"

He lets the pause hang heavily in the air.

"…I expect there will be some unfortunate accidents around her."

He nods meaningfully at Darius, turns, and walks back to his car without another word.

Malcolm's security men follow, Frank tipping his ram's head cane to his hat and nodding a meaningful salute to Darius before he turns and follows his boss.

They climb back in the car and drive away.

Darius stares after them. He feels weak with the sickness of fear.

The ugly scene inside the boat swims before him, playing over in his mind. The fear he saw in the old man's eyes when the union boss came to witness the bloody scene himself.

Darius pales. He raises a shaking hand to his face.

His mouth hardens into an angry line, his eyes following.

"Did they do it? Was it a warning? For us or for the Shipbuilders' Union?"

The wind picks up, buffeting at him.

The weight of this new revelation on his shoulders, Darius turns and seeks shelter inside the hull of the Gypsy Queen.

The rain comes on the heels of the wind, being whipped against the Gypsy Queen.

Chilled by the sudden drop in temperature, Darius finds his blanket and wraps himself in it, huddling in a corner for warmth.

The wind blows through the unsealed cracks of the hull, bringing the spray of wet from the rain with it.

The lantern sits forlornly on the floor in front of him. The sky darkening with the clouds rolling in puts the inside of the boat in shadow.

Darius sits there huddled in the corner, the pouring rain battering the Gypsy Queen, and the unfinished boat giving him only partial shelter.

A crack of thunder booms in the sky almost in unison with the bright flash lighting it.

***

It has been weeks since the strange accident that drove the union workers from the boat and the sudden spurt of progress has slowed to a crawl with Travis and Darius working on the Gypsy Queen in the little time they have between working two jobs each and any casual work they can find.

The first thing they did was to clean up the residual blood spattered mess, sanding the surfaces and replacing sections of lumber to get rid of the blood soaked into the raw wood.

A lot of the actual tearing down and building work is done now and they are working on the slow process of rebuilding.

In those weeks, Travis has made sure to run into Amelia at every opportunity, sometimes just standing outside her home in the dark hoping to get a glimpse of her.

Darius walks down the street with the work-weary slouch of a man who has put in too many hours of hard labour without a rest.

He nods to the old man sitting on the bench outside the store, not expecting a response, and pauses outside the door of the lumber store, looking in the window before he goes in. There is no one in sight inside the store.

Walking inside, he looks around, still finding no one.

Darius goes to the desk and rings the bell.

Hearing the ding of the bell, Amelia leaves the crates she is checking in the back room and walks through the doorway into the store.

Her heart speeds up at the sight of Darius standing at the desk. His back is turned to her and he does not see her.

"I haven't seen you here in a while," Amelia says, smiling brightly at him as she approaches. "How can I help you today?"

Darius turns, guilt tingeing his eyes. He cannot deny that he is glad it is her and not her father. His own heart beats faster at the sight of her and the sound of her voice.

A playful comment dies on his lips.

"Keep it to business," he thinks.

Amelia's smile falters just the smallest bit.

"I came to look through the catalog," Darius says.

Amelia breezes past him, her perfume lingering in the air to tease his nostrils. She goes around the desk and pulls out the catalogue from a shelf under it. Plopping the heavy book on the desk, she breezes past him again.

"I have work to do," she says icily. Amelia feels the burn of rejection. He is not there to see her.

"Why is she mad at me?" Darius thinks, confused by her sudden turn of mood.

He starts flipping through the pages looking for prices on items they need for the boat.

Amelia stops in the doorway to the back room, turning to look back at him.

"Just leave him and go back to work," she admonishes herself. But she feels the urge to push it, to go talk to him and see if just maybe he is there for more than just to order a few parts or tools.

"I probably should see if he needs help," she tells herself.

She returns to the desk, watching Darius flip through pages.

"Are you finding what you are looking for?" she asks.

Darius glances up and quickly looks back down at the pages. He feels awkward near her and her scent is filling the air like a soft kiss, making him more self-conscious.

"Not yet."

"How is your boat coming along?"

"Fine."

Amelia feels the flush of irritation at his short impersonal responses. She purses her lips and thinks.

"I have been running into your friend around town," she says finally, feeling him out for a response. "A lot. It almost seems like he is stalking me."

Darius pushes down the rush of jealousy.

"He probably wants to ask you out," he says.

She blinks at him. The idea is not a surprise. She has been suspecting as much, and that Travis simply has not built up the nerve yet.

"That he is bringing it up means he probably is not interested himself," she thinks, feeling the burn of disappointment. "I thought Darius likes me. He is a nicer person than Travis."

She frowns inwardly. "Travis is the sort of man you have fun with. He is exciting and fun and heats your blood. Darius is the sort of man you marry. He is kind and reliable and does not talk down to me or treat me like my ideas don't matter for not being a man."

"You know," Darius says, pretending to focus on the catalogue page as he turns it, "if he does maybe you should consider it."

Disappointment burns hotter in Amelia's stomach.

"He is actually telling me to go out with his friend," she thinks. Her heart races faster and her chest feels tight. "He knows. Somehow, he knows that I have feelings for him. He is pushing me to his friend instead."

The thought is a pain in her heart.

"Now you are being ridiculous," she thinks. "You like them both and you know it and you cannot have them both."

"He stands outside my house," she says. "Don't you think that is unusual?"

Darius shrugs. "He likes you."

"It is strange and creepy."

"He is not always very tactful in his approach to women."

"That is for certain."

Darius wants to look at her, but also does not. He glances at her and back to the catalogue page. If he looks at her, he might not be able to say what he is going to say next.

"You should give him a chance."

"Maybe I will," Amelia says, her voice a little tight.

Her words are a stab to his heart. Darius stiffens his resolve.

"It is better this way," he thinks. "She might be the distraction Travis needs to get him to obsess less over that boat."

Darius nods, tapping the page as though he found what he is looking for. It is an inconsequential little item for a small enough price to pay for the ruse of coming in here to see her.

"I'll order one of these."

Amelia moves stiffly, leaning over the book and jotting the information down.

Her sudden close proximity is a heady perfume filling Darius's senses; her soft hair, the curve of her cheek, her lips.

He pushes down the urge to reach out and lay the slightest touch on her, afraid it would make her evaporate into thin air.

Amelia feels the heat of his proximity too.

"Is that everything?" she asks, straitening up when she is done. Amelia glances away. She can't look him in the eyes. She is afraid he will see something there she does not want to show him.

"Yes, thank you." Darius nods farewell and walks a little too quickly out of the store.

Amelia watches him go, regretting not saying anything.

"What would you say anyway?" she mutters. "That you would rather date him? How would you say that when he has no interest in you? You have no idea."

Two hours later Travis comes into the store.

Amelia looks up to see who came in. She feels startled by the sight of Travis and like a woman who has just cheated on her lover although he is not and she has not.

Travis takes the blush flushing her cheeks to have another meaning.

He ambles through the store, feeling his charms working, and making a pretense of perusing the items on a shelf.

"Hello Travis. How may I help you?" Amelia asks, approaching him and stopping a proper distance away. "Are you interested in purchasing that?"

He does not pick up on her businesslike tone and demeanor that has replaced her prior playfulness towards him and Darius when they saw her.

Feeling suddenly shy, Travis swallows, trying to find the courage he had a moment ago. It was false courage that carried him through that door, propelled by a certain fear.

He tries to look her in the eye and can't.

"I thought, maybe, you would like to have supper with me?" he manages.

Amelia's heart flutters and she looks away, stiffening.

"I don't know if I should be angry he has the nerve to ask or thrilled," she thinks.

"I hardly think my parents would approve," Amelia says.

Travis looks at his feet sheepishly.

"Yes, I guess they have good reason not to, since your father thinks I robbed his store."

He looks at her earnestly.

"Is there no way to convince him I am innocent?"

Amelia flushes. "I'm not so sure you are," she thinks.

"You are an adult," Travis says hopefully. "You should not need your parent's permission like a child."

A rush of defiance fills Amelia.

"He is right," she thinks. "They treat me like a child. I am a grown woman."

"All right," she says.

"What?" Travis is unsure of her meaning in his surprise. He was fully expecting, even preparing to argue against, a stern refusal.

"All right," Amelia says again. "I will have dinner with you. It might not be a good idea to let my father know. Not just yet."

Travis nods eagerly, willing to agree to anything.

***

With her father still very much against everything the young man is, Amelia's dinner date with Travis has to be kept a secret affair.

Making her excuses and promising to not be late, Amelia leaves her home and hurries down the road to meet Travis.

Travis walks with a spring in his step and a smile he cannot stop. His smile gets bigger when he sees her in the distance.

They meet under the street lamp at the entrance to the park. She smiles shyly and he feels like he will faint.

"You look beautiful," Travis says, making her blush.

He draws his arm away from his body, kinked at the elbow, offering his arm to her. She slips her hand into the hole it makes, delicately holding his arm as they begin walking down the road together, exchanging small talk while trying to think of something clever to say. The stars sparkle in the sky above and the moon casts its glow across the land so that it is bright for the late hour.

They do not reach the restaurant before a figure steps out of the shadows ahead of them.

The fat man.

"Good evening," Norman says, tipping his hat to Amelia. The gentlemanly gesture is ruined by the leer that accompanies it.

Something about the man puts her on edge. She can't identify what. It is a subtle feeling that makes her feel somehow dirtied by his presence.

Travis stiffens and Amelia feels him tense beside her, adding to her feeling of unease.

"Evening," Travis says, his tension and distrust coming through in his tone.

"Fine evening, isn't it?" Norman says. He looks towards the nearby restaurant. "You two kids wouldn't be going for dinner, would you? Does a young man like you even have the money to treat a lady to dinner?" He chuckles nastily. "I'm sure you have some other, uh, commitment requiring your money? Debts to be paid. Some commitments don't take to being ignored, even for a pretty young piece of ass."

Travis leans forward, glaring at him angrily.

Amelia pulls back on his arm to restrain him. She looks at the fat man in astonishment, sensing there is some unspoken message between them.

"A gentleman should always look after his commitments first, shouldn't he?" Norman continues. "You wouldn't want your business to affect that pretty tart on your arm, would you?"

He looks Amelia up and down, making his meaning very clear.

Travis opens his mouth to talk, a barrage of insults and threats on the tip of his tongue, but he isn't given the chance.

Amelia is pulling on his arm, trying to drag him away.

"Let's just go," she pleads.

"Yes, go on with your evening my little friend," Norman chuckles. "You know where to find me. Just don't blow too much of your wad on the lady." He turns and walks off into the darkness, laughing vulgarly.

Travis is shaking with anger, his eyes blazing, and his hands clenching and unclenching into fists as if he can't decide whether to pummel the man or tear him apart.

Amelia looks up at him with concern.

"Travis," she says timidly.

He looks down at her and visibly struggles to control his anger, to push it away.

"I'm sorry," he says, meaning both the unpleasant confrontation and his show of anger.

Amelia nods. "Let's go have dinner."

Travis gradually calms down over dinner, managing not to make it a completely awkward time, but Amelia can't help but pick up on the anxiety that clings to him the whole time.

With dinner finished, they are leaving the restaurant and Travis isn't ready to let the date end just yet.

"I have to think of something to keep this date going," he thinks. He tries to come up with ideas to put off taking her home as they walk towards her home, dismissing each one instantly. Then he comes up with an idea, wondering why he didn't think of it sooner.

He turns to her, pausing in the street.

"You need to come see her," Travis says excitedly, "the Gypsy Queen; you need to come see how far we have come along."

Amelia looks at him a little skeptically. It is dark and the idea of crawling around a boat in the dark is not very appealing to her.

"Come, please," he begs. "It will only take a few minutes. I'm dying for you to see her."

"All right, but I have to get home soon. I promised I would not be late," Amelia relents with an uncertain smile.

Travis beams with joy and leads the way.

The Gypsy Queen is dark when they get there, the light of the stars and moon casting a sallow illumination outlining her dark bulk, giving the impression she is looming over them larger than real life in the darkness.

Amelia looks up at the boat with a little trepidation, uncertain about making the climb up the ladder to the deck waiting above. For a moment, she wishes she can see what lies waiting above beyond the railing edge, as if some sinister creature might lay in wait.

Goosebumps break out on her skin despite the warm night and a chill shivers down her spine, making all of her flesh suddenly go cold.

"It's ok," Travis says, mistaking her hesitation, "it is not that long a climb. You can go first. Don't worry about falling, I won't let you."

"It's just a boat," Amelia tells herself. "You are not going to let a boat beat you, are you? Come on Amelia, you are stronger than that."

A small part of her is hoping Darius will be there. She blushes at the thought, feeling the burn of her betrayal.

"Don't be so foolish," she admonishes herself. "You are on a date with Travis. You can't be hoping to see another man."

With a swallow and a nervous glance up, Amelia starts the climb, Travis following behind. She feels a trepidation she cannot place the cause of.

"Am I really being scared of the dark? Of an old boat?" she thinks as she concentrates on going hand over hand and foot over foot up the ladder. "I should have made him go first. Just in case."

Amelia pushes away the urge to look down and make sure Travis really is following her up. She feels like she is entering the den of the beast.

"You really are quite ridiculous Amelia," she thinks. "Since when do you scare so easily?"

Amelia breaches the top to find that nothing waits for them above except an empty deck.

An almost empty deck.

In the middle of the deck a blanket is spread out with a couple of cushions to sit on, a covered basket, and a pair of glasses next to a nail bucket filled with melting ice and a bottle of white wine nestled in its icy bed. Beads of chilled perspiration wet the outside of the bucket, slowly growing until they slide down the side of the bucket to wet the deck. Candlesticks with unlit candles and unlit lamps wait to light the deck.

Reaching the deck, Travis is even more surprised than Amelia to see the nighttime picnic waiting for them.

"Darius," he thinks, "always the romantic. He must have thought we would come back here."

He lights one of the lanterns to give them light.

"Come, let me show you around," Travis says, taking Amelia by the hand, nervous and excited all at once. He drags her around like a proud little boy showing off his fort, showing her every detail, every room. His eyes shine as he tells her about their plans for the boat and how grand she will be as she gently coasts down the river with her cargo of wealthy gamblers winning and losing large piles of money while musicians play in the background and the stars shine in the sky above.

Amelia is duly impressed both by the beauty coming out in the rebuilt boat and how much work they have done. The last time she saw the Gypsy Queen, the boat was a hollowed out hulk of rotting worm eaten wood sagging into itself on the ground.

The tour finished, they settle themselves into the picnic on the deck. Travis lights the other lamp and the candles, pours the wine, and unwraps the basket to find it filled with fruit, little breads, and cakes. They talk, laugh, and snack until much later.

Finally, looking at the night sky with a regretful look and the unpleasant knowledge her father will be waiting up and furious about her late night, Amelia decides she has to go home.

"It is pretty late. You had better take me home."

Travis nods, wishing he doesn't have to, and leans forward to blow out the candles.

A sudden breeze gusts through, lifting Amelia's hair and puffing out the candles just as he leans in towards them; gone as abruptly as it came. Closing out the flames of the lanterns, Travis leads the way down the ladder to the ground below.

A crash comes from above just as Amelia's feet touch the ground.

They both look up.

"The wind must have knocked over the bucket," Travis says.

Travis walks Amelia home.

They stop on the sidewalk in front of Amelia's house.

"There is a light on. Are your parents waiting up?"

Amelia nods. "My father will be."

"He will be angry I kept you out so late?"

"Furious."

"You are a grown woman."

She nods, her eyes shining with defiance despite her chest pounding with the fear of the coming scene.

"I am not sure my parents are aware of that."

With a kiss and a regretful pause on the sidewalk in front of Amelia's house, Travis releases her and she runs up the walk to her home, the light inside testifying to the fact her father is indeed waiting up for her.

Travis watches from the shadows beyond the yard until the door closes behind her before he heads home to the Gypsy Queen.

Travis does not get far before he is stopped by a figure heading him off in the road.

It is not Norman this time. This man looks rough and rugged and has the charm of a wharf rat; lean and nasty. It is Walter, the loan shark they resorted to borrowing from to pay the union men's wages. This man is much more dangerous than Norman.

He doesn't waste time playing at pretend pleasantries.

"You are late on your payment," Walter says, standing stiffly in the road before him.

Travis starts sweating nervously. He instinctively looks over his shoulder, worried that somehow Amelia might be there to see.

"Your girlfriend is safely inside," Walter sneers.

"How did you find me here?"

"I went to your boat to see you and I saw you leaving. I followed you."

"I wish you didn't," Travis says, seeing the other man looking past him to Amelia's house with interest.

"You are late on your payment," Walter repeats.

"I've made all the others. You know I'm good for it."

"I know you are a couple of assholes in over your heads. You are not good for it or you would not have had to take the money from me in the first place."

"That's a pretty girlfriend you have," he says, looking past Travis again as if he might be able to catch a glimpse of her.

It makes Travis reflexively turn and look behind him too, as if Amelia might actually be there.

Walter makes his move.

The moment Travis starts turning away; Walter leaps forward, swinging. The large wool sock he held behind his back and out of sight swings in an arc, the heavy pair of wooden croquet balls stuffed inside the toe bulging and deadly, swinging for the back of Travis's head.

Travis sees the movement from the corner of his eye, instinctively ducking and putting an arm up to protect himself from the damaging blow, spinning around towards his attacker.

Catching the empty stretched part of the sock on his arm, the ball-laden sock's blow is deflected, the balls and sock wrapping around his forearm and striking it with bone numbing force.

Despite the pain, Travis pulls his arm back, trying to snatch the weapon out of Walter's grip, pulling him closer in the effort.

Walter comes at him, holding onto the sock and punching him with his free hand, forcing Travis to duck and cover himself with his arms against the blows.

Not an experienced fighter, Travis is at a disadvantage. He usually ducks and runs before trouble can find him. Since taking on the Gypsy Queen, he is learning a few new moves the hard way.

He spins around Walter, keeping his arms up to protect his head, forcing his attacker to follow him around, the ball-heavy sock still locking the pair together. He sticks a foot out, tripping Walter, but Walter is a better fighter, experienced in winning fights, and dances his feet, easily unhooking the tripped one from Travis's foot and keeping his balance.

Walter yanks viciously on the sock, pulling Travis off balance and simultaneously sending his other arm straight into Travis's stomach, twisting his body into it for maximum impact.

Travis doubles over with a grunt as the air is forced out of him. Knocking the wind out of him also knocks the fight out of him and Walter gives him a couple of extra punches to the head to drive the point home.

Travis is sitting on the ground with his arms wrapped around his head now, hoping only to shield his head from as much damage as possible.

Walter takes his sock back and pulls Travis's head up roughly by the hair, forcing him to look up at him.

"One week," he hisses. "Double the missed payment plus the next one or I'll pay a visit to that pretty girlfriend of yours and take what you owe me out of her."

He shoves Travis's head away roughly as he lets go of his hair and slinks off into the night.

Tears spring to Travis's eyes. Feeling sorry for himself, he lets them come and sits there in the middle of the road sobbing.

There is no one around to see anyway.

***

Darius is nestled in a bed of straw, light coming in the cracks between the slats of the old wood barn walls. He stretches stiffly, scratching himself in a few places the poking straw made itchy, and runs his fingers through his hair in an effort to both knock out the pieces of straw and straighten it into something he hopes is presentable.

Opening the barn door a crack, he looks out at the morning light, looking for any sign of the farmer. He slips out of the barn, avoiding the house and hoping to not be seen.

Darius first goes to the docks to see the Dock Master to pay him his bribe money.

The docks are busy, as always. Crowds of men working to unload and load cargo, transferring it from and to trucks parked on the docks. Hopeful men queue up, milling around in hope of getting work.

The Queen Rhiannon is there at the docks. Darius cannot help but stare at the ornate casino boat looking out of place amid the larger cargo barges. There is no activity at that one boat, making it more out of place amid the activity bustling around the barges.

Darius pulls his attention away from the boat and makes his way through the swarm of activity to the Dock Master's office. He glances at one man a few times; unsure if the man is watching him. It gives him an uneasy feeling.

Pausing outside the door, he pushes it open; half hoping the Dock Master is not there.

The Dock Master looks up at the sound of the door and, after a pause of a few heartbeats, a smile creases his lips. He gets up and comes to the counter to greet Darius.

"How are our two newest boat builders doing?" His tone is a little too happy, his smile a little too big, and his eyes unreadable.

"We are doing all right."

"What can I do for you?"

"I am here to pay our fees," Darius says, feeling the urge to call it what it is, a bribe.

Fishing in his pocket, he hands the money over.

Basil takes the offered money, laying it out on the counter one bill at a time as he counts it with a greedy glint in his eye.

His focus on the money, he does not look at Darius when he speaks.

"You have made amazing progress with that boat. It really is quite impressive."

Darius nods acknowledgement, his stomach tightening. "I have a feeling I know where this is going," he thinks.

Basil continues, seemingly unaware and proving his suspicion correct.

"You know, the price for holding your slip at the dock will be going up soon, now that the boat looks like she might actually someday touch the water again."

Darius stands stiffly watching him count the money. He does not know what to say.

"I hope the price doesn't go up too much," he thinks. "I don't know where we will get the extra money."

Finished counting, Basil retrieves his ledger from its place, opens it to the page bookmarked with a fine ribbon, and carefully notes the payment. He is a meticulous man in every way.

Just as carefully, he takes out the cash box, placing the money inside and putting it away. Then he places the ledger back in its place.

He looks at Darius with a businesslike smile.

"Thank you for your business. I look forward to seeing you again." He holds out his hand.

Fighting the flush that threatens to rise up his neck to his cheeks, Darius steps forward and awkwardly takes his hand and shakes it. Basil makes him uncomfortable.

Darius nods and Basil releases his hand.

"I'll be seeing you around," Basil says.

"See you," Darius says quickly and ducks out of the office back into the sunshine and busy docks. He walks quickly through the crowd, dodging men laden with goods.

It is a long walk to his next stop. Instead of taking the road, which most people take and might have offered the opportunity to hitch a ride, Darius opts for a less well-trod path. There is a path along the riverbank that some of the workers use to travel between the docks and the shipyard.

It is shorter, but a rougher trek. The ground is not even, winding up and down with the river and sometimes moving away from the river to work its way around larger trees and rocks. It is an ideal path for someone who may be hoping to avoid running into the authorities.

Darius just wants the feeling of solitude the path through the trees along the riverbank offers.

The solitude is imperfect.

As he walks along the rough path, Darius listens to the sounds of the trees; the leaves hissing as they rub against each other in the wind, insects buzzing, and birds chirruping.

He hears the crack of a snapping branch before he sees motion through the trees ahead.

Darius tenses, the wad of cash in his pocket suddenly bulging more and weighing his pocket down harder.

He walks on stiffly, hands balled into loose fists, his eyes forward and head high, hoping his stance is enough to make a would-be thief pass him by without giving him any trouble.

Soon he can hear the footsteps of the approaching men, still catching glimpses of them through the trees.

They come into view. They pass each other on the path, each moving over to make room for the other, tense and walking stiffly. The two men give him a curt nod, only one making steady eye contact while the other looks away to avoid his gaze. Darius nods back and they are past each other and moving on in opposite directions.

Some time passes before Darius relaxes, listening for the dull pounding of running feet on the dirt path, wary they might decide to come back for him.

Darius continues, alert for any sounds that don't belong. It is apparent that those two have other business, but that does not mean there are no thieves waiting on the path.

When Darius hears the snap of another branch some time later, he ducks off the path into the trees and hides to watch.

Seconds later, he hears the footsteps of another traveller.

A man dressed like a laborer comes into view. He stops, looking around and listening. Finally, he moves on. Darius hears his footsteps moving on up the path and then breaking into a jog, fading into the distance.

After he is sure it is clear, Darius steps back into the path.

"He could have been following me. I should have taken the road. I think he was one of the dockworkers. His face looks familiar. But, why would he be following me? Was he going to rob me? Does he know I have a pocket full of cash for the Shipbuilders' Union?"

Darius waits, listening for the man to turn around and come back. He feels uneasy at the man having such a head start.

"If he was following me he could be running to catch up to me because he lost me. When I get close to the shipyard, I will have to leave the path and enter cautiously. Try to spot him and see what he is doing. He could be waiting ahead at any point to jump me.

He could be one of the Dock Master's men, or one of the union men. Either way, I'm sure he was sent to keep an eye out on me. I had the feeling I was being watched at the docks and that man was milling around. I caught him looking at me a few times. I think he could be the same man."

Uncertainty swims in his gut. He could be wrong. The man might have been looking at someone or something else. It could be coincidence he is now travelling the same path to the shipyard. It might not even be the same man.

Darius starts walking again, alertly listening for any sounds. He makes it to the shipyard without encountering anyone else on the path.

As he approaches the end of the trees, he moves off the path, pushing his way with some difficulty through the denser brush. At the edge of the clearing that opens up into the shipyard, Darius stops to study the yard.

He sees no one watching the path. He can't even spot any man who could be the one who passed him on the path or the man from the docks.

"I am making myself crazy," he mutters.

Darius leaves the trees, making his way down the embankment to the shipyard.

The yard is not nearly as busy as the docks, but men still move purposely, going about their business building boats. The hulking skeletons of two large river barges in progress stick out barren and ugly from the sand while men work to bring them to life.

Head down, Darius walks across the yard to the union office building. A few men notice him and look up to see who the visitor is. Some watch with more interest than others.

Darius enters the building nervously. He pauses, looking around awkwardly, frozen until the receptionist notices him. The receptionist at the union office gives him a coldly polite nod, knowing his face now, and waves him on into her boss's office without so much as a greeting.

She turns her attention back to her typewriter before he breaks his paralysis and moves.

Darius goes down the hall, knocking nervously on the open doorframe and hesitatingly poking his head around the corner, revealing himself to the man inside.

Desmond is sitting at his desk reading papers from a file. He looks up at the knock, smiles a smile that is a shade less than friendly, and waves Darius in, closing the file on his desk as he does so.

"Come in," Desmond says with a wave that is all business. "Have a seat."

Darius enters the office nervously, looks blankly at the offered chair, and sits down, fidgeting. He nods a greeting.

"Good morning, sir."

"How is she coming?" Desmond asks politely. "That is too bad about the accident. I guess she will be sitting in dry dock for a lot longer now."

"Yes sir," Darius nods. He fishes in his pocket and pulls out the wad of bills and change, sliding the money across the desk top.

"Our union dues sir."

Desmond looks at the crumpled pile of money without moving to reach for it. He looks at Darius, reading him, judging him by what he will say next.

"I am curious," Desmond says casually, the stiffness of his posture belying that the question is anything but casual, "just what are your plans at this time for that old paddlewheel boat of yours?" He pauses. "If... when... you get her in the water?"

"We are going to turn it into a pleasure boat sir," Darius says. "A mini floating casino."

Desmond's eyes remain on him, the look steady as he considers this.

"That is a pretty big undertaking for a couple of young men like yourselves," he says at last. "Do you know what you are getting yourselves into?" His look says that he clearly does not think they do.

"A casino is a big business to get into, especially for a couple of inexperienced businessmen like yourselves."

"I think we will be able to manage sir," Darius says. "We just have to take our time; get the equipment used and fix it up."

"How do you plan to come up with the casino equipment?" Desmond asks. "The tables, roulette wheel, the machines. Even used they are very expensive." His tone and expression show his doubt that they can pull this off.

"Do you really know what you are getting into?" he asks doubtfully.

It is obvious to him that Darius is completely innocent of these matters.

"You are having a tough time of it now with the building materials, the men's wages, union dues, the Dock Master's fees..." He steeples his fingers thoughtfully, trying to bring to mind the list of things the young men would be coming up against.

Desmond gets to his feet as he continues talking, walking around the desk and motioning Darius to his feet, walking him to the door.

"The gaming world is a very small world. Tight. It is closed to outsiders, unless they come from a lot of money. Casinos have a lot more officials that have to be bribed than the docks do. There are the bureaucrats with the gaming commission, the liquor commission, and the food handling board. And those are just the government agencies. The casino workers have a union too and they are far more difficult to deal with than the Shipbuilders' Union. The food handing board is union too, but they are a weak union. And then there is the Barlow family. They own the casino businesses here. I think you gentlemen are biting off a whole lot more than you can chew."

The meeting is over. He has his money and cured his curiosity.

"Thank you Mr. Moloney," Darius says, shaking the union boss's hand as if he had just done him a favor. "We will keep it in mind."

Darius is leaving his office, Desmond staring at his departing back.

Desmond calls out one last parting shot to the retreating man. "Be careful. Casino owners don't like competition."

He watches the young man leave the building, thinking to himself how unfortunate this is. He shakes his head.

"I kind of liked Darius, although I find his partner Travis to be a bit of a wild card, reckless and foolish," he says regretfully.

Eugene comes out of his office, catching Desmond before he can return to his office.

"How are our two young boat builders doing?" he asks.

Desmond lets out a little chuckle.

"They are actually planning on turning that boat into a casino," he says.

Eugene's reaction shows on his face. This news clearly bothers him, leaving Desmond wondering why.

Desmond thinks about his question for a moment before speaking.

"The old man who originally owned the Gypsy Queen, Thaddeus Barlow, is he even still alive?"

30   The Good Old Games

It may be a strike of pure luck that brings Travis to the town hardware store on that particular day at that particular time.

As he is about to enter the store, he nods to the old man sitting on the bench out front. He has walked past the old man and nodded a greeting to him every time he has gone to the hardware store. Each time the old man seems oblivious, just looking up and down the street as if he is waiting for someone.

The old man is a fixture of the town. Every day, rain, shine, or snow, it doesn't matter, he spends his days sitting on the bench before the hardware store watching the town go by.

He has for as long as anyone can remember.

Different people bring him food. Old Mrs. Carberry brings him muffins and coffee Tuesday mornings. Mr. Harrow always has a spare sandwich in his lunch on Thursdays when he happens to stop in the hardware store at noon. The baker sits with him Fridays to share whatever is on sale that day, saying he needs a break from the hot kitchen. The waitress at the restaurant runs over with Monday's breakfast special, always a customer ordered it then left before it could be served.

The old man is always looked after and eats something every day.

While most people don't know the old man's name, they know him the moment they see him. Unkempt and wiry thin; his too big clothes hang off him as if he had suddenly dropped from a healthy weight in mere moments. His clothes need mending and his hair a good comb. He sits always with his hat in his hands watching the town go by and leaning forward eagerly now and then only to sink back in apparent disappointment.

It is also well known the old man is entirely senile, his mind lost years in the past, no one is sure how long.

He sits there every day waiting and watching for his love who was supposed to meet him all those years ago at the bench in front of the hardware store. His love who will never arrive to meet him.

But today is an unusual day.

For the first time when Travis walks past him and nods a greeting, the old man turns to look at him and nods back with a spark of recognition in his eyes.

The old man stares after Travis as the store door bangs shut behind him, the dim interior of the hardware store swallowing him up. He sits there staring at the door, waiting for something to happen.

As Travis is leaving the hardware store ten minutes later, he walks by the old man, not thinking anything unusual is about to happen.

Then the old man calls him back.

"Hey!" the old man calls gruffly, his voice weathered and unused to vocalizing.

Travis turns around in surprise, staring at the old man and wondering if he had called him or if he just imagined it.

The old man waves him over.

Travis comes back and stands before the old man seated on the bench.

The old man pats the bench for him to sit down so he does.

He stares into Travis's eyes, his eyes unusually bright and alert.

Travis finds it a little disconcerting.

"You are the one fixing that old boat aren't you?" the old man asks, although it seems more a statement of fact.

"Yes sir," Travis nods.

"I hear tell you're planning on making the Gypsy a casino again." The old man seems to be staring right through him now, looking at something far away, perhaps in a distance of time. He goes silent.

"She was the very first floating casino," the old man says.

Travis is surprised he is still on the topic; certain the old man had drifted off again into the void of his lost mind.

"She was a grand beauty, the Gypsy, in her day; filled with riches and rich folk, fancy music and fancy people, and money spilling out of pockets onto the tables. Her master, Mr. Thaddeus Barlow, prized her above all else, putting on lavish parties on board her and allowing only the best people to board her. He had her special made and had her guarded night and day.

Up and down the river she went with a grace no other had, outshining every other boat on the water, heads turning her way in awe of her dark beauty. In her glory days..."

The old man's voice trails off as he talks, looking into the past, degenerated now into barely intelligible mumbling to himself.

"...and her eyes, dark and luring; her beauty and grace, the deep sadness, not like my Josey who is so bright and alive."

He looks around suddenly, looking for someone.

"Josey, she'll be here any minute," he mutters.

He snaps out of it suddenly, turning to Travis, his eyes clear and intelligent with no trace of the fog of confusion that had filled them a heartbeat before.

"Do you know what happened to the old casino equipment the Gypsy originally carried?" His eyes are eager, a hint of knowing amusement.

Travis thinks about it. Equipment like that is very expensive. It's not likely to have just been tossed out. Most likely it was sold off decades before when she was decommissioned.

"Sold off probably," he says with a regretful shake of his head.

The old man chuckles, making Travis wonder what he is up to. Travis has a sudden uneasy urge to pull away when the old man leans in close.

"I know where it is," the old man whispers conspiratorially. He leans back, talking in a more normal tone again.

"I was given charge of it all those years ago. Mr. Barlow was intent that no part of the Gypsy would ever be used again. I worked for him, you see, one of his security men. He paid me to dispose of the equipment. It was to be smashed and burned.

But I knew the value of that equipment. It was worth more on the underground market than I made in a year, in three years. I had it hauled off instead with a little help and stored it away in a barn on my family's farm. I was going to haul it off someplace far away and sell it, but I got cold feet."

He lifts his feet off the ground one at a time, looking down at them as if physically feeling the pain of his feet freezing suddenly. His voice has been growing more distant again as he relives the past once again.

"I was afraid of what would happen if Mr. Barlow found out. Anyone with half a head of smarts knew to be scared shitless of that man." He shakes his head, chuckling at his own foolishness.

The old man turns to Travis with a sudden urgency in his eyes.

"It's still there," he whispers, "in the barn where I left it, untouched all these years. The farm is no longer worked, hasn't been in years since I got too old. Took it over when my father passed. My brothers had no interest in taking over the farm, wanted jobs in the city instead, bunch of fancy pants." He sounds bitter at this, something Travis has never imagined this dotty old man capable of.

He leans in towards Travis again, looking up at him, his once large frame shrunken with age, self-induced starvation, and his forever waiting motionlessly.

He puts a hand on Travis's leg, patting it in an old person gesture that often makes the young feel awkward and uncomfortable. Travis has the urge to leap away off the bench, pulling the old man's aged knobby and wrinkled hand off him. He makes himself stay motionless, allowing the old man who he had never heard utter more than an unintelligible word or two to talk.

"You can have it," the old man whispers, "all of it. It's all still there in the old barn."

Travis's mind reels with this, barely hearing as the old man rattles off directions to his old family farm.

"Can this be real?" he thinks incredulously. "Can the original equipment still exist, spirited away and hidden all these years? Would it even still be any good or would it be rotting like the abandoned boat?"

"How much?" Travis asks, afraid of the answer.

"I don't want anything for it," the old man says. "Just take it. It belongs to the Gypsy."

Excitement fills Travis.

He grabs the old man's hand in both of his; pumping it enthusiastically, thank yous pouring out of his mouth in his overwhelming gratitude.

"You have no idea just how much this means to me; how much it will help us if the equipment can be made useable again."

Thanking the old man repeatedly, Travis gets up eagerly, unable to hold himself back from searching out the farm and finding the casino equipment.

Travis turns and leaves with an elated spring in his step, his head in a cloud of euphoria.

A strange gleam comes into the old man's eyes as he watches the young man walk away. The light in his eyes goes out like a candle flame suddenly snuffed out and he returns to his usual vacant stare, droopy posture, and senseless rambling as he watches the town go by, waiting for his beloved who will never arrive.

"Coming soon, my Josey, coming soon," the old man mumbles.

***

Travis finds Darius at the lumberyard behind the store. Pausing at the entrance, Travis looks around nervously as he enters. He is not welcome there and might find one of the workers confronting him with the intention of giving him a beating for being on the property.

Amelia's father still has not forgiven him, convinced that Travis is the one who broke in and stole tools and other building supplies.

Travis can't hide his eagerness when he spots Darius.

"Darius!" Travis rushes to him.

Darius looks at him in surprise, his mouth open to ask what is going on.

"I have great news!" Travis says. He is almost giddy with it as he excitedly tells Travis about the old man in front of the hardware store and the equipment.

Darius listens skeptically. When Travis finishes and is staring at him eagerly for a reaction, he shakes his head.

"I don't believe it. It sounds too good to be true and that is never good," Darius says. "This is the same old codger who is crazy as crazy can be and sits night and day outside the hardware store?"

Travis nods, a flush of disappointment crossing his face and taking a little of his enthusiasm away.

"Are you sure you did not imagine the whole thing? That old man never talks. He can't hold a conversation."

"I didn't imagine it." Travis is defensive, but it still is not enough to completely kill his eagerness. "It's real. He told me how he was supposed to destroy everything that was on the Gypsy Queen, but he hid it instead."

Darius shakes his head regretfully, disappointed in Travis's gullibility.

"Even if he did talk, if he did tell you this, the old man is stir crazy out of his mind. I can't believe you believed anything he said."

"He was lucid, I'm telling you. I believe him. We just have to find the barn," Travis says. "We've got it made now. We didn't know how we would come up with the equipment. We thought we would have to run her with just one table, getting more one at a time. But now we've got it all just being given to us free and clear!"

Darius looks at him doubtfully.

"Free. That should tell you something. Nobody gives away anything for free. Even if it is there, it can't be in good shape after all these years. Look at the boat. It was rotting to nothing."

"We can fix it up, just like the Queen. Just think," Travis blinks at him eagerly, "the original equipment!"

Darius sighs.

"All right. We will go take a look," Darius reluctantly agrees.

"We are not renting a wagon just yet," Darius says in response to Travis's excited eagerness.

Travis deflates a little.

"We will go take a look first," Darius says, "see if the barn is even there. See how bad the equipment is, if it even exists. Then we will figure out where to go from there."

Travis practically dances in his eagerness.

"Let's go. This way." He starts leading the way.

They go off on foot, walking and hitchhiking the long distance in search of the old barn.

Darius is well past the point of being ready to give up the search when Travis spots the barn through the trees. With an eager yelp, Travis is off and running towards the wooden wall he got a brief glimpse of through the trees.

Darius follows at a walk, a feeling of uneasiness descending on him for no apparent reason.

The barn has a long abandoned feeling to it. The paint has long ago cracked and mostly flaked off the outside, leaving the bare wood to the mercy of the elements. There is a sag to the roof and the whole structure leans a bit towards one side.

Darius looks at it uncertainly, hoping it doesn't cave in on them.

The barn doors are sagging on their hinges and it takes both of them to lift and swing one open wide enough to slip inside. A hole in the roof above, together with windows clouded with decades of dirt, lets enough light filter in so they can see.

Darius looks up. The hole to the sky above is not immediately visible. A second floor where bales of straw are stored acts as a secondary roof; blocking out the rain and sun from gaining direct access to the floor below.

They stand in the entrance staring, dumbfounded.

Just as the old man had said, the old casino equipment is still there, untouched and filled with an old charm that the newer machines don't have still visible even beneath the decades of dust.

They move forward at last, looking the equipment over, game tables and a roulette wheel, one-armed bandits, and a moveable bar. It is covered in dust and cobwebs but otherwise seems untouched.

The conditions in the barn seem to have protected it. The straw absorbing the musty damp before the hardwood could, preserving the equipment in mint condition.

A fat old barn cat with an odd voice jumps down from his perch, startling them. Ignoring them, the cat digs his claws into a squealing flailing rat it landed on and carries it off with an air of superiority. The well-fed animal apparently has also served to keep the rodents from chewing on the casino tables and games.

Darius stares around him in disbelief. Travis looks around in excitement.

"We aren't ready to start hauling it to the boat yet," Darius says. "It needs more work before we can start filling it up with tables."

"We can work on the tables here," Travis says, carefully rubbing the thick layer of dust off a spot on one machine to reveal the dull gleam of wood beneath. In his mind's eye, the wood gleams with an enticing lustrous warmth.

Darius nods. "It will take a lot of work. We will have to clean and polish each table slowly and carefully, restoring them to their original glamour. We might even have to strip some of the machines down and oil them to make them work."

"Let's do it." Travis's eyes are gleaming with an eager look that always makes Darius a little nervous.

31   Those Eyes

Between finishing their day jobs and starting their night jobs Travis and Darius are catching what sleep they can. They are still working multiple jobs each to pay the Shipbuilders' Union and the Dock Master and working on the Gypsy Queen in what little time they have left.

Travis is dreaming of the glamour and glory of the Gypsy Queen as she will be when they finish fixing her up. Wealthy men and women in well-tailored clothes schmooze and adore him, each vying for a brief moment of his attention. The young ladies follow him with their eyes, enamoured and begging his attention.

The Gypsy Queen glides along the river elegantly, bright lights shining off the luster of her polished wood. The music of the band playing in the background is slowly infiltrated by an annoying bleating noise. He winces at the racket, trying to figure out what it could be. Eventually it creeps into his dream enough, waking him.

Travis looks around groggily, his mind filled with fuzziness. The sound is still there. It takes a long moment to wake up enough to realize it is a car horn blaring outside the boat.

Darius's dream is less happy. The Gypsy Queen moves across the river's surface, sliding silently on the water. Strangely, the paddle wheel on the back is turning over, propelling the boat forward, the water churning beneath it, being carried up on the wheel's paddle blades and raining back down to the river, absolutely silently.

Her lights are muted and the polished wood dull. The raucous laughter of the wealthy gamblers sounds wrong, somehow hollow, threatening, and far away. The music from the band trickles from the deck, muted and tinny.

He stares around him at the over-crowded boat, feeling trapped. He can't move in the crowd. He needs to get out of there, to escape.

Then he sees them.

The eyes.

Dark and sensual, they flash at him. The eyes are all he can see of the woman's face as she moves easily through the crowd, eyes fixed on him, hidden to him by the people crowding the room as she slips behind them and reappears again, circling him, moving closer.

Darius cannot take his eyes off those eyes, searching for them when she vanishes behind an over-perfumed over-dressed woman. He is unable to tear his eyes away when those eyes appear again, fixed on him as she passes out of sight again behind a handlebar mustached man.

Those eyes fill him with an unpleasant feeling; a mix of excitement and fear, desperation and the ill feeling of doom.

Someone is talking to him.

Darius tries to tear his eyes away, unable to fight the urge to find those eyes in the crowd again. He has to force himself to look at the powdered white-haired woman talking to him, only managing to by convincing himself he can look behind her for those mesmerizing eyes.

The woman's mouth opens and closes, jaw clapping and wrinkled lips yapping at him, her words coming to him unintelligible and garbled.

And then they turn into an annoying bleating.

"Beep beeeeep beeeeeep blaaaaat beeep," she says and he wonders what is wrong with this woman. Why is she making that noise?

He wants to look away, to find the eyes.

Travis shakes him awake, and Darius wakes with a start, wondering why the woman's bleating is still in his head as he blinks his eyes and slowly realizes he had been dreaming.

"I'm awake aren't I?" he asks.

"Yeah, get up," Travis mutters.

"Why is that woman still making that noise?"

"It's a car horse, wake up," Travis says.

Getting stiffly to his feet, Darius follows him out to the deck where they look over the railing.

On the ground below a man is standing beside a car, the driver's door open, and is leaning in, pressing on the horn. The incessant bleating finally stops when he spots them and he waves at them to come down.

"What the hell," Travis mutters. He waves the visitor to come up.

The visitor just keeps waving them to come down.

Darius and Travis exchange a look.

Unhappily, they climb down the ladder to the ground below, their visitor apparently unwilling to come up to meet them.

Desmond waits below next to his car for them to climb down.

"Good evening gentlemen," Desmond says as they approach.

Travis looks at him moodily. He wants only to be still sleeping right now.

"Good evening sir," Darius says, a little relieved to have been woken from his dream despite his exhaustion. "I take it this is not a pleasure visit?"

"No it is not," Desmond says. "Although, it might be a pleasure for you. I have good news for you."

"We don't have to keep bribing the union?" Travis asks testily.

Desmond ignores the rudeness of the comment.

"As you may be aware if you have been keeping up on the news, there has been a downturn in ship building in recent months, with the poor economy and everything. Bad things all around," he shakes his head, tsk tsking about the state of the economy. "A number of contracts have been cancelled in the last few weeks and a lot of men have found themselves suddenly out of work."

"How is this good news for us?" Darius asks, suspicious that he knows what the man is getting at. The question is how bad will it be.

"Faced with the choice between a hungry family and an old cursed boat, some of the men chose to work," Desmond continues.

He looks at the two men as if expecting them to show gratitude. He ignores their lack of it and continues.

"It won't be a full crew, but I have men ready and willing to show up tomorrow to work on this boat of yours. You, gentlemen, are back on track."

Darius holds in his breath of relief, not wanting it to be obvious. This is better than he was imagining as Desmond kept talking. He thought the man was going to force a full crew plus more, maybe even two or three full crews of men on them. They can't pay one crew right now.

His stomach is still a tight knot of dread, "When we can't pay..." He drops the unpleasant thought unfinished.

"They will be here first thing in the morning," Desmond says as he gets in the car, not giving them a chance to respond. He turns his car around and drives away.

"Damn!" Travis swears after him, rubbing a frustrated hand on his head.

Weary, Darius just turns around and climbs back up the ladder, hoping to get one more hour of sleep before going to his night job.

An hour and a half later, Darius is on his way to his night job while Travis is on his way to somewhere else.

Walking through town, Darius recognizes the approaching man instantly and stiffens, watching him warily.

It is the loan shark Walter Cuthburt. They are still behind in their payments to everyone, struggling from day to day with too much debt and not enough income.

Walter stops in front of him, looking too casual; working too hard to look casual in order to seem superior to the man he is confronting.

"Hey there," Walter says.

"Hello Walter," Darius says, trying to move past him.

Walter moves to block his path, making him stop. Darius looks at Walter impatiently.

"I saw your buddy the other day," Walter says as if it is entirely unimportant. "You might want to remind him that I promised to pay a little visit to that girlfriend of his if, you know, you two don't catch up on your payments to me."

With that, Walter winks at him and slinks off, leaving Darius to digest this.

Darius stares hard after him, his hands clenching into fists. He feels the urge to follow him and shake him. Instead, he goes on his way, heading for work.

***

The next morning Travis is arriving back at the Gypsy Queen, finished working for the night and with little time to spare before heading to his day job. As he is approaching the boat, he looks up in surprise to see a car parked by the boat.

It is too nice to belong to one of the work crew.

Eugene is standing leaning against the car, waiting. The old man looks up as he approaches. His old eyes do not miss a thing, taking in the exhausted slouch and the grainy eyes, the lines that were not there before at the corners of Travis's eyes and the dark circles beneath them.

"Come on up," Travis offers grudgingly, walking past him towards the boat. If he stops moving now, he is afraid he won't be able to make it up the ladder.

Eugene shakes his head, eying the boat warily, making it clear he refuses to set foot on her.

He looks at Travis levelly, his eyes haunted.

"Abandon her," Eugene warns. "Burn her to the ground."

Travis stares at him in shock, shaking his head as if he had just been asked to brutally butcher his beloved.

"If you do insist on putting her in the water," Eugene sighs heavily as if the weight of the world hangs in his words, "at least do one thing for me… for you."

His eyes implore Travis.

"What?" Travis asks.

"Rename her and make her anything but a casino boat. Malcolm Barlow will not take kindly to the competition. If you make her a casino boat, you will have trouble from him. You can be sure of that."

His look suggests something more than Malcolm making them suffer is weighing on his mind. It is a warning, not a threat.

Travis sees fear in the union CEO's eyes.

Eugene turns, his shoulders slumped with the tremendous emotional weight he carries, and gets back in his car.

Leaning out the window, he repeats his warning,

"You have been warned. Destroy the Gypsy Queen. Abandon her."

He turns the car around and drives away, pausing for one last look back, a haunted look that leaves Travis wondering and sends a cold chill down his spine.

Shaking it off, Travis once again sees only the glory and glamour of the casino boat. The union boss's words only reinforce his dreams as he fantasizes about the richly dressed people greeting him as someone important. Money flashing and falling into his lap, the ringing and clinking of coins and game chips singing in the air, as the melody of the band plays in the background to the muted voices and laughter of the rich players.

A dark haired dark eyed beauty approaches him from across the room. There is a natural sensuality to her smooth movements. Her eyes lock on his as she approaches and he is powerless to pull his eyes away. It is all he will remember seeing of her. Those eyes.

The muted voices suddenly sound like harsh whispers and the music becomes tinny and hollow with a sinister edge. The sound of coins and chips becomes menacing and he closes his eyes to the image, shaking it all off with a nervous laugh.

Darius arrives at the boat just then. His expression turns grim the moment he sees Travis.

"I ran into Walter," Darius says. "He was waiting for me."

Travis's face pales a little.

"You did not tell me he threatened to hurt Amelia," Darius says, anger making his voice hard. "Was she with you when he threatened her?"

"No," Travis says quickly, worried that Walter had approached one of them again. That means she is in even more danger of Walter following through on his threat.

"We had better find some money and fast or your girlfriend is going to suffer the consequences," Darius says gravely.

32   Strange Things

Travis and Darius are sleeping curled up on the floor in their respective corners of the boat, each wrapped in a worn blanket, when the sound of vehicle engines and doors disturbs the morning quiet.

Groaning, Darius stretches stiffly and gets up, moving like an old man, his joints and back ruined with stiffness from too much work and not enough sleep on a hard floor.

Travis shifts, turning on the hard floor, and trying to remain sleeping.

Voices outside the boat and more doors slamming disturb his attempt.

He blinks his eyes, rubbing them and unable to get rid of the dry itch of exhaustion. He gets wearily to his feet, stiff and bent over, and tries to stretch and crack the stiffness from his back.

The movement reveals the stark reality of the weight he has lost since their endeavor with the Gypsy Queen began, his frame gaunt and his clothes hanging off it.

"They are here."

Travis and Darius wearily make their way down. They nod to the union men on their way past them. Some of them ignore them, a few nod back. The foreman, Herman, sneers.

"Let's get to work," Herman orders.

***

Hammers are pounding and saws cutting. The Gypsy Queen is filled with the heady odor of freshly cut lumber.

With the union men back on the job, the rebuilding of the Gypsy Queen is once again in full swing. She is progressing quickly in spite of the problems that plague her. The hull is mostly complete and they have turned their focus to the inside and deck.

Some of the crew are standing around outside the boat. A sleek black car has joined the work trucks. Desmond is facing off against the work crew.

"I don't get how we can be expected to build this thing without plans," the Foreman, Herman, complains.

"You're a smart fellow, you'll figure it out," Desmond says.

Herman shakes his head.

"We need blueprints, something. The hull is one thing. We built that following the curve of the old rotted wood. But the insides are another matter. We can't do any more work without the blueprints."

"I doubt these guys even know what a blueprint is," one of the workers says.

"Fine," Desmond sighs. "I'll see what I can do. This is a rebuild. The original plans should still be on file. Sit tight. You are getting paid whether you can work or not. I'll be back."

"Break time," one of the men chirps, getting a few chuckles from the others.

Desmond gets in his car and drives back to the shipyard.

Back at the shipyard, Desmond goes to the shipbuilding office next door to the Shipbuilders' Union. He goes down the hall to the basement stairs. The old files are stored in the basement.

Descending the stairs to the darkness, Desmond gropes for the light at the bottom of the stairs. Finding it, he snaps it on and the lights flicker to life to reveal a long hallway with ceiling lights at regularly spaced intervals doing a poor job of pushing the darkness back. Shadows cling to the lower walls between the lights.

Following the hallway, he passes a few doors, stopping at a door marked storage. The door is not locked and he opens it to reveal little in the dark room.

Sliding his hand along the wall inside, Desmond finds the switch and turns it on.

The basement room is large, dusty, and poorly lit, more resembling a tomb than storage. Rows of tall shelving containing dusty crates fill the room, leaving little room between them.

Against the wall by the light switch is a rectangular cabinet reaching the height of his shoulders and twice as long. It looks like a filing cabinet with oddly small drawers. Each drawer has a handle with a holder for a card the size of a business card. Each is labelled with a code revealing the contents of the drawer.

Desmond scans the drawer labels, finding what he is looking for, and opens it. The drawer is filled with three by five-inch index cards, sized just right for the height and width of the drawers. He flips through the cards, disturbing the dust coating their top edges. Not finding what he is looking for, he closes the drawer and moves on to another.

The fourth drawer has the card he wants, revealing the shelf location of the files he is looking for.

He wanders up and down the aisles until he finds it and pulls the crate out, scraping dust from the shelf ledge as he pulls it out. Wiping some of the dust off the lid and opening it, he carefully rifles through the contents.

Picking up an item, Desmond looks at it.

"Curious." He puts it back and turns his attention to the large rolls of papers. Unrolling them one at a time, he inspects them, re-rolls them, and sets them aside in one of two piles.

When he runs out of rolls, Desmond puts one pile back in the box and returns the box to its dusty shelf.

Desmond picks up the rest of the rolls from the floor and carries them out, turning off the light and closing the door as he exits.

***

"This is a waste of our time," one of the work crew waiting outside the Gypsy Queen complains. The hammers are now silent and they are all sitting around in the grass waiting for the union boss to return, hopefully with plans for the boat.

"Would you rather be wasting your time not getting paid?" Herman gives him a hard look. "Someone else could be sitting there instead of you."

The complainer looks away sulkily, not wanting to push his luck. There are other men at the shipyard who were sent home. There isn't enough work to go around. They have taken to drawing straws to see who works and who does not.

A sleek dark car is approaching on the road.

"Finally," Herman mutters, getting to his feet and watching the car approach.

The car pulls up and stops. Desmond gets out and nods to them, walking around to the trunk, and opens it, pulling out the large paper rolls.

The men gather around the trunk, suddenly interested. Talk has spread about the famed Gypsy Queen. Mostly rumor and hearsay, but the richness of her beauty lives on in the stories.

Desmond's eyes are lit up as the men crowd around him.

"These are the only copies. Look after them. I want them back in good condition," Desmond warns them.

"Seeing this old girl restored will be something to behold," Desmond says. "Old Thaddeus Barlow was obsessed with this boat. When it came to designing her, he commissioned the best boat builders and casino equipment designers in the world. Artists too."

He looks around at the men, lowering his voice.

"I heard a rumor once that Thaddeus Barlow commissioned them to build the most breathtakingly beautiful casino paddlewheel boat that would ever grace the rivers. No expense spared. With that in mind, they came up with a sternwheeler steam boat with an elegance surpassing any other ever found on the water. Their vision was inspired by a woman who worked for the old man."

"That must have been some woman," one of the men laughs, imaging one of the casino resort dancers in their skimpy costumes over-decorated in garish oversized feathers and bangles, and little else.

Desmond looks at him.

"You boys just keep to the plans. You will see what I mean."

A greedy glint shines in his eyes and a small smirk plays at the corners of his mouth.

"There is no way these guys are going to come up with the money to rebuild this heap," one of the men pipes up. "But I am curious to see what she looks like."

"These guys are determined and desperate. They will surprise you, but in the end they will have to abandon her unfinished," another says.

"What happens to her then?" a third asks.

Desmond looks around at them.

"That depends on how far you get. She could be worth a lot of money. The union might just lay claim to her to cover part of their debts and sell her at auction."

His thoughts turn to his plan. It came out of nowhere on the drive back here. If old Thaddeus Barlow is alive, he would probably pay handsomely to possess her once again. If not, his son Malcolm will probably do the same.

Either way, there is a lot of value in this boat if they finish rebuilding her.

"Keep me up to date on your progress," he dismisses the men, waving them off to work. They take the plans to go lay them out and start working.

Desmond turns to leave and pauses, waving the foreman to follow.

They stop at the driver's door.

"I want you to push these guys. Only the best. As much as you can. Where you can't, you come and see me and I will make sure you have what you need. She will be worthless if they go cheap on her. I want this boat to be as valuable as the day she touched the water for the first time."

Herman nods understanding.

"Keep this to yourself." Desmond gets in his car and drives away.

Herman turns back, walking to the boat. His lips form an angry line at the sound of arguing.

Walking around to the other side of the boat, he stops to watch three men standing around, two of them staring each other down angrily.

"You took it," the first man accuses.

"I did not. You just can't keep track of your tools," the second man counters.

The third is just bearing witness to the argument.

Herman sighs in exasperation.

"What is going on?"

The three men look at him.

The first one points. "He took my hammer."

"I didn't touch your damned hammer."

"How do you know he took your hammer?" Herman asks.

"I had it in my hand. I put it down right there next to the nail bucket to fill my nail pouch. After Mr. Moloney brought the plans, we started collecting our tools. When I reached to pick up the hammer it was gone."

"I didn't touch your damned hammer," the second man repeats defensively.

The offended just glares at him.

"How do you know he took it?" Herman repeats.

"He was the only one nearby," he says angrily.

Herman looks to the third man. "Did you see anything? Did you see anyone touch the hammer?"

"No sir, but I was looking right at him. He was gathering the markers and stuff. He dropped the level and cracked it. Look." He points to the damaged level. "I did not see him go near him or touch his hammer."

Herman scratches his head, looking around. "The hammer has to be around here somewhere." He starts moving things around and stops.

"How do you know which is your hammer?"

"It has a notch just below the claw; about a quarter inch down."

Herman kneels down, coming up holding something. He holds it up for all to see, the notch just below the claw visible to all.

"You didn't put it where you thought you did."

The hammer man looks shocked and confused. He looks down at where he could swear he had set it down. "But…but I…"

He shakes his head and steps forward sheepishly to take the hammer. Giving the other two a suspicious glare, he slinks off to join the crew on the deck of the boat.

Herman looks at the remaining two men hard.

"You had better not be playing games." He turns away to join the others on the boat.

The observer looks at the accused with a smile over his co-worker's vindication. The accused does not smile. He looks at where the hammer man says he left the hammer then at where Herman found it.

"I swear he put it down there too," he says.

The observer's smile falters.

***

"Okay gents, it's time to call it a day," Herman calls out two hours later, walking down the length inside the paddlewheel's curved hull. Half the lower level floor has been put in, raising it above the curved hull.

"Time to clean it up and pack it up."

Men nod as they go by, collecting their tools to clean up the job site and climbing down from the boat.

Herman enters the first room to inspect the progress. Satisfied, he nods and moves on to the next. When he reaches the final lower level room he stops and stares at the wall. The boards are not straight.

"Were they drunk when they nailed them on?" he complains. Walking forward angrily to take a better look, he stops and stares, realizing why the boards look off. Some sit straight, others lean one way or the other. Some are not even touching the wall.

"What the hell? They aren't even nailed down. They should have been finished this section."

Herman approaches the wall, testing the looseness of some of the boards. Something makes a noise under his work boot and he looks down.

Nails litter the floor.

He shakes his head.

"Sloppy."

Annoyed, he goes to the toolbox and grabs a hammer. Returning to the wall, Herman begins angrily hammering the nails in, straightening and nailing the boards in place.

***

Darius is walking wearily up the road in the deepening dusk. He stiffens at the sound of boots scuffing the road behind him, the sound changing with the pace of the steps.

He turns to see Travis jogging to catch up and stops to wait for him. Travis's posture is sagging and his booted feet hit the road clumsily with exhaustion, arms flailing more than they should for a determined run.

Travis's head rolls a little as he slows and stops when he catches up, panting from the run.

They walk on together, their boots occasionally wearily scuffing on the road and kicking up dust.

"So, we have union men again," Darius says dispiritedly, "just when we looked to be getting caught up on our debt payments."

"We do," Travis says, his voice a little too chipper for Darius.

"You aren't happy about it, are you?" He looks at Travis for a response.

Travis just shrugs as they walk.

"There is no way we can pay them," Darius continues. "Walter already threatened Amelia because we are behind on his payments. You didn't even tell me about that. Were you planning to?"

"I thought I would get it sorted out," Travis says.

"We can't keep this up. You know we are going to have to give it up sooner or later. We will never get that boat in the water. It's better that we cut our losses now, before someone gets hurt."

The implication hangs heavily between them. Before someone innocent gets hurt.

"You mean before Amelia gets hurt," Travis says. "I won't let that happen."

"I don't think you can stop it."

Travis stops walking, turns, and looks at him hard. Darius stops too.

"I'm not giving up on her."

"Amelia or the boat? It's just a boat, a ruined salvage left to rot."

"She has come a long way. We have come so far in rebuilding her."

"We have a long way to go too and no way to pay for it."

"We will find a way." Travis walks on, determined.

With a regretful shake of his head, Darius follows.

"I should have stopped this before it started," he mutters.

The work crew is just packing up for the day when they reach the Gypsy Queen.

Travis and Darius nod to them. Some don't acknowledge them. A few give them uneasy nods.

"You don't actually sleep in there, do you?" one of them asks as he picks up his lunch kit and tools, walking past them. His expression is grim and his eyes hold a strange look.

Darius turns to look at him, thinking the exchange odd.

"What was that about?" Travis says. He shrugs it off and climbs the ladder to the deck. The sound of hammering can still be heard inside.

"Someone is working late."

"They had better not be expecting us to pay overtime."

They enter the hull to investigate.

"Hello," Darius calls out. "Everybody else is leaving."

"It's time for you to go home," Travis says loudly.

They follow the sound of hammering and find the foreman, not recognizing him with his back to them.

"The day is over buddy," Travis says to the man standing with his back to them hammering away. "We aren't paying you guys overtime."

Herman turns to look at them, his face an angry mask.

"Don't worry, you aren't being charged overtime for this. Bloody guys should have had this done. Sat around most of the day doing nothing, and then when they can finally work they can't even nail the damned boards on properly. I won't leave until it is done."

Darius retrieves a hammer from their tool box and goes to stand a few feet from Herman. He starts hammering nails in.

Herman looks at him and returns to the job of nailing the boards down.

Travis watches them for a moment, shrugs, and gets another hammer. He joins them, their three hammers pounding nails into wood reverberating through the boat.

When they finish nailing the last board on, Herman gives them a nod.

"Thanks," he says dryly. He is not a man accustomed to thanking others, or having a reason to thank them.

"Thank you," Darius says.

He watches the foreman gather his few tools.

"Say, how about you have a drink with us," Darius says.

Travis shoots him an unimpressed look.

"Maybe another time," Herman says, heading out and climbing down from the boat.

"What are you doing?" Travis hisses at Darius.

"Just trying to be on good terms," Darius says. "It can't hurt."

Travis shakes his head. "Maybe, but he is still the enemy."

"Shut up and go to sleep," Darius says good-naturedly, his voice rough with exhaustion.

***

The next morning the foreman is on site before any of his men arrive.

Travis and Darius come out bleary eyed and fumble their way down the ladder.

Darius spots Herman sitting on the hood of his truck and nods to him.

Herman just watches them, taking in the obvious signs of strain and exhaustion, and how their clothes hang off them in a way they did not the first time he saw them.

Travis is oblivious and walks past him.

"Hey," Herman calls.

Darius stops and looks at him.

"What have you guys been eating?"

"What we manage," Darius says, trying to be elusive.

Herman waves them over.

Travis does not hear, walking on.

"Travis," Darius says sharply, getting his attention.

Travis stops and looks back, looking startled to see the foreman sitting there waving them over.

They approach reluctantly, suspicious of his motives.

Herman's arm snaps out twice in quick succession, tossing something at each of them.

Darius reacts instinctively, snatching it from the air and almost missing.

Travis's first instinct is to duck, but he manages to catch his too.

They both look down to find a fat wrapped sandwich.

Herman shrugs.

"The wife made them."

They both nod their appreciation.

"Thanks."

Herman nods back and they start the trek down the road to work, waiting until they have put the foreman behind them and are out of his sight before they hungrily tear the wrapping open and wolf down the sandwiches while they walk.

Herman watches them go and gives his head a slow shake.

"It's a rough spot the bosses put those two in."

He can't help it.

"Travis does not seem a man worth the bother, but Darius seems like a pretty decent guy."

He waits for his crew to start showing up. When most of them have arrived, he rounds them up, waving them to come over to talk.

"Come here guys. Over here."

Herman gives them a serious look.

"I looked over the site after you were all done and I was disgusted by what I saw. Down in the hull, in one room the boards were all loose and the nails tossed all over the floor. You had plenty of time to get that done and clean it up."

Some of the men are staring at him expressionlessly. The few who were working that section are looking confused.

He singles them out, staring them down.

"That was some damned sloppy work and I won't have it on my job site."

"But, we didn't…"

"We nailed all those boards in…"

He silences them with a look, his eyes hard and the set of his mouth a clear warning to shut up.

"I had to nail them all down and clean up your mess before I left. If it happens again you will not be back on my site."

They look at him unhappily.

"Now get to work," Herman growls.

They all turn and start working their way to their respective workstations. The two guilty men give him insolent looks, muttering under their breaths.

Herman turns his attention to the blueprints for the boat. He is studying them when he hears the men calling him from inside the boat.

With a sigh, he leaves the plans and makes his way up the ladder and down into the hull.

"What is the problem?" Herman asks, judging there to be some issue from the tone of their voices.

The men are huddled around the opening to the area he had finished hammering together the night before.

They move back, clearing the scene when he gets there.

He steps forward and stops, standing there staring slack jawed at the scene before him.

The two men he called out for not doing the job are smirking.

He gives them each a cold hard glare.

"You did this."

"No sir, it was like this when we came down here."

"It was sir," one of the others confirms.

"Son of a bitch," Herman mutters, his scowl hardening.

Those same boards he had hammered in himself with the help of Travis and Darius are sitting just as he had found them the day before, loose, not hammered down, the nails littering the floor.

****

The union crew have been back to work for a couple of weeks. Darius returns to the boat after work, stopping in the road to stare at it from a distance. Framework has gone up for another two floors added to the structure on deck.

"What the hell? We never discussed that."

Seeing the workers getting ready to leave, he breaks into an exhausted jog, managing to push it to a run, and arrives out of breath. He waves down Herman.

Herman looks at him curiously.

Too out of breath to talk at first, Darius can only wave nonsensically at the boat.

He finally manages to gasp the words out.

"What are you doing?" He keeps pointing in shock at the added framework. "Why are you adding floors?"

Herman nods, putting up a hand to motion him to wait.

Pulling out the blueprints, he spreads them out to show Darius.

"We got Mr. Moloney to pull the original blueprints."

Herman shrugs at Darius's unhappy look.

"We needed something to work by. We were working blind. Besides, you want her to be rebuilt to what she was, don't you?"

Darius is shaking his head in disbelief.

"Nobody told us about this," Darius mutters. "Nobody said a word. And, no, we are good with it without the extra floors. We don't need them."

Inside he is feeling the reality of the extra cost two more floors will add on like a physical assault inside him. They can't possibly manage it. He feels sick with it.

"Take it down," Darius says. "We don't want the extra floors."

"You want her to realize her full potential, don't you?" Herman says. He looks at Darius levelly. "At the very least, if you do have to give up and sell her, you will get a lot more for her if we stick to the original blueprints."

He pauses.

"Mr. Moloney thought it best we stick to the blueprints to the letter. Don't worry, we can keep the supplies coming. You won't have to worry about that."

His words are a distant buzz in Darius's ears. The world suddenly seems very far away. He looks at Herman, hearing him but the words feeling unreal. He feels like he is going to faint.

Herman is looking at him with concern.

"Are you okay?" Herman asks. "You don't look so good."

All Darius can manage is to wave him off and stumble off towards the boat.

Herman watches him struggle to climb the ladder.

"You are okay with this, right?" he calls to Darius.

Darius waves him off, hearing the buzzing of his voice but not the words.

"I will take that as a yes," Herman calls to him.

With a shake of his head, Herman rolls up the blueprints and gets in his truck, driving for home.

Darius reaches the deck and stands there looking up at the framework towering above him, his head swimming with dizziness. He has to reach out to grab something for support, holding onto the rail.

He does not know how long he stood there.

Travis comes up the ladder, staring in shock.

"What is all this?" he asks, staring up at the framework above.

"They found the original plans," Darius says dully. "Apparently it has two more stories. They didn't tell us. I think they are working on their own objective."

Travis just stares, his expression a mix of surprise, horror, and delight.

"They found the plans? So she will be exactly what she was before?"

"Apparently," Darius says.

***

Over the following weeks, strange things keep happening to the workers, but with little work available, they have no choice if they want to be able to put food on the table for their families.

Tools and materials mysteriously vanish, appear, or are moved. Boards that were hammered in are found loose, their nails missing or on the floor.

Unexplained accidents happen.

The energy inside the Gypsy Queen is becoming increasingly tense as she takes shape.

Travis continues to be filled with fantasies about how grand the boat will be and how popular and rich she will make him.

Darius continues to have strange dreams, the dark eyed woman and the boat always prominent in them. They come more frequently as the Gypsy Queen comes together, grow darker, and the mysterious woman just a little more real and less ethereal. He wakes drenched with sweat night after night, the dark circles under his eyes deepening, feeling weak and listless as if the woman of his dreams is draining his life as he sleeps.

With the work continuing at its increased pace, the cost of materials and labour is sinking Darius and Travis in an ever deepening inescapable hole of debt to Walter.

The strain continues wearing Darius down, embracing him in its dark grip, sucking health and vitality from him.

33   Dance of the Gypsy Queen

Travis, Darius, and Herman are standing before the boat studying her prow. The Gypsy Queen has been largely rebuilt, the workers now focused on rebuilding and finishing the rooms inside. Only the front prow remains untouched, the desiccated wood discolored and chewed with rot in contrast with the lively elegance of the rest of the Gypsy Queen.

Aside from the game tables and furnishings, the main thing missing now on the Gypsy Queen is the restoration of the crumbled figurehead. That carved figure from a time of the past which clings to the prow of the boat forever watching the approaching waves that are destined to break over her, watching for dangers ahead and warding off evil spirits. A protective talisman as much as an artistic expression of the boat's spirit.

It is evident from what remains of the figure, an unusual fixture on a river steamboat, that it had once been that of a woman from the waist up. They are not sure, but they suspect the figure tapered off below the waist to become one with the boat, as though somehow melding into the wood of the hull beneath the prow.

"We should just leave it off," Darius says. "It is an added burden we don't need. If we just smooth it out, nobody will ever know."

"We have to replace that wood anyway," Herman says. He looks at Travis quickly and turns his attention on Darius.

"I know you wanted us to leave that part untouched, and I suppose you might be having some sort of sentiments about whatever might have decorated the prow before. But, that wood is as rotten as the rest. If we don't cut it out and replace it she won't be seaworthy."

"I have no sentiments about this thing," Darius says. "He didn't want it touched." He indicates Travis.

"She will know," Travis says so quietly they almost can't hear him.

Darius flashes him a look and turns his attention back to the boat.

"The boat will look just as good without anything fancy on the front. We will just put a nice curve on it."

"I think we should find someone who can recreate her," Travis says. "She is meant to be there. The Gypsy Queen just won't be the same without her."

The foreman studies the front of the boat.

"I have to agree with Travis. I think it will finish her just right. You should have the decoration carved again just like it was on the prow before."

"How?" Darius asks. "It's not in the blueprints with enough detail to recreate it." He shakes his head. "I say we cut the cost and not bother."

"It will make her a very fine boat," Herman says. "Unique. I don't know of any river boats with a decoration on the prow."

Travis looks at them. His look is urgent. "We have to rebuild her just as she was."

Darius frowns doubtfully at the boat.

"Where would we even find someone to carve it?"

"I know of a guy," Herman says. "Won't cost too much either. Travis is right. You've gone this far, you should go the rest of the way with restoring her just the way she was."

Darius looks at the others, taking in Travis's rapturous eagerness and the foreman's calm confidence. He has a sinking feeling in his stomach.

"You have pushed us to go expensive on everything else and, like a fool, Travis keeps signing off on it. If I were here, I would have said no every time. Now this. I am afraid to find out what this will cost."

Travis grins eagerly. He knows that means Darius has caved. "Who is your guy?"

"Do we have to pay up front?" Darius asks.

"Some of it," Herman admits.

"How do we know he's any good?" Travis asks.

"It's what he does," Herman says. "Don't worry. You will be pleased. In fact, I think it was his grandfather who carved the original Gypsy."

"Is that what she was?" Darius asks, looking at the boat prow again, trying to imagine what the carved image may have looked like.

"Of course," Herman nods. "That's the name of the boat."

"All right," Darius agrees reluctantly. "I just hope it won't be too gaudy or too expensive."

"If it is, that will be just fine," Herman says. "She's a casino boat. She's meant to be gaudy. I'll have the artist come tomorrow. For now, we still have work to do before we call it a day."

***

Inside the boat, three workers are vigorously buffing the woodwork on the walls of the casino floor. The room is empty except for a couple of sawhorses with a plank over them for a makeshift worktable and the supplies for the finishing touches laid out on the table.

One of the workers falters in his vigorous motion, the hairs on his arms and the back of his neck raising.

He pushes on, scrubbing back and forth with the polisher, the dull lathered on film rubbing closer to a deep lustrous sheen beneath his hands with each pass.

The worker stops, turning to look at one of the others.

"Did you say something?"

The other man looks at him, not pausing in his own vigorous scrubbing of another section of woodwork.

"I ain't said nothing." He nods towards the third man in the room. "I ain't heard nothing. Maybe it was Charlie."

He turns his attention back to the wall, scrubbing back and forth with the polisher.

"Charlie?" the first man asks.

Charlie grunts back in response. He is not the talkative sort.

The first man turns his attention back to scrubbing the wall with the polisher.

A chill slithers down his back, pushing the hairs on his arms and neck to attention.

"Jesus, it's cold in here," he mutters. A faint trace of fog hangs off his breath.

He works harder at polishing, his arms moving back and forth with strong strokes.

He stops again, turning with a look of annoyance to look at the others. They both have their backs to him, arms working and diligently polishing the woodwork.

"What?"

Charlie glances at him, not breaking his stride, the polisher going back and forth.

The other man turns to look at him, still polishing. "What?"

"You said something. One of you said something."

"Nobody ain't said anything."

"You are messing with me. I heard a whisper in my ear."

"I ain't messing with you," the other man says defensively. He stops polishing and turns to face his accuser. "Now how do you think I'm gonna whisper in your ear from across the room?"

"I heard it. Clear as day. And there is no one in this room but us, so it had to be one of you and Charlie doesn't speak much."

"Girl," Charlie says so quietly it does not register.

"I ain't said nothing." He puts down the polisher, hot headed and getting angry at the baseless accusation.

"Look, I'm not trying to accuse you of anything." His expression and body language are accusing despite his words. "You can talk. Nothing wrong with that. I just didn't catch what you said."

"When I say I ain't said nothing, then I ain't said nothing."

"Girl," Charlie says again, looking around the room for something.

"Whatever. Just go back to work."

The hotheaded worker takes a step towards him.

"First you say I spoke when I ain't said nothing and now you tell me to get back to work like it ain't anything."

Charlie puts down his polisher and starts edging towards the open door.

The hotheaded worker continues, ignoring Charlie.

"You calling me a liar, ain't you? I ain't no liar."

"It's not important," the other man sighs. He wishes he had ignored it. "Maybe I just thought I heard a whisper."

Noticing Charlie's movement, he turns to him.

"Where are you going Charlie?"

Charlie turns to him, his eyes wide with that caught in the headlights stare he gets when he's startled.

Charlie points at nothing across the room and ducks out.

"Let him be," the hotheaded man says, picking up his polisher again. For all his bravado, he doesn't want to get into a fistfight either. "Charlie's a bit thick in the head if you know what I mean."

The other guy shrugs and turns his attention back to polishing the wood.

Only Charlie noticed the faint plumes of vapour hanging on their words as if the winter chill had set in already, although it is still a few months to winter.

Charlie hurries down the ladder to the ground, head down and moving intently. He passes the men on the ground studying the prow of the boat.

Darius looks at him, curious about his purposeful walk.

"He's in a hurry to get somewhere."

Herman looks. "Charlie, where are you going?" he calls as Charlie is passing them.

Charlie stops and looks at him. His eyes have a haunted look of fear.

"Charlie? Is something wrong? Did something happen?"

Charlie points back to the boat.

"Girl," he mumbles quietly, leaving the foreman and Darius wondering if they heard right.

"Amelia?" Travis asks. "She's here? Is she inside?"

Charlie shakes his head, looking more distressed by the delay, tucks his head down, and starts walking quickly away.

"Charlie!" Herman calls after him, but Charlie just keeps going.

Travis starts for the boat.

"I think he said a lady is here. It must be Amelia."

Darius looks at the boat doubtfully. "Even if she were here, I doubt she would just go in the boat."

Herman watches Charlie go with a bad feeling in his stomach. He follows Travis to the boat, climbing the ladder after him.

Travis reaches the deck first. Just as he is climbing over the rail, the two men polishing the woodwork come tripping out of the room and rushing towards him. Their faces are pale and panicked. Their skin is pasty, drenched with fear sweat.

Pushing past him they reach the ladder, jockey for a heartbeat for position, each trying to go down first, and stop when they realize the large frame of the foreman is filling the ladder below them.

They are almost dancing in their urgency to descend the ladder, impatiently waiting for the foreman to reach the top.

The moment Herman breaches the top; the hotheaded worker pushes past the other and scrambles down the ladder with trembling hands. There is nothing hot tempered about him now.

The other worker gives Herman a quick apologetic glance and hurries down after him.

"Hey, where are you going?" Herman calls down after them.

One of them points back at the boat quickly and they both hurry away from the job site, not taking the time to collect their things.

"What has gotten into them?" Darius wonders aloud.

Travis heads inside the casino floor room. "Amelia? Are you here?"

The game floor is empty save for the makeshift worktable and the polishing equipment abandoned on the floor where the three men had been working.

Travis moves on, searching the rest of the boat and calling out to Amelia.

Darius and Herman step into the gaming room, looking around it with puzzled looks.

They are still there when Travis returns.

"I don't know what he was talking about. There is no woman here. None of the other men have seen anyone."

***

The next morning, the union crew is milling around, curiously waiting for the artist to arrive. The three men who left the day before are missing.

Herman arrives at the boat. He gets out of his truck and looks around at the men.

"What are you waiting for? Get to work."

Still living in the boat, Travis and Darius climb down the ladder to the ground just as the foreman is sending his crew up.

They have a moment of jostling at the bottom of the ladder, trying to get down while the others are trying to climb up.

Travis looks around

"When is the artist getting here?"

Darius walks to Herman, exchanging looks.

"Morning."

"Morning."

"He should be here any time now," Herman says. He turns to Darius.

"Whatever those three saw in there yesterday, they are refusing to come back to work for you," he says.

Darius looks at him with alarm.

"Was there an accident? There were no signs of one."

Herman shakes his head. "No, and I couldn't make any sense of anything they said. Charlie is a bit slow, the result of a childhood accident. All he would say is girl. He just repeated it over and over."

"And the others?"

Herman's eyes get an odd look and his jaw tightens.

"Some nonsense about ghostly apparitions."

He looks away, makes a decision, and looks at Darius.

"The Gypsy Queen has a history you know."

"I bet it does. It's an old boat."

"No, I mean she has a real history. She's got a past. Most of it is rumours, but just like the sailors who pilot them, the men who build boats are superstitious too. Rumor is the Gypsy is haunted and that was why a perfectly good boat was decommissioned and left to rot."

"So, the accidents, mislaid tools and everything…"

Herman nods.

"Rumors and superstitious folks. These guys really believe she is haunted, so anything happens that they can't explain and they think it is ghosts and spooks."

Darius almost laughs.

"Of course."

"Someone is coming," Travis points up the road.

Travis is almost giddy at the sight of the lone figure making his way unhurriedly up the road towards the boat with a sack slung on his back. His progress is painfully slow for Travis.

As he approaches, they spot another, smaller, figure following behind him.

"That will be the artist," Herman says.

"Who is that with him?" Darius asks, trying to make them out in the distance.

"I have no idea."

Heads start popping over the top railing, men above trying to get a look at the artist.

When the artist arrives, the union crew mill around curiously. Most stay safely on the deck and out of Herman's sights. Some pretend to be working while they watch. A few make excuses to climb down to the ground for tools they don't really need.

Travis and Darius glance up at the men above.

Herman ignores them indulgently.

"They have all heard of the master artisans who carve the figureheads," he says, "but few have had the opportunity to actually see one in person. It is believed that the figurehead is what gives the boat spirit and that they somehow infuse the spirit into the figure when they carve it. Another belief is that the spirit finds the figurehead itself, confusing it for something living without a soul, allowing it to inhabit it."

"They actually believe these figureheads have some kind of spirit or ghost in them?" Darius asks. He chuckles. "That's nonsense."

Herman glances at Travis's rapturous face and then at Darius, and back at the approaching figures.

"Only the sailors know for sure, and any one of them would tell you their boat has a spirit, a life of its own."

"Good or bad?" Darius asks.

Herman smirks and Darius wonders if he is just toying with him.

"Depends on the crew and the figurehead. Depends too maybe on the artist."

He nods towards the approaching artist.

"This lot, him and those in his family who came before him, are as superstitious a lot as the sailors."

The approaching figures grow as they come nearer, finally coming close enough to make them out. Dressed in the worn clothes of those with very little money, the man and boy arrive.

The artist stops before them, drops his sack on the ground with a heavy clunk and jangle, and nods to Herman before giving the others an acknowledging nod.

"This her?" He studies the Gypsy Queen as if the presence of the men is of little matter to him.

The artist is a past middle-aged man with long grey hair and a beard that reaches his pants buckle. The creases of his eyes suggest he either squints or laughs a lot. The rough sound of his voice suggests he does not find very much to laugh about.

The boy stands behind him, dressed just as poorly, his hair overdue for a cut and his shoes looking as though it is only his willpower that holds them together. He eyes the men shyly from behind the artist.

"This is Darius and Travis," Herman says, pulling the artist's attention back to the introductions, "the current owners of her. And this is the artist who will make her whole again, Albin."

Albin reluctantly takes his eyes off the boat to nod acknowledgment of the introductions.

Darius holds his hand out to shake hands.

"I don't shake hands," Albin says, ignoring his hand and looking at the boat again.

"And this," Herman continues, "is her, the Gypsy Queen."

"When you told me it was her I didn't believe you." Albin turns his attention back on them. "Why her?"

"Pardon me?" Darius asks.

"Why her? Of all the boats you could have found, why her?"

Darius glances at Travis. He does not have an answer.

"I don't know," Travis admits. "I was just out walking and I kind of kept walking. It was like something drew me there, wanted me to go down that dried up tributary. And there she was." He pauses. "I guess you can say it's more like she found me."

He looks at the others sheepishly.

"I think she whispered to me," he says quietly, knowing how crazy it sounds.

Darius looks at the others with mild alarm.

Feeling the tension, Herman looks at the boy.

"Who is this lad? Yours? Has he come to watch his father work? Learn the trade?"

Albin almost glances at the boy, dismissing him immediately as unimportant.

"This is William," he says, "my new apprentice. William McAllister. His family left him in my care for a few months; had to go away on some kind of family business. Couldn't take the boy with them. I'm not sure the boy will work out. We will see how the world speaks to him." He shrugs.

Albin turns his attention on his new employers.

"What she becomes is what she is already," he says cryptically. "Do you have any vision for what you want on her?"

"The Gypsy Queen," Travis says, his eyes flashing with the excitement of the riches to come. "A long haired dark eyed beauty. Beautiful and mysterious to match the boat."

Albin's look flashes to Herman.

"This is a rebuild. Everything as close to original as possible," Herman says.

"I'm an artist. I can carve something, but I can't promise it will be exactly as before. That ornament was created under the hands of another."

Herman nods. "Just do your best."

Albin walks away towards the boat, studying the still rotten worm-eaten wood of the as yet untouched prow.

"You left this part untouched. The wood is bad. Soured."

"We will have the prow torn out and rebuilt by the time you are done carving a new figurehead."

"Can you do it?" Darius asks.

The artist studies the prow or a long moment, the boy shyly studying the people around him.

Albin finally speaks, not taking his eyes off the boat.

"My better judgement tells me to walk away right now."

Travis's heart sinks.

"I will study her first," Albin says. "Get a feel for what she wants. When I am ready, this," he motions to the rotten prow and the ruined remains of the figurehead that once proudly adorned the front of the boat, "will be ripped away. Every shred of rotten wood. It will be taken to my workshop."

"What will you do with the rotten wood?" Darius asks.

"Burn it, carve it. It will be the heart of the new figurehead. The soul of the boat, what is left of it, is there still in the ruined wood. I will lure her out and place her heart within the new figurehead."

Travis and Darius exchange a look. The unspoken message between them, "This guy is crazy."

"William," Albin turns to the boy still hiding behind him. "Get my things set up."

Shyly, the boy nods and hurries to do as he is bid.

***

Albin comes every day for a week, making the long walk to the Gypsy Queen and home with the boy trailing behind. He spends the week just staring at the boat, studying the blueprints, and studying the Gypsy Queen's prow from every angle, with extra care on the remnants of the original figurine that once adorned it.

It is a little disconcerting when Travis and Darius find him there in the dark of night, silent and motionless, just staring at the boat by the dim light of a sliver of a moon and the scattered stars. Always, the boy is his companion, sleeping on the cool grass in the night.

Albin spends a second week drawing sketches of the front of the boat and the remains of the ruined original figure.

Finally, at the end of the second week, he gets up and motions to the boy to gather his things.

Travis and Darius are gone to work, the work crew is working around him, and Herman is studying the blueprints spread out across the hood of a truck.

Albin walks up to Herman and stops.

Realizing someone is behind him, Herman turns to him.

"Have it ripped out and brought to my workshop. I am ready to begin."

Albin turns and walks away down the road, leaving the boy scrambling to finish collecting his things and jogging after him with the too heavy sack slung over his shoulder.

"Now that guy is an odd duck," Herman mutters. He turns away from the blueprints to give the workers the command.

"All right boys; let's start tearing out that rotten prow. Careful to keep it as intact as you can. The Gypsy is getting a new face."

***

That night, Travis and Darius return to the boat from their day's labours to find the front of the boat missing.

They stand looking up at the dark empty maw, feeling as if it is some wooden sea creature about to swallow them whole.

"They really did it. They took the whole front of the boat off." Travis's voice is incredulous with a touch of loss.

"They had to. Herman said it was rotten. Even the wood carver said the wood was too rotten."

"It just," Travis pauses, "feels like they took a part of her away."

"They did." Darius looks at him. "They will rebuild it. The prow will be strong."

"Yes, I guess so." Travis forces himself to turn away from the unsettling view of the boat missing its front, filled with a hollow emptiness that threatens to overwhelm him.

"We need to talk," Darius says.

Travis looks at him. "I know that tone of voice."

"We are out of money again," Darius says. "We are out of materials for the job. We haven't more than a few pieces of leftover scrap lumber. Herman said the union would keep that coming, but we can't pay for it. We have to pay the Dock Master, the crew's wages, and the Shipbuilders' Union. We also have to pay Norman and Walter."

The weight of his tone is as heavy as the payments are on his shoulders.

"So, we are screwed," Travis says unhappily. "What are we going to do?"

Darius shakes his head. "We can't afford to go any further into debt. We have already sunk too low. I don't think we can ever crawl out of our debts."

"We can't take on any more jobs," Travis says, a panicked inflection in his voice to match his eyes. "We already spend most of every hour day and night working."

Darius sighs wearily. He looks at his partner levelly.

"We have no choice. We have to call it and sell the boat."

Travis stiffens with the fear that surges through him. He knew this was coming.

His hands ball into fists and he unconsciously steps one foot forward into a fighting stance as though ready to fight his only friend over the Gypsy Queen. He shakes his head and it feels too heavy on his neck with the sorrow filling it. The sorrow washes down to his chest, plugging it like thick toxic syrup that threatens to suffocate the life from him.

His eyes meet Darius's and the look in them sends a chill down Darius's spine.

"We are not giving up on her," Travis says coldly, his voice choking with loss on the last word. "I am not giving up on her."

He steps forward, looking at him pleadingly.

"Look, she is almost there. We are so close. I've been working on the tables and they look like new. They are still good under the dust. A little cleaning and oiling and they are perfect."

"There is a big hole in the front of the boat," Darius says lamely. He regrets it immediately, knowing it can only give fuel to his friend's fire.

"We can't sell a boat with the front end missing, can we?" he thinks.

"I'll work even harder," Travis pleads as a boy might plead with his father for that dog he cannot have. "I will scour every town for work, for any deals I can get on materials, even used."

"I can't," Darius says. "We can't. We have nothing left to give this damned boat."

"We will sell anything we can."

"We have nothing to sell except the boat."

Travis turns on his heel, pacing angrily, his desperation and anger colliding. He spins on Darius, taking quick angry steps towards him, and visibly deflating as he stops and stares him down.

Darius looks down, touched by his pain and loss despite his resolve to stand his ground.

"Fine, we will talk to Walter about borrowing more money." Darius feels sick to his stomach over it.

The hope on Travis's face flutters into being and almost fades at the empty look of defeat in Darius's eyes.

"I have another job," Darius says quietly. "It will fill in the gap a little. Six hours a night from midnight to the early morning hours. It was meant to try to catch us up if we had to."

Travis looks alarmed.

"But, you are already over extended. That will have you working twenty-four hours a day seven days a week. When will you sleep?"

Darius chuckles a dry humorless sound.

"Twenty-eight and a half, actually. Let's hope no one notices the overlap. It's a simple job at least."

"What is it?"

"Bell ringer."

Travis looks at him in surprise.

"I didn't think that was still a thing. I mean, I thought doctors and science were advanced enough that mistakes like that couldn't happen anymore."

"There aren't many cemeteries that still have them," Darius says. "Just a few old school church run cemeteries. My guess is they have accidentally buried someone alive, or they just don't want to let go of the past. I don't expect to hear any bells ringing. I will probably just sleep."

"Not right on anyone's grave, I hope," Travis says.

Travis shudders at the thought of sitting alone in the dark silence of the graveyard, surrounded only by tombs and graves of the dead, listening to the silence for the tiny peal of a small bell to alert him that the dead does not sleep.

"Does it really happen that often?" Travis asks.

"What? No. There are no spirits trying to call the living. No dead waking up. Just the odd person afraid of that rare chance they accidentally bury someone who has not passed."

"I can't imagine it, waking up buried alive."

"That's why they have the bell ringers," Darius says. "The ones that bury the dead can't imagine it either, but their family can."

"Back to this," Darius says, tired of the morbid topic. "We will talk to Walter tomorrow. If he won't loan us any more then we sell the boat."

Travis blinks and turns away. It is not an acceptance of the deal, nor is it an outright refusal.

Around the curve of the hull and out of site, Herman stands listening to their conversation. With the conversation done, he quietly sets down the tools he was cleaning up and slips off into the night.

***

Herman arrives at a tidy two-story home in a nice neighbourhood. It is larger than many of the homes around it. Not a mansion by any means, but nice in a smaller way.

Approaching the door nervously, he pulls his hat off his head, holds it in his hands, and knocks.

After a long moment, he hears footsteps inside and the door opens.

Desmond stands in the doorway looking at him as if he half expected him.

"Mr. Moloney," Herman nods deferentially. He looks at his superior, waiting for permission to speak.

"Yes Herman, what is it?"

"They are done. Travis and Darius are done. They are in too far over their heads and can't come up with any more money. They can't take any more and they can't finish the boat. Darius is ready to sell the boat."

"He was ready to walk away from the start. What about his partner?"

"Travis is still determined to hold onto her. He doesn't want to give up, but he's done too. He just doesn't know it yet."

"Where does she stand? How close is she to complete?"

"Almost there. The artist is working on the figurehead and we have taken off the rotten prow. It's just a matter of closing up the hole and installing the figurehead. It's just flat deck at the prow. Then the engine and boiler, and finishing work inside, walls, electrical, plumbing, and furnishings, and she is ready for the water."

Desmond nods understanding.

"Our poor gentlemen friends. So close, and yet so far. The loss will be bearable if they can get enough money for her."

"I suppose."

Desmond meets Herman's eyes.

"Finish her. As I said before, it is in the union's best interest we don't see this investment sink, if you will forgive the pun. The union will cover the costs."

"They are going to that loan shark again to borrow more money."

Desmond smiles and the crease of his lips is a little sour with what he is doing.

"See the loan shark first. Let them think they are borrowing from him. Keep the union out of it. But really the money and materials will come from us, from our pocket."

"Why are you doing this?" Herman is a little afraid of his own question.

Desmond stares at him, unblinking. He is afraid to blink; afraid to show his own doubts about his actions.

"There is too much invested in that boat and I know of someone who would pay very well to have her back in the family."

"Old Thaddeus Barlow. Is he even still alive?"

"Or his son. Either way, the old man will want her returned. The son will too, although probably more for the profit and because he can't let that boat be owned by anyone else. It would sit too sour in his gut. An insult."

Herman nods as though he understands, but really, he does not.

"Good night Herman."

Desmond closes the door, leaving Herman both in the dark outside his door, and wondering at his motives.

The following day Travis and Darius pay a visit to Walter, coming away feeling soiled, threatened, and in shock. He was too easily agreeable to another loan arrangement and it makes them both feel at odds with the world.

34   The Father's Madness

A pair of sleek cars pull up at the dock. They look out of place before the rough planked buildings with their dirty windows, the stink of the river, and the cry of the gulls hanging over the large cargo barges bobbing against their dock slips with the splashing of waves breaking against their hulls and the wooden legs of the docks.

Tough looking men get out the first car. The cut of their suits, attitude of their stance, and eyes shifting in constant surveillance of their surroundings, makes it clear they are armed bodyguards.

Frank, the head security man, exits the front of the second car, gripping his thick cane with the heavy silver ornament. He walks around and opens the back door of the car and Malcolm Barlow gets out.

Malcolm looks around with distaste. He does not normally come to the docks except to come and go from the Queen Rhiannon. If he needs to meet with somebody, they come to see him, no matter who there are.

With a nod to Frank holding the car door, Malcolm steps forward and Frank closes the car door behind him. He moves forward with his entourage to the Dock Master's office.

One of the men moving ahead of him thrusts the Dock Master's door open with a bang, entering with two more men and quickly assessing the room before giving the subtle signal it is safe.

The startled Dock Master jumps and spins in his chair when the door bangs open suddenly, almost knocking his coffee cup across the desk. He stares at the men fearfully, knowing as soon as he sees them who is about to walk into his office.

Malcolm walks in with an air of owning both the place and the man at the desk. His expression is stone-faced anger.

Basil starts getting weakly to his feet, his desk chair scraping too loudly against the floor and making him cringe.

"What do you know about the Gypsy Queen?" Malcolm demands, immediately turning his baleful glare on the Dock Master.

Basil shrinks into himself in fear. He knew this was coming but knowing does not make it less frightening. He had been anticipating and getting more worked up with fear as he waits for the coming confrontation.

"I-I don't know how she ended up sold in a salvage lot. That had nothing to do with me. She was marked for destruction. Somehow, she got included in a salvage lot sold to Norman. He left her to rot up a tributary that dried up. Norman was planning to try to sell her, to you or to the highest bidder. I-I don't know why he abandoned that plan." Basil is trembling as he speaks, his voice shaky.

Malcolm stares at him with hard eyes.

"So this is *the* Gypsy Queen, the original one my father had built?"

Basil nods. "It is the same. When the boat was sold for salvage the boat and any contents became fair game to be resold, destroyed for scrap, or anything else the salvage yard decided."

Malcolm paces angrily.

"I never thought they would get this far rebuilding her." He turns on Basil.

"What are their plans for the boat?" Malcolm demands, stepping closer threateningly.

"I-I don't know," Basil lies. He is sweating profusely, the stink of fear sweat coming off him.

"You are lying," Malcolm accuses, his voice rising with his anger. "They are building a casino. A casino! I am the only one who can have a casino around here!" Spittle is flying by the time he yells the last few words.

Malcolm makes a visible effort to control his temper.

"What addresses do you list for them?"

Basil swallows. "Why do you want their addresses?"

"We are going to pay their families a visit." Malcolm grins wickedly. "Their addresses. Now."

Basil turns to his large ledger with trembling hands, making a pretence of having to look it up. He does not trust his tongue or his mind right now. His hands shake as he opens the large ledger and turns the pages until he finds the entry for the Gypsy Queen.

Basil shakes his head. His voices trembles.

"There is none listed. I think they said they would be living on the boat."

Malcolm scowls at this. It confirms what Frank told him.

"They list no creditors, no family. They bought a boat left to rot up a tributary and rebuilt her with no money and no family. How could they manage this?"

"Yes sir," Basil quivers. "She was. She is. These guys are not from money, I believe. Living hand to mouth. I-I don't think they have anywhere to go."

"So how the hell did they manage to buy my father's boat?"

"Sh-she was cheap, sir."

Malcolm frowns.

"You don't buy and rebuild a boat like the Gypsy Queen without a lot of money. They are getting money from somewhere. Someone is helping them. Who? Who is helping them?"

Basil shakes his head. "I don't know sir."

Malcolm scowls.

"I want to know who it is."

He turns and leaves the Dock Master's office, not bothering with the niceties of further conversation or goodbyes.

Frank gives the Dock Master a warning look before following his boss out the door, the others following behind. The glass in the windows rattles with the loud bang of the door when they close the door hard behind them.

Basil slumps down into his chair, trembling and staring at the door, half expecting them to barge back in. He listens for the sound of the cars before trying to get up. He suddenly has to pee urgently and is grateful he had not done so in his pants from fear while the casino boss was still there. He gets up shakily and makes an urgent rush for the bathroom.

Frank opens the door to the sleek car and Malcolm gets into the back seat. He closes the door, shutting his boss inside the car before moving to get into the front seat. The other men pile into the first car and the cars drive away.

"Take me home," Malcolm orders his driver.

"I am going to have to find out more about these men and their plans for the Gypsy Queen," he says. "Some phone calls will probably give me some answers, but that would not answer all my questions."

Malcolm falls silent, lost in thought. He had heard only some of the rumours about the Gypsy Queen, knowing that bad things happened on the boat right before his father had it decommissioned and sent it to be destroyed at the salvage yard. The boat had been in perfect condition and worth a lot of money. It was a lot of money to just throw away.

At the time he had thought it was the whim of an aging man who had grown tired of his toys and decided to move on to new ones. That wasn't unusual. Like his women back then, his father quickly got bored with his playthings and looked for something new. But he could never understand why his father would just decommission the boat and sell it for salvage when it had been worth so much. Why not sell it and get its value? There had always seemed something strange about that, and his father and his men had been very secretive about it all.

And, the Gypsy Queen was special. His father had been obsessed with her.

"What I do not know yet is what the secrets of the Gypsy Queen's past are, and the real reason my father had the boat decommissioned."

He is burning now to know why. If only his father would tell him.

He thinks as the car drives on, the world slipping by in a blur as he turns his focus instead on the memories inside his head, memories of the past and his confusion at the time…

Thirty-five years ago or so:

Malcolm is just a boy, sitting in the parlour reading.

There is a commotion at the front door. He looks up, curious and a little startled.

The door opens, banging into the wall, and his father, Thaddeus Barlow, comes stumbling in surrounded by men in suits and rough looking men.

Thaddeus Barlow is middle aged, his hair salt and peppering and lines around his eyes and mouth. He has a hard mouth, accustomed to cruel smiles and words.

Malcolm blinks in surprise, his breath coming faster. There are a few well-dressed security men who come to the house. They display impeccable manners and calm. He recognizes them as the men in suits with his father, but the other men he has never seen before. They are dressed how he imagines ruffians would dress. They are looking around, their eyes darting as if expecting trouble to jump out from any corner.

A couple of house staff rush into the front foyer to investigate, quickly turning and fleeing with shocked expressions.

Malcolm cranes his neck, trying to get a good look.

"Father is with them, but I cannot see him."

With a shocked sound, the head maid steps into the foyer, blinks at the men, and hurries back out to alert Mrs. Barlow of the trouble.

The men are speaking at once, their voices loud and alarmed. Malcolm cannot make sense of their conversation.

Mrs. Victoria Barlow comes brusquely into the front entrance, her voice starting firm and quickly turning shrill and anxious.

"Thaddeus, why are all these men in my… oh, oh! What? What has happened?"

She falters, her voice turning shrill when she sees the state Thaddeus is in. She motions quickly at the maid who nervously followed her back to the entrance, motioning to the parlour door.

The maid's stricken face appears in the doorway looking at Malcolm, blinking as if surprised to see him there where she had left him with his evening snack.

She quickly closes the double parlour doors, leaving Malcolm alone to stare at the closed doors wondering what is happening on the other side.

He sits there, woodenly chewing on his snack, staring at the door.

He can hear his mother's shrill voice on the other side, the men's voices too loud through the door. The door muffles the voices, which are drowning each other out in a cacophony of noise so that he cannot make out most of what they are saying. He can only understand half the words, making their meaning disjointed.

"Father dislikes loud voices in the house," he thinks.

Malcolm slips from his chair, crossing the room quietly, and putting his ear to the door to listen.

Blood.

Where is it.

Everywhere.

Stop him.

Coming from.

Burn it.

Mr. Barlow.

Who.

Evil.

Cursed.

Destroy it.

Those are some of the disjointed words, or possible words, he hears in the muffled bedlam of voices. Some are only partial words.

He also hears his mother's voice, shrill with strain, repeating his father's name as if to get his attention.

Swallowing and holding his breath to keep quiet, Malcolm slowly opens one of the doors a crack and peeks out. Immediately he can hear the conversation, the loud angry and alarmed voices hurting his ears.

His father's words are muffled as if someone is trying to keep him quiet; like that night he came stumbling in drunk and the maid put her hand over his mouth to quiet his loud bellowing. But this time his words are low and unintelligible, muttering what sounds like the same few phrases repeatedly.

"Now Mrs. Barlow, you should not be in the middle of this," one of his father's well-dressed security men is saying, his hands out in front of him in a gesture of appeasement or supplication, or perhaps to ward her off. Malcolm is not sure which. His tone is gently firm.

His mother's hands are up in the air in front of her in a stressed gesture, reaching out to someone on the other side of the security man.

"Mrs. Barlow, please," the maid simpers, her voice trembling with fear. She is reaching for his mother. "Come. Let me take you to your room."

"Thaddeus, what has happened?" Victoria whimpers, ignoring their attempts to draw her away from her husband.

She steps forward and Malcolm gets a look at her eyes. They are full of fear and worry, and something else he cannot identify at his young age.

She is reaching, moving forward.

The maid moves to take her arm and lead her away, but Victoria shakes off the maid's hands.

The security men move to intercept her, looking at their leader, the head of security who had just spoken firmly to her, afraid to lay a hand on their boss's wife. He hesitates when she brushes his hands aside to move past him.

Malcolm's father is still muttering unintelligibly, seeming oblivious to what is happening around him.

"BLOOD. (Unintelligible). Where is it (whispered)? Everywhere. It's everywhere (whispered). (Unintelligible) COMING FROM. Burn it. Burn it. BURN IT! (Unintelligible). Who? It's evil (whispered). Cursed (whispered). Cursed. CURSED. (Unintelligible). Have to- I-I have to… I have to destroy it (whispered). Destroy it."

Victoria's hand makes contact with her husband and, with explosive suddenness, he lashes out.

He might as well have struck her.

Thaddeus's arms flail out, warding her off. He half steps, half stumbles forward, his voice now booming in the foyer.

"AWAY FROM ME WOMAN! GET AWAY FROM ME!" he bellows and it echoes through the large house.

Malcolm gets his first real look at his father since the commotion in the foyer interrupted his evening snack.

Thaddeus's face is stricken with a grimace of fear and loathing and shock and heartbreak. It is waxy pale like Malcolm has never seen any man. Like he imagines a dead man might look.

His face, clothing, even his hair, are covered in blood, soaked with it, splattered with it. He leaves a smeared trail of blood on the floor from his shoes as he stumbles forward as though to attack his wife.

She looks utterly terrified by his sudden attack and is quickly stumbling back, keeping just out of his reach.

The maid cries out, falling back behind her, using her mistress as a human shield from his madness.

Thaddeus's eyes are wild and as deranged as the deranged state he seems to be in.

It is the only time in his life Malcolm has ever seen his father look afraid.

Malcolm pulls his eye away from the crack in the door, his heart pounding in his chest and his breath coming in ragged too loud pants, which he is sure they must be able to hear on the other side of the door.

He presses himself against the door fearfully, tearfully, listening out of sight.

Malcolm does not know what he is more afraid of, being discovered peeping on them at such a dramatic moment, or his father's bloodied deranged state.

He can still hear his father's ranting loud and clear, his back pressed to the door still holding it open a crack.

Thaddeus's disjointed rants are wild and confusing, and his orders yelled loudly in a voice cracking with strain.

"BLOOD. (Unintelligible). BLOOD! EVERWHERE!

Where is it (whispered)? Where is it (whispered)?

Everywhere. It's everywhere (whispered). IT'S EVERYWHERE!"

(Unintelligible) COMING FROM. Burn it. Burn it. BURN IT! I'M TELLING YOU NOW, BURN IT! WHY ARE YOU ALL JUST STANDING THERE? BLOODY WELL BURN IT!

(Unintelligible). Burn it to nothing, to ash (whispered). (Unintelligible).

It's evil (whispered). Cursed (whispered). Cursed. Evil! CURSED! (Unintelligible).

Have to- I-I have to… I have to destroy it (whispered). Destroy it."

Thaddeus seems to partially snap out of it now.

Malcolm hears his voice come steadier now, commanding and firm. The father he knows and fears and who does not terrify him with deranged terrified madness.

"I WANT THAT BOAT STRIPPED AND HER AND EVERYTHING ON HER DESTROYED! That boat is to be decommissioned! Pulled from the water immediately!"

There is a sound only of muffled rustling. Malcolm imagines them all bowing and mewling like pathetic little creatures to appease his father, rushing to make his wishes happen.

Everyone always rushes to make his father's wishes happen.

"Some day that will be me they all bow to," Malcolm whispers under his breath, making a promise to himself.

Thaddeus's voice comes again, commanding like an apocalyptical priest proclaiming judgement on his sinners.

"I swear to my last dying breath and beyond, that boat will never touch water again!" He commands like a man might swear vengeance on an enemy after suffering an emotionally mortal blow at his enemy's hands.

"The Gypsy Queen-,"

Malcolm believes the voice is that of his father's head of security.

"DO NOT SAY THAT NAME!" Thaddeus bellows. "NOT EVER. THAT NAME WILL NEVER SOIL MY EARS AGAIN! NO ONE IS EVER TO SAY THAT NAME AGAIN! DO YOU HEAR ME? NOT EVER!"

The head security guard nudges the door open just a little, looking in. Malcolm looks up at him, terrified, caught and startled.

The security guard only gives him the smallest of nods, no smile; merely an acknowledgement that he has shared that moment with them. And then the door closes and he is gone, the voices on the other side muffled again.

They move away. They must be taking his father away someplace. "Probably to the den," Malcolm thinks, picturing the room filled with his father's large richly gleaming mahogany desk, large overstuffed chairs, bookcases, and a well-stocked bar.

The present:

That is not all Malcolm remembers of that night.

"Other people came and went from the house all night that night," he thinks. "Angry people; women wailing and men crying. The police came and went. My mother was so distraught that they sent her away, all the while she was cursing and swearing at my father, trying to tear his eyes out as she was dragged away."

Years later, Malcolm was a young man when he had been suddenly thrust into the figurehead position as head of his father's company and his father began receding from the public. His father made his appearances at first, when needed, to make sure everyone knew that his son was little more than a messenger boy, an impotent figurehead, and the real power was watching, unforgiving and strong, from the shadows.

His father's public appearances increasingly became fewer until they stopped altogether.

What those outside the household did not see was his father's increasing rants, his maniacal behavior, the haunted look in his eyes, and the hollowness of his cheeks as the man seemed to be physically sinking into himself, eaten from the inside by his growing insanity, seeming to age decades in only years.

Malcolm's attention is brought back to the moment as the car pulls to a stop before the sprawling mansion.

Frank gets out, walking to the back door, and opens it, standing aside for his boss to exit the vehicle.

Getting out, Malcolm squints in the sunlight and turns to Frank.

"Find out everything you can about the men who have my father's boat."

Frank nods.

Malcolm turns to the house, walking purposely up the steps with his security entourage following and leaving Frank behind.

Frank watches them go in before getting back in the car. He motions the driver to go.

35   The Gypsy Queen Comes Home

Today is the day the new figurehead is to be finished. The artist had sent word five days ago promising they could pick her up today.

They hired the largest wagon they could find, uncertain how large the artwork would be, and headed out with a second wagon filled with union men following behind to load it.

The wagons lurch up the dirt road into the farmyard, Herman driving the lead wagon and Travis and Darius sitting to either side of him. He steers for the large barn in the distance.

Hearing the approaching wagons, the door to the small farmhouse opens and a woman and assortment of children spill out into the yard, watching them curiously. They stop there, not allowed to approach the barn, which is the artist's workshop.

Albin exits the house, walking through the throng of kids.

Seeing him, Herman pulls the wagon to a stop before him.

Albin nods a greeting to the men in the wagon as they leap down from the wagons. They are all itching to see the results of the man's labour.

In the lead wagon with Herman, Travis and Darius are both fidgety, afraid it will be a disaster. The three men in the lead wagon are slower to climb down, standing next to their wagon. Albin meets them with a serious look that almost dampens their excitement.

"She is this way," Albin says, leading them across the yard towards a large barn in the distance. "You will have to bring the wagon closer to load it."

Herman gestures to his men and they climb back in the wagon, men taking the reins of each wagon to follow them to the barn. Travis, Darius, and Herman follow Albin across the yard on foot.

Albin talks as he leads the way.

"To rebuild her, I started with building on what was left of the damaged figure, letting the remnants guide me. There wasn't much there to go by. After that I just created by impulse, let the creativity flow and let her be whatever she would become."

He pauses, turning to them with a strange look.

"You are taking her away today, right? You won't be leaving her with me another day?"

"Yes," Darius nods. "We came prepared to take it today."

"Good." Albin walks on and they follow.

The finality of the word and the touch of relief in it make Darius wonder.

They reach the barn.

With heavy movements, Albin pulls the big doors open one at a time, letting the light fill the interior of the barn.

Inside, a large object towers to the rafters covered with thin sheets sewn together to make a large enough cover.

Albin walks in ahead of them and stands beside it, turning to face them.

"Ready?" he asks.

Travis and Darius nod eagerly.

With a heavy breath of air as if the task carries an impossible burden, he reaches up and pulls the draped cloth. The cloth hesitates, catching on something as if perhaps the woman beneath it is shy to have herself exposed to their prying eyes and grips it to remain covered, before slithering over and down the sculpture towering over them to reveal the figurehead beneath.

Travis and Darius just stand there gaping at it as the cloth slips away in a pool of fabric to reveal the secret beneath it. They both gasp.

Staring at the figurehead, they hear the union men come in behind them, their feet shuffling to a stop and a couple of muffled whispers.

A beguiling dark haired dark eyed beautiful young woman stares down at them. Her limbs, supple and graceful, are wrapped in a gesture against her bosom, covering it with a suggestion it may be clothed or not, depending on the observer's desire. They cannot be sure if the gesture is welcoming or not.

Her eyes are partially hooded by her lids as if they carry some deep secret she is unwilling to share. Her mouth has an indefinable sadness about it that only adds to her beauty. Her long hair falls in waves that cascade down her back to tangle into the smooth wood behind her and her head is encircled with what looks like a crown of gold coins linked together with the fine links of a chain, a necklace for her delicate brow.

Her dress is merely a suggestion, curving down and around and spreading in rolling ripples that could be soft fabric or the waves washing over the prow cutting through them to become one with the boat once the figure is attached to the prow.

She truly looks like a queen, a Gypsy queen.

Darius stumbles forward, staring in awe, feeling cold fingers creep down his spine. It is the very same woman from his dreams, whose dark eyes haunt him, leaving him to wake in a cold sweat with his heart beating fast and his limbs trembling with a fear he cannot explain.

He is mesmerized by the sight of her. He feels her lifeless eyes staring back at him, looking into his soul.

"How could this artist have created the very same woman?" he thinks.

Travis's grin spreads across his face from ear to ear. She is the same beautiful woman in his dreams; the woman who was a part of the beauty and glamour of the Gypsy Queen.

"I can't wait to see her grace the front of our boat," he breathes, "to show her off proudly. I can't wait for Amelia and the world to see her."

Herman and his men stare raptly at the Gypsy Queen.

Albin breaks the spell she has on them.

"Load her up. Get the witch out of my barn," he says gruffly, quickly moving to the other side to pull on a rope that pulls ropes up through pulley's in the ceiling. The ropes raise the sheets back up and pull them over the figurehead to hide the Gypsy Queen once again from the lustful eyes of men.

With the figurehead covered, they blink and look around. Herman looks around pointedly to his men, directing them to get to work.

Travis and Darius watch them work.

They bring the larger wagon, turning the team of mules around and backing it into to the barn. It takes them a few hours to load the figurehead and strap it down.

Watching them, the artist can't seem to get rid of it fast enough.

With the statue loaded, they climb into the wagons. Darius looks back to see the look of relief on the artist's face as they drive away with his art and wonders why the man is so anxious to get rid of it.

He shrugs it off, thinking the man must have some other pressing work he needs the room for.

Behind them, Albin makes the sign of the cross over his chest.

"Good riddance Witch," he mutters before turning to limp for the old farmhouse he calls home.

"I don't remember him having a limp," Travis says absently, looking behind them at the artist as they drive away down the road.

***

It took the union men a week to attach the figurehead to the prow.

At last, the Gypsy Queen is ready. It is time to put her in the water.

Travis and Darius arrive at the docks, Travis grinning hugely and walking with a happy bounce to his step. Beside him, Darius's expression is serious and his walk carries the weight of the troubles weighing down his shoulders.

The docks are as busy as always, teaming with people, wagons, and trucks loading and unloading the river barges.

Pushing and dodging their way through the crowds, they pause outside the Dock Master's office, Darius frowning at the building.

"Don't look so eager," Darius complains. "We talked about this."

"Are you sure?" Travis asks, unable to stop grinning. "We already paid him a lot of money."

"I am sure," Darius says. "It has all been a money grab every step of the way with everyone we deal with. The Dock Master will demand extra money on top of what he already told us we have to pay when we need the slip to park the boat in. Some new hidden fee he forgot to tell us about."

"But once we find a more secure place to keep her moored, we can keep her there and only have to pay the Dock Master when we need the dock to load or unload passengers, equipment, and supplies," Travis adds.

"I hope so," Darius shakes his head doubtfully. "But, I don't think that is how it will work."

"He won't care that we have her parked somewhere else. As far as he will know we are running her up and down the river somewhere and only coming here when we have to."

"Maybe. I still think he will expect us to keep paying for the slip or we lose the privilege of docking here even for an hour."

Darius shoves his hands in his pockets, feeling for the wads of cash there.

"Let's go," Travis says eagerly, his eyes shining with excitement and unaffected by his partner's sullen mood.

He pushes the door open and Darius follows him in.

The Dock Master is sitting at his desk when they walk in. He looks up at the sound of the door opening and turns around with a surprised look.

"Good afternoon gentlemen," Basil says, rising from his chair and walking to the counter between them. "I wasn't expecting to see you today." Of course he was not. They aren't due to make another bribe payment for another two weeks.

"Good afternoon sir," they both say, approaching the counter.

Basil looks at Darius's serious expression and his gaze settles on Travis's grinning visage. He can't help but grin. Smiles tend to be infectious and Travis is grinning like a fool. A very happy fool.

"So, what is up?" Basil asks.

"We are ready for that slip for the boat sir," Travis says eagerly, staring him down and waiting for his reaction.

Basil is taken aback by this. He knows the Shipbuilders' Union has been squeezing them for months and that is even more reason to believe they would fail miserably in rebuilding that rotting old boat. He is surprised they managed to hold out as long as they did.

"Are you sure the boat is seaworthy?" he asks suspiciously. "I can't be having any sunken boats causing a hazard at my dock."

"The Shipbuilders' union has signed off on her," Travis says, his grin getting even bigger with the other man's surprise. "She is ready to hit the water. All that is left is the finishing work."

Basil looks to Darius for confirmation. He has always seemed like the more level headed of the two.

Darius nods gravely. "It is true sir. We've done it. The Gypsy Queen is rebuilt. We are not quite there yet to start running the boat. The inside walls are still being built. The electrical and plumbing needs to be done. We need equipment, staff, and furniture, and to get the licences before we can start business, but it is ready for the water. The union men said we should get the boat in the water soon so they can find and seal any leaks before we start bringing everything in."

"Right they are," Basil nods. He steeples his fingers, mulling it over.

"These aren't the usual experienced men I am used to dealing with," he thinks. "If they were, they would know they have to pay extra money now."

He glances at Darius.

"He's smart enough. He probably figured it out," he thinks. "That's probably why he looks so sullen. But these guys wouldn't know how much. I could get away with gouging these two deeper.

I'm not worried about them finding out and coming back on me for it later. They won't likely be around long enough before they lose their shirts, their boat, and anything else they have and take off for other parts.

It is almost a shame. I kind of like them and was even rooting for them, but that's the price of business."

He leans forward conspiratorially.

"This is your lucky day gents," he says. "It just happens that I can manage to cut you a bit of a deal today on your fees."

Travis's eyes light up, but Darius is skeptical. They had scratched hard to put together what money they could and barely managed to come up with what they hope would be enough. A deal now would be a blessing.

Their hearts steel when Basil gives them a number, and sink when he gives them another and then another, adding charges onto charges.

Basil pauses as though something just occurred to him. He meets their unhappy looks.

"We do have a bit of a problem my friends," Basil says.

"Here we go," Darius thinks.

Basil continues.

"You did not give me advance warning so I don't actually have a slip available right now. I could do a bit of juggling to make room, but it means I will have to pay off a few captains." He pauses. "Or, should I say, you will have to pay off a few captains."

He gives them a dollar amount.

"That should just about do it I believe, if you are lucky and the captains are feeling generous."

"And if they are not feeling so generous?" Darius asks suspiciously.

Basil shrugs. "They may want more. But I know of a few who are usually the more generous sort and who have had good business lately. Just give me a day to talk to them and make some room for you."

"Why do we have to pay off more than one captain?" Darius asks.

Basil blinks at him as though the question is a surprise.

"None of the boat owners actually own their dock space," he says. "They pay for time at the docks, not space. I will have to juggle their docking schedules to fit you in."

Travis and Darius exchange a quick look. The money they scraped together is not nearly enough to cover the added bribe and the other payments they have to make. This is only one of the stops they need to make today.

Darius's eyes shift and he looks at Basil and away, digging unhappily in his pockets. He pulls out the money and counts it, laying it on the counter.

All business now, Basil counts the money. He pulls out his ledger, turning to the correct page, and carefully notes the payment down. He glances at them, and then makes another notation next to the Gypsy Queen's name, noting that she is no longer dry-docked.

"Sign here please." He turns the ledger to them and hands over the pen.

He leaves the ink to dry while he puts the money away in the cash box and then closes the ledger and sets it back on its shelf.

He turns to his two customers with a smile.

"Congratulations gentlemen, you are officially masters of your own boat, and thus of the waterways."

Travis manages a sickly smile and Darius only nods, his expression still grim.

They turn and leave the Dock Master's office with heavy hearts. Basil grins behind their backs, wallowing in his own happy greed.

Travis and Darius pause outside the building. Travis looks at Darius with a frown.

"Now what?" Travis asks.

"Now we have to find some more money in the next two days to pay the Shipbuilder's Union, Norman, and Walter." Darius swallows the lump in his throat, his eyes threatening to tear with frustration.

"Damn it," Travis pounds his fist into his other hand. "No matter what we do, how hard we try, we just can't get ahead."

Darius's gaze shifts away. He can't look him in the eye. "Maybe we should sell some of the equipment."

Travis looks at him, startled.

"No, we can't. We need it to run the casino. We could never afford to replace it."

"We don't need all of it. We can sell a few."

"No," Travis is adamant. "She must be exactly like before. Every part of her."

Defeated, his shoulders slumped, Darius starts walking. "Let's go."

***

The next day dawns with a lacklustre cloud-filled sky. Travis and Darius have taken the day off work. It is a big day.

The Gypsy Queen is to be put to water today.

Travis has not been able to sleep at all, lying restlessly on his blanket on the deck of the Gypsy Queen staring at the sky. There were no stars and moon to light the sky with the clouds hiding them from sight.

Darius slept fitfully, his broken sleep filled with dreams of the dark haired dark eyed beauty mounted to the front of the boat coming to life, her eyes full of dark secrets and her lips with sadness. She keeps whispering things to him, but her mouth moves soundlessly and her warnings unheard. He woke bathed with a cold sweat, shivering, and his heart pounding with a fear he could not explain.

They both stand on the deck now, watching the growing crowd below.

Travis can't help the excitement that fills him. Their months of hard work have finally paid off. They are about to launch the Gypsy Queen.

Darius scans the crowd, looking for one face in particular. Amelia is coming to watch. It is going to be her first time seeing the outside of the boat finished, and her first time seeing the figure on the prow.

News that the old rotting boat that months ago had been dragged unceremoniously down the river and onto an empty un-owned piece of shore along the river was being rebuilt had become a popular topic for gossip in town. People walked by just to see how the boat was progressing, if at all. After a while, they got bored with it.

When news that the boat is actually going to be put in the water began to spread, people became interested again. Bets were made whether or not the boat would sink or float, and guesses were made as to what purpose the two young men were going to put the boat to.

With very few exceptions, Travis and Darius had decided to keep tight lipped on their plans for the Queen.

"Why are there so many people?" Travis wonders, surveying the still growing crowd. "This was supposed to be a secret. We wanted our grand opening to be grand. We wanted to build up suspense and hype, stir excitement in the people, and let them come and make the discovery when they come for the grand opening."

"Word got out I guess," Darius says.

The crowd of spectators had begun to gather long before the union men even showed up to start preparing the boat to be rolled into the water, and they have been at it for hours now.

There is a festive atmosphere to the crowd. Some brought and set up family picnics. Kids are running around playing and men are drinking beer while discussing the making and workings of a paddlewheel boat, whether they know anything about it or not, and women chatter about the local gossip while they wait for the entertainment to start.

Travis's excitement is contagious, spreading through the gathering crowd. Or, perhaps it is their excitement that is infusing him with an almost giddy sense of thrill.

"There she is," Darius says, spotting Amelia in the crowd.

Travis looks, doesn't see her, and he points her out.

"Let's go down," Travis says, leading the way down the ladder to the ground.

They work their way through the crowd until they spot her again.

Young women titter behind their hands when Travis rushes forward excitedly at the sight of Amelia and leads her forward by the hand to show off his prize.

He leads her around the hull towards the back, showing her everything he possibly can, leaving the figure at the front for last. They stop at the paddlewheel so he can explain its mechanisms to her, and then move around the other side of the boat towards the front.

When they finally reach the figurehead, Travis stops and stares at Amelia, eagerly waiting for her reaction.

Darius stands back, watching them, his expression carefully unreadable.

Amelia looks up at the carved woman who seems to be growing out of the front of the boat like a ghostly figure emerging from the wood.

It sends an instant chill down her spine.

"It feels like she is staring at me." Amelia feels a little alarmed by the sight. "Like she is looking right into my soul with those dark hooded eyes."

She stares back into the Gypsy's eyes, wondering at how they seem to be depthless wells filled with secrets she might whisper to you if you only turned away and paid her no attention. She studies the mouth, the slight downturn at the corners hinting at a deep sorrow. She is beautiful and elegant with a grace any living woman would envy.

She feels too real.

Amelia has to hold back against her urge to step forward and touch the figure to make sure it really is only wood.

She is afraid it would feel like flesh, soft and supple and warm, instead of the smooth hard wood it is made of.

Amelia turns to Travis with a confused look and a question in her eyes that pulls at her breast, but unsure what she wants to ask.

"Go ahead," Travis says, grinning. "You can touch her if you want."

Amelia instinctively draws back at the thought of touching the wooden woman, as if somehow knowing the carved woman would not like it.

"We are ready," Herman interrupts the moment.

Travis looks at him and back to Amelia, his grin widening further.

Travis leaps forward and grabs Amelia's hand, startling her. Her first impulse is to pull away. He pulls her forward before she can react.

"Come on, I want you to do the honor," he says. "You are supposed to break a bottle of champagne on her before putting her in the water, kind of a baptism for boats. I want you to do it."

He drags her along eagerly.

Amelia looks back at the woman on the boat's prow, her motionless eyes somehow seeming to follow her with their silent secrets and filling her with unease.

She looks around for Darius, for someone to help her.

While everyone waits, the Shipbuilders' Union men put everything into place to drag the boat into the water, they work quickly at preparing the Gypsy Queen to be moved from the grassy ground that had sunken under her weight to the nearby river. Ropes and pulleys are already set up, logs to roll her on, and logs to push her with.

A tugboat chugs up the river to them, its squat chimney stack belching foul smelling black smoke, sending a new surge of excitement through the spectators. It slows, stops, and backs into place along the riverbank. Ropes are tossed across the water and tied off.

The tug is ready to drag the Gypsy Queen to the water.

The crowd moves closer, excitement coursing through it at all the activity. It is about to happen.

Amelia is still looking around for Darius when she turns, startled, to see him next to her on the other side. They exchange a look, both their expressions showing their reservations.

"Let's do this," Travis eagerly rubs his hands together, grinning at each of them.

Amelia shifts closer to Darius, unconsciously seeking safety.

Travis waves them to come and leads them to the prow. He stops there, looking at the crowd importantly and up at his Gypsy Queen with rapture.

"She approves," he thinks, staring into those dark eyes that stare back into his.

Travis, Darius, and Amelia take their places and Herman joins them, holding a champagne bottle with a large dark red ribbon tied to its neck.

"Red like blood," Amelia thinks, looking at the bottle and quickly looking away. She tries to push down the thought and the uneasy feeling it brings to sickly life in her stomach.

Travis says some words she cannot hear, his words drowned out by the chugging tugboat, the blare of a horn of a passing river barge, and the murmurs of the crowd. Everything sounds muted, like someone pulled a thick sack over her head. Suffocating and muted.

Oblivious that no one heard him, Travis motions for Amelia to break the champagne bottle on the boat.

She looks dully at him and then at the bottle being held out to her, seeing only the bottle and not the man holding it. Suddenly she has the urge to flee. She hesitates, not wanting to touch the champagne bottle. If feels somehow tainted.

Travis motions towards her with the bottle, urging her to take it.

Behind her, Darius moves closer, touching her elbow.

Amelia turns and looks at him and the moment their eyes meet a cold chill fills Darius. The expression in her eyes haunts him. He gives her a small nod to let her know he is here for her.

Turning back to Travis, Amelia takes the champagne, grasping the bottle too tightly and a little surprised to feel the solid reality of it in her hands. She just stares down at it for a long moment.

"Go on," Travis says, leaning in and nudging her. "Smash it on her. You won't hurt her."

It pulls her back to reality from whatever dark place she receded to in her mind.

With a nervous glance at the men around, the crowd watching, and finally looking up and staring back into the eyes of the ever-watching Gypsy Queen, Amelia pulls the bottle back and swings it in a wide arc with more force than she intends.

It connects with the Gypsy's hull with a thud and a crack, shattering in an explosion of champagne that drenches the hull, dripping down like watery colorless blood.

She shudders at that sudden image of blood splattered everywhere, dripping and soaking into the ground instead of the clear champagne it really is.

Darius starts motioning people to back away and Travis leads Amelia away to a safe distance. She stumbles along behind him, unable to take her eyes off the Gypsy.

Travis stops and is looking down at her hands. She looks up at him, feeling disoriented.

"You are bleeding," Travis says, reaching for a handkerchief in his pocket. "You cut yourself."

Amelia can only look down at her bloodied hand as he gently wraps the cloth around it.

With a shrill whistle from the foreman, the men lined up along the lengths of heavy rope like tug-of-war teams pick up the ropes and start walking, taking up the slack. They heave together on the ropes when they grow taught, throwing their weight against the weight of the boat, pulling the wrong way, away from the river. If the boat slips into the water too fast they might damage her hull.

The tugboat's motor farts and belches thicker clouds of black smoke, rumbling louder as its captain opens the throttle just a little, and it pulls ahead slowly until the tow rope hangs in a taught line.

It hesitates as the motor chugs harder with the throttle being opened more, its back end digging into the water pushing the nose up. The boat tilts almost imperceptibly towards the river.

Herman signals and, with a yell, the men heave on the ropes as the tugboat captain lets off on the throttle, idling the motor.

There is no discernible movement from the men pulling on the ropes.

They need to rock her lose from the sunken ground before they can jack her up onto the logs and roll her to the river.

Herman signals, a man on shore waves his flag, and the tugboat captain opens the throttle again, giving another surge of pressure on the towline, and down throttles again.

With the change in pitch of the tugboat's down throttle, the men yell and heave again, the boat rocking with the tugging back and forth.

"Stop!" Herman yells and the flagman signals to the tugboat.

The tugboat's throttle is choked back to an idle and the men drop their ropes, rushing in to jack up the boat and roll the logs into place. This takes a few hours with the men working together quickly in coordinated unison. A line of logs leads down the short slope to the river.

They nod and step back to the ropes as each man's job is done.

"Ready!" Herman yells and the flagman signals the tug.

The men pick up their ropes again, taking up the slack, and prepare to battle gravity and the tug for the Gypsy Queen prize.

"Heave!" Herman yells, signalling the men to go with a wave of his arm.

The flagman signals the tug and the captain opens the throttle full, the men on the ropes pulling the opposite way to slow her descent to the river.

Nothing happens for terrifying heartbeats.

The crowd watches expectantly, holding their collective breaths. Amelia's hand comes to her throat protectively. Darius blinks a slow blink, feeling as if his heartbeat is actually slowing down with the slowing of time. Travis's mouth falls open, watching with fear and hope.

The Gypsy Queen shivers and then at last begins to reluctantly move towards the water, the logs carrying her weight rolling with her.

The tugboat pulls, its throttle eased open more to increase the pull. The men heave, and she slides forward, gaining speed on the slope once the momentum starts.

The men heave harder, digging their feet into the ground and throwing all their strength and weight against the ropes, being dragged towards the river by the heavy boat.

The Gypsy seems eager now for the water, slipping down the slope too fast, men yelling, and the rolling logs she rolls on clattering and cracking beneath the weight pushing down on them.

Somehow, as the boat slips towards the water, a man standing where he should not be is caught by the rolling logs.

A woman watches in silent dawning horror as his shirt snags on the log and then yanks him forward. The first shocked soft scream passes her lips as he is pulled by the shirt, dragging him along with the log. The snagged shirt twisting with the turning of the rolling log pulls the struggling and flailing man in. The desperate cries of the trapped man are cut off swiftly.

The woman finds her voice and her first piercing scream shatters the joyous moment as she witnesses the twisting shirt and rolling logs pulling him in between the rolling logs and beneath the sliding boat, crushing and grinding him to a bloodied pulp.

Realizing too late, men yell and dart forward. A few men heaving on the ropes drop them and scramble to help. Others fall, valiantly trying to keep up the fight and are dragged until they let go.

Most of the onlookers cheer, watching the boat with glee, ignorant of the drama unfolding.

The woman screams again.

The shrill scream of the traumatized woman shatters the moment, causing some in the crowd to pause and look around curiously.

She screams again and points for those who turn to look at her, her reaction slowly trickling through the crowd. Those down the line with a view of the other side of the boat begin to push and shove, swarming over to see what is happening, their morbid fascination overruling common sense.

The Gypsy Queen continues to slide along, taking the rolling logs down the bank with her and ignoring the growing shocked reactions of the horrified people watching as this all took place in a span of heartbeats, leaving a red smear along the bottom of the boat and on the grass in its wake.

With a surprisingly subtle splash that sounds like a strange sigh, the Gypsy Queen dips her toes into the river and glides effortlessly in. She bobs as if nodding to the tugboat pulling her and then drifts on the water like a serene swan, her abandoned ropes trailing down the slope behind as she slowly moves off into the current, washing the blood away.

Behind her, scattered Shipbuilders' Union men get to their feet to watch her.

The tugboat captain scratches his head with a perplexed look.

"That was odd. I've tugged many boats in my life, and have been a part of putting many boats into the water, but I have never witnessed such a soft plash of one this size hitting the water. Nor have I heard such a sound before as a boat settled into the water. It was but a soft sigh of displaced water and air that sounded almost like a nearly silent cry of sorrow gasped on a near silent intake of air, as of someone doing so as they gulped a big breath of air to hold under the water knowing they are about to drown."

In the Gypsy's wake, people in the crowd rush forward as if they might actually be able to help the mutilated man. Realizing it is pointless, some stop to stare at the boat in stunned shock.

The drifting boat continues moving out towards the center of the river, dragging the loose ropes behind, the tugboat captain waving and shouting to the people on shore.

"The ropes! The ropes!"

Herman snaps from his shock and comes to the realization they are about to lose the last ropes needed to pull her back into shore so some men can clamber onto her and steer her into dock. He jabs one of his men in the ribs and races forward, grabbing another, and points to the escaping boat.

They bolt down the slope, dodging and leaping the scattered and broken logs, to grab the trailing ropes and pull, yelling to others to help. One by one other men, union and spectators both, run forward to grab ropes, pulling the unwilling Gypsy back to the edge of the shore.

Others look around in stunned shock.

Travis and Amelia stand together, their faces ashen with shock and unmoving. Darius is trembling, his face pasty and his body drenched with sweat. He feels ill.

Everything seems to be happening far away.

Travis blinks. Someone is yelling at them; standing right in front of them and yelling at them. It does not register through his shock. It is Herman.

Someone else walks up, another union man, and Herman stops yelling and turns to him, enraged by the stress of the moment.

"Where is the man who is supposed to be on the boat to steer her when she hits the water?" Herman demands.

The new arrival turns, face waxy and pale, and points at the meat mulched between logs and smeared on the ground, a shred of bloody cloth fluttering in the wind.

"I think that was him."

Herman's shoulders sag and he runs a trembling hand through his hair.

"Get someone on her. We need someone to steer her into the slip when the tug gets her to the docks."

The man runs off on unsteady legs to do as told.

Herman turns back to the shocked boat owners. The sooner he gets them out of here the sooner they will snap out of their shock.

He grabs Travis, Darius, and Amelia each by their shoulders one at a time, shoving them on and getting them moving. They stumble forward woodenly and he herds them like a dog herding sheep too stupid to move, shoving and barking at them until he gets them inside a waiting car.

Getting into the driver's seat, he starts the car and drives off to bring them to the docks to meet their boat.

Numb, Darius can do little but move as he is moved.

Putting the boat in the water had been nerve wracking from the very first moment for them both. Travis had wanted to do it on their own. Watching these experienced workers do it made it very clear they had no business moving boats themselves. If they had tried to do it on their own, he is certain they would have sunk the Gypsy in the process and probably killed themselves.

He stares out the window of the car, not feeling the pressure of Amelia squeezed in between him and Travis pressing against him. He is watching the spectators try to pull their world back together and make sense of what they just witnessed.

Swimming out with powerful strokes, one of the union men gropes for and grasps a rope trailing in the water. Dragging himself hand over hand through the water along the rope, he reaches the boat and pulls himself out of the water and scrambles up the rope. Climbing over the railing, he makes it to the deck of the Gypsy Queen.

Two more men follow. He runs across the deck to the wheel room while the others move along the deck quickly tossing off the ropes restraining her by the men on the shore. If left, the trailing ropes would have snagged on deadwood along the shore and beneath the water, mooring the boat until she could be cut free.

The man in the wheel room waves to the tugboat driver and the tug chuffs forward, taking up the slack once again in the towrope and slowly dragging the Queen up the river to her new home.

The trip goes without event, the tug slowing as it draws nearer to the empty slip in the docks waiting for the Gypsy.

Dockworkers turn to watch curiously as the new boat is taxied in. The Dock Master comes out of his office to watch, surprised at the elegance of the rebuilt boat as she glides in towards her place. He is drawn to the figurehead at the front, the beautiful carved woman sadly riding the boat in.

"I wonder why they made her look so sad. And yet, that sadness seems only to enhance her beauty and mysteriousness."

The Gypsy glides forward, expertly steered by the man in the wheelhouse, dockworkers rushing forward with mooring ropes ready to snag her and restrain her to her bed.

She turns and glides smoothly into the waiting slip without a hitch… except for the hapless seagull that dives into the narrowing gap chasing after the delectable flash on the water's surface that might have been a fish, diving at the wrong moment to find itself crushed between the boat and the bumper hanging from the dock.

The bloodied feathers are washed from the boat by the lapping water as the wind drives the waves in towards the dock, banging all the boats against their moorings and the padded bumpers protecting them from damaging themselves on the docks.

The dockworkers toss their ropes, lassoing the mooring anchors on her side rails and tying them off on the dock. The two men on deck throw ropes to the dockworkers and they are tied off, securing the Gypsy against any chance of her escaping her mooring.

The Gypsy Queen is secured. She is home.

Ignorant of the tragedy on the shore downstream, the gathering crowd cheers, chattering excitedly over the elegant paddlewheel that looks so out of place among the ugly river barges dwarfing her.

***

The car arrives at the docks just moments before the boat is slowly taxied into her slip. Herman drives in as close as he can get to the dock and parks.

"We're here," he says, "and just in time to watch them bring her in."

They get out of the car and make their way through the crowded docks, standing far enough back from the dock slip to not get in the way.

A crowd is gathering, watching the paddlewheel boat come in. It does not take them long to figure out the three men and one woman watching with mixed expressions belong to the new boat.

Darius watches the boat taxi in, still feeling ill from the events on the riverbank. He does not let his mind think about anything.

Amelia is in dazed shock, not really taking it in and simply allowing herself to be jostled and moved wherever someone might choose.

Herman's expression is torn by his conflicting thoughts and feelings warring against each other.

Travis stands stiffly in disbelief.

"We did it. We actually did it," Travis says.

Shock and horror are being pushed out by the happy excitement around them. He can't help it. After working so hard for so long, he cannot help but let the mood on the dock affect him.

"These people here have no idea what happened," Herman thinks. A chill still fills him.

Together, they watch her being expertly manoeuvred into place and suffer the congratulatory slaps on the back as men rush in to toss ropes to the men on deck. The excitement of the gathering crowd has partially broken the spell of the earlier tragedy and they look around in muted elation.

Amelia just stares at the boat, one thought that refuses to leave her mind. "A man died for this."

As the mooring ropes are tied off, Travis finds himself grinning with the crowd.

It is done.

Travis turns to Darius, grins, and claps him on the back.

"Let's go celebrate," he says, taking Amelia by the hand. The three turn and walk away, heading for town to celebrate their success.

Darius and Amelia exchange a look. Neither feels like celebrating.

Herman catches the Dock Master's eyes across the dock and they stare at each other for a moment as people unknowingly pass by between them.

Basil breaks it off first, turning to return to his office.

Herman turns and jogs after the others, easily catching up with them.

"We'll take the car."

Feeling like everything is suddenly right with the world; Travis claps him on the shoulder, including him in their group.

***

The Queen Rhiannon is coming in from her evening cruise. Her guests are growing tired, most are drunk, and the casino workers are hoarse from barking away trying to push their guests to bet more money.

Malcolm is standing on deck as the boat slows and turns, being steered in for a delicate landing, the windblown waves making the job more difficult as she dances and bobs on the waves.

As they draw nearer, he notices the newly refurbished boat at the dock.

He watches the boat curiously as the Queen Rhiannon approaches it, the docks and river barges giving him only broken partial views of the new boat.

The Rhiannon breaches the last obstructing barge and the telltale paddle wheel on the back of the boat comes into view.

Malcolm whistles as his boat slowly draws alongside the new boat, impressed with the elegant beauty.

His eyes flash and his jaw clenches, showing the slow anger simmering, his eyes glued to the boat.

The Queen Rhiannon continues on, slowly drifting towards the front of the new paddlewheel.

Malcolm has to look again when the name carefully painted on the side comes into view, rereading it.

"Gypsy Queen!" he breathes.

As the Queen Rhiannon continues to its own slip, the dark haired Gypsy on the prow is revealed.

Malcolm stares at her dancing and bobbing on the water on the front of the boat.

36   Celebration

The noise of the pub seems strangely muffled with the shock still clinging to the foursome. They are sitting at a table with celebratory drinks on the table before them.

Amelia looks around, feeling awkward and out of place.

"My father and mother would be furious if they knew I was in a place like this."

She instinctively ducks into herself, making herself smaller and less noticeable.

Darius looks at her, taking notice of her discomfort.

"They won't have to know, and you are a grown woman who can make up her own mind and choices."

Amelia gives him a small thank you smile.

Travis just grins around the table at everyone.

"We did it.," Travis says. "I knew we would, but I have to say, I kept having doubts we could ever pull this off. I mean, wow."

He stares around at them, his train of words lost; speechless with his own amazement.

Herman takes a long drink from his glass, studying each of them over his glass. He eyes the room to see who is there and if anyone is paying attention.

Putting the glass down, he leans forward and looks at each of them seriously.

"Now what?"

"What do you mean?" Travis asks.

"Now that you have her in the water, what are you going to do?"

"Sell it," Darius mutters under his breath, staring down at his glass. He picks it up and takes an angry swallow.

Amelia looks at each of them, feeling the tension growing.

Travis's eyes flash and his jaw clenches, but he pushes Darius's words away. He meets Herman's eyes, staring into them. His expression is serious, but his eyes are gleaming with a hint of mischievousness.

"Can I let you in on a little secret?" Travis asks.

Darius's eyes flash a warning at him, but he ignores it.

Herman leans forward slightly, closing the gap a little and staring at Travis with more interest.

"We are going to run her as a casino boat, just like she was originally built."

He stares at Herman, waiting for his reaction.

It is not the reaction he is looking for.

Herman leans back and barks a laugh out. He shakes his head in amusement.

"A casino boat. You guys are flat broke. Hell, you are broker than broke. You are so far in debt that you don't even know who you are in debt to."

He looks around the room as if to check who else is in on the joke, takes a long swallow of his drink, and leans in towards Travis again.

"How much do you owe?"

Travis just blinks at him, not answering. His jaw works and his fists have tightened without his realizing.

"Where are you going to get the money for the game tables, and to pay off the Gaming Commission? If you think the Shipbuilders' Union is run like a mob; that is nothing to the Gaming Commission."

Travis is breathing heavy, his eyes blazing.

Herman shakes his head in amusement.

"Your partner is right," Herman says. "You should just sell her. You might even make a profit now that she's finished, if you didn't borrow at too high of a price."

Darius is reaching out to touch Travis, to give him a warning to keep his mouth shut.

It is too late.

"We have the tables," Travis blurts out, staring Herman down. "We just need the rest of the furnishings."

Herman blinks at him in surprise. It takes him a long moment to be able to find the words to speak.

"You have gaming tables? Where? How? Where did you get them?"

Travis cannot help the involuntary grin that forces its way across his face, half a grin of pleasure at besting this man's argument and half-pleased with acknowledging their success, and just a little sick feeling.

Darius is shaking his head in defeat, wishing he would stop talking.

"We got our hands on the original tables."

Herman blanches just a little.

"The original tables? You mean from before she was decommissioned?"

Travis grins larger, nodding.

Herman shakes it off, thinks about it, and a slow smile spreads across his face although his eyes are still serious.

"My boys and I are off the clock, but what can we do to help?"

***

Eugene is sitting in his office at the union building in the shipyard. He looks even older somehow, the weight of his thoughts wearing him down. He pours himself a drink of dark amber liquid from a fancy crystal carafe sitting on his desk into the old fashioned crystal glass next to it.

Relief that the Shipbuilders' Union's dealings with the cursed Gypsy Queen are over sits uneasily in his gut.

"Almost over," he reminds himself.

He has one last thing he has to do.

Taking a large swallow of the neat cognac with a grimace, he picks up the phone receiver and dials. It rings a number of times in his ear before it finally stops with a click and a pause of dead air that he imagines hissing back at him across the wires into his ear.

Finally, after an interminable pause, a raspy voice answers.

"Hello."

"She's back," Eugene says.

37   The Gypsy

"Let's take this one first," Travis says, indicating a sheet enshrouded object a little more than shoulder width wide and chest height. Travis and Darius are in the old barn where the Gypsy Queen's contents had been stored so many years ago. The cracks between the boards of the walls allow enough light to see easily enough, splashing lines of light across the floor and shroud-covered contents. Straw dust dances in the light, disturbed by their presence.

Darius walks over to it, lifting one corner of the sheet to reveal the gleaming wood and metal slot machine.

"It cleaned up pretty nicely."

"It took a lot of work. I had to take it apart to get the mechanisms greased and working again, but it works beautifully."

Darius pulls the sheet up and over, draping it down the machine's back like the dust-filled train of a gown.

Fishing in his pocket for a coin, he puts it in. The coin slides down its track, setting off a short joyous ring before falling into the empty holding tank with a dull clunk. Gripping the ball at the end of the arm, he pulls it down and releases it. The machine bursts to life, the wheels on the front spinning to flash their pictures through the rectangle glass window with near silence. The same mechanism turns the cylinder with bumps and notches, the needles of thin metal strips tripping over them in a musical dance, plinking out repeating bars of some banal wordless song.

They watch the spinning wheels spinning too fast to clearly see the pictures. They begin to slow, first one and then another, each eventually rolling to a stop to reveal a line of matching images.

The perfect juxtaposition of matching pictures triggers something inside the machine's mechanism and the music switches to a triumphant few bars of a new song interspersed with ringing bells. The turning mechanism inside stops dancing the bells. The spinning musical cylinder continues for another couple of turns and a spring-loaded arm is released, dropping open a door that would release a gush of coins to the tray below if there were any to be released.

The single coin slides down into the tray, its face staring up at them.

The spring pops back and the door snaps shut, and the machine falls to almost surreal silence again.

The old resident tomcat eyes them balefully from his resting place.

"Well, I'd say that's good luck," Travis says with a grin.

"It would be better luck if there was a jackpot inside it to win," Darius says, looking at the solitary coin.

Somewhere outside an insect starts its raucous hissing buzzing timpani.

Darius returns the sheet covering the slot machine and they each take a side, struggling to lift the heavy machine.

"This thing is bloody heavy," Darius complains.

"It's all the gears inside. You should see it all."

They waddle to the waiting wagon, backed in with its tail just inside the large barn doors that are flung wide open. The sunlight spreads its fingers across the barn's interior in a hazy attempt to touch everything inside the door. Carrying the heavy machine between them, muscles straining and popping, they set it down carefully next to the tail end of the wagon.

"How are we going to get it in the wagon?"

"With a lot of determination?"

Darius studies the problem. He isn't sure the two of them will be able to lift it high enough from the ground up to the wagon bed.

"We should have four men for this job."

"Yes, but we don't want anyone to know where we are keeping the casino equipment."

"I have an idea."

Darius returns to the barn, searching around inside and out of it. He finds an old tractor tire outside the back side of the barn and drags it over.

Travis watches him curiously.

Darius finds an old crate and tests it, stepping on it with one foot and pressing his weight down. His foot breaks through the rotting wood without much effort. He shakes his head and continues his search. Finally, he goes up to the hayloft inside. There he finds a stack of crates that are not ruined by the elements.

He picks through them for sturdy looking ones and tosses them down to the floor below.

"Take those to the wagon."

Below, Travis looks at them, shrugs, and carries them two at a time.

When Travis returns he looks up to see Darius pulling at the planks of the hayloft. The nails of one board give with some resistance and an unhappy squeal and the board pops loose.

"Take the other end," Darius says, feeding the board down to Travis.

"What is this for?"

"A ramp. Just like the boat."

Travis grins. He takes the end being fed to him and lowers the board to the ground, careful not to hit any of the equipment.

They continue until they have enough boards for a makeshift ramp two boards thick and the width of the wagon bed.

Satisfied, Darius climbs down from the hayloft and goes out to the wagon. He inspects their collection, thinking, and starts piling it up. With the tractor tire and wooden crates, he builds a two step rise and lays out the boards from the top step to the wagon bed.

Seeing what he is doing Travis nods appreciatively.

"Okay, let's try this."

They each grasp a side of the slot machine, grunting and heaving, and manage to lift and waddle it over. With one more heave, they get it up onto the lower level. The wooden crates groan in protest to the weight, but hold.

"Okay, one more. Lift."

Shifting their grips and grimacing with the effort, they strain and lift it to the next level.

Darius looks at Travis over the machine.

"Let's hope these boards hold."

They both climb up onto the ramp, one in front of the machine, and the other behind. They drag and waddle-walk the machine across the boards towards the wagon. The boards groan and bend under the weight, causing them to worry they will break or slip.

The machine passes into the wagon bed, its springs creaking as the wagon slouches a little with the weight.

Travis releases the breath he had been holding without realizing it and looks at the machine with relief.

"Let's get it against the end and make room for more."

They move the machine into place and jump down to the ground.

"The tables are a lot lighter," Travis promises.

Picking a sheet enshrouded table, they repeat the process. As promised, the table is lighter than the slot machine, but it is still very heavy.

They struggle with the game table, straining to lift and carry it into place and walk it up the makeshift ramp onto the wagon.

Returning for more, Darius takes a moment to study the contents of the barn around him. Beneath the sheets covering the carefully cleaned and polished pieces, the wood, paint, and chrome gleams.

The pieces still waiting to be repaired and cleaned sit covered with sheets, some with only a shroud of dust and cobwebs to cover them.

"This guy really did save it all, didn't he?" Darius says.

"It looks that way. Just the gaming tables and equipment though. We still need to furnish and stock the kitchen galley and fill the boat with all the other furnishings we need."

A guilty flush creeps up Darius's neck. His thoughts are on how they might sell the game tables to pay off some of their debt while they try to sell the boat.

"What else is in this stuff? Have you gone through it all?"

"No. I just started working through it one machine at time."

"We're here. Maybe we should take an inventory."

Travis nods. "I guess we should have done that already."

They start exploring the dust-coated shapes in the barn.

Tucked away in a dark corner, Travis finds some old steamer trunks. He opens one, seeing nothing of interest, and closes it.

He opens another trunk and looks inside. It is filled with belongings from a woman. The clothes are very old and outdated looking. There are tarnished broaches with broken clasps and missing stones and a hairbrush and ornate combs missing teeth. The worthless possessions of a young woman spirited away when they were no longer needed.

"Nothing but junk."

He reaches in and pulls something out, turning it over to look at it. Something is wrapped in a red cloth tied with a ribbon. Travis carefully unties it, unwrapping the square of cloth the size of a large handkerchief to reveal a deck of cards too large for casino cards.

He looks at them with fascination. It is a deck of tarot cards with pictures of a Gypsy woman painted on the back in fine detail. Her dark eyes stare out mysteriously from the back of the cards, her dark hair caught up in an ornate headscarf. Large gold hoops hang from her ears and an elaborate necklace drapes at her neck. All of it, her tan skin, clothes, jewelry baubles, and headscarf look like the stereotyped Gypsy portrayed in film and other media.

He flips quickly though the cards, the scenes on their backs varying slightly from card to card. Each card had been painstakingly painted individually. The Gypsy woman is attractive, but not as attractive as the carved woman decorating the prow of the Gypsy Queen.

Travis studies her face more closely.

"It's not the same women." His voice holds a hint of wistful disappointment. "Of course it isn't. The likelihood of two made up visions of women, one carved recently and the other painted and printed on the backs of cards locked away in a trunk for decades, being the same is impossible. It would have been interesting, though, if they were the same."

He turns the cards over to examine the card faces.

The faces of the cards are also painted with painstakingly detailed pictures depicting different scenes, no two cards the same. He studies one card closely.

A regal man stands with one foot resting on the head of a dog lying at his feet. The dog's tongue lolls out and its eyes stare blindly at a cup overturned on the floor, its contents spilled. The man holds two more cups in his hands and is staring back at him laughingly. There are more cups. He does not count them.

Travis replaces the card in the deck and starts wrapping the cards back in the cloth. His hands fumble and he drops them. The cards scatter as they fall, some falling in clumps and others fluttering down, turning over on the air as they fall to the floor.

Travis starts picking them up, putting the deck back together.

He stops, staring fixedly at one particular card that landed face up. A rather gruesome depiction of Death stares up at him. He is suddenly filled with an uneasy feeling. Thinking himself foolish, he continues gathering up the rest of the cards quickly.

With the cards roughly stacked in his hand, the lopsided pile revealing the edges of many of the cards, Travis moves to a table where he sets the reunited deck down. Most of the cards show him their backs, the Gypsy woman on the top card staring at him with her mysterious look. He can see from the edges that some cards are face up.

Travis reaches out one hand, spreading the cards across the table to reveal the face up cards. One by one, he pulls them out, setting them aside.

The first card shows a man who appears to be strangled, hanging upside down. His eyes are bulging and his mouth gaping with his tongue partially protruding. Travis cannot decide if he is supposed to be dead or pleading for help. The Hanged Man.

The second card depicts a sinister creature, frightfully horned with cloven hooves and goat legs standing atop a pile of what appears to be human corpses writhing in pain. The creature smiles wickedly, enjoying the torment of those below. The Devil.

The third card shows a crumbling tower, thorny vines crawling up its sides as though the plant is strangling the structure, tearing it apart with its wickedly long thorns. A man is falling from the tower, his arms and legs flailing and his face twisted in a scream. Looking closely, he thinks he sees the shadow of a woman inside the tower window, but he cannot be sure.

The fourth card is the death card that first caught his eye, its picture just as twisted and gruesome as his first impression of it. He looks more closely this time. Death is clothed in a long rotting robe that appears to hang weightlessly off him. He notices this time in the darkly ornate background, a dark figure hunched on a stool painting a portrait on an easel. He cannot make out the unfinished portrait, but has the sense it is of a man.

Frightening ghostly apparitions hang in the air above, barely there. Dark gossamer rotting fabric hangs from them, their wings carrying them effortlessly. Wicked clawed fingers are reaching and tearing the souls from their victims, the victims falling from the sky to litter the ground Death walks on. One apparition stares directly at him, faceless. A sick chill slithers into his stomach and he feels as if blood red eyes that are not there are staring directly into his soul and weighing it.

Travis turns the card over with a nervous laugh. He picks up the last card and studies it.

The final card disturbs him the most. The woman wears a flowing dress, her dark hair tumbling down and becoming one with the dress, both melting into the background as though she is not entirely there. Like she is a spirit growing out of the dark cloudy picture behind her where thorny branches twist around each other before a distant castle on a cliff. Her dark eyes stare back at him.

"I feel like they are staring into my very soul," he whispers.

Her eyes look haunted, shadowed eyes that hide some dark secret. Her mouth is curved in a hint of a smile that suggests a deep sadness. Behind her the waves crashing against the cliff reveal the suggestion of a boat that appears about to be smashed against the bottom of that rocky cliff.

Travis's eyes focus on the woman, her face.

The hauntingly beautiful woman bears an uncanny resemblance to the figurehead of the Gypsy Queen.

A chill shrivels his spine. He feels stiff, unreal, trapped in a surreal existence with no way to return to the real world.

Travis blinks. He rubs his eyes and closes them, silently praying for the world to come back to him. A part of him deep inside is afraid that admitting that fear will make it true that the world is gone.

When he opens his eyes again the picture on the card is not what he remembers. The woman has only the barest hint of a resemblance to the Gypsy Queen figurehead on the prow of his boat. Her regal dress is no longer melting into the background. The waves crashing against the cliff behind her no longer hold the suggestion of a boat.

He scoops up the cards with shaking hands, returning them face down to the rest of the deck and quickly tapping their edges on the table so they fall together neatly before he rewraps them with the red cloth he had found them in, tying the ribbon as if to keep those images from escaping to come after him.

Travis hesitates. He has a sudden image of himself throwing the cards into a fire, watching them curl and char as the heat licks at them and finally bursting into flames to be destroyed

"No." He quickly shoves the cards into his inside jacket pocket.

Travis looks around for Darius.

"Let's get this stuff to the boat. We can come back to do inventory," he says.

"All right. We have room for a few more tables. Let's grab this one." Darius indicates a table.

Picking another sheet-covered table, they carry it to the wagon, shove it into place, and return to grab another table, grunting with the effort of lifting it to move it.

The resident old tomcat has been eyeing them suspiciously since they arrived. He meows at them with his strange strangled voice, seemingly not impressed they are taking away his barn's furnishings.

He hisses at them with bared sharp teeth, staring with his expressionless and creepy yellow eyes as they carry the table past where he lounges.

Once they have the last piece for that day's load on the wagon, they return to give the barn one last survey and close the doors securely behind them.

The old barn cat appears next to the barn, exited from some hole somewhere, stalking them as if hunting for human prey as they chain and lock the doors and return to the wagon to climb up for the drive home.

Travis takes up the reins, giving them a shake and clicking at the mules. With the creaking of harnesses, they lean into their harnesses and start pulling, the wagon rocking on the uneven road.

Travis glances back at the load, worried something might be damaged from the rocking motion of the wagon.

"They will be fine," Darius says. "They are covered with cloth and we left enough room between each piece so nothing should rub or bang together.

They drive on, the wagon continuing its rocking and bouncing down the road.

After travelling some way, they notice a man walking along the side of the road ahead.

Hearing the approaching wagon, he stops and turns, waving to them.

Travis slows and stops the wagon when they reach him.

"Hop on up," he says, indicating the seat.

Darius moves over, making room, and the man climbs up with a grateful nod.

"Where are you headed?" Travis asks.

"Wherever the road takes me," the man grins.

He is an older man, in his sixties, and having the wiry thinness of a man whose ropy muscles are stronger than his size suggests. His clothes and face are weather worn and lined, and his smile reveals gaps in his yellowed teeth. His dark hair is faded to more grey than black, and his dark eyes appear almost black in his face darkened by the strong tan of a man accustomed to being outside.

"Bit of a transient spirit, huh?" Darius says with a chuckle that does not cover his uneasiness.

He cannot pinpoint what, but something about the man makes him feel unsettled.

"I've never been one to settle down for long in any place," the hitchhiker says.

He turns to look at the contents of the wagon.

"What are you hauling?"

"Just some equipment," Darius says evasively.

"Looks like casino tables to me."

Travis and Darius both eye him warily. The same thought crosses both of their minds.

"Hope he isn't planning to rob us."

"You must be headed for the Gypsy Queen," he says. "I heard she has been found and fixed up. You might be looking for some experienced help?"

"We are heading that way with this load," Travis says. "We aren't looking for anyone just yet. But we will be when we are ready to start rolling her down the river."

The man looks at Travis pointedly.

"You might find yourself short on people willing to work on a haunted boat."

Travis smirks, but it falters under the older man's steady stare.

"Ghosts. There is no such thing."

The man laughs. It is the laugh of someone who knows something you do not.

"I'll be getting off here."

Travis stops the wagon, looking around. There is nothing around but grassland and bush.

The man climbs down and nods a thank you to them.

Travis clucks the mules into motion, the wagon rattling and bouncing down the road again.

"That was odd," Darius says, glad to be leaving the strange man behind.

"It was," Travis agrees.

When they arrive at the dock, they load the game tables onto the boat with the help of Herman and one man from his crew, placing each table where they think they want it and leaving the sheets covering them to keep them clean and protected.

Setting one table in place; Travis stops and checks inside his jacket pocket. Satisfied the cards are still there, he heads out to help bring in the last table up the gangplank.

***

"You shame your whole family with this nonsense," Amelia's father rages on. "Associating with that man, a man who robbed your own father. You went to the launching of that boat against my orders. You made a public disgrace of yourself breaking a bottle on that boat!"

Amelia stares back at her father defiantly.

Roman towers over her more with his temper than his size. He is not a large man. He is furious, his finger jabbing at the air as he yells at her.

Amelia rolls her eyes in exasperation.

"I am a grown woman and yet my father treats me like a child to be chastised and told what she can or cannot do," she thinks.

"Do not you roll your eyes at me!" Roman roars, stepping closer and raising a hand as if to strike her. He is angry enough that he needs to lash out and strike something, but would never actually hit her.

"You will not see that man again if I have to keep you locked in this house. Do you understand me? You will not see Travis again."

***

Darius is alone in the casino room, the game tables they brought over looming under their white sheets like ghostly apparitions in the dark, waiting for the rest of the equipment from the barn to join them. It is not completely dark, the lights of the moon and stars above and the lamps on the dock sending more than enough light through the un-draperied windows to see.

He turns. He thought he heard a sound.

The muted sound of distant music comes to him, a hollow tinny sound to it. It seems odd, with the same unnerving sensation of danger he got from the music playing in his dreams, the live band that somehow had that same tinny sound like it wasn't real, or perhaps he was hearing it echoing to him through metal ducts instead of on the evening air outside.

The music is too soft, sounding far away.

"It must be coming from another boat."

Darius turns again, peering through the semi darkness. He thought he caught a fleeting glimpse of movement at the edge of his vision. It is gone in a flash and then there again.

He whirls again, trying to catch it, but catching only the hint of the afterimage of a dark figure teasing his retina like the flicker of a ghostly image. But again, there is nothing there.

He turns quickly, thinking he saw movement again.

There is only the gentle flutter of a sheet draping one of the tables, as if someone had just walked by, brushing against it, but there is no one there.

Unnerved, his heart pounding, Darius leaves the room quickly, going upstairs to the room that will be his. There are no furnishings in his room yet, except his blankets and pillow folded in a corner and an oil lamp. He spreads the blankets out and settles in for the night, falling asleep, his dreams haunted by visions of the wooden Gypsy Queen on the boat's prow gesturing to him, calling to him soundlessly.

***

Malcolm is sitting in his opulent office in his large home. The morning light does little through the curtains and the lamps offer the room muted light that leaves shadows in the corners. His expression is serious as he reaches for the telephone. He phones the bank and is put through to the bank manager.

"George, Malcolm here," he says when the other man answers. "I have a favor to ask you."

"Go ahead," George the bank manager says.

"Two gentlemen rebuilt an old paddlewheel. They would have to have money for a big job like that, either family money or financing. The family names are not known, so it is unlikely they have money. See if your loan manager remembers anything about it."

The bank manager nods. "Alright, give me a minute."

He covers the mouthpiece on the phone with his hand to muffle any sounds and calls his secretary in.

She comes in and waits for orders.

"Get Shannon in here."

She nods and quickly moves to do so.

A minute later Shannon Whitaker comes into George's office, simpering up to his boss.

"Yes sir, you wanted me?"

"Yes. A couple of gentlemen may have come in for financing to fix up some old boat. Do you know anything about it?"

Shannon blinks in surprise.

"Oh, yes sir. That was quite a while ago. They had nothing. No collateral. Just a worthless old boat. No credit, no money. I sent them away. I wouldn't give them a loan; it would have been a complete write off. They never could have paid it. They came back a second time, saying they were building it all themselves and working to pay for the materials and thought they could borrow money with the boat stripped down. They had union men working for them then or something. It still wasn't worth anything. Besides, they were not business types. Not loan material."

"Nothing? No money at all?" George looks doubtful.

The loan officer shakes his head.

"I think one of them was working shovelling shit and the other at the slaughter house. I doubt they had the money to pay their rent."

The bank manager nods.

"That is all I need," he says dismissively, waving the man out of his office and returning to his phone call.

"They were here," George says into the phone. "No money, no property, no backing. They tried to get a loan for it but had no collateral."

"So where did they get the money to rebuild a boat?" Malcolm asks.

"Not here," George says. "But they did try to get a loan, twice. Had some guys from the Shipbuilders' Union working for them."

"Thank you." Malcolm hangs up.

He dials again, listening to the ringing of the phone on the other end in his ear.

Eugene answers. It is his private line.

"Hello, Eugene Randall here."

"Eugene, Malcolm here. I am looking for a bit of information. The two young gentlemen rebuilding the Gypsy Queen had a union crew working for them."

Eugene narrows his eyes, nodding.

"Yes, we had to muscle them a little. They thought they could do it without the union, but we straightened them out."

"How did they finance it?"

"I don't know," Eugene says. "Hold on, I will check with Desmond. He did the dealings with them."

Covering the mouthpiece, he calls Desmond into his office, his voice ringing through the office and back up the phone line.

Desmond comes in.

"Yes sir?"

"Those young fellows rebuilding that old paddlewheel, how did they finance it?"

Desmond shrugs.

"As far as I could tell they worked their asses off, working nearly around the clock at every job they could get. They barely made their payments, always late on them too. I am pretty sure they resorted to a loan shark when they were too short."

Eugene nods.

"That is all I need." He waves Desmond out and puts the phone back to his ear.

"Worked their asses off to earn it, borrowed where they could, loan shark most likely, probably stole too I imagine. They are broke. No bank would touch those boys."

"Thank you Eugene," Malcolm says, hanging up the phone.

He stares down at the silent phone, contemplating.

"Now how the hell did two boys with no family and no money manage to pay the union and rebuild a boat?"

Malcolm is completely mystified and, he has to admit grudgingly to himself, a little impressed.

***

Darius wakes up feeling disoriented. He gets up; wondering what woke him, and goes to the deck.

He almost immediately realizes he is not alone. He looks around and sees a man in the casino room through the windows.

Going to investigate, Darius recognizes the uniform of a police constable the moment he enters the room.

The constable is nosing around the casino room, looking under the sheets covering the tables. He looks up when Darius enters.

"Do you have a permit for these?" the constable asks.

Darius immediately becomes nervous, sensing trouble.

"Not yet sir," Darius says. "We still have more equipment to get. We can have it here as long as we don't start running the casino before we get the permits."

"I am just here to make sure." The suggestion is clear in both the constable's look and his tone.

He continues.

"If I was to come here and it appears this stuff is being used, I would have to take you into custody for illegal gambling and file a report with the Gaming Commission. That would be regretful. All of your equipment would be seized, your boat, everything."

Darius stares at him with a deer caught in the headlights look. They would never get the permit, and they would be fined at the very least.

"What does he want?" he thinks. "A bribe?" Darius almost panics.

"Be calm. Just act casual," he warns himself.

He surreptitiously pulls money out of his pocket and slips it onto one of the sheet-covered tables. His hand trembles as he pulls it away.

"If I am wrong, this will go badly," Darius thinks.

"You won't have any problems with us," he says, trying to act casual as he moves to put the machines between him and the constable.

"We won't do anything to get ourselves into trouble."

The constable follows him around the machines.

"You are already in trouble. A man died moving this boat onto the water. You could be charged for careless endangerment causing death."

Darius swallows.

"I-I believe the Shipbuilders' Union was taking care of that."

"Lucky for you, they are. I will be back to check on you periodically." The constable saunters out.

Darius's knees are weak and he takes a moment to just stand there and breathe, his blood pulsing in his ears. When he finally feels like he can walk, he makes his way around the machines.

The money is gone.

"So this is how it's going to be," Darius mutters, fingering his empty pocket where what was left of their cash had been moments before.

38   Demands and Questions

Three sleek cars drive into the deserted dockyard. Somewhere a security man is keeping an eye on things, but at present he is nowhere to be seen. The cars drive right up to the wooden docks, parking before the Gypsy Queen.

Malcolm looks out his back seat window at the boat, taking her in. He cannot help the mixed feelings of approval at the job done on her and grudging respect for the men who pulled it off.

Car doors are already opening and closing as his security men exit the vehicles and do a quick sweep of the area. Satisfied, one of them returns to the cars and knocks on the front passenger window while the rest take up defensive positions.

His head of security, Frank, looks back at him from the front passenger seat. Malcolm nods and Frank opens his door, stepping back to open Malcolm's door for him.

Malcolm gets out and takes a moment to look around.

"It's not too often I see this place at night when no one is around. It's quiet. It stinks just as much as during the day. Let's go."

Frank signals to two men nearby and the three lead the way up the gangplank to the Gypsy Queen.

Frank waits at the top while the other two make a quick circuit of the deck. They return and nod the all clear.

Frank signals down to the dock and Malcolm steps onto the gangplank. He immediately feels the motions of the plank moving with the boat's movement with the water. He mounts the plank, stepping off onto the deck above.

Behind him, the men left on the dock keep watch.

"Let's take a look around," Malcolm says. "See who is home."

"Yes sir." Frank signals the two men to move ahead, clearing the way before them. With little to see on deck, they find the casino floor.

Malcolm steps through the doorway onto the casino floor, taking a moment to take it all in.

The rich dark wood shines with a well-polished lustre, the carved accents painted in brilliant colors that bring out the beauty of the boat rather than making it look gaudy.

Malcolm walks over and lifts the edge of a sheet covering one of the gambling tables, peeking under it. He arches an eyebrow and pulls the sheet off to reveal the table. He is surprised to see the heavy wooden ornately carved table that would have filled a wealthy casino decades ago; but have all long since been replaced with more modern sleeker and lighter weight tables.

He walks to another, pulling the sheet off to reveal the same. He continues, de-shrouding a roulette wheel and slot machine. Each machine is of the same fine quality, heavy and richly made, elegant and not gaudy.

Malcolm stands in the middle of the room, feeling as if he has been swept back in time to the Gypsy Queen of his childhood. Ghostly memories of the now outdated clothes and perfumes the past fill the room; the sounds and smells of his youth. He remembers being on this very same boat.

He looks to the doorway, half expecting to see his father come strutting in with a pack of wealthy patrons mewling around him, simpering to gain his favor.

"And something else," he thinks. "There is something else I am forgetting."

He closes his eyes, letting the memories wash over and through him, feeling the gentle rise and fall of the floor beneath his feet move with the swell and fall of the water lapping against the docks.

He can hear the lapping sound too, that low guttural sound of the water trying to push the boat off the dock only to suck her back in as though trying to gently bash her against the wood. The bump of the boat against the bumper pads protecting her from the dock is almost inaudible here.

The gentle rise and fall of the boat… "Like a woman's soft breast," he finishes the wordless sensation.

Frank and the two men wait silently for him to be ready to move on.

"It is almost like I can reach out and touch the moment," Malcolm says quietly, reaching one hand out to grasp only air. "It is like I can feel the presence of someone who is not here. I can almost smell…"

He almost says 'her'.

Malcolm snaps out of it.

"Let's finish searching the boat. They have to be here somewhere."

Taking their cue, the two men move on, clearing each room before Frank and Malcolm enter. They search the rest of the boat only to find it deserted.

They stop on the deck. Malcolm looks out over the water of the river, the reflection of the moon dancing and roughened on the water's surface. The stink of the river suddenly feels cloying.

Malcolm's eyes are hard.

"These guys have done a surprising job of refurbishing the old boat," Frank says. "The boat still needs to be furnished and stocked, and a new boiler, but otherwise she is ready to take passengers."

Malcolm scowls.

"They have a long way to go," he says coldly.

He stalks off down the gangplank, leaving Frank and his men to follow.

"They are not here," Malcolm complains.

"They did not know you were coming, sir," Frank says.

"I assumed someone would be here. I do not like having my time wasted. They should have been here."

Returning to the dock, Malcolm walks around to the prow to take one more look at the figurehead. The beautifully carved figure seems to be watching him. It makes him feel uncomfortable, sending a shiver through him; those secretive dark eyes and the small sad curve of the mouth that suggest she might whisper secrets in his ear that would shock and torment him for life.

Unable to shake the feeling that unnerves him, Malcolm returns to wait by the cars, pacing impatiently.

"I am not leaving without dealing with these men," he complains, crossing his arms and leaning against the car in an angry posture. He stares off at nothing.

At last, a tired and dirty looking man comes walking into the dockyard and up the dock. He is just one of many such men who would move through the crowd of dockworkers and men looking for work; any kind of work.

Alone at the empty dockyard he is an anomaly who does not belong.

Darius is exhausted and wants only to fall onto his blankets and sleep. He walks around the corner into the dockyard, immediately noticing the cars and men parked next to the Gypsy Queen.

"Why are they parked next to the boat? It must be a coincidence. They must be here for business with someone else. We have paid everyone except Norman and Walter. They would not be here in expensive cars," he tries to convince himself.

It does not work and Darius's stomach is a tight knot in his gut.

Darius catches Malcolm's eye long before it becomes apparent he is heading his way.

Malcolm watches the approaching man absently, becoming interested only when he gets close and it becomes clear he is coming to the Gypsy Queen.

Darius takes a furtive look at the men as he approaches, recognizing Malcolm. He stiffens.

"Shit. This is not good."

Darius tries to keep his expression blank, fighting the urge to run for his life. The man has tried to kill him once already.

Darius barely looks up as he is about to walk past the cars and waiting men. They all watch him, surprised he seems oblivious to their presence.

Malcolm sees differently. He notes the stiffening of Darius's shoulders and the set of his expression.

"He knew we are here the moment he stepped into the dockyard. The cars parked next to the boat, us waiting here, it leaves no room for doubt who we are waiting for. He is playing like he doesn't see us."

"You are right," Frank says, eying the approaching man suspiciously. His hand moves instinctively towards his handgun, his other tightening its grip on his ram's head cane.

"Hello there," Malcolm calls to Darius. "Where are your bosses, the boat owners?"

Darius stops, wishing he is anywhere else, and looks up to meet Malcolm's stare.

"That's me," he says.

Malcolm looks him over doubtfully.

"I was told you were just a pair of labourers but I didn't believe it."

"It's the truth."

Malcolm looks at him closer. For the first time a sense of familiarity rings in his memory.

"Do I know you from somewhere?" he asks.

"I do not believe so," Darius says, hoping he does not make the connection.

"Let us get right to business," Malcolm says. "I have wasted enough time already waiting for you. I am here to make to you a very generous offer."

Darius looks at him suspiciously.

"I don't think I am going to like where this is going," he thinks.

Malcolm continues.

"I have been told you are planning to operate a casino boat. That is not a wise choice. I own the only casino boat on the water and I intend to keep it that way. If you continue with this plan of yours, you and your boat will have an unfortunate accident."

Darius shifts uncomfortably, trying to keep his expression calm despite the anger and fear simmering inside.

"That sounds like a threat."

Malcolm lets a slow grin spread across his face. His eyes show only malice.

"I do not have to mince my words with the likes of you. I have the Gaming Commission, Casino Workers Union, the Dock Master, and the police all in my back pocket. I am untouchable."

"However, I am also a reasonable man," Malcolm says. "You just happen to have acquired a boat that once belonged to my father; a boat that held a very special place in my father's life and his heart. I would like to have that boat back in the family. I will allow you to sell me the boat and any equipment you may have procured; for a reasonable price of course."

"I have a feeling your idea of a reasonable price is at a substantial loss to what we have already paid and still owe."

Malcolm's grin turns cold. "I did say at a reasonable price. Reasonable for me."

"I am not at liberty to talk for my partner," Darius says, his voice trembling despite his attempt to control it, "but I have no intention of selling the boat."

"Funny. I heard differently," Malcolm sneers at him.

"The boat is not for sale." Darius is struggling to control the tremor threatening to take over his whole body. He can't stop the fear sweat that breaks out. He feels clammy with it.

Malcolm looks at this man who dares to defy him. He sees his fear.

"I do know him from somewhere," he thinks. And he suddenly knows where. He narrows his eyes, studying the man.

"I know where I know you from," he says. "You and your partner snuck on my boat. You and your friend decided to go for a little swim. Tell me, is your partner the same fool you were with then, or did you find another fool?"

Darius steels himself. He is terrified inside. "Don't let him see your fear," he thinks. He stares back, his expression blank and his eyes hard. He clenches his fists at his side to try to stop their trembling.

"I remember," he says evenly.

"Sell it all to me at my price and just walk away; otherwise you two will not be walking anywhere at all." Malcolm eyes Darius, shifting his gaze meaningfully to the open water then back to him again.

Malcolm signals his men and they move in closer, surrounding Darius.

With a wicked grin, Malcolm turns back to his car as Frank opens his door.

Malcolm gets in and leans out, directing his attention back to Darius.

"I will be expecting to hear from you."

He nods to Frank, leaning back and staring straight ahead as the security man closes the door and gets into the front seat, giving Darius a hard look as he does so.

The rest get into the cars and they begin driving away.

Frank opens his window and tips his stout ram's head cane to salute Darius. With a grin he closes the window, the car turning and driving across the dockyard with the others following behind it.

Malcolm chuckles.

"I have to tell you; I don't know if I should laugh or yell. I can't believe the gall of these two, yet at the same time I have to grudgingly admit that I feel a stirring of respect for them."

Darius watches the cars drive away, letting the fear take hold of him at last. He cannot stop trembling and feels sick.

***

Malcolm paces the opulent office at his home with an old fashioned crystal glass of expensive brandy in his hand.

The image of the carved woman on the prow of the Gypsy Queen is stuck in his mind. He feels a sudden need to possess that woman, the boat. His desire for the boat before was nothing more than the need to not have competition and the jealousy of someone who cannot stand to let anyone have anything better than him.

Now it fills him with a fiery hunger to own, to possess.

"The Gypsy Queen is more elegant than the Queen Rhiannon. I will have the Gypsy Queen and make her into my casino boat. I will have the old equipment pulled out and replace it with the sleek modern style I prefer. The lights will be replaced with something fancier and the trim on the walls repainted in more garish and lively colors.

She will replace the Queen Rhiannon as the only floating paddlewheel casino on the water. I will have the Queen Rhiannon stripped and repainted in muted colors and sold.

My casino boat will be better, richer, more beautiful and grand."

The image of the dark haired dark eyed beauty on the boat's prow follows him as he paces. He cannot make that image go away.

With a grunt, Malcolm swallows the rest of his drink, putting his glass down too hard with a thud on the wooden table, and leaves the room.

Ascending the stairs, he goes to his bedroom and changes for bed.

Malcolm climbs into bed, drawing the blankets up, turns off the lamp, and closes his eyes, breathing heavy drunken breaths. He lays there staring at the darkness behind his closed lids.

His wife on the other side only rolls over, turning her back to him.

Slipping into the foggy half conscious state between sleep and wakefulness, the Gypsy beckons to him in that darkness behind his closed eyes; her eyes hooded against revealing their secrets and the small sad smile on her lips as she whispers soundlessly to him.

Malcolm wakes in a cold sweat, his heart pounding in his chest sending a sharp pain down his arm. He sits up and looks around his large bedroom as if expecting to see the Gypsy woman there. His wife sleeps next to him, completely unaware. His pyjamas are soaked with sweat.

Malcolm is filled suddenly with an urgent need.

"I have to know why my father had the boat decommissioned and tried to destroy her despite her obvious value. I need to know the real reason my father had that boat taken from the water.

It is time to get some answers."

Malcolm gets out of bed, grabbing his robe and slipping it on over his sweat dampened pyjamas as he leaves the room. He goes down the hall and practically runs down the wide stairs to the main floor.

There he hesitates, turning to look down the hallway towards the back of the mansion. On the far end down that hallway, in the rooms furthest from where he sleeps with his wife, are the rooms occupied by an old man.

His father.

"After all these years, decades during which everyone had assumed the old man had died and been quietly buried, my father has hidden in his rooms, still alive. Out of the sight and the knowledge of the world."

Malcolm walks down that darkened hallway and stops at the end, staring at the closed double doors. He grips both door handles, turns them, and pushes the doors open. For the first time in his life, Malcolm does not bother to knock when he enters his father's rooms.

The old man is sitting in a chair before the fireplace, shrivelled with age and infirmity, seeming to be swallowed by the large chair.

The flames in the fireplace dance and flicker low, giving off little light, slowly burning down as they consume the wood.

The old man's balding head shines beneath the wisps of white hair that refuse to give up and fall out like the rest. Age spots and the odd mole mar the nearly bare scalp. The face beneath is barely more than a skull draped with skin, the skin ruined with age spots and wrinkles. The boniness of the old man's frame is hidden beneath the now too large housecoat covering it. One arm is visible halfway between the wrist and elbow, resting in his lap, skeletal and frail. Like the head and arm, the hand is ravaged by wrinkles and age spots, impossibly thin, veins bulging where flesh should have covered them, roadways of blue beneath the paper thin skin.

Malcolm's breath catches in his throat.

"The old man has finally died," he thinks, feeling a mix of remorse for having those answers he desperately needs stolen from him and relief at being rid of the old man.

He can detect no sign movement, not even of a single breath rattling in or out of those ancient lungs.

The corpse opens its eyes. The eyes stare at him, sharp and intelligent. He is alive.

Malcolm walks forward, approaching the chair, feeling like a small boy again trying to get the courage to face the towering man who was his father.

Now he towers over the frail creature swallowed by the chair; the weak creature who was once his father.

Swallowing, Malcolm forces the words out.

"Tell me about the Gypsy Queen."

The old man chuckles a dry raspy sound more resembling a death rattle than a laugh.

"What interest do you suddenly have in an old boat?"

"She wasn't destroyed. Did you know that?"

Malcolm studies his father for a reaction and the old man only keeps staring at him with that unsettling intelligence.

"No, you wouldn't know. How would you; locked away here in a prison of your own making? Yes, the salvager did not destroy the Gypsy Queen as you ordered. Instead she was sold in a salvage lot and then left to rot."

"And you want to bring her back to life." The old man's voice is a dry sound that rubs on his nerves.

"Someone already did. She's been rebuilt."

The old man grins a toothless grin.

"You feel the pull of her don't you? She calls to you, making you need to possess her. You fool. You were always stupid. You were a stupid boy and now you are a stupid fool of a man."

"Stop playing. She was the most valuable boat on the river. Why did you have the Gypsy Queen decommissioned? Why did you order her destroyed?"

"You think you can possess her beauty. That you can control it. Own it. You can't. Her beauty will own you. She will devour your soul."

"Stop it old man. Answer my question."

"She cannot be owned. Not by me or you. Not by any man."

"Father..." Malcolm's fists are balled and his voice is as angry as his face.

"She is evil."

"Why did you take her off the water?"

"The water gives her power."

"Why did you have her decommissioned?"

"She destroyed me. She will destroy you."

"Why did you order her destroyed?" Malcolm is shouting now, his anger building.

"Blood gives her more power. Death."

The old man is shaking his head now as if regretting some long ago choice.

"She cannot be destroyed and she cannot be allowed to exist"

Malcolm struggles to control his temper. The overwhelming urge to punch the old man has him stepping forward as his arm draws back. He wants to pummel him. To beat him into oblivion.

"I am not going to leave without answers," Malcolm says with cold anger.

"The old fool is not of sound enough mind to give me those answers," Malcolm thinks, his frustration surging.

Malcolm grins and it shows only malice towards his father.

"You have always been the stupid one, old man. You abandoned the most valuable boat on the river to the scrap heap. You abandoned a profitable casino business. And for what?

I heard the rumors old man. Oh yes, I know all about them. Your womanizing. The one woman who would not have you."

"No one would say no to me," Thaddeus hisses at him.

"She did," Malcolm sneers. "Oh, you could take her, possess her, own her, but you could not truly have her. She refused you that."

Thaddeus is leaning forward in his chair, gnarled bony hands gripping the chair arms, eyes blazing with fury.

"What happened old man? What happened the night you came home covered in blood?

Everything changed that night. You started your decline. You started to become a recluse, and you finished when you put me in your place as a figurehead at the top of your casino empire the moment I came of age. You pulled the strings from the dark for a while, but you aged quickly. From the night you came home covered in blood and raving like a lunatic, you aged quickly. And from the moment you stopped making public appearances you began to deteriorate."

Malcolm taps his head for emphasis.

"You began to pass into a vague world of an infirm mind lost to ramblings and haunted by the ghosts of his past."

Thaddeus looks like he would rise from his chair and throttle his son if he were not too infirm to do so.

Malcolm grins, full of spite and hatred for his father.

Thaddeus sits back and starts to chuckle. It comes out a dry wheezing cough and builds, his shoulders rising and falling to it, and then his whole body shaking with it.

"It is suiting in a way," he says. "The son who was made the figurehead of an empire, a puppet under the control of his father, the puppet master, now stands before the withered old man, drawn there by a figurehead; under the spell of a wooden woman adorning the very boat that seemed to have put his father spiralling into infirmity."

***

Darius turns and starts walking out of the casino floor. He stops. Something red caught his eye.

He walks through the cloth-covered tables and stops. Darius looks at the door.

"Did the constable leave this? No. Not likely. Mr. Barlow?"

He eyes it warily. The red cloth-wrapped object appears harmless.

Darius picks it up hesitantly. He unwraps it to reveal a deck of cards. He flips through them quickly, noting the picture of the gypsy woman on the back and the tarot card faces.

Travis walks in and freezes, staring at the cards in Darius's hand.

"Where did you find that? I must have dropped it."

He feels the need to claim it, but also feels relief it is in someone else's possession.

"Right here on the table." Darius looks at him.

"What is this?" he asks as he turns it over, looking at it.

Travis looks at it almost hesitantly, reliving his fear for just a moment before pushing the fear away.

"Tarot cards," he says. "I found them in a chest at the barn. They look like they probably came from someone pretending to be a Gypsy card reader; maybe a real one even. I thought you might find them interesting. Wasn't your mother a Gypsy?"

Darius nods.

"She was Roma, but you know that whole stereotype thing is actually pretty insulting. That is not who they are. It is curious, though, considering we are about to start running a business that revolves around card games and luck, and on a boat called the Gypsy Queen with that same stereotype plastered on the front of it."

He rewraps and pockets the cards and starts walking out to the deck.

"I'll look at these later. You found them in a trunk? Was there anything else there like this?"

"I didn't really look," Travis admits. "We can look when we go back to the barn tomorrow."

Travis follows Darius out. They stand on the deck looking out over the dockyard.

"We had a visitor," Darius says.

"Who?" Travis is instantly alert and wary.

"The police constable."

"What did he want?"

"What does everybody else want?"

"A bribe." Travis chuckles a humorless laugh and Darius nods.

Darius mulls over telling him about the visit from Malcolm Barlow when something catches his eye.

"Hey, what's that?"

"What?" Travis cranes to look. "I don't see anything."

"There." Darius points. "I think someone is down there."

"Let's go check it out." Travis starts for the gangplank and Darius puts out a restraining hand.

"Wait. We don't know who it is."

"Okay, then let's sneak up on him and find out."

Moving cautiously, they duck low and try to leave the boat unseen.

Stepping lightly, they approach the person on the docks from behind.

"You aren't very good at sneaking," the man says as they are getting close.

Darius blanches and Travis looks startled.

Herman turns around to face them.

"Why are you here?" Darius asks.

Herman shrugs. "With all that equipment onboard and all the trouble you have been having, I figured you need someone to guard it."

Travis and Darius exchange a look, both suspicious of what his true motives might be.

"You work for the Shipbuilders' Union," Darius says. "Why would you be guarding our boat?"

39   Warning

Amelia steps out of the dress shop and walks down the side of the road.

"I have one more stop to make before going home. Father has kept an eagle eye on me ever since the launching of the Gypsy Queen into the river and his tirade over my presence at the event."

Her pace quickens angrily at the thought of it.

"This is the first time I have been able to leave the house without him and I will relish in the freedom of it," she says stubbornly.

Amelia is startled when she is suddenly brought back to reality by a man blocking her path.

He is a frighteningly rough looking man and puts her immediately on edge with his presence. He has a feeling of danger about him.

"I do not appreciate the way he is looking at me like I am a piece of meat on a dinner plate he is about to bite into," she thinks.

"Hey girl," Walter says.

"Excuse me," Amelia says, moving to go around him.

He moves, keeping his eyes on her and preventing her from passing him.

"Let me pass," she says indignantly, stiffening her back and trying to push past him without touching the vile man.

He moves, blocking her path again.

Amelia stares at him. "I have a very bad feeling about this," she thinks.

She turns and runs, lifting her skirts to keep from tripping, the man chasing her.

Amelia turns down another street and then down another, running as fast as she can, her breath coming in ragged hiccupping sobs, the man in pursuit and finally gaining on her.

He grabs her arm, spinning her around off balance and pulls her into the darkness behind a building.

She struggles and tries to scream, but he pulls her close, wrapping one arm around her while covering her mouth with the other, muffling her cries.

Walter drags her further behind the building.

Once he has her deep in the shadows he stops, pinning her against the wall and leaning against her heavily. His breath is sickening and the odor of his body revolting.

Amelia is terrified.

"If you struggle or scream I will hurt you," he hisses in her ear. "Behave and maybe I won't. Understand?"

She nods; her eyes wide like a frightened doe, tears springing to them.

"I like the way you tremble," he says roughly, reaching up to grope at her breasts over her dress.

She whimpers.

"You are the little bird that was with my friend, Travis," he says, shoving his hand inside the top of her dress and groping roughly.

Amelia squirms, trying to break free; but he holds her harder, hurting her, leaning harder and crushing her against the wall.

"Your boyfriend owes me money. I warned him what I would do if he got behind on his payments." He licks her neck with his disgusting tongue.

Amelia struggles, kicking at him and trying to bite him. A scream escapes past his hand as he struggles to control her.

He grabs her hair, pulling it hard and forcing her head back. Pinning her to the wall with his body, he slaps her hard enough to leave a mark across her cheek.

A trickle of blood dribbles from her nose and he slams her against the wall, banging her head with a dull thud that makes her dizzy as the pain explodes in her skull.

He shoves his hand between her legs, grabbing her through her skirts, groping hard and squeezing, pulling her to him suggestively.

"Tell your boyfriend if he does not pay up I will be coming back for you; take my interest from here."

He gropes at her between the legs again, making his meaning more than clear enough.

Walter shoves her away roughly, making her fall to the ground, and walks away, leaving her shaken and only a little hurt to give Travis the message.

Amelia sits there sobbing on the ground; covering her face with her hands.

40   The Old Gypsy Trunk

Travis and Darius open the door of the barn, letting the light splash across the dust-laden air and the straw and dusty tables.

"Okay, so we'll load up some more tables to bring back and take another look at those old steamer trunks," Travis says.

They load up the tables and then stand in the middle of the barn, looking around.

"The trunks are in the back corner," Travis says.

They go to the back corner, standing over the old steamer trunks.

"That's the one with the cards," Travis says.

Darius looks at the trunk, its lid still left open from Travis's previous visit and its contents only hastily rummaged through. The trunk itself looks to be in decent enough shape.

He pulls it out. It is heavy, scraping against the floor as he turns it, looking it over.

"This trunk doesn't look too bad," Darius says. "We could use it for storage. Do you think there might be anything else like those cards in here?"

"Could be. I didn't really look through all the stuff in there."

Darius starts going through the contents of the trunk, shifting them around and doubting there will be anything but the clothes that stink of age and mildew.

"I only looked through the tarot cards quickly. Did you notice the slight variations in the pictures of the Gypsy woman on the backs?" Darius asks.

"Yes. I thought that was interesting, and curious. With a little distraction and the nervousness I imagine someone might feel getting their fortune read, the fortune teller's customer likely wouldn't even notice the differences. However, the fortune teller would know with each card exactly what picture would be found on the flip side."

"So, a cheating fortune teller."

"A card counting fortune teller," Travis laughs.

There is an edge to the laugh that makes Darius look at him, wondering if the cards somehow bother him.

"I never thought Travis was superstitious, but he sure seems bothered by those cards," Darius thinks.

"I suspect the owner of the cards was no real fortune teller," he says, "but rather used the marked cards to trick their paying visitors into either believing their powers or paying extra money to learn their fortunes. I can see no reason why the cards would be markedly different on the back side otherwise."

"They are pretty detailed for a charlatan. The intricate details of the painted pictures on both sides surprised me."

"I'm the so-called Gypsy here, and I don't believe in this stuff. You aren't buying into those cards belonging to a real fortune teller with some kind of powers, are you? The pictures were all disturbing in some way, and I didn't even give them much of a look. I expect that is intended to add to the con. And it is only that, a con."

"It does fit the motif of our casino boat," Travis says. He goes back to rummaging in his trunk.

Darius looks at the other trunks. This one that held the tarot cards looks different from the rest. The others are basic steamer trunks, the type commonly used for packing to travel long distances when a suitcase would not be enough. They are plain and functional. This trunk is a little smaller and decorative with a similar feel to the cards. He does not know much about what would be considered Gypsy style, but to him the trunk feels stereotyped Gypsy.

"That makes sense," he thinks. "If someone is going to play the stereotyped Gypsy part to con people, they would go all out with the costume, cards, trunk, and all."

He looks at the clothing with a frown. They don't look like much. Garish colors of age-rotten cloth that is yellowing in blotches.

"Well, I'm not finding anything else in this one," he mutters.

Looking around quickly, he grabs some handfuls of stuff that looks like Travis had yanked it out and left it on the floor on his previous visit, shoving it carelessly back in the trunk. His hand hits something hard inside as he does.

Darius looks at the jumbled clothing. Reaching in and shifting the contents, he finds the object and pulls it out, holding it up to examine it.

It is a flat wooden board, decoratively painted like the tarot cards. The paint is cracked with age and the wood looks on the verge of splitting down the middle. Strange markings and lettering is painted on the front face of the board.

He gets an odd feeling just looking at it, like the board might somehow be connected to something spiritual, drawing unseen forces to it.

"Nonsense," Darius thinks. "You don't believe in that nonsense. It was probably just one of the gimmicks the fake fortune teller used to trick money out of her clients."

Returning the board to the trunk and covering it up, he closes the trunk and picks it up to carry it out to the wagon.

"You are taking the chest?" Travis asks.

"I thought I'd go through it more carefully later," Darius says. "It goes with the cards."

"I don't think we can fit anymore," Travis says, getting up. "Let's go unload. We can go through these trunks later."

"Suits me. It's going to take us a while to unload," Darius says.

Darius loads the chest and they strap the load down and drive back to the boat.

They unload at the boat, piling the load inside.

Darius brings the chest to the empty room that is his sleeping quarters instead of leaving it with the rest of the stuff to be put in place later. He spreads a blanket over it before returning to the deck.

"I am going to return the wagon and mules and see if I can find Amelia," Travis says. "We haven't seen her since we put the Queen in the water."

"All right. I'm going to get some sleep."

After dropping the wagon and mules off and paying the livery man, Travis starts on foot in search of Amelia. He walks the town, trying to think of where she might be.

"I have been trying to see her at every chance I have since we put the Gypsy Queen in the water, but with no luck."

"She is probably at home. I can't just go to her house. Her father would never let me see her. Hell, he would probably chase me off with an axe or some other weapon."

Travis grins despite himself at the image of Amelia's father chasing him and waving some houseware instrument of his destruction.

He frowns.

"What if she is avoiding me after the shock of witnessing the man killed beneath the Queen when we put her in the water? That would have been pretty traumatic for her to see."

"I need to see her, to talk to her. I need to make sure everything is all right after she witnessed that terrible accident."

He looks up at the stars starting to come out.

"Come on Lady Luck, give me some luck tonight."

***

Amelia staggers up the front walk to her house on wooden legs that do not want to work. Grasping the door handle, she fumbles with it and thrusts it open, stumbling inside and closing the door too quickly behind her with a slam.

"Is that you, Amelia?" her mother's voice calls from the kitchen.

"Yes, it's me," Amelia manages to mumble out.

"You don't sound right."

Lena steps from the kitchen, walking briskly to the front entrance, and stops. Her face drains of color and she stares at Amelia.

Amelia stares back at her with haunted eyes. Her hair is dishevelled and her dress dirty and in disarray. She is still visibly shaken, pale and trembling.

Lena stares at the mark on her face and red smear of blood from her nose. The spell breaks.

"What happened?" Lena wails, rushing forward.

She is putting her hands all over Amelia, searching for injuries. All Amelia can feel is that deplorable man's hands on her. She tries to ward her mother's hands away.

"Are you hurt? Were you run over? Trampled?" Lena's voice is high with stress.

Her mother's distress brings on new waves of sobbing. Amelia breaks down sobbing harder and babbling incoherently about the man who chased and attacked her in the street.

Hearing the commotion, her father comes in from the parlor. He freezes, staring at his daughter in shock, noticing her dishevelled appearance, face splotched with tears, the mark from the man's blow, and the smeared blood.

He pulls himself together with a visible effort, looking shaken himself now.

"What happened?" Roman demands in a hard cold voice that quavers a little.

"A-a m-m-man," Amelia manages, her teeth chattering with her trembling from shock. "A s-strange m-man. He-he attacked me."

Amelia feels faint, her body suddenly washed in a wet chill. Her face turns pasty and damp.

"She is about to faint," Lena wails.

Roman lunges forward, grabbing her as her legs give out and holding her up awkwardly.

"Help me get her to bed," he urges Lena.

Together they manage to half carry and half drag the weak woman to her room and lay her in her bed.

Lena covers her face, sobbing as she flees the room.

Roman closes the door, returning to the front hall and the beginning of the scene.

He paces angrily from the front entrance to the parlour, pulling back the curtains to look out at the offending world for any sign of his daughter's attacker. He moves on, pacing to the kitchen where his wife is sobbing in a chair at the table and looks up to him to make it right.

He continues pacing angrily.

"I am going to get my boys together and go after the man," he swears loudly. "Whoever did this is going to pay."

He turns and stalks to Amelia's room, flinging the door open, Lena following anxiously.

Amelia starts with a jump at the sudden intrusion, her eyes wide with the fear still gripping her from the incident in the street. She looks at them as though she does not quite recognize them.

"Who did this?" Roman demands.

"I-I don't know," Amelia manages.

In his fury, Roman looms over her and grills her, throwing questions at her faster than she can answer, repeatedly asking about the details that stuck in his mind, needing to identify the man who attacked his daughter.

Her mind in a jumbled confusion of shock and trauma, Amelia starts mixing things up. She is stressed over the attack and her father's bullying inquisition, worrying he might find out that the attack is Travis's fault.

She blurts it out.

"The man who attacked me said it is a message to Travis to pay his debt!"

Roman falls suddenly silent, glaring at her. Behind him, Lena looks horrified. The silence in the room is a physical entity.

Amelia can see the very moment Roman goes from frenetic anger to shock, to deadly rage.

"What have I done?" she thinks sickly.

His mouth claps closed, his face turns purple and seems to puff like a balloon, and his breath stops.

She thinks he might drop dead of a heart attack right in front of her.

Then he explodes.

The expulsion of expletives that pour from his mouth is shocking. Lena covers her mouth and eyes in shock, as if the act will somehow gag Roman's foul lips.

Amelia covers her ears, the volume hurting them.

Finally, Roman whirls on Amelia, leaning over her, threatening; his eyes bulging and purple face inches from hers. She cannot help but stare at that vein visibly throbbing in his temple, certain it will suddenly burst at any moment.

"He is responsible for this," Roman says. He did this. Travis."

"You. Will. NOT. See. That. Man. Ever. Again." His words come slow and in a deadly low voice she has never heard from her father before. Each word coming out apart from the one before and after it, a pause between each that makes each word all the more lethal.

Roman turns and walks out of her room. He leaves the house without another word.

"He is going to kill Travis, isn't he?" Amelia whimpers.

Lena does not answer, staring after the open door. "He just might," she thinks. She retreats from the room.

Roman's words do not have their intended effect. They echo in her mind. "You will NOT see that man ever again."

"I have to see Travis; no matter what Father says. I have to know that he is okay. I am afraid of what my father might do. And that man who attacked me; he will go after him. I need to warn him about the man who attacked me before he hurts him."

Amelia gets out of bed and moves to sit at her dressing table, looking at her stricken face staring back at her in the mirror.

"I need to make sure Father does not hurt Travis. Or Darius either. He could get hurt too just for being there."

She swallows, fighting back the tears. She also wants to hurt Travis herself with the knowledge of the man's attack on her and that it is his fault.

She stares at the mirror for a while, looking at herself. The face staring back at her looks angry, traumatized, and hollow-eyed.

"I look different. I feel different."

She makes a face and presses her fingers against her features as if that will fix them.

"Everyone will know. They will take one look at me and know that I have been violated."

She can still smell the stink of the vulgar man on her; feel his foul hands on her. Her body still throbs with the revulsion of his touch and where he touched her. Her heart beats fast and her body tremors with the fear she cannot let go. Sour sickness rolls in her stomach.

Amelia's eyes burn with hot angry tears and her cheeks with shame.

Her bottom lip quivers and she stares harder in the mirror, holding onto her anger like a life preserver.

"I am so angry," she tells her mirror self. "I am angry that foul disgusting lout dared to put a hand on me. I am angry that I am soiled and afraid. I am angry about the attack I suffered at the hands of that disgusting man over Travis's debts and I want nothing more to do with Travis. Ever."

But at the same time she yearns to see him.

"I should tell Travis what happened. Make him know what he did. Make him hurt for hurting me."

"Tell Darius." The idea worms its way in and Amelia does not know which she wants more. To see Travis hurt for hurting her, to make sure he is safe, or who she wants to see more.

That yearning wells up through the sickness rolling in her stomach and through the pain and fear swelling her chest, filling her with worry over him. It catches in her throat, making it difficult to breathe. It forces the tears to flow from her eyes.

Amelia rubs the tears away angrily, hating what she sees in the mirror.

"I cannot hide what happened."

She hears her mother somewhere in the house and looks quickly at the door.

"Please do not come in," she whispers.

***

Travis and Darius are at the Gypsy Queen putting the gaming tables and machines in place.

"We just need to get some decks of playing cards, chips, and dice, and we are in business," Travis says, grinning.

"And the permits, furnishings for the rest of the boat, food and alcohol, and staff," Darius adds, his face a serious mask of exhaustion. "And a new boiler."

"You look exhausted," Travis observes. "Why don't you go have a sleep? I'll finish setting up here."

Darius nods and goes to his room. He stops, looking around the empty room. The only furnishings are his pillow and blanket and the old steamer trunk.

The blanket covering the trunk is carelessly tossed aside and the trunk lid is wide open.

Darius looks around quickly as if he might spot the culprit.

He walks to the chest. He hadn't had a chance to look through it yet, so he would have no way of knowing if anything is missing.

"Did Travis go through the trunk?"

Darius turns to the door intent on finding out.

He stops.

A single card lies on the floor before the door.

"That wasn't there when I came in, was it? I don't remember seeing it."

Darius picks it up, staring at it.

A dark eyed dark haired Gypsy woman stares at him from the card. Her tumbling locks of long hair flow into her dress, both seeming to melt into the background as if she is only partially there, materializing from some ghostly plane that is the picture behind her. Her eyes appear heavy with the weight of some secret she dares not tell, her lips curved in the smallest hint of a sad smile. Behind her a castle sits on a cliff, waves crashing against the cliff as though to tumble the castle down to be destroyed on the rocks below. The rolling waves hold the suggestion of a boat about to be dashed against the cliffs.

He can't stop staring at her, drawn to her eyes and pulled into their mysterious depths.

"It can't be," he whispers.

The woman on the tarot card is the very same woman adorning the front of the Gypsy Queen.

He has to force his eyes away from the card, blinking and keeping them closed while he counts the heartbeats of his wildly pounding heart.

When he opens his eyes again the picture on the card is different. The woman is different; standing instead of beckoning. Not melting from the background. It is not her.

Darius looks more closely at the waves, unable to find any hint of the boat that had been there.

He feels shaken.

Darius turns and looks at the open chest. He goes to it, kneeling to move the age-rotten faded and once garishly colored fabric.

There, exactly where he had left it, is the deck of tarot cards carefully wrapped in the red cloth and tied with the ribbon.

Darius picks the deck up and unties it, his hands trembling. He unwraps the cards, searching through them and expecting this one to prove to be a duplicate, somehow dropped or planted.

The card is not in the deck. Replacing the card, he wraps and ties them again, and then wraps them in a shirt for good measure before putting the deck back in the trunk and closing the lid.

Darius feels a chill tickle down his back, as though the very lightest of touches traced down it.

Embarrassed, he decides not to mention the trunk or the cards.

"I'm getting punchy."

He takes his blanket and pillow, does his best to make himself comfortable, and tries to go to sleep.

The eyes of the woman on the card haunt him into his sleep.

41   Maiden Voyage

Travis and Darius are in the boiler room, grease soiled and slick with sweat. They are staring at the old rebuilt steamer boiler. Fire glows inside the open door, most of the smoke rising up the chimney stack.

"Do you even know anything about this kind of boiler?" Darius asks.

Travis scratches his head, a heavy wrench in his other hand.

"A boiler is a boiler. They all work on the same principles. I still can't believe the shape it's in. I didn't even consider being able to rebuild it."

Darius looks at the boiler skeptically.

"These boilers are nothing like the other boilers. They don't go through the same kind of abuse a steamboat boiler does."

Travis tries again to start the boiler. It makes noise and dies.

"I don't get it. We cleaned and checked every inch of it."

"Maybe it's ceased," Darius says.

"Not possible. I've never seen a cleaner boiler and this thing sat for years. Old Thaddeus Barlow babied her. He went high class all the way. This is not some poorly designed or maintained boiler. There was not a dent or scratch on her. No one abused this baby."

"Just a lot of rust," Darius says. "No matter how well maintained, it has probably weakened with age."

"She will start. Maybe she's not hot enough."

"Just go slow. I don't want to be in here if it blows up."

Travis adds more wood to the fire, stoking it hotter.

He tries starting the engine again. It chugs, rattles, and dies.

"Are you using the right fuel?" Darius asks.

Travis shrugs. "Wood is free everywhere. Just cut up some deadwood."

"Maybe it's supposed to be coal."

"We don't have the money for coal."

"Maybe it's the wrong kind of wood? Some burn hotter than others."

***

Malcolm Barlow is furious. He is standing on the deck of the Queen Rhiannon glaring at the Gypsy Queen. The slow trail of smoke from the smokestack thickens. He hears the belch of the boiler trying to start, stalling, and silence.

He grits his teeth.

Frank stands behind him silently while he rants on.

"I have threatened them, offered to buy her, bribed everyone, and finally hired a couple of dock workers to sabotage the Gypsy Queen, and it all failed. Everything I did to make them give her to me failed. Those idiots are completely unaware of most of my attempts to ruin their plans."

He turns to look at Frank with his baleful glare.

"How have I not won? How are they still carrying on? The two fools I had unceremoniously tossed from my boat to drown are succeeding when I was so sure they would fail.

They know nothing about running a steamboat or a casino. That is the only reason I have not outright had them killed yet."

He turns back to glare at the Gypsy Queen.

"I am going to enjoy watching them fail. And when they do, I will scoop up their boat for a song. For nothing. They will beg me to take her."

***

Amelia arrives at the dockyard. She looks across the empty yard to the docks where two fancy steamboats are tied among the looming dark shapes of the ugly river barges.

The two paddlewheel boats are a stark contrast to each other. They are both stern wheeler showboats with a single large paddle wheel on the back of the boat.

But where one is an ugly gaudy carnival of color and design, the other is even more elegant in contrast.

Swallowing her fear of being in the dark and silent dockyard at night, she forces herself to walk on towards the docks.

As Amelia is nearing the docks, she stops and listens; sure she heard the soft sound of footsteps somewhere in the dark.

She looks around and sees nothing.

"It's your nerves," she whispers to herself. "There is nothing there. Nobody."

Amelia is filled with the urge to turn back and call it off.

"You can't quit now. You have to confront Travis about the man who attacked you."

She pushes the other thought down, the need to see him and confirm that he is okay. Amelia steels herself against it, trying to hold on to her anger.

"You can't confront someone you feel sorry for."

Amelia reaches the docks and her shoes make a soft thocking sound against the wood. She tries to walk quieter, unnerved by the silent darkness, the only other sounds the water lapping against the docks and licking up the supports beneath them, and the occasional bump of a boat against its padded bumpers keeping it from hitting the dock.

She pauses at the bottom of the gangplank for the Gypsy Queen. The boat is quiet and dark, but there is smoke rising from the smokestack.

Docked nearby, the Queen Rhiannon's lights cast a glow across the deck of the Gypsy Queen.

"They aren't here. It's too dark and quiet."

The sound of the engine trying to come to life reverberates through the boat, chugs, and dies.

"Okay, so they are here then."

She steps onto the gangplank, walking up it almost soundlessly to the deck above. Amelia looks around. There is no sign of anyone onboard. She moves along the side, finding a door and taking the stairs descending to the level below.

***

Another fart belches from the Gypsy Queen's boiler next door as it struggles to start and fails again.

"I've had enough just watching and waiting," Malcolm growls.

His anger still growing, he spins away from the deck railing and paces back and forth then stalks across the deck. He moves purposely down the gangplank.

His security team is unaware he left.

Malcolm stops on the dock and stares up at the Gypsy Queen, his eyes glittering with a deadly intensity.

"When I confronted my father about that boat, the old man just stared at me vacantly and talked nonsense. But I could see the intelligence in those eyes, measuring, always measuring me. I knew the old man was in there."

The old man's refusal to answer his questions had only made more questions burn inside him and fuelled his anger.

"And then he came out."

Malcolm starts walking up the Gypsy Queen's gangplank to confront the men who possess her.

***

"I don't know what is wrong with her," Travis says. "She just won't start. We checked everything. It doesn't make sense. The boiler should be heating up enough. The engine should start."

"It sat for a long time. Maybe the boiler has to be replaced after all," Darius says.

They come up a ladder and through a hatch in the deck floor at the back of the boat, standing on the deck just ahead of the paddle wheel.

They both stop and stare.

A man is coming up the gangplank, a dark form in the night shadows.

"Herman?" Travis calls out.

He stops at the top and begins stalking across the deck towards them. His stance and walk trigger a warning in them both.

Darius takes an instinctive step back.

Travis holds his ground.

Seeing his quarry, Malcolm moves across the deck, speeding up as he goes. He notices one taking a step back.

"He's trying to make a cowardly escape," he growls under his breath.

Halfway across the deck Malcolm moves from the shadows into the light coming from his own boat.

Recognizing him and seeing the rage on Malcolm's face, Travis does not want to meet him without a weapon to defend himself with.

He glances back at the open hatch.

Darius sees his look.

"It's too risky. He'll catch you with your head out and unable to protect it," he warns.

"I told you not to try running a casino boat!" Malcolm yells across the deck, the anger carrying his voice further. "I offered to buy the boat! You will sell her to me. I will have the Gypsy! You will give her to me!"

Malcolm pulls out a gun, stopping before them and pointing it between the two men, ready to move it the small degree necessary to hit either one.

A flash of movement, something dark in the shadows behind them, catches his eye.

He looks past Travis and Darius.

"Who is here with you?" Malcolm demands.

"There is no one else here," Darius says.

Malcolm continues to focus past them, looking for whoever is there, ready to aim and shoot them too.

"Come out!" he demands. "Whoever is there come out right now!"

There is no movement or sound; just the gentle rocking of the boat on the water, the lapping of the water on the docks and the soft bumping of boats against bumpers.

He turns his focus back to the men before him.

"Whoever is with you is a coward," he spits the words out at them, "hiding and sneaking off in the dark."

Distant music comes to them, tinny and muted.

Travis and Darius notice it immediately.

Each is pulled into their own memory of the music. It is the same music each thought he heard before on the Gypsy Queen. The same music that played in their dreams before the strange dark haired dark eyed woman appeared. The same woman the artist had carved for the figurehead.

The music is coming from behind Malcolm.

Malcolm hears it now.

He turns towards the casino room, keeping his gun trained on Travis and Darius.

Dull light diffuses through the casino room, softly glowing through the windows, the source of the light unknown.

Sound echoes distantly in the room, muted and soft as if a far away crowd mingles. People laughing and calling, gambling; dice clattering, dealers barking, and slot machines jingling and ringing happily fills the room despite its emptiness.

"What is going on?"

They all turn to focus on the source of the voice.

Amelia is standing there staring at them in confusion, her dress pale in the moonlight against the deck she stands on.

She gasps when she sees the gun.

Travis opens his mouth to tell her to run, ready to lunge forward and grab Malcolm's arm holding the gun.

Darius looks around, stunned, lost in the sounds and lights, barely registering the danger they are in from Malcolm. Lost in his fog he does not know Amelia is there.

Darius hears a soft whisper behind him.

Amelia stands before them, behind Malcolm, staring fearfully at the gun.

Malcolm looks at Amelia in confusion, not realizing the gun turns with him to point at the young woman.

"Where is that sound coming from?" Malcolm asks.

Amelia turns to the casino room, her eyes widening at what she sees.

The others are drawn by the surprise in her face, turning to look.

Travis reaches out, grabbing Darius's wrist and tugging on it.

Pulled out of his vision, Darius blinks and looks around in confusion. He sees Malcolm and the gun. The gun pointed at Amelia.

It feels unreal, more a dream than the dream he was in. It all seems to be moving very slowly.

The look on Amelia's face registers and he follows her eyes to see what the rest are staring at.

There, where he just stepped off the gangplank onto the deck, stands a withered old man, the faint wisps of white hair and his nearly bald head bringing attention to the moles and age spots that ruin the almost shiny scalp. Thaddeus Barlow.

The old man trembles with the effort of standing, the suit sagging on his wasted frame, his withered hands hanging at his sides. He raises one gnarled hand, pointing.

Another old man stands next to him, not offering any help. This man is not as old. Not as infirm.

Eugene Randall looks from the withered animated corpse beside him to the people before them.

"Father," Malcolm gasps.

Thaddeus steps forward, his pointing finger aiming at Malcolm accusingly.

"Fool," he rasps, his voice papery thin.

"Eugene, what are you doing here?" Malcolm asks, turning his eyes on him, taking them off his withered father with difficulty.

"Mr. Barlow called me," Eugene says, meaning the infirm man beside him. "I picked him up and brought him to her, the Gypsy Queen."

Thaddeus does not seem to be aware of the others' presence anymore. He stumbles forward on nearly crippled legs, staring at the rebuilt boat in awe and fear.

They watch the old man, the weight of the strangeness of it all weighing heavily on each of them.

Eugene steps forward.

"You don't know what you have done," he says. "You don't know about the Gypsy Queen."

"The Gypsy Queen was the first of her kind, a floating casino. Paddlewheel pleasure boats were going out of style and your father, Thaddeus, could have easily bought a whole fleet of them and fixed them up for the money he put into this one boat.

But the boat wasn't the real prize. Thaddeus owned the casino world. He was the cartel boss and he could have anything in the world he wanted. He didn't have to ask. He just took it.

Then a young woman came to work at the casino. She was beautiful, dark haired and dark eyed.

Thaddeus fell hard in love with her the moment he laid eyes on her, this beautiful young woman. Being wealthy, powerful, and used to being able to take what he wanted, he took that ability for granted. He never asked the girl what she wanted. In his world that did not matter.

Thaddeus thought he could own her heart and soul by right of his position. He expected that she would be loyal to him. He was so blindly enamoured with her that he was unable to see that the feelings were not mutual.

He just took her.

But he was a jealous man too and could not stand to share anything he treasured. No man but him could be allowed to even look at her.

Thaddeus needed someplace to keep her safe. He also needed to show off his prize. It wasn't enough to possess something; everyone had to know he possessed it.

He had the boat built, obsessing over the smallest detail. She had to be as elegant and beautiful as his Gypsy girl was. He commissioned a figurehead in her image for the prow even though it was unheard of on a riverboat.

He named the boat in the young woman's honor, calling her his beautiful Gypsy queen. She was a prisoner on board the new floating casino, never allowed to set foot off the boat, security men paid just to guard her.

Thaddeus spent more and more time on the boat, taking his young Gypsy queen to bed and completely ignorant of the young woman's sorrowful sobs afterwards.

The heartbroken young woman had tried to commit suicide a number of times; each time prevented that escape by Thaddeus's security men.

She swore curses against her captor and his men, and when she was allowed out of her room when the boat left the dock without guests and the barest of crew, she roamed the boat silently, slipping through its halls like a ghost, heartbroken and looking wistfully to the freedom that lay always beyond her reach across the water.

There were a number of different rumours floating around back then about the fate of the beautiful dark eyed young woman rumoured to be kept imprisoned on the Gypsy Queen. Some said she committed suicide and others that she died in a tragic accident in a desperate attempt to escape. Still others said that she was murdered at the hands of her unwanted lover, Thaddeus.

Even the stories of her murder varied. Some believed it happened because he was frustrated at her refusal to return his love and others that he murdered her in a jealous rage when he discovered she was in love with one of his security men.

The young man, her lover, turned out to be a young Romani man who had infiltrated Thaddeus's security men to rescue her. He was her true lover, and the man she was promised to marry before Thaddeus kidnapped her.

Nobody knew what happened to the young Romani man after her tragic death. Without a body, some even doubted the Gypsy girl ever existed. But, of course, there could be no body. Thaddeus was not about to go to jail.

The one thing the stories agreed on is that the Gypsy Queen was haunted by the spirit of the unhappy young woman seeking vengeance for the wrongs committed against her."

Thaddeus turns to them, pulling himself away from staring at the boat he had tried to destroy. His eyes hold an incredible sadness.

He looks at Malcolm.

"Your mother never understood, calling the boat my obsession. She only learned of the young woman later, after I had her on the boat for a while. She was furious when she found out."

"That's when she divorced you," Malcolm said.

"Yes," Thaddeus said. "She divorced me and I happily paid her what she wanted. I never loved her. Our marriage was more of a business arrangement. She tolerated my indiscretions and I ignored hers. She gave me an heir and I gave her anything she wanted. The only thing she really wanted was power, and she never had that. To have power over me I would have had to love her."

"But you loved the Gypsy woman," Amelia said softly.

Thaddeus looks at her.

"I don't know if you could call it that. Was it love?" He shakes his head. "I honestly don't know if I was ever capable of such a thing. I owned her, possessed her, but I don't know if I actually loved her."

"So, you destroyed this woman over a selfish loveless passion, a need to own something."

Thaddeus nods regretfully. "She was another trinket. A mere bauble. Something to own that was better than what anyone else owned. More beautiful and mysterious."

"I think she might even have been a witch." This last comes out so softly that not all of them heard it.

Amelia did. So did Darius.

"I paid the price for my foolishness," Thaddeus says. "Things happened on the boat after. Terrible things. The night of her death was horrific, but it did not stop. I had the Gypsy Queen pulled from the water, put in dry dock, but it didn't stop. I decommissioned her and sold her for salvage. She and everything on board was supposed to be destroyed. She was never to be on the water again."

"And that ended it," Darius says.

"No," Thaddeus says. "It never stopped. She would not let me go. My Gypsy queen followed me, haunting me, tormenting me night and day."

He turns now to his son.

"That is why I put you in place to run the business for me. People were starting to talk; to think I was crazy. Maybe I was. I stopped going in public. She was everywhere. I knew then. I have always known. She will not stop until I die and I am going to a special kind of hell when I do."

Thaddeus shakes his head morosely.

"She was so innocent."

He stops, looking around fearfully. "She is here, now."

"What happened to the young Romani man?" Darius asks. "Did you kill him?"

"I tried," Thaddeus says. "She saved him. After that I don't know."

He looks more closely at Darius now, recognition in his eyes. At the same time a fog creeps into them. A distant memory.

"You," he whispers.

Darius stares back in confusion.

Thaddeus shakes it off.

"You look just like him," he says, "her young Romani lover."

"What happened to her?" Amelia asks. "Did you kill her?"

"It does not matter now," Thaddeus says sadly.

A sudden chill fills the air and their breaths float on it in clouds of vapor.

Thaddeus looks startled. His eyes widen and he staggers backwards. Behind him, Eugene opens his mouth as if to scream, staring in mute fear.

Something unseen slams into the boat, rocking it violently and tossing them around on the deck like dolls.

Thaddeus falls and the deck surges up to meet him, fracturing his age-fragile bones with the force as he strikes the immovable hardwood of the boat deck.

The swelling water washes over the docks and dances the barges on their lines, banging them ruthlessly against the docks.

The sudden surge is like riding the back of a great whale rising up. When the deck falls away again on the retreating swell, it drops away beneath their feet, sending everyone falling.

The spray of water filling the air with a fine mist turns to slush in the cold air gripping the boat, washing over the deck and railings and coating them with ice.

Thaddeus looks at them from where he is sprawled. The intelligence in his eyes is a sharp contrast to the frail body he is trapped in. He is dying.

An unseen force picks him up and tosses him, leaving him broken and unmoving on the deck.

Travis and Darius watch in mute shock.

Malcolm is struggling to his feet on the icy deck.

Eugene stays down, afraid for his own age-brittle bones. He is trying to slide towards the gangplank.

Malcolm flails his arms as if against an invisible attacker. With no warning, he flies across the deck and slams against the wall between the large windows of the casino room with such force the glass on either side crackles, a spider web of cracks spreading across each window.

Almost silently, the glass comes apart, cascading down in a shiver of the soft light inside and from the boat next door sparkling off the shards.

Travis staggers to his feet, sliding and lunging across the deck. He grabs Amelia, wrapping his arms around her protectively.

"Please, don't hurt her!" he cries to the wind and the sky.

Amelia screams as an unseen force strikes them, sending them flying over the railing to the water below.

Half risen to his feet, Eugene steps forward, his face stricken with terror. A tight fist grips his heart, squeezing. Sharp pain courses down his arms, turning his fingers numb.

Darius runs to the railing, screaming, looking over the edge to the dark water below.

"Amelia! Travis!"

His screams are whipped away on a sudden wind that threatens to send him over the railing too. It dies as suddenly as it came, leaving the Gypsy Queen strangely silent and still.

"Amelia. Travis." The words are a sob now.

Darius suddenly realizes the night has become darker than night. He looks around, trying to see past the darkness enveloping the deck of the Gypsy Queen.

"When did it get so dark?" He looks around fearfully. "Where are the boats? The dock? When did we leave the dock?"

Eugene falls to the deck clutching at his heart, in the midst of a heart attack.

The boat rocks violently, tossed by suddenly thrashing waves.

Eugene slides across the deck, slamming against the thick round spool of heavy rope coiled on the deck before continuing to slide across to the railing before the paddle wheel.

There is a groaning within the bowels of the boat. A dull clunk. Chugging shudders through it and then levels off.

With the grinding shrieking of unused metal catching on metal, then slipping and moving, the grease slathered on beginning to be worked through the moving parts, the large paddle wheel slowly begins to turn.

Water is drawn up on the large paddles, falling to reclaim its home as they reach their apex and go over and down, water raining down to the black river water soundlessly.

Darius's breath hangs heavily in front of him. Silent.

It is as if all sound has been sucked out of the world.

Dark clouds fill the sky, descending to fill the deck with a dense fog.

Darius looks around in terror, alone.

She comes out of the fog, her long dark hair tumbling down, seeming to become one with the billowing fabric of her dress, both whipped by the silent winds, both seeming to almost meld into the deck and fog that has become the entire world. Dark haired and dark eyed, moving with a supple grace most women would envy, she comes.

Darius is pulled into her eyes, unable to look away, feeling as if he is being sucked into them as he stands motionlessly on the deck.

Her shadowed eyes hold dark secrets. Her mouth is turned up in the slightest of smiles, a smile filled with eternal sadness. Her lips hold the promise they might whisper those secrets in your ear if only you turn away for just a moment and do not look at her.

Darius is powerless to do anything but stand there and watch her come.

In a room above, a single card lays on the floor.

The Gypsy Queen on the card smiles sadly, seeming to come like a ghost from the background, the waves crashing against the cliff behind her as if to tear the castle above down from its perch. The tossing waves below the cliff hold the suggestion of a boat about to be smashed against the rocks at the base of the cliff.

Her lips are slightly parted as if to soundlessly whisper her dark secrets.

Another card flutters down to join it, partially covering it.

The card is the death card that first caught his eye, its picture just as twisted and gruesome as his first impression of it.

A figure is clothed in a long rotting robe that appears to hang weightlessly off him. He is walking, mindless of the carnage happening around him.

Frightening ghostly apparitions hang in the air above, barely there. Dark gossamer rotting fabric hangs from them, their wings carrying them effortlessly. Wicked clawed fingers are reaching and tearing the souls from their victims, the victims falling from the sky to litter the ground Death walks on.

One of these creatures seems more real than the others. Its victim hangs from its grasp, screaming soundlessly as its other claw ruthlessly tears his soul out. A withered old man.

The creature stares directly out of the card, faceless, as if staring directly into your soul and weighing it. There is a sense of blood red eyes that are not there, sending a sick chill slithering into your stomach.

In the dark background a dark figure hunches on a stool painting a portrait on an easel. In the portrait a beautiful young woman adorns the prow of an elegant paddlewheel steamboat. Her partially hooded eyes suggest they carry some deep secret she is unwilling to share and her mouth has an indefinable sadness about it. Her long hair falls in waves that cascade down her back to tangle into the smooth wood behind her and her head is encircled with what looks like a crown of gold coins linked together with the fine links of a chain, a necklace for her delicate brow. Her dress is merely a suggestion, curving down and around and spreading in rolling ripples of waves washing over the prow to become one with the boat.

On the deck, a man stands staring at a faded apparition, the suggestion of a woman.

An almost invisible gossamer thread joins them together.

It is broken.

On the boat deck, Darius is still mesmerized by the apparition before him.

She comes at him and he tenses. He is off balance with the heaving of the boat on the waves still battering the boats against the dock, adding to the confusion filling him. His mind screams at him to do something. Anything. React. Defend himself somehow or run. He is helpless to do anything, his mind numbed from all rational thought and muscles frozen with fear.

An icy blast hits Darius, making him stagger back, almost falling. As suddenly as it hit, the waves making the Gypsy Queen rock and heave are gone, the boat sitting still at her mooring and only the soft guttural sound of water gently lapping the dock posts is left.

The clouds thin and the fog evaporates, bringing the world back to normal.

He does not know when the music stopped or the casino floor room went dark.

Darius looks around in muted confusion. She is gone.

Malcolm lies slumped against the wall where he was thrown, motionless. His eyes staring emptily at nothing.

Thaddeus is a broken crumpled heap of withered and broken old man. The light gone from his eyes, already drying, staring into the face of Death itself in the form of the apparition of the young woman which is now gone but forever imprinted on his soul, whatever Hell it has been sent to.

Eugene's hand quivers and reaches weakly towards the gangplank. It drops to the deck and he lies motionlessly.

Darius blinks, finally realizing that it is over. He runs to the rail, grasping it and leaning over, yelling to the quiet water below, his eyes searching the darkness.

"Amelia! Travis! Amelia!"

There is a faint splashing sound and a muffled call.

"Here!" It is Travis's voice.

Darius looks around in urgent panic for something, anything, to throw overboard. There is nothing.

He races down the gangplank, stepping and almost tripping over Eugene's prone form, skidding to a stop and looking around urgently.

Darius spots the life preserver hanging on a post and races for it. Grabbing it, he races back, almost putting himself over the railing in his rush when he hits it. He scans the water below frantically, trying to spot them.

"Travis! Amelia!"

The weak call comes again from somewhere in the darkness below.

"Here."

He spots movement. A hand waving on the surface of the water.

Wrapping the end of the rope around his hand and swinging it back for extra leverage, he throws the life preserver overboard. It hits the water with a dull splash.

There is more splashing.

His heart seems unable to work. It feels like a cold hard lump in his chest. He can't swallow. Can't breathe.

"Pull us in."

He looks around uncertainly. It comes to him. The dock.

Grasping the rope with both hands, he drags the life preserver along, hearing the bumping against the hull, walking the railing of the boat.

Reaching the front, Darius looks at the carved woman.

"How do I get around it?"

"It's okay!" Travis yells from below. "Drop the rope! I can swim for the dock!"

Un-wrapping the rope from his hand, Darius balls it up, judges the distance, and throws it as hard as he can. The rope is unravelling as it sails over the figurehead, draping it on the way down.

There is a tug from below and the rope falls, vanishing into the darkness.

Darius races back down the gangplank to the dock and stands there staring anxiously into the dark. He is not sure if he hears the splashing of Travis swimming or only the water lapping against the dock and boats' hulls.

A hand reaches up, grasping at the dock, and Darius starts. He lunges forward, grabbing the hand in both of his.

Travis's head pops over the edge, followed by his other hand with the rope gripped tightly. Darius moves to pull him up.

"No, take the rope. Pull her up!"

Darius barely snatches the rope before Travis drops back down, leaving him staring after him with the life preserver rope hanging from his hand.

Taking the rope in both hands, Darius starts reeling it in, almost immediately taking up the slack. He pulls it in hand over hand until the weight of a body makes it difficult.

Travis's hand appears again, then the other, and finally his head. He crawls onto the dock and joins Darius pulling.

"Hold on tight!" Travis yells down to the water.

When the top of a wet bedraggled head begins to appear over the edge of the dock, Darius is struck with a sudden sickening foreboding, half expecting it to be the ghostly apparition from the deck.

Relief floods him when he sees Amelia's stricken face staring up at them. She is sitting in the life preserver, clinging to the rope.

Travis rushes forward, reaching for her.

She hesitates, staring at his offered hand before tentatively letting go of the rope with one hand to reach for his.

Grasping her hand, he pulls her closer until he can get both hands.

With Travis pulling her by the hands and Darius pulling the rope, they get her safely on the dock.

Amelia stands there shivering with shock, her knees weak, staring up at the Gypsy Queen as they help her out of the life preserver.

Reaching blindly, Amelia grasps Darius, clinging to him for dear life.

"We are alive," Travis says numbly, staring at the figurehead with an icy chill coursing through his veins.

"For now," Darius says softly.

END

Other books by L.V. Gaudet:

The McAllister Series:

Where the Bodies Are

Are you ready to step into the twisted mind of a killer? What kind of dark secret pushes a man to commit the unimaginable, even as he is sickened by his own actions?

A young woman is found discarded with the trash, left for dead. More bodies begin to appear.

The killer's reality blurs between past and present with a compulsion driven by a dark secret locked in a fractured mind. Overcome by a blind rage that leaves him wallowing in remorse with the bodies of victim after victim, he is desperate to stop killing.

The search for the killer will lead to his dark secret buried in the past.

The McAllister Farm

Take a step back in time to meet the boy who created the killer and learn the secret behind the bodies in Where the Bodies Are.

William McAllister is a private man who does not like to have attention on his family. His family history is as dark as the secret hiding in the woods.

Just as he begins to bring his troubled son into the family business, a serial killer starts preying on local young women. The McAllisters quickly find themselves drawn into the spotlight when the town decides William McAllister is the killer.

The attention is a threat to both William McAllister's profession and his family. He has no choice but to find the killer himself.

He might not like what he learns.

Hunting Michael Underwood

Step deeper into the twisted mind of a killer as he slips further into madness.

Hunting Michael Underwood follows on the heels of book one, Where the Bodies Are, bringing the first two stories and their characters together as the search for the killer continues.

Michael Underwood has vanished and Detective Jim McNelly will not stop until he finds him. Working with the detective, Lawrence Hawkworth is still chasing the bigger story he knows is behind the bodies.

Jason McAllister knows he must stop the killer he created before he goes too far. He may be the only one who can stop him.

Unable to let go of his barely remembered past and the search for his sister, the killer goes looking for Jason McAllister's past and his family.

Killing David McAllister

Sometimes the only way to stop a monster is to kill it. He has gone by many names, but he was raised as David McAllister, and finding what he is looking for is not enough to quiet the darkness inside him.

Other Books:

Garden Grove

Who wants to stop construction at the new Garden Grove residential development? Garden Grove is a hotbed of complications from costly mistakes and vandalism to sabotage and the poisoning of the work crew.

While the construction crew struggles to stay on schedule, they face growing problems and, with them, a growing sense of unease.

A group of local housewives drawn into the growing mystery uncover a secret that brings Garden Grove deeper into a new mystery connecting all the suspects.

The mystery deepens with the discovery of old human remains that have their own dark past recently planted at the jobsite.

When all attempts to shut the site down permanently fail, two long time elderly residents step up their own efforts. Each with their own family secrets, the pair of quirky old birds are pitted against each other and their longstanding family feud is brought to the boiling point.

Old Mill Road

Twelve years ago four kids found something in the woods that tore their innocence away. They made a vow to keep it secret. Now, impossibly, someone found it again.

The abandoned mill off the old Mill Road has a dark history that has been told for generations, a story about something sinister haunting the woods.

Unable to remember the events of twelve years ago and troubled by the haunted look he sees every time he looks at his sister's eyes, Nick has returned to learn what happened when they were kids.

Still obsessed with Felicia and Nick's family suddenly vanishing in the night after their childhood discovery, David is determined to get answers from Nick, while his brother Ian tries to temper his obsession.

Felicia's return to help Nick will trigger new revelations about the mummified bodies of children appearing in the woods decades apart.

About the Author

L.V. Gaudet is a Canadian author, a member of the Manitoba Writers' Guild, the Horror Writers Association, and Authors of Manitoba.

L.V. grew up with a love of the darker side; sneaking down to the basement at night to watch the old horror B movies, Vincent Price being a favorite; devouring books by Stephen King, Dean Koontz, and other horror authors; and has had a passion for books and the idea of creating stories and worlds a person can get lost in since reading that first novel.

This love of storytelling has this author working writing and editing into a busy life that includes work, family, and supporting the writing community. L. V. Gaudet volunteers with the Manitoba Writers' Guild, is the editor of the MWG newsletter, proofreads for the HWA newsletter, and visits schools for I Love to Read month.

L.V. Gaudet currently lives in Manitoba with two rescue dogs, spouse, and kids.

Follow L. V. Gaudet:

Facebook: https://www.facebook.com/LVGaudet.Author/
Instagram: lv_gaudet
Twitter: @lvgaudet
Wordpress: https://lvgaudet.wordpress.com